Love to Pat!
Mattie

EVERYBODY KNEW PETE

Marian Mathews Hersrud

Marian Mathews Hersrud

April 23, 2010

AuthorHouse™
1663 Liberty Drive
Bloomington, IN 47403
www.authorhouse.com
Phone: 1-800-839-8640

This book is a work of fiction. People, places, events, and situations are the product of the author's imagination. Any resemblance to actual persons, living or dead, or historical events, is purely coincidental.

© 2009 Marian Mathews Hersrud. All rights reserved.

No part of this book may be reproduced, stored in a retrieval system, or transmitted by any means without the written permission of the author.

First published by AuthorHouse 9/24/2009

ISBN: 978-1-4490-1499-5 (e)
ISBN: 978-1-4490-1497-1 (sc)
ISBN: 978-1-4490-1498-8 (hc)

Printed in the United States of America
Bloomington, Indiana

This book is printed on acid-free paper.

To cousin Judy Holmes and innkeeper Marian Burns who introduced me to a new and exciting world in Maine and to my family who were my support group.

ACKNOWLEDGEMENTS

My list of those who provided much-needed information that saved the author total embarrassment and possible lawsuits, includes a wide variety of talents and occupations. My thanks to all of you.

Because our heroine, Jenny McKnight, is a psychic, Mary Dean, Minneapolis, MN, and Linda Denerley, Warwick, NY, shared their own experiences that make Jenny's visions believable.

Hero, Charlie Brewster's routine as a crime reporter, is authentic, thanks to Prudy Taylor Board, Delray Beach, FL.

Legal consultants, Bruce Hubbard, Sturgis, SD, Fred Newman, Naples, FL, and Preston Rand, Brewer, ME, provided law enforcement and legal details plus a complete floor plan for the theater's courtroom scene.

James O'Grady, Lead, SD, converted our imaginary Legion Club into a theater. Richard Reeder, Minneapolis, MN, filled in technical details, and Patrick Pins, Mandan, ND, assisted with the duties of the director, committees and publicity.

Betty and Sol Wise, Saratoga Springs, NY, provided information about Skidmore College.

Luigi Longo, Naples, FL, endowed my Guido with a real Italian personality and vocabulary.

Special thanks to my editor and confidante, Joyce Wells, Bloomfield Hills, MI, and Naples, FL.

Again, thank you. I am eternally grateful.

Other novels by
Marian Mathews Hersrud

Sweet Thunder

Spirits and Black Leather

PROLOGUE

October, 1998, Sowatna, Maine. Midnight.

Misty rain obscured the moon, the empty streets dark and wet. Perched high in a gnarled oak tree, an owl hooted. The chill October wind carried the sound off to the Atlantic Ocean's churning waves.

Under the glow of a solitary streetlight, two figures hunched into sweatshirts, hands in jeans pockets, heads bent against the wind. High school girls, their giggles and whispers broke the silence.

"Did your dad wake up when you left the house?" Jenny asked.

"I don't think so," Erin replied. "Have you got the roach clip?"

"Yes, and I borrowed my dad's key and a flashlight."

The girls hurried to the Presbyterian Church on the corner of Fifth Street and Maple Avenue. They walked around to the side door, and Jenny unlocked it. She aimed the flashlight toward the stairs. Still giggling, they climbed the steps that led to a small room above the sanctuary. The massive bell that tolled a welcome to the parishioners filled the space leaving only enough room for the girls who sat down and leaned against it. Emptying their pockets, they brought out stashes of marijuana – clip, papers, and matches.

"I hope nobody saw us," Erin whispered.

Jenny leaned out of the open window overlooking the street. "I don't see anyone."

They relaxed, rolled their joints, and lit up. Jenny watched as Erin slipped down, eyes closed.

"Mmm," she murmured.

Jenny who really didn't like the stuff had inhaled only once. She studied her friend. Why had Erin passed out after only one joint? Jenny remembered a faint smell of alcohol on Erin's breath as the climbed the stairs. Had she been drinking before they met?

Maybe they'd been crazy to sneak out tonight. Her dad would take away her driving privileges if he found out. She stood and walked to the window. The mist had turned into a gentle rain, and the streetlight cast an eerie glow.

As she looked up the street to her left, a man moved into the light. Bent over, he carried someone, maybe a man, on his back, his feet dragging along the sidewalk.

"Erin," Jenny whispered, "come and look."

Erin moaned softly. Eyes closed, she curled into a fetal position. Jenny turned back to the window. The man trudged past the church, hauling his burden down the street toward the pier. Other streetlights picked up his descent, but gradually he vanished into the darkness and rain.

Jenny chewed her lip, staring into the distance where she had last seen the man. A light breeze rustled the few remaining leaves that clung in defiance of winter's approach. The sharp sound of a car door slamming shattered the quiet, followed by a motor humming to life. The sound faded as the car moved away. Jenny shivered and sat down beside Erin's inert body.

Jenny checked her watch with the flashlight. An hour had passed. It was time to leave. She shook Erin who sat up and mumbled, "Time to go?"

"Yes," Jenny answered. She gathered up their materials and helped Erin down the dark stairway.

As they left the church, Jenny said, "I'll see you tomorrow."

"Okay."

Erin would seen forget about their visit to the church. Jenny, however, would live with what she saw that night. The rain, the wind, and the man who dragged another down the street toward the pier.

CHAPTER ONE

The scream that erupted from Jenny McKnight's throat was high-pitched, gut-wrenching. She sat up in bed and turned on the light. 4:00 a.m. She shivered as she recalled her recurring nightmare. A man came toward her from the shadows of a tree-lined street and stopped under a bright streetlight. He advanced slowly. She couldn't see his face. Each time she experienced the nightmare, she awoke screaming before she could recognize the man.

Her roommate, Kate, called from the other bedroom. "Are you okay?"

"Yes. Sorry to wake you." Jenny got up, grabbed a robe, and went to the kitchen. Maybe a cup of tea would put her back to sleep. Kate came in and slipped into the other chair. Jenny filled two mugs with water and put them in the microwave.

"What are you going to do about those nightmares?" Kate asked.

"I don't know," Jenny said. "Teaching's done for the summer. Maybe I'll drive up to Sowatna and visit my family. Maybe a change of scene will end the problem." She smoothed back her auburn hair and rubbed her eyebrows.

"I'm curious," Kate said. "Something must trigger them. Do you suppose it's something that happened in the past?" She made tea and gave Jenny a mug.

Jenny sipped her tea and stared out the window over the sink. "I don't know." She watched as dark clouds hid a half-moon, breaking and reforming. Drops of rain began to pelt the window. "The only thing I remember is a crazy night when I was a high school senior ten years ago. My friend, Erin, and I sneaked out and smoked pot upstairs in the Presbyterian Church." Jenny laughed. "You can't believe how cool we thought we were."

Kate laughed. "Who didn't smoke? My boyfriend and I tried pot on the fifty yard line at the high school stadium."

Jenny nodded. "I've never told anyone this before. She paused. "It's difficult to talk about, but something weird happened that night."

Kate leaned forward. "Really? What?"

"I remember it, every detail. The wind, the cold rain. It was late October. Erin and I brought our marijuana stuff and climbed up the stairs to the steeple. At the top was a small room. Just enough space for us and a huge bell. Erin did most of the smoking and went to sleep on the floor. I took just one drag, put it out and went over to the window. The mist had turned to rain." Jenny shivered. "I looked out and saw..." She stopped and stared at Kate, her eyes wide, not seeing her.

Jenny's mind had left the kitchen and was at the window of Sowatna's Presbyterian Church in October, 1998. "There's a streetlight on the corner, and I see a man bent over, carrying the body of someone on his back, the feet drag along on the sidewalk. The man moves slowly, but I can't see his face. He walks past, dragging his burden down the street toward the pier. Now he's beyond the streetlight. I can't see him any more, but I hear a car door slam, and the sound of a motor starting up."

"Did your friend see the guy?"

Jenny blinked, and memory faded back into the past. "No, Erin was asleep. I had to shake her to get her down the stairs and point her toward her house."

"Have you ever talked to her about that night?"

"No. After graduation, we lost track of each other. She works here in Portland, but we haven't seen each other. I've called and left messages, but she hasn't returned them. Now I'd like to see her again. Play catch-up." She finished the tea. "Maybe what I saw that night is related to my nightmare." Jenny stood. "Thanks for listening, Kate. I sometimes wish that I didn't have these psychic moments. Last Christmas, I went skiing. I stopped at the side of a run and watched a guy whiz past me, totally out of control. As he went by, his body looked to be all dark, almost black. When I reached the bottom of the run and saw the ski patrol and the stretcher, I knew that he was dead. They told me that he had run into a tree and was killed instantly. That's not fun, Kate."

"Do you have brighter happenings?"

"Oh, yes. I've seen my mother late at night just before I go to sleep. Mom died when I was eight. I remember the perfume she always wore, Patchouli. Sometimes my bedroom is filled with that scent, and I can see a faint shadow in the corner of the room, a shadow with a beautiful white aura around her. I know she's with me, Kate, and that's pure joy."

That night, she tried to erase ten years of nightmares from her mind and hoped that talking about it with Kate had erased her fears, but sleep was a faint hope as she turned over, punched her pillow, and turned again. After thirty minutes of turning and punching, she picked up the phone.

* * *

"Louise, he's back." Her niece's voice on the bedside phone was a quivering whisper. Now fully awake, Louise switched on the light and checked the clock.

"Jenny?" she asked, already knowing the answer. No one but Jenny would call at this hour.

"I hated to wake you, but I'm scared."

"When was the last time you had that vision?"

"Tonight. I want to come home."

"Of course. You can stay with me."

Jenny's sigh of relief was clearly audible. "Thanks. Yesterday was our last class. My third graders have all gone home, and I can drive up this morning."

"Good. Come in time for lunch." Louise replaced the phone and lay back in bed.

Sleep would return slowly as she thought about Jenny lying awake and afraid in Portland. Her niece loved to teach, but her visions had marred the experience. When she had returned to Sowatna during Christmas vacation, she'd told her aunt about the man who appeared mysteriously at any hour. "He's big, heavy set. I can't see his face. He walks toward me, then disappears."

Jenny's visions were not unusual. Psychics often had presentments that baffled and plagued their lives. Louise had great respect for friends and family members who experienced strange visions. Maybe it was their Scottish ancestry. She'd experienced strange disappearances and reappearances, a new black dress gone from its box in her closet and her sorority pin, no longer in its cushion, both of them mysteriously

3

reappearing months later in their original places, and the chilling premonition of her sister, Betsy's sudden death. Louise's experiences were minor compared to Jenny's.

"I usually know who's calling before I answer the phone," Jenny had confided one afternoon as they shared a Coke at Louise's craft shop. "It's a creepy feeling."

Louise laughed. "But just think, Jenny, you don't have to pay for Caller I.D."

Louise recalled other, less pleasing incidents in Jenny's life and hoped that peace of some sort might be possible for her niece. At last she rolled over and fell into an uneasy sleep.

The next morning, Louise dressed, ate a hurried breakfast, and walked downtown to her craft shop on Sowatna's Front Street. She liked the morning's walk. Five blocks down to the pier where waves of the Atlantic Ocean lapped against tall-masted sailboats, yachts, fishing schooners, and a wharf that stretched out into the sea. Her walk took her past the Presbyterian Church whose steeple reached up into the sky, past homes of her neighbors where friends nodded and waved. Sowatna, Maine's six thousand inhabitants got up early, went to bed early, and knew almost everyone in town.

"We're just a small fishing village," Louise explained to friends in faraway places. "Lobster mostly."

She stopped in front of the craft shop, picked up a discarded soda can and unlocked the door. The sign, 'Sew What?' etched on the glass panel produced her usual smile. Summer visitors returned each year asking for new designs and assistance with last year's patterns. Neighbors and people from an ever-spreading local area kept her busy during the rest of the year.

Six years prior to opening her shop, Louise, an accomplished seamstress, began to order craft supplies for her friends. Word got around. "Ask Louise, she'll get it for you." Soon her living room became mired in cross-stitch kits, knitting supplies and needlepoint yarns and patterns. Once her interests broadened into quilting and weaving, passage into the kitchen became an obstacle course around, through, and over looms and quilt frames. It was time to either move herself or her craft supplies. David McKnight, Jenny's father and her brother-in-law was president of Old Maine Bank & Trust Company.

Louise had done the paper work and had shared her portfolio with David. "You have a keen mind for investments," David had said. "No need to call in the Small Business Administration. We'll give you what you need."

Louise found an empty building on Front Street, located the owner, and six months later, 'Sew What?' was open for business.

Inside the shop, she reversed the 'closed' sign, turned on the computer and plugged in the coffee maker. As she sat down at her desk in her office at the rear of the store and began to attack yesterday's mail, she heard the front door open. She walked to the front counter and welcomed a young man who looked around at the store's merchandise. A tangled mop of brown hair framed a sun-tanned face. A firm chin softened by a dimple. A pleasant-looking young man, Louise noted, and yet he had a serious, almost solemn look about him.

"Hi, I'm Charlie Brewster. I'm new. Just got a job with the Chronicle as a reporter."

"I'm Louise Campbell. Where are you from?" The usual question to a newcomer.

"Florida. I was a crime reporter for the Miami Herald, but I did a lot of articles on all kinds of fishing. My life sort of changed, and I wanted something new. I remembered summers in Bar Harbor with my folks, checked the internet, and here I am, ready to do lobsters and deep-sea fishing."

Louise smiled. "We have a lot of both, but we're pretty quiet. Not much excitement."

"*Sowatna* is an odd name. Sounds Native American."

"It's *Abanaki*, one of the tribes that lived here before we came over and displaced them."

Charlie picked up a cross-stitch leaflet, glanced at it briefly and laid it on the counter. Almost casually he said, "I read about a murder that happened here about ten years ago. They arrested a guy, but he wasn't brought to trial."

"Yes. I remember it well. It was rather exciting. The victim was Pete Clampton. He grew up here. Was a lobster fisherman and ran a charter service. Pete knew the best fishing areas, and he had a thriving business."

"They found him on his boat, didn't they?"

Louise nodded. "He was slumped over the wheel. Stabbed. Funny thing. He was stabbed from the front. Somebody had moved him."

"And they found a guy on the pier and charged him with the murder."

"Yes," Louise said. "The man overdosed on heroin and was out cold. He testified before the grand jury that he'd made an appointment with Pete and went on his boat to buy heroin and to arrange some sort of a trip with Pete. He said that Pete was dead when he got there, so he searched the boat and stole some drugs."

"And the grand jury didn't arraign him?" Charlie sounded incredulous.

"It was circumstantial evidence. No witnesses. There was something strange about the entire affair. He refused to talk about his planned trip with Charlie, and the grand jury didn't pursue the matter. They said the trip was irrelevant and immaterial. And the man had been too high on drugs to make much sense anyway. He had a drug problem, but I didn't think that he was a murderer."

Charlie nodded. "Sometimes it's hard to tell. They come in all shapes and sizes. I learned that in Miami. But I read his testimony. It's an interesting case."

"Interesting, yes, and we'll probably never know who killed Pete." Louise shrugged her shoulders.

Charlie shook his head. "I've had enough excitement working at the Herald to last a lifetime. Now I want to get the feel of a small town again." He grinned. "And I might find time to work on the play I started last year after I read about the murder."

He turned around as the door opened, and Jenny ran past him. She put her arms around Louise and kissed her forehead.

"It's great to be here," she said, then turned to acknowledge Charlie who stood back and smiled.

"Jenny, this is Charlie Brewster from Miami. He's going to work for the Chronicle."

Jenny shook his hand. "Glad to meet you. I'm Louise's niece. I just drove up from Portland."

"Hi." Charlie walked to the door and looked back. "Maybe I'll see you around."

He left quickly, and Louise sensed that he didn't want to linger. Odd, she thought. Jenny was a beautiful young woman. Long, thick auburn hair, brown eyes, classic features, and great legs. Men usually took a second look.

* * *

Charlie's second look was inside his mind, shoving visions of Dierdre aside. He shook off his memories of their Jamaica honeymoon in 2004, nights on South Beach, beer and a blanket, sex and sea grass. He tried to block out the morning three years later when he found Dierdre's e-mail on his lap top. "Charlie, I don't want to be married any more. I'm filing for a divorce. I've met someone else." An e-mail! She could have called, and he could, at least, have heard the sound of her voice. They could have had lunch at the pier. She could have held his hand, spoken kindly.

He shoved his hands in his pockets and walked to the wharf. Here were rocks and a heavy Atlantic surf. Not Miami, Charlie. Get real. He locked his car, and walked up the hill to Pine Street. A four-block walk helped to clear his head. He located the newspaper office between a florist shop and a bakery. He opened the door, and familiar odors and sounds welcomed him. The chugging and churning of the presses, the smells of paper, coffee, and cigarettes. No one was at the reception desk, so he walked toward the nearest office. The door was open. He saw a woman seated at a desk, telephone in one hand, a sheaf of papers in the other. On her head, a black, wide-brimmed hat trimmed with a massive black feather that swooped and fluttered as she spoke.

"Goddammit, George, I need that release ASAP. Now!" A deep voice, raspy, harsh. She slammed down the phone. Charlie grinned. The cast of characters may have changed, but the dialogue was the same. It was good to be home.

"Hi, I'm Charlie Brewster, your new reporter. You must be Charlotte Quincy, the editor."

The woman nodded. "Sit down. I read your resume and your articles. I like your style. We don't have much crime around here, but there's a lot of news to report." She pulled out a package of cigarillos and lit one. The first drag produced a hacking cough. "Oh, shut up," she said before Charlie could open his mouth. "I never have time to finish one of these." She leaned back in her chair. "When do you want to start?"

"Tomorrow's fine. I've moved into a motel and..."

"You don't want to get permanent yet, huh? That's okay. Be here at 8:00. Talk to Sara on your way out. She does salaries."

Charlie moved to the door and took a last look at the editor. Under the plumed hat, a tumble of hair in shades of gray and red. Green eyes dressed in horn-rims. A sharp nose. She wore a white shirt covered by a heavy purple cardigan sweater. Sixty-something probably.

"I suppose you wonder about the hat," she said. "I raid my grandmother's trunk sometimes. She was one of the first newspaper women in North Dakota. I like the continuity."

Charlie laughed. "I'll bet she was a good one."

Charlotte swiveled her chair around to face a computer behind the desk. The interview was over.

Charlie found Sara in the next office. Dimples, blonde pony tail, low-cut T-shirt. "You're Charlie," Sara said, cracking her gum. She worked her computer, turned on a printer, and handed Charlie a form. "This is salary and a job description. The last part is pure conjecture. You'll like it here." She flapped her heavily mascaraed eye lashes and smiled. "Is there anything I can do for you?"

"Not right now, thanks." He paused. "Were you here when the Clapton murder trial took place?"

"No, I was just a kid in Bangor."

"Okay. I'll see you tomorrow."

Charlie walked back down to Front Street and headed for the pier. He thought about his meeting with the women at the craft shop. Louise, the owner, would be a source of information when he had time to work on his novel. Her niece was good looking, but she wasn't Dierdre.

***

As Louise waited on her morning customers, Jenny checked her e-mail and answered the phone, and, two hours later, looked at her watch.

"I'm starved," she said. "Can you close the shop for lunch?"

"Of course. We can walk to The Lobster Shack."

Over crab cakes and coffee, Jenny described her recurring vision. "It usually happens during a thunder storm. It's so ugly. When the vision ends, I'm in a cold sweat." She sipped coffee and looked around the cafe.

Louise realized that the discussion was over but sensed that something lay deep and hidden within Jenny's mind. She paid the bill, and they walked back to the shop.

"I'm going to visit my high school friend, Erin Gregory, this afternoon," Jenny said. "I called, and she's expecting me. I want to see Dad too, so I'll stop at the bank. I'll come back when you close the shop, and we'll go out for dinner." She paused at the corner. "I needed to come home, Louise. I want to put an end to the nightmares, and I think that I can do it here."

* * *

Jenny dodged afternoon traffic as she walked to Erin's home. Her five-block walk along Front Street was a refresher course in Maine's coastal environs. The crash of waves against a rocky shore, the fresh odor of salt and sea, and rows of offices and residences, all snuggled up against rocky cliffs. It was good to be home.

Jenny rang the doorbell, and as she waited on the step, she noticed that the Gregory residence needed paint and attention. Erin opened the door and stepped back.

"It's great to see you, Jenny. Sorry I was out when you stopped in at the rehab office in Portland last month."

"I miss seeing you too. We need to talk."

Erin motioned her friend to a worn orange velveteen sofa. "Soda?"

"No, thanks. I just had lunch." Jenny settled on the sofa. "Do you remember the night we sneaked out to smoke pot at the church? We were seniors and thought we were so cool."

"I don't remember much. I guess I passed out. Why do you ask?"

Jenny studied her friend. "I'm bringing it up because I saw something that night, and now I'm having nightmares. I don't know if they're connected to what I saw, but I think they are, and I want to get a decent night's sleep."

Erin looked interested. "What did you see?"

"Out of the steeple window, I watched a man drag a body down the street. A dead body; I'm sure of it. A car started up and drove away."

Erin nodded eagerly. "Oh, my gosh! And the next day Pete Clampton's body was found on his boat."

"I was scared," Jenny said. "When I heard about the murder, I was sure that was Pete's body being dragged, but I couldn't tell my dad. I'd have been grounded for the rest of the year."

"So you never told anyone?"

"No. And when the grand jury dismissed the case, I didn't need to report what I'd seen."

"Would you have come forward if there had been a trial?"

"Of course. So why am I plagued with the nightmares?"

Erin pondered the question. "Maybe you need to find out who really did kill Pete."

The women stared at each other.

"And maybe that's the answer, but where would I start?" Jenny asked. "That was ten years ago. The murderer may have moved. Maybe he's dead."

"I could help you ask around. What do we know about Pete? A lobsterer. What else?"

"I don't know. I have to think." Jenny stood, hugged Erin, and walked to the door. "I'm going to stop at the bank and visit with Dad. I'll call you tomorrow. When do you go back to Portland?"

"Next week."

"Do you like your work?"

"Yes. It's strange being back at the rehab center as an employee, not as a client. Those four weeks I spent in rehab four years ago changed my life, and now it's good to help other alcoholics. Been there. Done that."

Jenny kissed Erin's cheek. "I don't have to worry about you any more, and I'm so proud of you. Not an easy road you've traveled."

"No, but when you hit bottom, you have nowhere to go but up, and I'm still climbing."

* * *

That afternoon, Ann Thompson entered the craft shop. Over her arm, she carried a plastic bag filled with quilt pieces. She dumped the contents on a counter. "I can't do it, Louise," Ann announced. "Nothing fits or looks right."

Louise looked at her friend. Ann resembled that bag of fabric. Nothing fit or looked right. She wore a faded red T-shirt, pink striped shorts, and worn brown sandals, not her usual smart, coordinated attire.

"Let's spread the pieces out on a table and put them in order." Louise gathered up the material, rearranged them, and now the colors fell into place. "I'll pin them together, and you can start over."

"Thanks. I needed help. Maybe I need help with the rest of my life." Ann sighed. "Glenn's in Bangor on a big highway project. I don't see him much. The kids are in college. Guess the 'empty nest syndrome' has hit me." She smiled. "Maybe you were lucky not to have a husband and kids, Louise. You get used to their being around, and when they're not, you feel empty."

Louise nodded. "Maybe you're right." *No husband and kids? Lucky?* Louise looked down at her left hand. She could still feel that engagement ring and the warm glow of a future marriage, a marriage that wasn't meant to be.

The afternoon hours flew by as customers came and went. At 5:30, as Louise turned off her computer and unplugged the coffee urn, Jenny returned. "I visited Erin and stopped at the bank to see Dad. He wasn't in his office. One of the cashiers told me that he'd left for the afternoon. Didn't know where he went."

Jenny helped Louise put the craft shop back in order, the 5:30 routine. Louise's motions were on automatic pilot, but her mind steered her through the skies of memory — her little sister Elizabeth, Jenny's mother, dead at thirty-five. Too young for a massive heart attack. Doomed from birth, the autopsy proved. David, Jenny's dad, worked his way through grief and loss, raised Jenny with help from paid employees, friends, and especially, Louise. He'd risen from cashier to president of the bank, and Louise saw him less frequently.

"How about pizza?" Jenny's voice cut off the memories.

"I have one in the freezer. Let's go home."

CHAPTER TWO

Jenny's father, David McKnight, unlocked his gray Lincoln Continental that was parked behind the bank in the "Reserved for Bank President" space and headed east toward Lake Narriguagus. It was 2:30 p.m. Ann would be at the cabin at 3:00.

Twenty minutes later, he turned off the highway onto a rutted graveled road that was canopied by tall pines and white birch trees. As he approached the cabin, he saw Ann's white Pontiac convertible parked under a maple tree. The lake beyond the cabin was a shimmering blue, blending with the sky. Gentle waves lapped against the rocky shore. The cabin, built in 1938 and purchased by David's father in 1974, was post card perfect – hewn log exterior, cedar-shakes roof. Picture windows now enhanced the view from inside, and the garage had been enlarged. Nothing else had been altered. The interior was warm and inviting. Flowered chintz at the windows, rustic, well-worn leather chairs and overstuffed davenports. A coffee table fashioned from a storm-tossed piece of driftwood.

Ann met him at the door with a lingering embrace. He stroked her lower back. "You wore black?" he asked.

"Yes. For you."

They walked slowly to the bedroom, theirs for the afternoon. "Let's see." He kissed her deeply, and sat on the bed.

Ann mouthed a kiss and unbuttoned her white shirt cuffs and the front buttons revealing her back silk bra. She slid her black skirt to the floor.

David said, "Oh, baby," as he saw her black garter belt and sheer black nylons.

"Now it's your turn." She bent over the bed and undressed her lover.

David's mind and body were engulfed in waves of passion, and he knew that Ann shared his emotions as they moved together, one with each other.

At last they moved apart. David kissed her gently and stroked her shoulders. "Oh, baby," he murmured again. There was nothing more to say. They slept.

Ann stirred beside him. "I must get home, sweetie. Glenn's coming back from Bangor tonight."

David groaned. "When are you going to leave him? You know I want us to be together, married, legal."

"And you know what's holding me back. Fear and family. The adulterous wife wants out. Not a pretty picture in a small town."

"But what about the abuse?"

"He never hits me where it shows or when the kids are present. Who'd believe me?"

David put on his trousers and brought two Scotch and sodas from the kitchen. He sat on the edge of the bed, Ann close beside him, sipping, thinking. His mind raced. There had to be a solution.

He remembered the first time he had met Ann three years ago. He hadn't wanted to attend the monthly Country Club dance. Too many twosomes, too many evenings with Betsy, gone for seventeen years. His sister-in-law, Louise, had almost dragged him to the club. "You need to get out, David. Meet people, see your friends. Pick me up at seven."

Dutifully and reluctantly, David followed Louise's orders. The club's dining room was filled with members and guests, most of whom he knew. Greetings were exchanged as he and Louise found a table for two.

Glenn Thompson, who had moved to Sowatna in 1988 and had established a thriving road contracting business, called from an adjoining table. "Come and join us. We have two empty seats, and we've just sat down."

Louise and David accepted the invitation and ordered cocktails. David gradually relaxed and made light conversation with Ann Thompson who sat on his left. She wore a simple black sleeveless dress, and her shoulder-length blonde hair fell in soft waves. A pretty woman, David thought and the thought surprised him. Dancing followed dinner, and David returned to his prior unease. He hadn't danced since Betsy died. Didn't want to hold another woman in his arms, feel her body close to his, sense an alien perfume.

"How about a dance?" Ann's voice broke into his discomfort.

The band played a long, slow version of 'That Old Black Magic.' David remembered the steps, and Ann followed easily. He didn't know when it happened – when his dread turned to desire, how her body close to his aroused a sense of desperate wanting, needing. My God, he thought, an erection? He must be crazy!

When the song ended, he led her back to the table, excused himself and raced to the men's room. He splashed cold water on his face and neck, adjusted his trousers and glared at the mirror. "You dumb ass," he said. "It was just a dance."

He returned to his seat, ordered coffee, and tried to make conversation with Louise, but when the band started again, Louise went to the dance floor with Glenn Thompson. Now David and Ann sat together surrounded by two empty seats, and David was as tongue-tied as a fifth grader at his first chaperoned party. He finally found his voice. "Thanks for the dance. It's been a long time for me."

"I know," Ann said. "Again?"

The music was another slow one, and he gathered her close. "I want to see you again, and I know that's off limits," he whispered.

He was startled when Ann said, "I want to see you too."

And that's how it started. Now as he and Ann sat together on the bed at the cabin, he was again tongue-tied, frustrated, hating reality, hating Glenn, hating himself. He finished his drink and took both glasses to the kitchen. He looked out at the lake and wished that he and Ann could sail across it, find a passage to another lake, then another and leave Sowatna forever. No luggage, no strings that tied them to former lives. Just the two of them together.

Their afternoon was over, and the bedroom darkened. David watched a heavy, dark thunderhead move across the sun at the western edge of the lake. Ann shivered and moved close to David. "Must it always grow dark eventually?" she asked.

"I hope not, my love." He stood, kissed her forehead and gently pulled her up from the bed. "You should leave first. Drive carefully."

When Ann was out of sight, David straightened the bed, washed the glasses and gave the cabin a last-minute inspection. A light rain began to fall as he started his car. His afternoon with Ann had begun with joyous anticipation. Now as he drove away, his mood blended with the heavy thunderhead, foreboding, a presentment of approaching squalls.

* * *

"Hi. I'm Charlie Brewster. I have a reservation."

The desk clerk at the Blueberry Inn shuffled papers. "You're in room six." She gave him a key and a registration form. "Sign here."

All business, Charlie thought. Down East aloof, maybe. He'd heard about those folks but hadn't met any in Bar Harbor. Small talk, get-acquainted talk might warm the chill, but he had too much on his mind. Being here in Sowatna with its pier, lobster boats, and the smell of ocean sent his mind into a file folder labeled 'Clampton Murder Drama.' He was anxious to learn more about the trial and to flesh out characters and background. He opened room six, threw his luggage on a chair. His first stop would be the local bank.

At the teller's window, Charlie stood behind three customers. While he waited, he visualized a bank scene in the play he was writing.

"Hi, I'm Charlie Brewster with the Sowatna Chronicle. I want to open a checking account."

The teller smiled and extended her hand across the counter. "Welcome." She gave him an application form and announced a non-stop litany of regulations and stipulations as Charlie filled out the application.

He handed her the completed form. "I'm also looking for a good lawyer, maybe one who might have worked on the Pete Clampton murder case." The last words were stated with a quizzical tone.

The teller nodded. "You'll want to see Colin Greene. He defended the man accused of the crime. His office is up the street on India Avenue. Two blocks from here." She pointed a finger toward the northwest.

Charlie left his car in front of the bank and walked up the street. Colin Greene's office was an unimposing, one-story building in traditional white siding. Green shutters framed two modest windows. A lion's head brass door knocker and a brass name plate on the solid dark green door informed the visitor that this was an office of solid, legitimate gentlemen of the bar. Charlie read the names. 'Sinclaire,

Greene and Hansen, Attorneys at Law.' The interior was understated respectability. Charlie walked across a tired Oriental rug that was centered on polished oak flooring. Sturdy brown leather sofas and arm chairs lined the walls that displayed paintings of ships, all in gilt frames. The receptionist behind a heavy, dark mahogany desk looked up and smiled.

"Do you have an appointment?"

Charlie shook his head and gave his name and occupation. "I'd like to make an appointment to see Mr. Greene. I need information regarding the Clampton murder."

"No problem. Mr. Greene's last client left five minutes ago. He might be able to see you now for a short time." She called, listened, and motioned Charlie to a seat. "He'll be right out."

Charlie shrugged and sat. Sowatna was definitely not Miami where he'd have waited for days, met the lawyer in his office, and converted the conversation into dollars per minute.

Colin Greene wore a white shirt, blue and white polka dot bow tie, chinos, and loafers. His gray goatee and steel-rimmed glasses softened a sharpness around the mouth and eyes.

"Mr. Brewster, how can I help you?"

Charlie stood and introduced himself. "I'm new at the Chronicle, and I'm interested in the Clampton murder. I've read articles, but I want more information. I'm working on a play and..."

Greene cut him off. "That was ten years ago, and most of the cast have left or have forgotten their lines."

Charlie laughed. "That's why I want to start with you, the guy who defended Tim Brennan. Where is he now?"

"I don't know. Come back to my office. I have a few minutes before my next client." He turned to the receptionist. "Will you get me the case file on the Clampton murder?"

The chair was overstuffed and comfortable. Charlie settled into it and accepted a cup of coffee that Greene poured from a decanter on his desk. "Can't function without this," the lawyer said. "Tell me about your play."

"I was a crime reporter for the Miami Herald for about eight years and read about the Clampton murder along with other unsolved cases. The locale, the people, all of it make for great drama. Now I want to flesh out the details, learn more about the victim, the accused, and the legalities of the charges."

"That's an imposing project, Mr. Brewster. When will you have time to work at the paper?"

Charlie laughed. "My first priority is taking orders from Mrs. Quincy. The play's my after-hours entertainment."

"Ah, you've met Charlotte. A brilliant mind hiding behind an outrageous façade. You never know what she's going to wear or say."

Charlie laughed. "She's kind of intimidating, but I'm looking forward to working with her."

"Here's the Clampton file." The receptionist placed a file on Greene's desk.

Charlie picked it up. "Not much here. I was expecting a ream of material."

"We don't keep a complete transcript. You can get all of it from the court reporter, but it'll be expensive. Ask my receptionist to make copies for you, and keep me informed. I've always been a theater buff. Did some acting in college."

"Thanks for your help. This is a good start."

He left Greene's office, stopped at the receptionist's desk, and gave her the file. "I need copies of this, and I also need the court reporter's name."

"Wait a minute and I'll make the copies. The court reporter's name is Troy Witherspoon." She went into another office, and Charlie picked up a copy of the Sowatna Chronicle and settled into a chair. So far, he thought, the move to Maine was the right one.

* * *

"It's good to be home." Jenny opened Louise's front door and ran to the kitchen.

"I'm glad you're here," Louise said. "I'm selfish. I thought you might want to stay with your father, but I hoped you'd stay here."

Jenny's smile was wistful. "I wanted to be here with you because of the nightmares, and Dad's gone most of the time. Besides, I practically grew up in this house, remember?"

Louise put her arm around Jenny. "Yes, this was home for you after your mother died. Your dad was so lost, so bitter. He sort of rattled around his house when he was there but spent most of the time at the bank and at the cabin."

"I was lost and bitter too, and I sometimes wonder why we couldn't share our feelings. Dad didn't seem to care that I spent so much time here with you. In fact, he seemed to welcome my absence."

"He loved your mother deeply and wasn't able to express his feelings. He was too proud and confused to ask for help from anyone."

"It's sad. We needed each other but didn't know how to reach out. I love my dad, and now as an adult, we have a good relationship. Maybe some day we'll be able to talk. Communication wasn't so important twenty years ago. Now maybe there's too much." She laughed. "I'll take my suitcase upstairs, then help you with the pizza."

Kitchen conversation was lively. Louise entertained Jenny with the day's events, and Jenny countered with third grade activities, the victories and defeats in the classroom and on the playground. The doorbell's ring interrupted and Jenny ran to open the door.

"Dad!" She threw her arms around him. "I'm so glad to see you. I stopped at the bank, but you'd left."

David smiled. "You look wonderful, honey."

"So do you." She smoothed his hair. "A little gray is becoming. Very distinguished. Come to the kitchen and have some pizza."

"I'd like that. How long can you stay in Sowatna?"

"I don't know. School's out until September, and I don't need to take more education courses this summer."

Louise set another place at the table and poured a glass of Chianti for David. "I'm glad you're here," she said, "because Diane Martin, the president of the Arts Council, called to say that our summer theater project has hit a snag."

"What's happened? Renovation of the old Legion Club is on schedule."

"It's the funding, David. Betty and Fred Gorder have withdrawn their pledge."

David sipped his wine and scratched his left ear. "I'll talk to them. Our National Endowment for the Arts grant money should cover our current expenses, and our volunteers are saving us a ton of money."

Jenny, surprised to hear their conversation, checked the oven, then turned around. "Summer theater? You never mentioned it, Louise."

"It slipped my mind. Sorry. I haven't been too involved." She winked at David. "Except for a healthy donation."

Jenny brought three cups of coffee to the table and sat. "Tell me more."

"Summer theater's big, Jenny. We're renovating the Legion Club and are hiring a director."

Louise added, "Anne Thompson was in the shop this morning and told me about the search committee. They're using the internet and asking theater groups in the area for possible candidates."

Jenny noticed a change in her father's expression. Concern? Almost embarrassment. Maybe he knew something about directors.

"What's the play?" she asked.

"We don't know yet," Louise said. "A committee is working on it."

"I'd love to get involved," Jenny said. "I've worked with the third grade Christmas pageants, and last year I helped with two high school productions. I learned a lot about building and painting sets."

Louise was busy slicing cucumbers and tomatoes. She put the prepared vegetables into a salad bowl.

Jenny watched Louise toss the salad. Her motions turned the process into a *pas de trois*, Louise in the center between two wooden salad spoons. Jenny heard portions of *Swan Lake* in her head, then quickly tuned in to kitchen conversation.

Louise turned away from the salad and leaned back against the counter. "So now let's think about the project. This first attempt won't be Broadway. No one expects a professional theater. We could manage without the frills."

"How about a Neil Simon, or are the royalties too high?" Jenny asked. "There's melodrama. Some of those don't have royalties." Jenny thought about high school productions. "And musicals are crowd pleasers."

"The Council's working on it, but the director may have his own ideas," David said.

Louise served the pizza, followed by apple pie while Jenny and David tossed ideas around. "I'll call Diane Martin tomorrow and tell her that you want to help, Jenny," Louise said. "With the help of miracles and angels, the curtain might go up on Labor Day."

***

The next morning after breakfast, Jenny called Erin. "Do you have time for coffee? I'd like to meet you at Jerry's Expresso."

"Sure. See you at nine o'clock."

Jenny walked down the hill with Louise and stopped on the sidewalk in front of the coffee shop.

"Will you tell Erin about our theater project?" Louise asked.

"Of course, but we have other things to discuss. I'll come back to your shop for lunch."

Jenny slid into a booth across from Erin who had already ordered coffee. She ordered a latte and squeezed Erin's hand.

"Let's go back to our adventure at the church. Can't you remember anything?"

Erin shook her head. "I'm sorry. I was so stoned that I can't even remember how I got home." She stared at Jenny. "But I do remember what happened at home. Mom and Dad were drunk and arguing. Dad threw a bottle at the cat and yelled horrible accusations at both Mom and me. I ran upstairs and locked my bedroom door."

"I didn't know," Jenny said. "You've been through hell."

Erin nodded. "You went to college, and I went to rehab."

"And now you're employed there. Do you like working with the people?"

"Yes. I've been there and know what they're experiencing. It helps to know the territory." She sipped her coffee. "But let's talk about your nightmares and how we can get rid of them. 'Find the killer,' you said. Where do we start?"

"I've thought about that body being dragged. Nobody's going to drag a heavy load too far, and the car was close to the church. Who lives near there?"

Erin thought before answering. "I think there are only three houses in the block west of the church. The minister lives in one, Glenn Thompson, a road contractor, and George Hendricks, the Ford dealer, live in the other two. I come home often, so I'm sure I have the right names."

"We might rule out the minister, though you never know." Jenny raised one eyebrow.

"Richard Evans, the minister who was here when we were in high school, left after we graduated."

"I remember now," Jenny said. "He was fired. Something about drugs and theft. It was an awful scandal. I wonder what happened to him."

"Let's hope that the church found help for him." Erin stirred her coffee. "That leaves Thompson and Hendricks. We can play Nancy Drew and ask questions. Who are their friends? What are their interests?"

"And what were you doing the night of the murder?" Jenny sighed. "We have to be careful. A killer can kill again. Which name do you want?"

"I've met both families, and I don't need a new car. I'll take Thompsons. And I'll be careful. Can we meet again before I go back to Portland?"

"The day after tomorrow, here, same time."

As they stood to leave, Jennie noticed Charlie Brewster in the next booth. "Hi, I'm Jenny McKnight. We met yesterday at my aunt's shop."

"I remember." He looked down at his coffee cup, and Jenny realized that the conversation had ended.

Jenny persisted. "You're with the Chronicle. I might have a story for you."

Charlie looked up and smiled. "Sit down and tell me about it."

Jenny and Erin sat down, and Jennie introduced Erin. "We've been friends since grade school."

"That's great," Charlie said. "Now, what's the story?"

Jenny leaned her elbows on the table. "The Arts Council is planning a summer theater production. They're renovating the old Legion Club and hiring a director."

Charlie pulled a spiral notebook from his pocket and took out a ballpoint pen. "Sounds interesting. Tell me more."

Jenny detailed the proposal. "They're thinking about a musical or a light comedy. If they can put it all together, they could be ready by Labor Day."

Suddenly Charlie smiled and took Jenny's hand. "Wonderful! I'm working on a play. I could furnish a rough draft and it would be perfect for your production."

"What's it about?"

"The Pete Clampton murder. It's..."

Jenny pulled her hand away. "No." She slid out of the booth. "We can't do a play about the murder. It just wouldn't work. We need something light and fun." She turned and walked away.

Erin gave Charlie a shrug. "Sorry," she said and followed Jenny outside.

Jenny stood at the curb, hands in the pockets of her jacket. "Charlie doesn't know anything about what happened, and he could stir up real trouble for us. We have work to do. No publicity and certainly no stage production."

"I know what you mean," Erin said. "Let's do our interviews and hope Charlie Brewster won't have time to work on his play. I'll see you the day after tomorrow." She hurried down the street.

"Hey, I want to talk to you." Charlie had left the cafe and took Jenny's elbow. "What's wrong with a play about the murder? You haven't read the script, and you don't even know if I can do drama. Can't we discuss it?"

Jenny looked at Charlie and paused. There was something familiar about him. Had they met before? Had she known him in another life as a friend perhaps, someone she could trust? Maybe it was the tumble of brown hair that matched his eyes. "I guess we could talk about it," she said. "Do you want another cup of coffee?"

They walked back into the café, sat down, ordered, and then Jenny plunged in. "I can't tell you why I don't want to see a play about the Clampton murder. You're working for the Chronicle, and..."

"And," Charlie picked it up. "You're afraid that I'll report what you might say."

"That's about it," Jenny said.

"I know that we've just met, but I can understand your feelings. I've been a journalist long enough to respect someone's reluctance to confide in me, and I respect your wishes, Jenny. Believe me, when I promise to honor confidentiality, I mean it."

Jenny pondered his statements. Was he sincere? Could he be trusted? She hoped so. The coffee was hot and strong and gave her the courage she needed to go on. "I will trust you, Charlie, just this once. I think I saw something that night that might have been tied in with the murder. I didn't testify because the grand jury declared that there would be no indictment, that there was insufficient evidence to merit a trial. The real killer's still loose. Maybe he's here. Maybe he's dead or moved away. I need to find out."

"And you don't want my play produced until you find the killer?" Charlie laughed. "Come on, Jenny. You can still play detective while we're in rehearsal."

Jenny shook her head. "This isn't trivia, Charlie. I can't sleep anymore. I'm having nightmares." She stared at him. "More like visions." Charlie didn't blink, so she continued. "I need to find out why I have these visions and why it's bothering me now. Please forget your play and just do your job on the Chronicle."

"I'm sorry about the nightmares, Jenny. That's not fun. Honestly, I promise to think about it." He finished his coffee and offered his hand as he stood. "And how about dinner tonight? You choose the restaurant."

Surprised by the invitation, Jenny agreed and gave Charlie her address. "The Dolphin's good."

As they left the café, Charlie said, "I'll pick you up at six-thirty. Can I give you a lift now?"

"No, I'm walking. Thanks."

She watched Charlie drive away, then she walked slowly down the street to George Hendricks's Ford dealership. Charlie's dinner invitation was a nice gesture, but did he have a hidden agenda? Maybe he wanted to change her mind so that he could get his play produced. Fat chance, she thought.

Now she stood in front of Hendricks Ford, and she hadn't even considered her approach. What would she say? What if Hendricks was the murderer? What if he would kill again to keep his secret?

CHAPTER THREE

Jenny left the coffee shop and thought about Charlie during her three-block walk to Hendricks Ford. He'd shown no interest in her when they met at Louise's craft shop, and now a dinner invitation. Maybe she shouldn't have agreed to join him. Maybe she shouldn't have told him about the nightmares. A crime reporter writing a play about a murder. Interesting. Obviously an experienced journalist. So why had he chosen to work in a small town in Maine? Dinner conversation ought to be revealing. And she liked the brown hair and the dimple on his chin and his Miami tan.

A salesman greeted her as she entered. "Hi. Can I help you today?"

"Thanks. I'd like to see Mr. Hendricks if he isn't busy."

"No problem. Just follow me."

George Hendricks's office door was open, and Jenny was surprised to hear a piano concerto above the sound of Hendricks's voice on an intercom. "I'll get the invoice, and we'll discuss it." He looked up, saw Jenny, and smiled. "Sit down. I'll be with you in a minute." He ended his conversation, moved a stack of papers from a chair to the floor and turned to Jenny. "What can I do for you?"

Jenny took a deep breath. Why hadn't she thought about what she was going to say instead of thinking about Charlie Brewster? What if Hendricks was the murderer? She smiled and spoke slowly, uncertain, on edge. "I'm Jenny McKnight, David's daughter."

"Of course. I haven't seen you lately. David tells me that you teach in Portland."

"Yes. I'm here for the summer. I just learned that the Arts Council plans to do summer theater, and maybe you can help."

"You need a car on stage?" Hendricks laughed. "We loan convertibles for parades."

Jenny relaxed and laughed also. "We may not need a car because no one's even chosen a play." She studied Hendricks's facial expression as she added, "A new journalist here is writing a play about the Clampton murder, and he'd like to have it produced."

Hendricks's eyebrows went up, and his cheeks flushed. "That's not a good idea, Jenny. It's been ten years since the murder. People wouldn't be interested." He stood and walked her to his office door. "Call me if you need a car," he said and turned back to his desk.

Jenny walked back to Louise's craft shop reliving Hendricks's brush-off. She had blown it, she thought. She should have established some kind of rapport with him, talked about his business, his friends. Dumb.

* * *

When Jenny left his office, George Hendricks gritted his teeth as he returned to his desk. Jenny could make big trouble, and he didn't need any more. Running the dealership was enough of a headache. Why had he become involved with two fast-food, take-out seafood restaurants fifteen years ago, adding another migraine to the one he already had? He remembered the deal he'd made with Pete Clampton.

"Sure. I can supply the lobsters for you, George," Pete had said. "Just give me twenty-four hours notice."

Pete had delivered, and George didn't ask questions about size or the location of Pete's catch. Payment was in cash. No need for the invoices and statements that complicated his car business. Too bad the operation hadn't continued as originally agreed upon.

He ran his hands through his thinning gray-brown hair. At sixty-eight, his stocky, athletic body had eased into a comfortable, portly build, and bulging biceps had settled into a softer mode. A modest gut now protruded above his trousers. He picked up the phone to call Doris. His hand shook, so he cradled the phone on his right shoulder.

"Hi," he said. "I had a caller just now. Jenny McKnight. Remember her? Her dad's the bank president."

"Of course," Doris replied. "What did she want?"

"I don't know. She said that some folks are thinking about doing a play this summer based on Pete Clampton's murder."

Doris's pause was so long that George thought she'd left the line. "Oh, my God," she said at last. "When you come home for dinner, we'll have a drink."

"Good. See you about six." George replaced the phone, put both elbows on his desk, his head resting on his hands. He wished that he hadn't called his wife. Doris would over-react as usual. Jenny had mentioned a new journalist. 'Journalist' was bad enough; 'new' was even worse.

* * *

Glenn Thompson a local road contractor, stood at his living room's picture window and studied the house across the street. It needed a paint job, and the lawn was a disgrace. Glenn liked neatness and order. His highway projects won approval because his crews cleaned up after the work was done. No trash, no unfinished road work. His men followed orders. If they didn't, they knew the consequences, so they put in long hours and accepted the wages guaranteed when they arrived. Glenn was proud of his working arrangements, the housing and meals. Men working and living together meant constant mediations, but Glenn's foreman, Oscar Mendes, was an expert. And he knew the language.

He was also proud of his own appearance, neat and well groomed. He kept in shape with a daily exercise program.

"Those damned Petersons ought to be sued," Glenn said as Ann walked into the room. "Their yard is a disgrace."

"Maybe you should call the mayor."

"For all I know, his relatives probably live there." Glenn turned and stared at his wife. "Where were you yesterday? You weren't here when I got home from Bangor."

"I was at the craft shop." Ann turned away and walked to the kitchen.

Funny, Glenn mused. The door bell interrupted his thoughts. He didn't recognize the young woman who stood outside. She wore jeans and a heavy blue cardigan sweater, and her blonde hair was swept back into a long braid.

"Hi," she said. "I'm Erin Gregory, and I'd like to visit with you for a few minutes if you have time."

Glenn ushered her inside and smoothed back his hair. "I don't think we've met. What can I do for you?" He didn't offer her a seat. She probably was a wild-eyed evangelist who wanted to save his soul or donate to her church's building fund. If she pulled out a Bible, he'd shove her out the door.

"I stopped by to tell you that our town is going to do a summer theater production, and I thought that you and Mrs. Thompson might be interested."

Glenn, relieved that she wasn't going to save his soul, smiled. Erin was attractive, young. Maybe available. "Sit down. We've already contributed to the project, but I haven't heard much lately." He joined her on the davenport.

Erin moved away and took a notebook from her pocket. "The Arts Council started the project, and I don't know much about it. I want to get some feed-back from people in town to see if there's enough interest to proceed."

"Putting on a theater project is a real challenge, but it can be done. Do you have a theater?"

"I heard that the old Legion Club is available. I don't have any details."

"I have some equipment that might be useful." He didn't notice that Ann had come into the room.

Ann extended her hand to Erin. "I'm Ann, and I'm already working with the Arts Council. I'm on the search committee to find a director."

"Do you think your friends might be interested?" Erin asked.

"They already are. I'm sure that David McKnight will be involved," Glenn said and looked at Ann.

"Yes," Ann said, "and maybe the Wilders. Their son is a drama major at the university."

Erin stood and moved to the door. "We're just beginning," she said. "We don't even have a play."

"I'm sure you'll find a good one," Glenn said.

"There's a new journalist in town who is writing a play about the Pete Clampton murder. He'd like the Arts Council to present it."

"I'd rather see a musical. Something light. The trial's old hat. People wouldn't be interested."

"You're probably right," Erin said. "Thanks for your time."

Glenn watched Erin as she walked to her car. He might call her some evening to check on the production, he thought, and that journalist had better forget about Pete's murder.

* * *

Jenny left the Ford agency and wandered down to the pier, her thoughts a jumble of what-I-should-have-said, and what-I-saw-in-George's-reaction. She knew that she had blown a good opportunity to learn more about Hendricks and his relationship with Clampton and might not have another chance to talk to him. She bought a Snickers candy bar at a kiosk next to the pier, found a bench, and looked out at the harbor. Lobster boats were securely tied up at the dock, and flocks of sea gulls hovered, skimming the waves above the boats. Cirrus clouds moved across an azure-blue sky, and a gentle breeze nudged the crafts that were tied to the pier.

She finished her candy and walked slowly across the street to Louise's craft shop. When she entered the shop, she saw Louise visiting with a man who looked vaguely familiar. Neither of them noticed her until she spoke.

"Hi, I've been to the Ford dealership," Jenny said. Louise glanced at her but turned back to the man. Jenny tried again. She reached for the man's hand. "Hi, I'm Jenny McKnight, Louise's niece."

Louise laughed. "This is Colin Greene, attorney at law." She looked at him. "That's a proper title, don't you think?"

Greene laughed also and winked at Jenny. "Sounds terribly legalistic, doesn't it? It's nice to see you again, Jenny. It's been a long time. We've been discussing the theater project. Are you interested?"

"I am. Did Louise tell you that there's a new reporter in town who has written a play about the Pete Clampton murder and wants to have it produced here?"

"The reporter came to my office yesterday. I loaned him the case file, and I suggested that I might want a part in the production. I don't think that he was impressed."

Jenny snorted. "I hope his play goes into file thirteen or the recycle bin on his computer. My reasons are personal." Jenny looked down. "The reporter's investigation might muddy the water for me." She looked up at the lawyer. "I was a senior in high school when Pete was killed. High school kids don't pay much attention to adults, so I didn't know him. Did you know him, Mr. Greene?"

"Of course. Everybody in town knew Pete." He paused and looked at Louise, then back to Jenny. "His dad started the lobster fishing business. Pete was brought up on a lobster boat, and he never left. He knew every cove, inlet and rock on the coast. He was a good man, a very private man. He didn't socialize much. Your dad probably knows more about him because of the bank. Ask him."

"I will. Thanks."

Greene smiled at Jenny. "I'm glad we met." He turned to Louise. "I have an appointment. I'll talk to you later."

After he left, Jenny asked, "Louise, do you have time for lunch."

"Absolutely." She took Jenny's hand. "I'm glad that you met Colin. We've known each other for a long time." Before Jenny had time to comment, Louise went to her office and returned with her purse. "Let's go,"

Lobster bisque at the Crab shack gave Jenny time to give Louise a full report.

"You told Charlie about the nightmares, and now you're having dinner with him," Louise said. "The conversation should be fascinating. And Hendricks didn't sound gleeful about Charlie's play. Hmm." She massaged her left shoulder and frowned. "What are you and Erin doing, Jenny? You said you were to meet her, and now you tell me that both of you are questioning people. What's going on?"

Jenny sighed and took Louise's hand. "I want to find out why I'm having nightmares. Maybe they're connected to Clampton's murder."

"Jenny, I know that you're a psychic, and that there are spirits in our lives, both good and bad. Have you thought that maybe that vision, that spirit, is a good spirit, not a bad one?"

Jenny's eyes widened. "Is he trying to tell me something? Prodding me to take some kind of action?"

"It's possible."

Jenny's mind raced. The visions, her need to return to Sowatna. Finding Erin at home. Even Charlie's play. Too many coincidences. She finished her soup and propped her elbows on the table.

"I remember every detail when we smoked pot upstairs in the church ten years ago." Louise leaned forward as Jenny described the experience. "If Brennan had been brought to trial, I would have told what I saw that night."

"But it's still bugging you," Louise said. "Be careful."

"Maybe I should visit with the minister. He lives across the street from the church."

"Mr. Conway is new and wouldn't be much help. Mr. Evans was our minister ten years ago. He left about eight years ago under some rather questionable circumstances. He moved to Portland and might still be there. Call him."

"I will because we're thinking about the people who live near the church. That's why I met with Hendricks, and Erin's calling on the Thompsons. Those are the only three houses in that block west of the church."

"That's right," Louise said, "but have you thought about the people who live behind the church on Fifth Street?"

Jenny laughed. "I should begin with you. You're right next door."

"Oh, sure," Louise said. She laughed too, but Jenny noticed a brief look around her aunt's eyes that was not amusement.

"And your neighbors next door own a bed and breakfast."

"Yes, the *Bella Notte.* That's Italian for 'Beautiful Night.' Guido's Italian. They bought the house about four years ago."

"I remember his wife Mavis when she worked at the high school lunch room. Pretty and plump. A big, tall girl. The boys couldn't take their eyes off her cleavage, but she could have knocked them all flat if they'd tried anything. She left town before I graduated. And now she's back with an Italian husband. Is their operation successful?"

"I think so," Louise said. "I have to admit that I wasn't happy to see a bed and breakfast next door. Noisy people, cars coming and going at all hours. The Biancis had to get permission from the city council to open the place, and a lot of us testified against it. In spite of our protests, the council approved their request. Maybe Guido charmed them with his beautiful dark brown eyes and wavy black hair. Mavis did all right."

"Have there been problems?" Jenny asked.

"Surprisingly, no, and they've been good neighbors. I don't see Mavis often, but Guido stops by the craft shop sometimes. Says his mother crochets."

"But the bed and breakfast wasn't here ten years ago."

"No, but Mavis was here. Her parents moved to Cape Cod about fifteen years ago, and Mavis moved into the Burchard guest house. Her parents rented it for her from a legal firm that handled the Burchard trust. The big house was empty until she and Guido bought it."

Jenny raised her index finger. "So Mavis is still on the list of suspects."

Louise looked at her watch. "I must get back to the shop. I hope you have a good evening with Charlie. I'd like to be a mouse in the corner."

Jenny laughed. "Careful. There might be a trap. If it's not too late, I'll fill you in tonight."

* * *

Charlie stood on the sidewalk outside of the cafe and watched Jenny as she walked up the street toward the Ford Agency. Nice legs, he thought. Maybe a nut case with those nightmares, but he needed her as a friend, not an enemy. He'd put too many hours into the play to forget it now. Of course he could turn it into a novel, maybe another like Capote's 'In Cold Blood,' almost a fictionalized version of a real murder. He'd read the book and seen the movie. Not a bad alternative. He looked again at Jenny's retreating figure. No, dammit, his work would be a play, and it would be produced here in Sowatna. He thought about the file that Greene had given him. He'd put it in a drawer waiting for the time to study it thoroughly. As a reporter for the Miami Herald, he'd learned that without careful preparation, time to study all the angles and all the evidence, his front-page news reports could result in, at the least, irate readers, and at the worst, expensive and damaging lawsuits. He'd have time on Saturday to give the file his full attention.

He walked to the Chronicle office and stopped at the reception desk. Sara had left her office and was now taking calls behind the counter.

"Hi," Charlie said. "Anything for me?"

Sara flapped her eyelashes, heavy with mascara, and cracked her gum. "Mrs. Quincy left a file for you. Here it is."

Charlie took the file and sat on a wooden, armless chair in the corner. The front office was bare with meager furnishings. A table piled with recent editions of the Chronicle, two wooden chairs and a floor lamp. Charlie gave the lamp a second look. The base was plain dark wood, but the shade was ornate, massive, too large for the base and covered in red velvet with long braided silk tassels hanging down.

Sara saw him eyeing the lamp. "That shade belonged to Mrs. Quincy's grandmother, so don't even touch it."

Charlie laughed and studied the folder. Inside was a clipping from yesterday's front page and a sticky note reading, 'Follow-up for tomorrow's edition.'

"When do we print?" Charlie asked.

"Whenever Mrs. Quincy thinks we're ready," Sara said. "You'll have time now."

Charlie read the article, a summer reading program for kids at the library. If he could find the library, he could be there in time to interview the librarian and some of the kids. Sara gave him directions, and when he arrived, the main reading room was filled with kids who giggled, jostled, poked, and shoved. Two women ran around the stacks looking for strays and finally led two six or seven-year-old boys back to the center of the room. Charlie took out his BlackBerry and introduced himself to the elder of the two women.

"Thanks for coming," the gray-haired, matronly woman said. "I'm Genevieve Upton, the librarian. And this is," she turned to her companion, "Diane Martin, the president of SAC."

"Sowatna Arts Council," Diane explained. "We started this reading program last summer, and it's been a great success. You read yesterday's article of course."

Charlie nodded and noticed that the president of SAC fit the role. Tall, a nicely contured body, great legs well displayed under a yellow tennis skirt, and long blonde hair pulled back into a pony tail. Diane gave Charlie a wide smile. "So you're the new man on the block," she said. "How do you like Charlotte? She's *tres formidable*."

Everybody Knew Pete

"We've just met. I like her," Charlie said, a bit on the defensive. Diane wouldn't get much out of him.

"Good," Diane said. She smiled. "Would you like to interview me for the paper?"

"Yes, and Mrs. Upton and some of the kids."

Diane motioned Charlie to a gray upholstered davenport next to the front window. She sat down close to him, hips touching, and looked at his BlackBerry. "You can take this down," she said. "I moved here four years ago from Evanston, Illinois. My husband got tired of Lake Michigan and decided to try the Atlantic. He sails."

"And you?"

"I'm a landlubber. Have you ever been seasick? Not fun. So I stay ashore. I organized the Arts Council three years ago because Sowatna could use a little culture, and I was bored."

"Children?" Charlie asked.

"Three, all under nine years old. So the reading program was a natural. We have other projects too. We work with the Maine Humanities Council and bring in guest speakers. And now we're thinking about summer theater."

Playing innocent, Charlie said, "Where would you present the plays, and what ones are you considering? It's a big undertaking."

"We can't build a theater yet, but the old Legion Club could be renovated. I'll appoint a play-selection committee to find something that won't charge huge royalties, something that would appeal to tourists and the locals."

"Do you get many tourists during the summer?"

"Yes. The natives call them 'rusticators,' people who come here for the summer. They rent cottages or stay at bed and breakfasts."

"Your selection committee might be interested in my play. I have to tie up some loose ends, get more detail. It's about the Pete Clampton murder ten years ago."

Diane smiled. "If the play's good," she winked at Charlie, "and I'm sure you know how to write, it ought to be a winner. I don't know anything about the murder or the trial. It's past history, but the locals might enjoy a rerun of the events. When you finish it, call me, and I'll give it to the selection committee. Of course I'll give it a big plug." She stood and took his hand. "Call me any time."

Charlie's cell phone rang as he stood up. "Mrs. Quincy's sending over a photographer, so line up some good shots," Sara told him.

Charlie replaced his phone and found the librarian busy with six pre-schoolers who sat on the floor in front of her. "The Chronicle wants to take some pictures, Mrs. Upton. A photographer is coming over."

"That's nice. The children will love to see their photographs in the paper."

Charlie watched as Diane corralled a group of middle school students and gave each of them a book. "Let's take turns reading," she said. Her smile was directed at Charlie.

When the photographer, a young man who could have passed as a high school student, arrived, Charlie watched and took notes. The kids loved the attention and scrambled for front row positions. "Okay, everybody, let's have some fun," the young man said.

Fifteen minutes later, the photographer and his subjects had had enough fun. The kids grabbed the books they'd checked out and, in spite of directives from Mrs. Upton, "Don't push, don't run, walk slowly," rushed to the front door like a stampeding herd of buffalo.

Charlie laughed. "Kids never change," he said.

The photographer nodded. "I'll walk back to the office with you," he said.

Charlie pocketed his BlackBerry and thanked Mrs. Upton. He was relieved to notice that Diane had disappeared.

As he walked toward the Chronicle office with the photographer, Charlie asked, "How long have you worked for the paper?"

"I just started this summer. I'm Adam Roberts. My dad worked for the paper even before Mrs. Quincy became the editor. I sort of inherited the job when my dad retired this year."

Charlie's mind did cartwheels. "Then your dad probably knew all about the Clampton murder."

"Sure. The police called him in to take pictures on Pete's boat."

"I'd like to meet your dad," Charlie said. "I'm working on a play about the murder, and he may be able to flesh out some of the details."

"Call him any time," Roberts said. "He's Adam too. I'm Junior." He scribbled a phone number and address on a note pad.

"Thanks. I'll call him."

They walked into the Chronicle's front foyer. Sara met them with raised eyebrows and signaled murder with a finger across her throat.

Charlie heard Mrs. Quincy's raspy voice behind her closed door. "Your ad is sexist and demeaning, and I won't print it." An emphatic bang meant that her phone conversation had come to an abrupt halt. The door opened, and the editor strode out, hands thrust inside skirt pockets. She glared at Charlie and Adam. "It's about time you two showed up. Got the pictures?"

Adam nodded and gave her his camera. "It's all in there, ready for printing."

She turned to Charlie. "And what do you have?"

"I interviewed the librarian, the president of the Arts Council, and some of the kids. Now I need a computer to write up the article." He pulled out his BlackBerry. "It's all here."

"Good. You can use the office next to mine."

Charlie finished the article, left it with Sara, and drove back to his motel. Four o'clock. He'd have time to check the Greene file before his date with Jenny. He opened the file and spread its contents on the bed. Pages of testimony, but, holy shit! No photographs! Charlie was stunned. He knew from experience that the photographer took precedence over the coroner and the police. "Don't touch anything until it's photographed" was the usual command, and everyone obeyed. So where were the pictures? Adam Roberts, Senior should have some answers.

CHAPTER FOUR

"Watch your step. These old stairs have been here since World War 1."

Jenny's warning came too late as Charlie stepped on a loose board. He grabbed Jenny's elbow and steadied himself. "The food had better be worth the climb," he said.

The Dolphin, Sowatna's claim to a five-star restaurant, perched above a tackle and gift shop next to the pier. The hostess greeted Jenny, eyed Charlie with interest, and seated them at a table by the window that faced east toward the ocean. The sunset behind them cast an eerie glow over the water. The sea gulls had nested. The tourists and fishermen had found shelter. Boats anchored at the pier rocked gently against their moorings. A peaceful evening.

There was nothing peaceful in Jenny's mind. High winds of anxiety agitated waves of tension, suspicion and, she had to admit, fear. Charlie had called for her at Louise's home. A gentleman in manner, he escorted her to his Ford Escort, opened the passenger door just as she reached for the handle, and made small talk as she directed him to the restaurant. Charlotte Quincy was interesting, and the library interview had gone well. He'd met Colin Greene who had given him a file. No details.

They ordered drinks and watched the pier fade into darkness. "How was your day?" Charlie asked as the martinis arrived.

"Nothing special," Jenny replied, following the casual, on-the-surface program Charlie had established.

Conversation ceased during dinner, and Jenny was relieved to turn her mind over to Caesar salad, lobster, and creme brule, but the tension returned during after-dinner coffee. Jenny excused herself and found the ladies room. As she applied lipstick, she wished that she could find a magic carpet to transport her back to Louise's home. The curly brown hair and the Miami tan weren't enough to attract her to Charlie. They had nothing in common, and his play-writing scheme was an anathema. She plastered a smile on her face and returned to the table.

Charlie held her chair for her, sipped his coffee, and cleared his throat. "The dinner was great. What's wrong?"

Jenny, startled, shook her head. "What's wrong is that I don't feel right. I'd like to go home."

Charlie nodded and called for the check. "Let's walk out on the pier," he said.

Charlie took Jenny's hand as they walked past anchors, coils of rope, and bird droppings. He stopped in front of an old lobster boat in need of a paint and scraping job. "I'm not much good at this," he said. "I know that you're upset about my play. I'm new in town. So much I don't know. I'd like your help, but I don't know where to begin."

Jenny smiled, and the waves of tension eased into ripples. She steered him to a bench and sat beside him. Where to begin, indeed.

"Charlie, we've just met. I've told you about my nightmares, but I know nothing about you, why you're here, why you're interested in the Clampton murder. You've met my aunt and my friend, Erin, and you must have now a sense of this place. So what about you?" And why should she even care, she asked herself.

"I came here because I'd visited Maine with my parents, and I wanted to get away from my life in Miami. A crime reporter suffers burnout after six years of looking at dead bodies, pushing the cops for more information than they want to give, and tangling with lawyers who are tied up in the legal systems." He paused. "And I wanted to forget a marriage that ended in a nasty divorce."

"I'm sorry," Jenny said. "I shouldn't have probed."

"That's okay. And you asked about the play. When you're doing crime in Miami, you see just about everything. The Clampton murder trial was juicy enough to whet my appetite, and it occurred in an area that sounded vaguely familiar but remote enough to get me away from my frustrations. Anger, too, Jenny. Dierdre didn't even have the decency to meet me. She sent an e-mail, for God's sake!"

"That's rotten," Jenny said. "No wonder you chose Sowatna." She smiled and took his hand. "Welcome to the nut house. You're among friends."

Charlie took Jenny's hand as they started across the street to his car. They had almost reached the curb when they heard a car approaching on their right. The car's headlights were bright. As it came toward them, the driver accelerated. Jenny stood transfixed, staring at the car.

"Move, Jenny!" he yelled and pushed her roughly ahead toward the curb. The car was almost upon him, and he heard Jenny's scream and saw her fall on the pavement as he lunged forward and fell down against her. The car whizzed by, missing them by inches. They lay against the curb, half of their bodies on the sidewalk, the other half on the street. Jenny sobbed quietly and moaned.

Charlie moved away from her. "Are you all right?"

"I think so." She sat up and rubbed her back. "He tried to kill us. Did you see anything?"

"No. There wasn't time. I think it was a Ford. A dark color, but I'm not sure. I'm sorry I pushed you so hard, but you just stood there."

"I know. It was the lights. Something about the lights." She shuddered.

Charlie helped her to her feet. They brushed off their clothes, and Jenny picked up her purse. "I'm okay," she said. "Let's go home."

She took Charlie's arm and tried to ignore the pain. She'd hit the pavement hard, and Charlie had fallen down against her increasing the pressure on her right hip.

"You're not okay," Charlie said. "Where does it hurt?"

"My right hip. I can walk, so it's not broken. I'll lean on you."

Without a word, Charlie picked her up, put her left hip against his body and carried her the few hundred yards to the car.

His gesture bought out the tears she'd tried to conceal and was angry that she'd been weak, and, darn it, 'feminine.' For five years, she had been her own boss, handled her own finances, filled her own gas tank and decided with whom she would eat and sleep.

She sat up straighter in spite of the pain and wiped away the tears. "Thanks, Charlie. I'll do the same for you some day."

They both laughed as they arrived at Louise's home. Jenny leaned on Charlie as they walked up the steps and crossed the front porch. When she opened the door, he kissed her gently on her forehead.

"I'll call you tomorrow to see how you are. It's been an unforgettable evening."

Jenny noticed a soft light purple aura about Charlie as he walked to his car. Nice, she thought, and 'unforgettable' was an understatement.

Jenny limped into the kitchen and found Louise at the table drinking a cup of tea. "Are you hurt?" Louise asked. "What happened?"

Jenny poured a cup of tea from the pot on the table. She winced as she sat down. "We had a fine dinner and a good conversation later at the pier. He told me about his recent divorce and his need for a change in his life. That was great, but I hurt my hip."

"How?" Louise asked.

"When we crossed the street, a car almost hit us. It was horrible, Louise. The driver *tried* to hit us. I couldn't move. Charlie pushed me out of the way, and we both fell down against the curb."

"Did you see who was in the car?"

"No, and we didn't get the license number. Who would do something like that?"

"Who knows? Maybe it's related to your inquiries about the Clampton murder."

Jenny sipped her tea and thought about Louise's suggestion. She'd seen George Hendricks. Had Charlie mentioned her search to anyone?

"I'll think about it." She paused. "Tomorrow, I'd like to talk to Mavis at the Bella Notte. I haven't seen her since high school, and she probably won't remember me, but she's in the neighborhood now."

Jenny finished her tea. Sleep didn't come easily. Her hip bothered as she turned in bed, and she envisioned the car lights as they came toward her. Why hadn't she run to the curb? Why did Charlie have to push her out of the way? Two hours later, she finally drifted off and dreamed of screaming birds that tore at her clothes.

* * *

While Jenny and Charlie sat at the pier, Erin and her father sat at their kitchen table, Jacob Gregory with a bottle of Budweiser, Erin with a can of soda.

"Why'd ya come home, Erin? Ain't nothin' here for you. We're okay, Gloria and me, and we don't need no lookin' after."

Erin nodded. She knew that arguing led nowhere. "I came because you're my parents, and I like to be with you." The last part was a lie. She came because there was always the faint hope that their lives might change. And one day at home always convinced her that nothing had changed. Her dad would continue to drink himself to death, and her mom would continue to rage and threaten. Erin knew the scene so well that she could lip-synch the dialogue.

"Gloria said you was with Jenny McKnight. Pretty fancy, I'd say."

"Jenny and I were friends in high school, Dad. She's interested in that murder ten years ago. Pete Clampton, remember?"

"Yeah. Funny you should mention it. I got a call today from Tim Brennan, the guy they arrested for killing him."

Erin looked up at her dad. "What did he say?"

"Said he was comin' up to Sowatna. Could I help him, he said."

"What did he want?"

Jacob looked down at his beer. "Nothin' you'd care about." He looked up. "Forget I said anything. He probably won't come."

Erin suspected that Tim wanted drugs. He'd been in treatment four years ago at the Thomas J. Moore Center in Portland, and she remembered him as one of their failures, one of the lost ones. But why had he called her father? Was he drugging too? She looked at his clothes. He wore a long-sleeved plaid shirt instead of his usual sleeveless T-shirt. Needle marks? She grabbed his left arm and pulled up his sleeve before he could stop her.

"What the hell are ya doin', for God's sake?" he yelled.

Erin saw the marks and fell back on her chair. Tears ran down her cheeks. It was too much. Her dad, a junkie. An alcoholic was bad enough. She covered her face with her hands. "I can't believe you'd do this," she said.

"It's my life, and I can do as I please. Now that you're in the big city, you're Miss Holier-Than-Thou. Big deal. Go on back to Portland." He swigged his beer and tossed the empty bottle into a trash can.

Erin ran out of the kitchen and collided with her mother who had just come in.

"What's going on?" Gloria Gregory asked. She took Erin's hand. "You're crying."

"Ask Dad," Erin said. She sat on the davenport and blew her nose.

Gloria put her arm around Erin. "That's okay, sweetie," she said. She stood and walked into the kitchen. "Dammit, Jacob, what did you say? What did you do?"

Jacob pulled down his shirt sleeve. "She's got no right," he said.

"So now she knows what a low-down skunk you really are!" Gloria said. "I don't know why I put up with you and..."

Erin put her hands over her ears and mouthed the next words. It was time to leave. She ran upstairs to her bedroom and threw her clothes into a suitcase. She couldn't stay here, couldn't listen any more. Crying had become dry sobs as she closed the suitcase and ran downstairs.

Her mother met her at the door. "Don't leave," she said. "We can work things out."

"No, Mom. You and Dad need to work things out yourselves. I can't help you."

She walked to her car, drove away and didn't look back. Four blocks from home, she stopped and considered her options. A motel, Jenny at Aunt Louise's home, a bed and breakfast? Her first choice made sense. She registered at the Blueberry Inn.

"Room seven," the night clerk said and gave her a key. "It's on the left."

Jenny unpacked, turned on the TV, and lay back on the bed. She stared at the ceiling and weighed her options. She wasn't to meet with Jenny until the day after tomorrow. She'd interviewed the Thompsons, recognized the come-on in Glenn's remarks, and didn't want to see him again. She looked up at the television screen and watched a road construction gang at work. Maybe a trip to Thompson's construction business might offer more information. She undressed, shrugged off her parents' life style, and fell into an uneasy sleep.

The next morning, Erin dressed and thought about breakfast. As she opened her door, she was startled to see Charlie Brewster emerge from the room next to hers.

"Hi," she said. "I'm Erin Gregory, Jenny's friend."

Charlie looked startled, and Erin laughed. "I moved in last night. Life at home wasn't much fun." She looked at her watch. "It's seven-thirty, and I'm hungry. Are you?"

Charlie nodded. "Where's a good place for breakfast?"

"The Sowatna Inn serves great pancakes. It's on Front Street. I'll meet you there."

They got into their cars, and Charlie followed Erin's car to the inn.

After breakfast, Charlie said, "The pancakes were great. Mind if I smoke?"

Erin shook her head and brought out a package of Camels. "I quit for a while," she said, "but struggling with two addictions was one too many."

Charlie's raised eyebrows induced an admission of Erin's victory over alcohol and her work at the Center in Portland.

"Did you know Tim Brennan?" he asked.

"Yes. He went through rehab with us twice, but he's still drinking and drugging." Should she tell Charlie about Brennan's return to Sowatna? She knew that Jenny wanted nothing to do with Charlie's play, but he'd bought breakfast. "My dad said that he was coming to Sowatna. He didn't say when. Maybe you'd like to meet him."

Charlie's smile brightened the dining room. "You bet," he said. "Can you arrange it?"

"I'll try. That means I have to connect with my dad again, something I don't want to do, but I'll do it for you." She smiled. "Thanks for breakfast."

She forgot about Charlie and Tim Brennan as she drove to Thompson's road construction operation three miles beyond the city limits. A sign on the corner of the highway and a narrow black-top road highway read 'Thompson Construction Company.' She followed the road that was bordered by rows of pine trees and stopped on front of a double-wide trailer, probably the main office, she guessed. She was surprised to notice a lawn and flower beds. Off on either side of the office were piles of gravel, almost two-stories high, and pieces of heavy equipment. The machinery was as clean as the lawn and flower beds. A two-story building stood behind a trailer, eight identical windows on each story.

She pushed open the door of the trailer and was relieved that Thompson wasn't at his desk. She walked around behind the office and noticed three men standing by a gravel truck. Dark-skinned with thick black hair, they looked to be foreign, maybe South American or Mexican. They were dressed in identical gray coveralls and wore heavy boots.

"Hi," she said. "If Mr. Thompson isn't here, I'd like to talk to you for a minute."

One of the men stepped forward. *"No hablo ingles,"* he said.

Erin remembered enough of her high school Spanish and her refresher conversations at the center to converse with the men. They told her that Thompson was on a construction site and that they were ordered to keep visitors away.

"What do you want?" The voice behind her was loud, firm, and heavily accented.

Erin turned and saw a man dressed in jeans and a brown sweat shirt. He carried a hard hat and a crow bar. He was dark-skinned with black eyes that glared at her. Although only slightly taller than Erin, his presence was threatening.

"I was interested in building a road," she said.

The man laughed as he touched her shoulder. "I don't think you want to build a road," he said, "but I can show you around. I'm Oscar Mendes, and I'm in charge when Mr. Thompson's away."

Erin hesitated. "That would be nice, but I can't stay long," she said.

"Come," Mendes said. He took her hand and led her back to the trailer.

As they entered and Mendes shut the door behind them, Erin was apprehensive. Maybe she should have said goodbye and hit the road.

Mendes didn't waste time. He grabbed Erin's neck and pushed her face against his. His breath smelled of garlic and beer. When his other hand reached under her T-shirt, Erin went to work. With all of her strength, she kneed his crotch, and when he released her, she shoved him against the wall.

"Don't touch me, you creep," she said. She opened the door and ran out before Mendes could reach her. Her hands shook as she started her car and drove away.

She relaxed as she entered Sowatna's city limits. So much for the Thompson Construction Company. She'd seen enough – the foreign laborers and, she was sure, their living quarters. She'd noticed that the three men had walked away when Mendes arrived. No help there if he'd raped her. She returned to her room at the motel, switched on the TV, and lay down on the bed. Maybe she'd call Jenny, and maybe she'd take a nap and try to forget Oscar Mendes.

* * *

Charlie paid the breakfast bill, located a telephone book and punched in Troy Witherspoon's number. Colin Greene, Brennan's lawyer, had said that the court reporter had a complete transcript of the trial, and Charlie needed details.

When Witherspoon answered, Charlie introduced himself and asked for an appointment. "I'm working on a play about the Clampton murder," Charlie said, "and I'd like to visit with you."

Witherspoon gave him directions to his home on Grant Avenue. "Ring the bell and come in," he said.

Witherspoon's home was Maine white. Charlie surmised that the white paint purchased in Maine was whiter than the white purchased in the other forty-nine states. Maybe it was because the air was more clear and the pine trees more green. Two steps led up to the front door, and Charlie noticed a ramp at one side. Witherspoon's lawn needed mowing, and the shrubbery was overgrown and tangled.

Charlie rang the bell and entered as instructed and was surprised to see the court reporter in an electric wheel chair. Witherspoon's curly hair was more gray than brown. He was heavy set, biceps bulging under his sport shirt. He wore navy shorts. One of his legs was missing.

"I left the other one in 'Nam'," Witherspoon said. "How can I help you?"

"I got interested in the Clampton murder when I was a crime reporter for the Miami Herald," Charlie explained. "I moved here for a change of scenery and to work out the details of the trial. Colin Greene told me that you had the complete transcript."

"Yes. Our job is to keep those transcripts for seven years."

"I can't afford to buy a copy," Charlie said, "but I'd like to visit with you about the murder."

"Of course. I'm not busy right now. Coffee?"

Witherspoon beckoned Charlie to follow him to the kitchen. He stood on one leg and poured out two mugs. He sat down again and took them to the table. "I have a prosthesis that I wear in court, but at home, I prefer the chair. Now let's talk about the murder."

"I know that the grand jury acquitted Tim Brennan for lack of evidence, but I'd like to know more."

"Brennan testified that he'd come on board to buy drugs and to arrange for some sort of a trip. Bill Daniels, the county attorney, decided that the trip was immaterial and irrelevant, and the jury agreed."

"But they did find Brennan on the dock by Pete's boat."

"Yes, and they found his fingerprints in the cabin along with a lot of others. But they couldn't find a weapon, and there was no blood. Obviously Pete had been killed somewhere else and placed in his captain's chair. Brennan's a little guy, probably weighs about one hundred and forty. Pete was big, probably weighed about one-ninety. Brennan couldn't have carried Pete anywhere, let alone lifted him into his chair."

"But they found heroin on the boat. Wasn't that a reason to investigate further?"

"Daniels said that the owner of the drugs was dead, so there was no point in a follow-up."

Charlie drank his coffee and stared up at the ceiling. "It's strange," he said. "Greene gave me a copy of the case file, and there wasn't a lot in it, not even photographs. I was a crime reporter for the Miami Herald for six years, and I know that the photographer is always the first one on the scene. Nothing is touched until he's done his work."

"True, and Adam Roberts took pictures. I don't know what happened to them. You'll have to ask him." He smiled at Charlie. "If you want more coffee, help yourself. Now tell me about your play."

"In the play, Brennan goes to trial. A big courtroom scene. The stage will be divided, and when something happens in the courtroom on one side of the stage, what actually happened in detail is shown on the other side of the stage."

"You're going to make a lot of people curious or perhaps angry."

Charlie laughed. "I'm changing all the names of places and characters. Of course the natives will recognize some of the plot because the first victim is a lobsterman.

"There's more than one murder?"

"Of course. No self-respecting murder drama has only one murder. Remember Agatha Christie's *"The Mousetrap"*? And I'm borrowing another gimmick from a play I starred in as a senior in high school, Ayn Rand's *"The Night of January Sixteenth."*

"What's that?"

"I'm going to have the judge select the jury from the audience. I saw that done in Deadwood, South Dakota. They did the trial of Jack McCall, the man who murdered Wild Bill Hickok. The tourists loved it."

"Will the accused be found guilty?"

"That's going to be up to the jury, and it's not important. The plot centers around the characters in the play, the hero and heroine, the legal folks and some inhabitants of the town. The town's name is New Bradford."

Charlie got up and refilled their mugs. "When I started writing, it all seemed to be cut and dried. Just another murder, and I'd seen too many in Miami. Now that I'm here, I know that Clampton's murder isn't cut and dried, and that interests me. Where are the photographs? Why wasn't there a further investigation after Brennan was released?"

"I can't answer, Charlie. At the time, we accepted the grand jury's verdict, and then it was business as usual. Maybe we wanted to forget what happened to Pete. Murder's not pleasant."

"And maybe somebody didn't want to see a further investigation." He drank more coffee. "Do you know Jenny McKnight?"

"Of course. I know her dad and her aunt better. Jenny teaches in Portland, and we don't see her often."

"She and her friend, Erin Gregory, are digging around about the murder. This is confidential, Troy. She says that she's having nightmares and thinks they're connected to something she saw when she was in high school, and she wants to clear the air. I can't give you any more details.

"Her dad told me that she was a kind of a psychic, so maybe there's a connection somewhere. Personally I don't believe any of that occult stuff."

Charlie nodded. "I don't understand it either." He leaned closer to Witherspoon. "The Arts Council here is planning to do a summer theater production, and I'd like to have them use my play. Jenny's against it, says it interferes with her investigation."

Witherspoon laughed. "Good luck, Charlie. I'll be around to pick up the pieces."

Charlie stood and shook hands with the court reporter. "I'll call if I learn anything new. Thanks for your help."

Before Charlie started his car, he found Adam Roberts's phone number and punched it in on his cell phone. Charlie introduced himself and asked for an interview after his work at the Chronicle.

"My son told me that you'd call," Roberts said. "Come about five o'clock."

* * *

Jenny awakened at seven o'clock the morning after her narrow escape in front of the Dolphin. She struggled out of bed. Her hip had throbbed all night, and she hadn't slept well. She limped to the bathroom, dressed and went to the top of the stairs.

"I smell coffee," she called. "I'll be right down."

Suddenly she felt a force pushing her forward. She fell down the steps, head to carpet, back to wall, knees to the banister. She fell totally out of control.

Louise heard Jenny's screams and ran to the stairway. Jenny lay in a crumpled heap at the bottom of the stairs. Blood gushed from her forehead. Louise ran back to the kitchen, grabbed a dish towel and her cell phone. As she punched in 911, she wrapped the towel around Jenny's head.

"My poor baby," Louise murmured.

"Something pushed me," Jenny said as she fought for breath. She looked back upstairs and saw a gray aura surrounding a gilt-framed picture that hung on the wall behind the stairway.

"Who's in that picture? she asked.

"That's my great grandfather, William Campbell. He was born in Bradford, Scotland, in 1864 and died there in 1892. He was only twenty-eight. There's no official record of his death. All I know is what my grandmother told me. She was only three when he died and didn't remember much about him."

"How did he die?"

"I don't remember. I'll have to look it up."

"I'd like to know. She tried to sit up but fell back onto the floor.

"Don't move. The ambulance will be here soon."

Six minutes later, Jenny was strapped on a gurney and transported to the emergency room of the local hospital.

The doctor ordered x-rays and while the film was being developed, he repaired the gash in Jenny's forehead.

"It took only four stitches," he said, "and the gash is close to your hair line. You'll never notice it."

A nurse entered with the x-rays. The doctor frowned at the results. "Your hip isn't broken, but your left ankle is. It's a clean break." He pointed to a spot on the x-ray. "Right here, see?"

Jenny couldn't see, but she felt enough pain in both her hip and ankle to accept his diagnosis.

"We'll cast it and give you a pair of crutches. Stay off of it for two weeks. We'll take another x-ray at that time."

Louise took her hand. "It could be worse, honey. You can still get around."

"I hope there aren't many steps up to the bed and breakfast," Jenny said. She patted the bandage on her forehead. "I must look terrible." She found a mirror in her purse and groaned. "I'm getting a black eye. I look like I've been in a fight."

"The other guy probably looks worse," the doctor said. "Try these for size."

He held out a pair of crutches, and Jenny pulled herself up from her chair. "They're fine," she said as she moved slowly across the room. "I haven't used these since I fell on the slalom course at Mount Abram. That time it was only a sprain."

As she and Louise left the hospital, Jenny said, "I guess I'd better wait until tomorrow to see Mavis. I'm feeling a bit groggy."

"Take the day off and rest. I'll take you back to the house before I open the shop."

She helped Jenny work her crutches up three steps into the living room and asked, "How well do you know Mavis?"

"Not well. I was in school when she worked in the lunch room. We didn't speak much. Why do you ask?"

"She's an odd duck. I don't know how she snagged Guido. Maybe she'll tell you tomorrow, but stay on her good side. Sometimes I can hear her screaming about something. She's almost twice your size, so be nice and don't ask too many questions."

CHAPTER FIVE

Charlie checked his watch after his call to Adam Roberts. Eight-thirty. Time for work, but first he needed to call Jenny. No one answered. Strange, he thought. He would try again later.

Charlotte Quincy met him at the door. "Come into my office, Charlie. We need to talk. Sara, bring us some coffee and take my calls."

Charlotte lit a cigarillo and leaned back in her chair. "Diane Martin, the Arts Council president, called me yesterday afternoon after her library reading class. The Council is working on a community theater project, and we're giving them as much publicity as possible. She said that you'd written a play about the Clampton murder." She blew a smoke ring. "Is that why you came here, just to finish your play?"

Charlie winced. "Partly," he admitted. "It's a unique story." He took a swallow of coffee and looked out of the window behind Charlotte's desk. "I came for several reasons, personal ones."

Would Charlotte really care about Dierdre's e-mail or why he'd remembered great vacations in Bar Harbor? She was his boss. She was entitled to know, so he gave her a brief and unemotional account.

"You made a wise choice," she said. "I liked the articles you submitted, and I like your style, but..." She blew another smoke ring and drank coffee. "I run a newspaper, Charlie, and I need a damn good journalist." She paused. "Full time."

"You've got one. I want to be a part of your team, and the play won't interfere, I promise." He leaned forward and looked intently at her. "But now, because of the play, I'm getting some information about the murder that might be a real scoop for the Chronicle. It won't be part of the play, but I'm finding unanswered questions."

"Like what?"

"Like where are the photographs of the murder scene, and why wasn't there a further investigation after the grand jury didn't indict Tim Brennan?"

Everybody Knew Pete

Charlotte stubbed out her cigarillo. "Funny you should ask, and I can't answer. Now after ten years and twenty-twenty hindsight, I wonder too. The boat was searched. There was an inquest. The Chief of Police brought in help from Portland. It was all according to the book."

"Maybe the book wasn't finished."

Charlotte walked to the window. With her back to Charlie, she said, "Okay, you may have a story that's worth pursuing but right now, we have deadlines." She turned back to Charlie. "The Arts Council theater project is worth a lot of copy right now, and I want you to take it on. Any questions?"

"Who should I see first?"

"Diane Martin, the president of the Arts Council, then David McKnight, the bank president, who is in charge of funding. He's also helping with the new theater. They've hired a theater architect, and the work is on schedule."

David McKnight. Jenny's dad. Charlie tried to keep a cool facade, not wanting to admit even to himself that he had already developed a more than casual interest in his daughter. "I'll call both of them this morning. Do you want pictures?"

"Not yet. Wait until we have something worth photographing." She paused. "You can keep on using the office next to mine. You have a computer, and Sara can find anything you need." She turned around to her computer. The interview had ended.

Charlie's office contained a desk, computer and phone. The window was a plus. He called Jenny. Still no answer. He transcribed his notes, stood and stretched. He looked out of the window. Boats rocked gently against the pier, and people strolled leisurely. A quiet scene. He forced himself back to his assignment, and David McKnight answered his call.

"I have a nine-thirty appointment," David said, "but you can come now."

Charlie walked to the bank, his step confident, knowing the route after just two days in Sowatna.

The teller smiled. "Mr. McKnight's expecting you." She gestured toward an office beside the front door.

Charlie heard McKnight's voice on the phone as he entered. "You what? Are you all right? Two weeks on crutches? I'm so sorry."

He looked up and saw Charlie. "I'll call back, Jenny. Charlie Brewster just came in." He listened. "You two know each other? I'll put him on."

David gave the phone to Charlie whose face had changed color remarkably. "I tried to call you this morning," Charlie said. "Did you break your hip last night?" He listened intently as Jenny described her fall. "I'll call you this afternoon. I'm sorry too." He gave the phone to David.

"I met your daughter, and we had dinner together last night." Charlie said. "A car tried to run us down, and she hurt her hip. And now falling downstairs. Maybe I'm a jinx."

David smiled. "It's not your fault." He gave Charlie a wry smile. "Unless you were with her this morning. Now what can I do for you?"

Charlie took out his BlackBerry, sat down in front of David's desk and put himself into the role of journalist, not a man interested in the bank president's daughter.

"I was a crime reporter for the Miami Herald, and now I'm working with the Chronicle. Charlotte's put me on the theater project and said that you would fill me in. Tell me about the theater."

"A theater architect came up from Portland and went through the old Legion Club. He pounded on walls and studied the building. He said that we could renovate it easily because the structure is sound with few weight-bearing walls. Minus the second story flooring, they can slant the first floor, and the stage will have the proper elevation for good viewing. Acoustically, it's quite good, and the architect recommended special materials for the walls and ceiling."

"How are you funding the project?"

"Local people have kicked in handsomely, and we received a grant from the National Endowment for the Arts."

"We'll need pictures as the work progresses." Pictures. Charlie's mind returned to a file minus pictures. "When I worked for the Miami Herald, I became interested in a murder that happened here about ten years ago, and now I want to find out more about it."

Everybody Knew Pete

David scratched his ear. "You move fast, Charlie. Two days in town and you're already dating my daughter and investigating a murder." He leaned back in his chair. "I'll take you to the theater when you want pictures and more details."

He looked at his watch, and Charlie took the cue. He stood and shook David's hand. "Thanks for your time, Mr. McKnight. I'll call when we have a photographer."

Charlie turned to the door and almost collided with Diane Martin. His first reaction was that Diane looked like an Easter chicken. Yellow everything - T-shirt, shorts, sandals, and topped off with a yellow scarf holding her ponytail.

"Hi," she said. "I have good news for David. You'll be interested." She took Charlie's hand and led him back into David's office.

"David, we've hired our director. I'm so excited. His credentials are excellent and fit our needs perfectly."

"How did you find him?" David asked.

"Our internet search paid off. He called me from Saratoga Springs where he'd been working at Skidmore College as a visiting director, not part of the faculty."

Charlie palmed his BlackBerry. "What's his background?"

Diane took a note pad from her purse. "He's worked with summer theaters in the midwest. Two years ago he moved east and helped to start a summer theater in Middletown, New York. He likes to work with new productions like ours and says that he can also double as a dance instructor if we do a musical."

"Did he have any suggestions about a play?" Charlie's mouth watered as he thought about selling his drama to the director.

"No. He said that he wanted to meet with us first. He had some ideas but a choice would be premature. He plans to drive up from Saratoga next week."

David made notes on a yellow pad. "Tell me more about his background, Diane."

She sat down and crossed her legs. The view from Charlie's position was awe inspiring.

"He started out as a dance instructor. He loved ballet and dreamed of being another Balanchine, creating his own ballets, so he had his own studio and…"

David interrupted. "Where was his studio?"

"St. Paul, Minnesota."

David's hand shook as he wrote the name. "What's his name?" David's voice was hoarse, almost a whisper.

"Michael Jamison."

Charlie noticed that David's smile was forced as he pushed back his chair and stood. "Thanks for the information, Diane. I'm anxious to meet the guy." He looked at the clock on the wall. "I'm sorry, but I have another appointment in a few minutes. Charlie, I'll call you when I have more details."

"Sounds like everything is moving right along," Charlie's reporter's nose smelled another story, but this wasn't the time to follow its lead. He walked out of David's office behind Diane and shut the door behind them. He couldn't see David as he pulled out his cell phone and punched in a number, and he didn't hear him speak in a jittery muffled voice. "Ann, we need to meet. The cabin at three o'clock."

Charlie walked outside with Diane. "Mrs. Quincy suggested that I interview you for the paper. I'll buy coffee if you have time now."

"Great. I'll meet you at the Expresso." She blew him a kiss and ran to her car.

She could have offered him a ride, he thought as he stood in front of the bank and pulled out his cell phone. Charlie heard a weak voice and listened to Jenny's report of her morning's activities.

"I'm so sorry," he said. "I have an interview now, but I'd like to see you when I'm finished."

"Good. The door's unlocked."

Charlie walked to the coffee shop and found Diane in a booth, already with coffee. She patted the seat beside her, but Charlie slid into the seat opposite. He ordered coffee and took out his BlackBerry.

"What triggered the Arts Council's summer theater idea?"

"I told you yesterday that I was bored, and I'd seen productions in Michigan. Sowatna's a natural with its summer visitors, and Labor Day is a big event here."

Charlie had to admit that a keen mind resided beneath the blonde ponytail with its bright yellow scarf. Committee assignments, theater reconstruction, and state regulations were understood and detailed.

An hour later, Charlie had enough information for three columns. He pocketed his BlackBerry and stood. "Thanks for the interview. We'll be in touch."

He paid for the coffee, ran back to the Chronicle office and drove to Louise's home. When he entered, Jenny welcomed him from the davenport, her leg propped up on a footstool. A pair of crutches leaned against the wall. Her forehead was bandaged, and her left eye was black and blue.

Jenny described her fall down the stairs, and she felt warm and comforted as Charlie stroked her arm. "It was sudden, and when I fell, it sounded as though I'd landed on a bag of potato chips. I heard the crunch before I felt the pain."

"How's the hip?"

"It's sore." She spoke slowly. "I lost my balance. There's a picture of Louise's great grandfather, William Campbell, on the wall above the stairway, and I think that old goat pushed me." Her laugh was mirthless. "He lived in Bradford, Scotland."

Startled, Charlie said, "New Bradford in the name of the fictitious town in my play. Is there a connection?"

"Who knows? How was your visit with Dad?"

Charlie grinned. "He thinks that maybe we slept together last night, and I didn't have a chance to tell the truth. He gave me some good information about the theater. Diane Martin interrupted our conversation to say that they've hired a director. He'll be coming next week."

"That's good news." Jenny shifted around and, with effort, moved her foot. "Damn, this cast is heavy, and I have to wear it for two weeks. I'd planned to see a woman today who might have known Pete Clampton, but I'll wait until tomorrow when I'm feeling better."

"Your ankle must hurt. I'm going to leave, but I'll call you tomorrow. Maybe you should forget about Pete's murder until you're back on two feet."

"I'm not giving up, Charlie." She glared at him. "And please don't show your play to the director. Let him make his own choice."

Charlie walked to the door, and then he slowly turned back. "I have to show him the play, Jenny. I've poured two years of my life into it. The characters are more real to me than some of the folks I've met.

They're real people. If you were a writer, you'd know the feeling." His jaw was set, his body stiff, unmoving.

Jenny sat up, both arms firmly on the davenport, fists pushing into the upholstery. "All right. Go ahead. But remember that I'm dealing with *real* people, Charlie. I'm a real person, not a figment of your creative imagination, and I have to get rid of my nightmares and learn the truth."

"We both want to learn the truth but for different reasons." He opened the door but looked back, his eyes narrowed and glaring. "I guess our reasons are insurmountable, Jenny. You go your way, and I'll go mine."

He closed the door behind him.

* * *

Jenny leaned back on the davenport and sobbed quietly. If her ankle didn't hurt, and if she could move without crutches, she wouldn't have cried. Damn! She picked up her cell phone and called Erin. "Where are you?" she asked.

"I'm at the Blueberry Inn." Jenny listened as Erin described her experience at the Thompson Construction Company. "It was horrible, but I'm okay." Jenny heard a change in her voice. "Tim Brennan's coming here to see Dad. I think that my dad's buying drugs from him." A sob. "And there's nothing I can do."

"I'm sorry. Life's tough sometimes." She paused. "Tim Brennan's coming? I'd like to meet him. Can you bring him here? I fell downstairs this morning and broke my ankle. It was bad enough being almost hit by a car last night. Now I'm stuck here." She didn't mention her disagreement with Charlie. She'd thrown out enough garbage.

"I'll come by and bring you a coffee. Okay?"

"Yes, please come." Jenny smiled wanly. A friend in need. She found the TV remote, turned on CNN and tried to forget Charlie's parting remarks.

She heard Erin's step on the front porch and called, "Come in. The door's unlocked."

Erin ran to her friend and hugged her. "This has been a bad morning for both of us. I don't want to go back home, but I'd like to see Tim. Mom said she'd call me when he came." She gave Jenny a cup of coffee in a paper cup. "Maybe this will help. Can I get you anything from the kitchen?"

"No, this is perfect. Thanks." Jenny sipped coffee and shifted her weight. "The cast is heavy, and I have to wear it for two weeks." She paused. "And if that's not enough, Charlie and I had an argument just before you came. I asked him not to offer his play to the new director, and he got mad. He's going to screw up our work, and there's nothing we can do."

"Men!" Erin exclaimed. "They're nothing but trouble. I'll never understand why my mom has stayed with my dad. She could have had a life without all the hassles."

"Maybe she loves him."

Erin snorted. "Love? It's eating her alive."

"Maybe your dad will go to treatment sometime. You conquered your addiction."

"Yeah, but it was hell. At first I hated rehab almost as much as I hated the cell I'd been thrown into. Four other women were in there, all facing D.U.I. charges. It was ugly."

"How long were you in there?"

"Just overnight. The next morning I was shipped over to the Thomas J. Moore Center in a van with those women. I had a sponsor who was merciless, and I hated her. I needed a drink, and the routine was boring."

"But you stayed."

"Yeah, and by the fifth week, everything changed. My sponsor seemed to care about me, and even the food improved."

"Maybe you changed."

Erin sat down across from Jenny and sipped her coffee. "That's true, and that's when I began to realize that this place offered hope to people like me. After I finished treatment, I asked to stay on and work with other alcoholics."

"You must have needed training courses."

"Oh, yes. They hired me as an assistant, and while I worked there, I took an on-line course that offered an associate degree in psychology. Now I'm a C.A.P., a Certified Addictions Professional."

"I'm proud of you, Erin. You climbed a mountain." Jenny hugged her friend. "It was easy for me, going to college. I knew that I wanted to teach, and I still love those kids."

"We've both knew that we wanted to help people, you with your students and me with my clients." She smiled. "Okay, what's our next step?"

"I'm going to call Bill Daniels, the County Attorney. He testified before the grand jury and might have some insights. I'll see Mavis Bianci tomorrow." Jenny smiled. "I don't suppose that you want to try the Thompson Construction Company again."

"Hell, no. Do you want me to visit Hendricks?"

"Good idea. I wasn't prepared when I met with him and didn't ask the right questions."

Erin stood. "I'll go there now and report back to you." She left, and Jenny lay back against the davenport. It was going to be a long two weeks.

* * *

Erin drove to the Hendricks Ford Agency and knocked on George Hendricks's half-open door. Hendricks looked up and invited her into his office.

"I'm Erin Gregory, Jenny McKnight's friend. If you're not too busy, I'd like to visit with you."

Hendricks's body language told her that he wasn't happy to see her, but she sat down across from his desk and forced a smile. "Jenny told me that she'd seen you."

Hendricks nodded. "She said that some guy was writing a play about Pete Clampton's murder." He picked up a pencil and tapped it on his desk. "I told her that nobody would be interested."

Erin pushed on. "Jenny doesn't like the idea either, but she is interested in the case. Did you know Pete?"

Hendricks put the pencil behind his ear. "Everybody knew Pete, and I had some business dealings with him."

Erin leaned forward. "Do you want to talk about it? I'm sure that Jenny will be interested."

Hendricks paused. "I own a restaurant here and one in Bangor. Pete supplied the lobsters, that's all."

Erin sensed that it wasn't all, but Hendricks picked up the phone.

"Now I have to make some calls. Do you mind?"

Erin stood. "Thanks for your time, Mr. Hendricks. I'll see you later."

Who knew when *later* would occur? Erin drove back to give her report to Jenny.

* * *

Charlie hit the wheel repeatedly with his fist as he drove from Jenny's home to the Chronicle office. Damn, but that woman was stubborn. Couldn't she understand his need to complete his play and see it produced? What about those nightmares? Maybe she ought to switch to decaf. He'd better forget about Jenny McKnight.

He spent the afternoon transcribing his interviews and was relieved that he'd passed his editor's scrutiny. "Good work, Charlie," she said as she scanned his work. "Take it back to the press room."

At four o'clock, he called Adam Roberts, the photographer's father, who gave him his address. "I'll be right there," Charlie said.

He saw Charlotte Quincy at her desk as he left his office. "I'm going to see Adam Roberts, the photographer. Maybe he can answer some of my questions."

"Good luck. Maybe you'll have a story."

Roberts met him at the door. "Come in and have a drink. Martini?"

Charlie nodded. Roberts's gray beard, neatly trimmed, completed a weathered, furrowed visage. Heavy eyebrows above horn-rimmed glasses. Brown leather elbow patches adorned a gray cardigan sweater, and his jeans ended in black sneakers. The living room matched – soft brown arm chairs and davenport, Chippendale and leather.

Roberts called from the kitchen. "Dry or dirty, and what do you want to know?"

"Dirty, and what happened to the photographs you took on Pete Clampton's boat?"

"I don't know." Roberts handed Charlie a martini. He sat down in one of the heavy armchairs and motioned Charlie to sit on the davenport across from him. He scratched his beard. "My son, Adam, told me that you were interested in the case. Why?"

"Two reasons. I'm writing a play about it, and now I'm finding a lot of questions without answers."

Roberts took an olive from his drink and chewed. "I'll tell you what I saw, and I hope you find the pictures to prove it. Pete was slumped over in his captain's chair, his head on the helm. His hands were at his sides."

Charlie worked his BlackBerry. "What did he wear?"

"A blue denim jacket, blue shirt, and jeans. He wore gray wool socks, but no shoes. I was ordered not to describe the crime scene, so that's not for publication."

"I understand. How about the cabin? Were there signs of a struggle?"

"No, and there was no blood. I took about ten pictures and gave them to the coroner when he arrived."

"Who called you? Did someone call 911?"

"Dispatch called me at two a.m. A patrol car had found Brennan on the dock."

"I'll check with Dispatch. I spent a lot of time with those folks when I was a crime reporter in Miami."

Roberts nodded and laughed. "A crime reporter in Miami doesn't get much sleep, I'll bet." He took Charlie's glass to the kitchen and returned with a refill. "Talk to Gary Latham, the coroner. He's in Bangor most of the time. I'll give you his cell phone number. When he comes down to Sowatna, we have dinner together. Lots of memories, and not many happy ones."

"When did you discover the cause of death?"

"Luckily Latham was in town and came right over. He talked to me, then he and a medic moved the body to a stretcher. When they laid Pete on his back, they unbuttoned his jacket and saw the stab wounds. Pete's shirt was covered with blood. Old, congealed blood. The killer must have buttoned the jacket after he'd killed him."

"Or dressed him in it. What time did Latham arrive?"

"About three o'clock. Latham figured that Pete had been dead at least three hours."

Charlie put down his drink and walked to the window and back to his chair. "I'm trying to get a picture of this. I've seen a lot of murder scenes, and I have a lot of questions. Who called the police? Where was Clampton killed?"

"And where are those damned photographs?" Roberts added.

Charlie finished his drink and shook Roberts's hand. "Thanks for the information and the drinks. I'll call the coroner and the county attorney. Maybe one of them knows about the photographs." He paused. "I was told that Tim Brennan, the man accused of the murder, may be back. I'd like to see him."

"Good idea, but he won't be much help. I was there when the police picked him up. The guy was stoned, totally confused. He babbled something about needing to see Pete. He'd obviously been on the boat because he kept repeating, 'He's dead. I didn't do it.' He was still protesting when they put him in the police car."

Charlie added a dozen more questions to his list as he left the photographer's house. He was relieved that his play was almost finished, neat and tidy, and now, he had to admit, far from the reality of Pete Clampton's murder

* * *

Pete Clampton's killer was uneasy. The killer had heard about Charlie Brewster, a new reporter with the Chronicle who had a play about Pete's murder. And those two women, Jenny McKnight and Erin Gregory, snooping around, asking questions. Trying to run one of them down with his car was a stupid move. What if they'd seen the license plate? No need to panic. If you'd killed once...

CHAPTER SIX

David drove to the cabin, his mind racing. Michael Jamison in Sowatna. Unthinkable.

Ann's white convertible was parked under a tree. He opened the cabin door, hugged her briefly, then without a word, went to the kitchen and returned with two drinks, a Scotch and soda for her, a Scotch and water for him. He put them on the coffee table and sat beside her.

"The Arts Council has hired a director for the theater and..."

Ann interrupted him with a laugh. "Thank heavens! I thought that someone had pulled a gun, shoved everyone into the vault and robbed the bank."

"I almost wish." David gulped his drink. "This is serious, Honey. The new director is Michael Jamison. He's Jenny's biological father."

Ann was silent for a moment. "I don't know what you mean or why that's so important. Lots of people adopt children, and you must have adopted Jenny."

David finished his drink and took Ann's hand. "That's true, but listen. Jenny doesn't know this, but her biological mother is Betsy's sister, Louise."

"Oh, my God!" Ann stared at David. "What will Louise do?"

"I don't know." David refreshed his drink in the kitchen and paced the floor. "Here's what happened. Louise was a student in Jamison's ballet school in St. Paul, Minnesota. They fell in love and sent invitations to their wedding. Two weeks before the event, Jamison wrote Louise a letter and left town. Louise didn't tell us what was in the letter."

"And she was pregnant," Ann said.

"Yes. She said that she hadn't told her fiance about the baby. Didn't want him to think that she'd pressured him into marriage."

"So you and Betsy adopted the baby?"

"Of course. Betsy couldn't have children, so Jenny was a blessing for us."

"And you brought her up and never told her about her real parents."

David sat down next to Ann and glared at her. "Dammit, Ann, we *were* her real parents." He stood and paced again. "Sorry. I didn't mean to get upset, but I don't know to handle this. Louise didn't want Jenny to know, and we respected her wishes."

"I didn't mean to be unkind. You've been a wonderful dad, and I'm sure that Betsy who couldn't have a child of her own was a perfect mom."

"But it hasn't been easy. When Betsy died, I resented Jenny. She interfered with my grief. I didn't need another set of tears." He looked at Ann, almost pleading. "I wanted to cry alone. Can you understand?"

"I don't know. I've never had to face that situation. Betsy was your real wife, and Jenny wasn't your real child. Were those your thoughts?"

"Maybe. Louise was our strong supporter. It was easy for her to love her own child and share our loss. She gave me the space I needed, often keeping Jenny at her home. I'm not good at in-depth discussions, but I'm sure that, for Louise, keeping the truth hidden must be unbearable at times."

Ann was silent and sipped her Scotch. "You must tell Louise about Jamison before someone else does. I can picture Diane rushing into the craft shop bubbling over with the good news."

David nodded. "I'll tell her as soon as I leave here. I wanted you to know the whole story. If any of this gets out, the rumor factory will be running into overtime." He took their glasses back to the kitchen, and Ann followed. They washed, dried and then embraced.

Ann put her head on David's shoulder. "I wish I could help, but there's nothing I can do."

"Just be there for me," David whispered. "I love you so much."

* * *

Louise's mind was not on her work. Customers came and left with packages, but Louise's thoughts were home with Jenny. Poor child. A sore hip and a broken ankle.

After breakfast, she had made a new pot of coffee and sandwiches for her lunch. What else could she do?

She was surprised to see her brother-in-law David enter the shop. He turned the 'Closed-Open' sign to 'Closed' and led her to the back room. She sat and stared at him.

"What's happened? You look like you've seen a ghost."

"Almost." He took Louise's hand. "I have to tell you this before someone else does. Michael Jamison is the new director."

"Oh, dear God," Louise whispered. "You're sure?"

"Diane told me this morning. Charlie Brewster, the new reporter, was there too, so it will be headline news."

Louise sat quietly, processing David's report in her mind. Her first reaction was to close the shop and fly to Tahiti. Then sensible assessments crowded in. Who knew the truth? Only David and her sister Betsy. No one else.

Louise leaned back in her chair, arms raised to the ceiling. She lowered them slowly to her lap. "I have to think. How much time do I have?"

"Diane only said 'next week.' Nothing definite."

Louise's hand shook as she poured two cups of coffee. "I have to settle my nerves." A hint of a smile appeared. "I haven't seen Michael in almost thirty years. Will he recognize me? Or even remember me? So long ago." She stood, coffee cup in hand, and tears welled up. "What should I do, David? Help me."

David put his arm around her shoulders and lifted her chin. "We'll work this out together. I'm here for you." He finished his coffee and walked to the front door. He turned the 'Open-Closed' sign around and called back to her. "It's going to be okay. Don't worry."

Don't worry? Louise followed David's retreating figure with her eyes, wiped them and stared at her computer. Maybe she could disappear into the monitor, become an icon on the screen saver, her symbol a retired ballerina.

She leaned back in her chair and closed her eyes. Time flew backwards for her as she relived those special days before her wedding. She'd made the three bridesmaids' dresses. Laughter and tears during alterations. Hurried evenings with Michael. Writer's cramp as they addressed the invitations. Last minute preparations. Her mother's

Everybody Knew Pete

timid remarks concerning the wedding night, shyly admitting that she'd sat on the bed filing her nails, a virgin too nervous to undress in front of her new husband. Louise had played the role expected of her, a virgin in her mother's eyes. She would smile telling her mother that the baby's birth, seven months after her wedding, was two months premature. Michael must never know of her pregnancy either. Only Louise and her gynecologist would know that the bride was two months pregnant. Louise had learned how to assume a role. As a member of the *corps de ballet*, she could smile as she first stood *en pointe*, her toes bleeding.

Michael's letter arrived two weeks before the wedding. She remembered how her hand shook as she opened the envelope. A sense of doom, a foreboding. As she read Michael's words, tears welled up and dripped onto the paper.

'I can't do this to you. I tried to be straight, tried to love you as a real man. I've heard the muffled jokes about gays in tights, and I didn't want to be one. But I am, Louise, and I don't want to hide in the closet any longer. I will always love you in my special way. I never wanted to hurt you. Please forgive me.'

How much more courage now playing a new role, canceling a wedding only two weeks before the event and offering limp answers to honest questions.

She told her sister Betsy about the letter and her pregnancy and was surprised and delighted with her reaction. "We can't have children. David and I want to adopt your baby."

Louise retreated to northern Minnesota to give birth and forget. Betsy and David in Sowatna, Maine, agreed to accept Louise's demands that her child, Jenny, must never know the identity of her biological parents, and when Louise moved to Sowatna after Betsy's death, the secret became a bond.

Now Louise sat in front of her computer and stared at the icons. No retired ballerina. She was not there. She was in Sowatna facing another stage presentation. Maybe this time she'd win an Oscar.

* * *

Erin left Jenny and worried as she ran down the steps to her car. She wanted to help her friend, but now that Jenny was house-bound, much of the foot work would be hers.

She called her home, and her mother answered, her voice a whisper. "Tim Brennan's here in the kitchen with your dad."

"I'll be right there."

Erin greeted her mother and walked into the kitchen. Her father and Tim sat at the table drinking beer. Both of them stared at Erin, silent, waiting, and Erin knew that she'd interrupted their conversation. Tim had changed since his last visit, three years ago, to the Thomas J. Moore Center in Portland. Older, his face, a druggie's pallor, eyes that betrayed a life of addiction. His hand shook as he smoked. A baseball cap, backwards on his head. A faded orange T-shirt and dirty, frayed jeans.

She gave her father an acid smile. "Sorry to bother you." She turned to the other man. "But I need to talk to you, Tim. Will you come out to my car for a minute?"

She knew that Tim recognized her but he gave no sign. He shrugged his shoulders and stood.

"Okay. Just for a minute. I don't have much time."

He followed her and leaned against the car. "What do you want? Are you going to invite me back to that shit house in Portland?"

Erin smiled. "No. Listen. I was a senior in high school when Pete Clampton was killed. Now a friend is having nightmares and thinks that what she saw the night of the murder might be connected to his death. She asked me to talk to you, and she'd like to see you if you have time."

Tim snorted. "Why didn't she come with you?"

"She's laid up with a broken ankle. Can you see her?"

Tim scratched a day-old beard. "I might. Gotta finish here first."

Erin fought back her tears. "I don't want my dad buying your stuff, Tim."

"It's his life."

"I know." She looked at her watch. "Meet us at Jenny's house in fifteen minutes. I'll give you directions."

"Okay, but make it short."

Erin drove back and found Jenny sitting in the kitchen, her leg propped on a chair. "Do you want lunch? Louise made sandwiches."

Erin shook her head. "I saw Tim Brennan, and he's coming here." Suddenly she remembered her promise to Charlie who also wanted to see Brennan. "I need to call Charlie. He's anxious to meet Tim."

Jenny scowled. "He was here earlier." She chewed her sandwich and sighed. "Okay, call him."

When Erin explained to Charlie that Brennan's time was limited, he said, "I'll be right over."

"Oh, swell," Jenny said. She took her crutches and hobbled back to the davenport. "Tell me about Tim."

Their conversation was interrupted when Tim Brennan rang the doorbell. Erin introduced him to Jenny who plunged into the first of a litany of questions.

"How well did you know Pete Clampton?"

"We met about a year before he was killed. He bought some stuff from me." Tim paused. "This didn't come out at the hearing, but after ten years, it doesn't matter." He took off his cap and twirled it around. "I bought some stuff from him."

"Where did he get the stuff, and what was it?" The question came from Charlie who stood inside the door. He walked to Tim and put out his hand. "Erin called me. I'm Charlie Brewster with the Chronicle."

When Charlie walked in, Erin looked at Jenny and noticed that the room temperature had dropped twenty degrees. An icy stare was her greeting. No words were spoken.

Tim looked from Charlie to Jenny, confusion in his eyes. He turned to Erin. "What's going on? You asked me to see your friend Jenny, nobody else."

Erin explained. "I'd promised Charlie, and you were in a hurry."

"Okay. So what do you guys want to know?"

"What did you buy from Pete?" Jenny picked up on Charlie's question.

"Good stuff from Colombia. Pete said that he sailed out of there often."

Charlie made notes. "Did you notice anything unusual about Pete's boat when you boarded that night?"

Tim shook his head. "When I saw that he was dead, I searched the cabin. I found the stuff I wanted, so I sat on Pete's bunk and snorted." He grinned. "Man, that was good stuff. I told Colin Greene, the lawyer they appointed for me, that Pete and I were going to take a trip, but Greene wasn't interested."

"Where were you going?" Jenny asked.

"Pete didn't say. Just told me to meet him on his boat at two o'clock in the morning. Said he wanted to leave in the middle of the night, and I didn't care."

Charlie asked, "How did you know that Clampton was dead?"

Tim groaned. "I told all that to the lawyer. He was dead as a door nail, slumped over the wheel. No blood, no shoes, but dead. I felt his pulse to make sure. Nothing."

"So what did you do?" Erin asked.

"I wasn't about to call the cops, so I went through the cabin, found the stuff and had a hell of a good time. I sort of remember leaving the boat, nothing else until I woke up in a cell in the police station."

"Who called the police?" Charlie asked.

"How the hell should I know? Isn't that in the file somewhere?"

"There's a lot of material that isn't in the file," Charlie said. "I've read through it."

Jenny looked at Charlie. "I'd like to see the file. May I?"

Erin noticed Charlie's reluctance to share. What was going on between them?

"Tomorrow maybe. I'll send it over."

Brennan stood and walked to the door. "I gotta leave. I need to stop at Hendricks Ford and get an oil change. The light came on when I left Portland. And I've got some other calls to make."

"Can you give me your address and phone number?" Jenny asked. "I still have more questions."

Tim laughed. "I don't have a permanent address." From his pocket, he pulled out a tattered note pad, scribbled and gave Jenny a page. "Here's my post office box number in Portland. You can reach me there."

He walked to the door and looked back at all three. "I'd be careful if I was you," he said. He took off his cap. "Ten years ago when they let me go, I was so glad to get out of Sowatna that I ran off and didn't look back."

"I don't blame you," Jenny said. "That must have be scary, knowing that you were innocent but not being sure anyone would believe you."

"Yeah, but later I was curious. After I went to rehab that first time," he paused and looked at Erin. "You probably remember me."

"Yes. We tried to help, and I had high hopes, Tim."

"We don't all get it, Erin. Anyways, I came back to Sowatna and looked around. Talked to some folks. Some things didn't add up."

"Did you talk to your attorney or anyone that might help?" Charlie asked.

"Hell, no! I didn't like what I heard, and I got out of Dodge, know what I mean?"

They nodded in unison.

"I was so rattled that I headed for the first bar out of town." He grinned. "That's the story of my life, kids." He looked at Erin. "Maybe someday I *will* get it, but not right now." He put on his cap and opened the door. "Be careful, that's all I gotta say."

Charlie joined Brennan at the door. "Thanks for your time. Here's my card. Call me if you think of anything else."

"Fat chance," Brennan said and ran down the steps to his car.

As Jenny watched Tim's departure, Erin noticed a change in her expression, a strange look of apprehension and fear.

Charlie followed Tim, closing the door behind him without looking back. Erin looked back at Jenny again and saw that tears had welled up in her friend's eyes.

"We didn't learn much," Erin said. She took Jenny's hand. "Something's wrong between you and Charlie, right"

Jenny nodded. "He's interfering with my problem, and he doesn't care." She sniffed. "I have to find out who carried Pete's body down the street. And now a broken ankle. I hope I mend fast."

"So do I. It's a bummer. I have to do some case histories for the clinic tonight. Do you need me?"

Jenny shook her head. "I'm okay. Louise will be home soon. I'll call you tomorrow after my visit with Mavis. I called her at the bed and breakfast next door. I think she remembers me from high school."

Erin drove back to the motel hoping that her mind could leap from Clampton's murder into the clinic's demands.

* * *

Jenny picked up her crutches and hobbled into the kitchen. At the sink, she splashed cold water on her face and breathed deeply. She had seen a black aura surrounding Tim as he walked out, and visions of the dead skier long ago at Mt. Abram crowded into her mind. Now she saw the skier again as he sped past her on the slope, schussing down, out of control, a black aura surrounding him. She knew that he was dead before she saw the stretcher and the ambulance. Now that same aura had surrounded Tim Brennan. Even if she were able to contact him, he'd have laughed and ignored her warnings.

"Hi, I'm home." Louise's voice was a welcome respite from her forebodings.

Jenny turned and exchanged a hug. Louise hung onto Jenny, then stepped back and smiled. "I've had a busy day. How was yours?"

"I'm not sure. Erin came and told me that Tim Brennan was in town. Charlie came and we..." She paused and studied an ant on the floor. "We had a sort of a fight."

"What's 'sort of'?" Louise laughed gently.

"He's impossible. Wants to have his damned play produced and doesn't give a hoot about my nightmares." She poured two cups of coffee and sipped hers slowly. "Tim came, and Charlie returned because Erin had promised him an interview with Tim. We asked questions. Nothing new, but..."

Jenny stared at Louise hoping for comfort, a denial. Perhaps her aunt could disable the ticking time bomb in her head. She leaned against Louise, her head against her aunt's chest. "When Tim stood at the door to leave, I saw a black aura around him. I've seen a black one only once, and I'm frightened."

She and Louise sat at the table and sipped their coffee. Jenny sensed that Louise's concern was a facade. She noticed deep worry lines between her eyes, a mouth tight, no upward curve. Louise had worries of her own.

Louise looked up from her coffee and smiled. I'm going to make up a bed for you in the den downstairs. I have a sleeper sofa. You'll be comfortable and won't have to negotiate the stairs. I'll bring down the things you need from your room."

"Wonderful. I'm okay with the crutches, but the stairs are a bit much right now."

"I stopped for some Chinese takeout and a new DVD. We'll have a nice evening."

"You're so special, Louise. What would I do without you?" She was startled to see her aunt begin to cry. "Are you all right?"

Louise nodded. "I'm fine. I'm home, and I won't be the dying swan from the ballet *Swan Lake*. See?" Louise stood and did a fast twirl toward the sink.

Jenny admired her movements but wondered why ballet had entered their conversation. She looked down at her bulky cast and shook her head. Sadly, she could only sit in the audience.

* * *

Tim had left Jenny, Erin, and Charlie at Jenny's aunt's house bothered by their questions. He shook his head as he ran to his car. Dumb people. They didn't know what they were getting into. Innocence can kill. He made calls on his cell phone. He had other interests that needed attention. He arranged his appointments and met with several acquaintances. He hadn't been in Sowatna for two years, and it was time to reconnect.

He stopped at Hendricks Ford just before closing time. An oil change was long overdue, and he didn't want engine problems. George knew he was coming. He drove to the service department, found a mechanic and went outside for a cigarette while the mechanic changed the oil. As he waited, George Hendricks called to him. "I'm glad you're getting your car fixed. What brings you to Sowatna?"

Tim hesitated, needing time to create a lie. "I met some friends. I thought we'd settled everything. Now I'm on my way back to Portland."

Hendricks studied Tim's green Pontiac Firebird. "Pretty fancy. You must be doing all right."

"I get by," Tim said. He noticed that his hands shook. He paid cash for the work and drove to his last appointment.

The evening sky darkened as he left Sowatna. Luckily he knew a short cut that took him away from the Interstate, the proverbial shortcut—narrow, pot-holed and lonely. It began to rain, gently at first, then a downpour that canceled visibility. He pulled over to the side of the road and stopped. This would be a good time to take care of the shakes. He found what he needed in the glove compartment. Nice, he thought as the drug took effect. He was glad to leave Sowatna. One of the people he'd seen after he'd left Erin could make trouble. Jenny and Charlie asked too many questions, and that could lead to more trouble. He had kept his side of the bargain for ten years. No need to worry now.

Car lights behind him broke into his musings. The car stopped behind him, and Tim worried. No flashing lights or sirens. Obviously not the cops. Suddenly someone opened his door and pulled him out into the rain.

"Oh, it's you," Tim said. "I thought we'd settled everything."

"Not quite." The knife entered Tim's chest with such force that he fell back against the car.

Tim stared at the killer as blood mingled with rain. "No," he gasped as the killer struck again. Another "no," whispered, gurgled. Tim's last words.

CHAPTER SEVEN

Warm and dry in Sowatna's police station, two officers sat at their desks and joked with Dispatch, Carol Taylor. They'd finished a tour of the surrounding territory and helped a Maryland driver with a flat tire. A quiet day.

Dispatch took the 911 call. "A car's in a ditch out on highway 125, about five miles west of here. The caller thinks the driver might be dead." The quiet, idling evening went into overdrive.

Eight minutes later, the county sheriff, the chief of police, and two highway patrol officers were at the scene. Behind them an ambulance and a fire truck. The rain had ceased, but the ground was soaked. Puddles of dirty rain and mud had obliterated footprints or any possible evidence needed for a thorough investigation.

Adam Roberts parked behind the fire truck and jumped out of his car, cradling his camera. He breathed deeply and rubbed his eyes. He'd thrown on some clothes as he left his home. The buttons on his brown striped shirt were in the wrong holes, and he finished zipping up his jeans as he ran down the slope to join the four men who stood by the car.

The sheriff spoke. "Start with the exterior of the car and pan the area, Adam. The ground won't be much help. We checked for footprints and found nothing. Everything's been washed away."

"Is the driver dead?" Adam asked. "I wish my dad were here. He's had more experience."

The sheriff opened the car door with a gloved hand and said, "Take as many pictures as possible from all angles, but don't touch anything. We'll open all the doors for you." Adam looked into the car and saw the driver slumped over the wheel, dead, obviously. There was no blood on the seat.

While the law enforcement people checked the car, the sheriff discussed the scene with Harry Pierce, Sowatna's chief of police. "We've found no evidence of a collision or an accident involving another car, so why is this vehicle in the ditch?"

"Someone must have pushed it," the sheriff's deputy answered.

"It was there when I called you." A new voice behind Pierce. Pierce turned and saw a well-dressed man in a tan sport coat and navy blue trousers. He carried a brief case. "I'm Henry Parsons. I called you on my cell phone. I was going to Freeport to see a client and saw the car."

"Did you go down to it?" the sheriff asked.

"No, I stayed up here."

"Good," Pierce said. He took out a pad and pencil. "We need your name and address."

As the men talked, Gary Latham, the county coroner pulled up behind them. "I was called," he said. "Has anyone touched the body?"

"No," Pierce said. "That's your job."

Three cars passed by heading toward Sowatna. They drove slowly to avoid the police cars and to take quick looks into the ditch. One was a dark blue Ford Taurus driven by a solitary figure.

* * *

Charlie left Jenny at Louise's house, threw his notebook into his car and climbed in after it. He was sorry about her broken ankle, but dammit, the woman was as stubborn as a cat with a mouse between her teeth. She'd never let go. He drove back to the Chronicle office and transcribed his interviews with Adam Roberts, David McKnight and Diane Martin.

Charlotte stuck her head in his door. "I'm leaving now. I'll see you in the morning." She lit a cigarillo and blew smoke rings. "Did you learn anything today?"

"The mind boggles," Charlie said. "Just when I find an answer, a hundred more questions come up. The theater project looks good. Diane's a smart woman. They've hired a director, Michael Jameison."

"What about the Clampton murder interviews?"

"Good feedback from Witherspoon and Roberts." He smiled. "And I met Tim Brennan just now."

"Anything new?"

"He and Pete bought drugs from each other. That's a surprise. He wondered about a trip he was to take with Pete because he didn't know the destination. I didn't have much time with him. Tim said that he had other appointments. I gave him my card, and I hope he'll call." Charlie shook his head. "I felt sorry for the guy, Charlotte. He looked like a sixty-year-old druggie. Eyes bloodshot, sallow complexion, stooped over. The grand jury may have dismissed the case, but he's paid for his freedom."

"Some people don't want help, and some can't give up the habit, no matter how hard they try. Maybe the guy tried and failed. Who knows?"

Charlie checked his watch. "I didn't realize it was so late, and I'm hungry."

Charlotte's phone rang interrupting his mouth-watering visions of crab cakes and beer. She ran back to her office and picked up the phone. "What?" Her voice was urgent, demanding. "I'll send someone right away. Give me the exact location."

She ran back the few steps to Charlie's office. "There's a dead body in a ditch. The sheriff just called. Here's the directions."

Before he knew what had happened, he was pushed out of the office, scribbled directions in his hand.

"Take highway 125, go west and hurry." In spite of the call's grim message, Charlie almost smiled as he ran to his car. Charlotte had a nose for news.

He had no trouble finding the crime scene. Cars, an ambulance, a fire truck, and clumps of law enforcement people and civilians crowded around the area. Headlights and spotlights zeroed into the ditch.

Charlie jumped out of his car and looked for a familiar face. He regretted that he hadn't taken time to visit police headquarters, introduce himself and meet the people in charge. Now in the midst of an investigation, the police wouldn't welcome an unknown reporter. He saw a uniformed man who appeared to be in charge and introduced himself. "I'm Charlie Brewster of the Chronicle. Charlotte sent me."

"Good. I'm the county sheriff. We knew you were coming. My deputy can fill you in."

Before Charlie had time to ask the location of his deputy, a younger man ran to him. "I'm the deputy. Here's what we know. The dead man is Tim Brennan."

"Oh, God!" Charlie shook his head as he took out his BlackBerry.

"Did you know him?" the deputy asked.

"We met this afternoon." This was no time for details. He worked his BlackBerry and watched the activity surrounding Brennan's ditched vehicle. He was relieved to see a familiar face when Adam Roberts, Jr. scrambled up the six-foot incline to the highway.

"I got the pictures," Roberts said. "Come down."

As Charlie half-slid and half-ran down to the car, he thought about the one and only time he'd met Brennan. His last words as he stood by the door were "Be careful." He must have known someone who had triggered that warning. Maybe if Brennan had followed his own advice, he wouldn't be sitting in a ditched car on a lonely road, cold and dead.

* * *

"Why can't we have a murder on Friday night instead of Wednesday?" Charlotte Quincy's voice blasted into Charlie's cell phone as he went to his car. "The murderer should have waited so that we'd have hot news for our weekly paper on Saturday."

Charlie's laugh was grim. "Yeah, well, he didn't wait. I've been here for an hour, and everything's about wrapped up. The body's been taken to the mortuary, and the coroner followed the ambulance in his car. A wrecking crew was called, and they've pulled the car up onto the road and loaded it onto a flat bed. All the law enforcement people have left, and I'm sitting here in my car wondering what the hell!"

"You're coming back to the office now, I hope. I'll be here."

Charlie thought about Brennan as he drove back to town. The poor guy, he looked like a loser, but who would have thought that he'd lose his life after he left Sowatna?

When Charlie drove into town, he saw the lights of the Chronicle office ablaze in an entire block of dark, empty buildings. Charlotte met him at the door. "Let's get to work," she said. "You look like you need a drink. I have some Scotch in my office. It'll cool your nerves."

"Thanks, I need it." He slumped down into a chair in Charlotte's office, his feet splayed out in front of him. Sipping a shot glass of

Scotch, he sighed. "I've covered a lot of murders in Miami, but I never knew the victims. Now here's a guy who's flesh and blood, a guy who spoke to me today, who even warned me to be careful."

"He said that?"

"Yes, 'be careful' he said."

Charlotte sat behind her desk drumming her fingers on the ink pad. Suddenly she stooped and picked up a black, wide-brimmed hat adorned with a massive black feather. She put it on her head. "I think better when I wear my grandmother's Sunday hat."

Charlie smiled. "You brightened my evening." He stood and downed the last of the Scotch. "Thanks. I'm going to work now. I'll have it all for you in the morning."

"I have to make some notes. Lock the door when you leave."

At 2:00 a.m., Charlie turned off the lights and locked the door behind him. He'd done his job. The story was front page and well done. He hoped that the turmoil inside his head would ease and that sleep would erase his wild flights of thought. And then there was Jenny. A good night's sleep shot to hell.

* * *

Jenny's bedside phone rang at six a.m. "Yes?" her sleepy voice answered. She looked at the clock and shivered. This wasn't the time for idle conversation, and she envisioned disaster. "Who is this?"

"It's me, Erin. Have you heard the news?"

Jenny couldn't find her own voice. It was stuck in her throat, stuck in foreboding fright. She forced the words. "Tim Brennan's dead, isn't he?"

"You heard!"

"No. I just knew." Jenny sat up in bed holding the phone. Should she tell Erin about the black aura she'd seen surrounding Tim as he left the house? No, she'd told Erin about her nightmares. No need to add more of the supernatural. "How did he die?"

"The radio newscaster said he was found in his car five miles from town. He was stabbed."

"Oh, God!" Jenny wiped her tears on the bed sheet. "I wish he'd told us who else he was going to see before he left. Now we'll never know." She swallowed her tears. "I guess we'll just have to keep going. I'm going to see Mavis after breakfast."

"Good luck. I'll call you from Portland."

* * *

At 8:30 a.m., Charlie called the Chronicle office. "I'm going to the police station this morning. Take my calls."

"Okay," Sara said. "See ya." Charlie heard gum cracking as she left the line.

The police station was in a post-murder mode. He knew that Tim's death was no longer a local event when he saw four TV uplink trucks, stations WVII and WLBZ of Bangor and two Portland trucks, stations WCSH and WGME. Three highway patrol cars had managed to squeeze in between the trucks. Charlie entered the building and saw six news reporters who studied reports. He had never met any of them, but they may as well have had 'PRESS' emblazoned on their foreheads. Chief Pierce had anticipated press coverage and had printed out details for the reporters. He had little time for interviews, but a news conference was inevitable. Charlie found Dispatch seated at her desk, headphones securely fastened. She studied her wide-screen monitor and worked the mouse. Charlie hated to interrupt her. He knew that her work was vital to the murder investigation, but he needed to meet her. As a crime reporter for the Miami Herald, he knew the value of Dispatch. They'd been his friends, his confidantes.

"I won't take much of your time," he said. "I'm Charlie Brewster at the Chronicle."

"I'm Carol Taylor. I heard that you were new in town." She put out her hand. "It's a zoo this morning. We haven't had the coroner's report yet. Here's what we have." She gave him a duplicate of Pierce's handouts.

"I started work on Monday and haven't had time to meet you people. I hadn't expected that a murder would be our first encounter."

"Fortunately we don't have many here."

"Have the next of kin been notified?"

"Brennan's mother drove in from Augusta after we called her and arrived at seven o'clock this morning. Brennan's identification was in his wallet, but there was no money."

"So robbery could have been the reason he was killed."

"It's possible." Carol's screen changed images, and she turned to take the calls. Charlie scanned the information sheet and followed the reporters into a room containing a long table, chairs, and a portable lectern. Chief Pierce welcomed the reporters.

"The sheriff asked me to give you all the information we have right now." He outlined key items. "We don't know who Tim Brennan saw while he was here, and we need that information."

Charlie shook his head. As a journalist, he didn't have to reveal the names, but his conscience pricked. After the briefing, he stopped Pierce in the foyer. "I saw Tim Brennan yesterday afternoon at Louise Campbell's home."

Pierce glared at him. "Why didn't you tell me that last night or before the briefing? Good God, man, this is murder!"

"I know. There wasn't time last night, and I just got here."

"Come to my office. I want details."

Charlie followed Pierce and sat down in front of his desk. "Brennan had been to see Erin Gregory's parents, and she was upset because Brennan was selling drugs to her dad. She, Jenny McKnight, Louise's niece, and Brennan were there when I arrived."

"Why was Brennan there?"

"Jenny's having nightmares and thinks that they're related to Pete Clampton's murder ten years ago. It's crazy, but she wanted information from Tim about the murder."

Pierce made notes. "I'll talk to the Gregorys and Jenny. Erin's dad won't be much help, but her mother's reliable. Who else did Brennan see?"

"He said that he needed to stop at Hendricks Ford to get an oil change and that he had other calls to make. No names." Charlie bit a fingernail. "He was nervous, edgy, and he told us to be careful."

"Maybe Jacob Gregory will know his contacts." Pierce stood. "Thanks for your help, Brewster. We'll be in touch."

* * *

Jenny finished breakfast and hobbled down the front steps with her crutches. She walked slowly to the bed and breakfast next door and stood on the sidewalk looking up at the old Burchard house, now the Bella Notte Bed and Breakfast. She hadn't seen Mavis since high school and didn't expect her to remember one of the many students who pushed, yelled and sometimes threw up in the school lunch room. She remembered Mavis as a heavyset woman who stayed in the kitchen most of the time but pushed massive carts of food during lunch hour.

Four steps led up to the front door. Up with the good leg, she remembered, but the good leg's hip wasn't in great form. One step and she sat and, thrusting her right leg in its heavy cast in front of her, pushed herself backwards up onto the other three. As she struggled to her feet, the door opened and Mavis rushed to her side.

"Let me help." She lifted Jenny up like a five-pound sack of flour.

Jenny brushed off her skirt, picked up her crutches and offered her hand. "Hi, I'm Jenny McKnight. I just broke my ankle. I'm staying next door with my aunt."

Mavis laughed. "I remember you from high school. Come in."

Jenny was impressed with the living room. The antiques looked real, the wall decor appropriate. She walked across an Oriental rug and lowered herself onto a green velvet settee.

"Coffee?" Mavis asked and, before Jenny could answer, Mavis was back with two steaming china cups. "I'll bet you were surprised to see me in Sowatna. I left about two years after you graduated. My parents moved to the Cape. I loved it there."

"Is that where you met Guido?"

Mavis laughed. "That's where I *landed* Guido. He and his parents were visiting from Rome. Guido said he liked big girls with big *le minne*." She patted her cleavage. "I never had a real boy friend in Sowatna. Guys thought I should be on the wrestling team or a line backer for the Sowatna Eagles."

Jenny thought about her own high school experience. Kids could be cruel. Everyone had to conform to acceptable patterns of behavior and appearance. She'd kept her psychic visions and premonitions secret, knowing the taunts and secret snickers that would occur from such disclosures. "It must have been pretty quiet."

"Yes, pretty quiet." Mavis drank coffee and looked down at her cup.

Jenny shifted her weight and picked up her cup. "This is off the subject, but did you know Pete Clampton?"

Mavis spilled her coffee and wiped her blouse. "Everybody knew Pete. Why do you ask?"

"Just curious. A new journalist, Charlie Brewster, is writing a play about the murder. The Arts Council plans to do a summer theater production, and Charlie wants them to do his play."

"That's crazy." She went to the kitchen and returned with a coffee pot. Jenny noticed that Mavis's hand shook as she refilled their cups.

"Ridiculous," she added. "People don't want to remember Pete's murder. The case was dropped. The Arts Council should do something light and funny."

"I agree." Jenny sipped her coffee. "What do you remember about Pete? I was in high school and didn't know him. Another lobsterman, that's all"

Mavis leaned back against the settee and looked at the ceiling. "He was a big man with the bluest eyes I'd ever seen."

Jenny was startled. She hadn't expected that Mavis would remember the color of a man's eyes. Perhaps Mavis knew that Pete Clampton wasn't just another lobsterman.

Suddenly Mavis stood and put her cup on the table. "I don't want to talk any more. I have work to do. Come back another time."

Jenny struggled to her feet and took her crutches. "I didn't mean to upset you." She remembered tales of Mavis's temper and was glad to leave. She opened the door and, using the crutches for balance, hopped on one foot down the steps.

* * *

Mavis watched Jenny struggle down the sidewalk to Louise's home, then shut the door and sat on the settee. She looked around the room as though she'd never seen it before. This was home now. This was her new life. Mrs. Guido Bianci, not Mavis Long, the tubby woman whom the boys sneered at behind her back. She'd heard their muffled laughter, their whispered ridicule.

But Pete Clampton hadn't joined the crowd. His boat, his arms, his bed were home to her, a haven, an escape. Mavis stood and looked out of the picture window that faced east toward the ocean. She could envision Pete's boat moored at the pier. She felt again the gentle movement of the waves that rocked the boat like a cradle, and she and Pete moving together in their own wave pattern.

She lay back on the settee, her immense body limp. She fingered herself and moaned softly as she remembered their lovemaking. Three seconds later, she sat up and opened her eyes that were suddenly wide and filled with glaring hatred. "You bastard," she said. "You deserved to die."

She took the cups back to her kitchen, and as she placed them in the dishwasher, Guido entered from the garage. He put two grocery sacks on the table and embraced his wife. "*Cara mia*," he said. He kissed her. "You were asleep when I left. I wanted to wake you, have some fun and start our family, but you looked so peaceful." He kissed her again. "I can wait." He rubbed her nipples that now were hard and evident under her blouse. "I must tell you good news. My nephew, Ernesto, in Rome and his wife, Rosa, are to have a baby this summer. He asked us to be godparents."

"That's wonderful. Maybe we could fly there for the christening."

"Yes, we must do that. How was your appointment yesterday? I was busy in the kitchen when you returned."

"It went well. The cleaning woman is interested in working for us." Mavis turned away from Guido and opened the grocery sacks. "I had a caller just now, Jenny McKnight, Louise's niece from Portland. The Arts Council plans to do a summer theater production."

Mavis stared out of the window above the sink. "We talked about Pete Clampton's murder."

"And you were upset?"

"Everyone in Sowatna was upset."

She picked up an engagement calendar. "No guests until next week. We'll have time to paint the back bedroom."

"Yes, and I've called a plumber to install a bathroom in the walk-in closet. We need another, and the closet's the perfect size."

Mavis was relieved to change the subject, to put Pete Clampton back in her mental closet where he belonged. One day perhaps she'd be able to tell Guido why she couldn't have his babies, his *bambinos*.

* * *

Jenny hobbled back to Louise's and called Erin. "Can you stop here on your way to Portland this morning?"

"Yes, we need to talk."

Erin sounded breathless and emotional, a carbon copy of Jenny's mood. Her accidents, Tim's death and her recent visit with Mavis were, in varying degrees, a succession of misfortunes.

Erin knocked, opened the door and plopped down on the davenport. "It's been a tough morning. I can't help my parents, Tim Brennan's dead, and my dad will probably be a raving maniac until he finds a new supplier for his drug habit."

"I don't blame you for wanting to leave. There's nothing you can do."

"No, and I still think about my trip to the construction company. Attempted rape sticks with you even when you try to forget it."

"I've never had that experience, but I'm sure that you can't forget. And let's face it. Brennan's murder has changed our first, fine careless rapture when we thought about finding Pete Clampton's killer. It would be an exciting adventure. Ta da! The killer is arrested, and my visions disappear. No complications, and of course no danger." Jenny sipped her coffee. "No danger," she repeated. "When that car came at Charlie and me, I was scared but dismissed it as having no connection with our search for Pete's killer. Just some crazy kid playing games. Now that Tim's dead, I'm sure that the incident was no game. Someone was dead serious."

Erin nodded. "And you could have been dead. Why did you stand there in the street without jumping out of the way."

"It was the car lights. Something about the lights. I can't explain it."

"So what will you do now?" Erin took Jenny's hand. "I don't want to do any more detective work, Jenny. It's too stressful, and I have a job that takes all of my strength, mental and physical. I'm needed at the center. I can't help my mom and dad." She blew her nose. "I don't want to come back to Sowatna now. I need space and order in my life."

"I understand, and I don't blame you. We're both scared. I need space and order too. Look at me! Almost run over and now, two weeks on crutches and Charlie and I can't get along. Maybe it's time for me to chill out for a while, take it easy, read a book." She smiled. "I'll call if I need you and, right now, I hope I don't."

Erin left, and Jenny turned on the local radio station. "And that's all we have for you now regarding the murder of Tim Brennan." Darn, she'd missed the news report. The TV wasn't much better. Summer reruns. She went to the kitchen and made coffee.

"How would you like to inspect the work being done on the theater?" Her father's phone call was a welcome relief.

"I'd like that, Dad. Erin's left, and I'm bored."

She took her crutches and walked from the kitchen to the stairway. She looked up the stairs to the portrait of William Campbell, Louise's great grandfather. "Good morning," she said. "Did you push me, or did I imagine it?"

CHAPTER EIGHT

"I'm glad you called," Jenny said when her father arrived to take her to the theater site. "I went to the Bianci's bed and breakfast this morning, and the trek on crutches was a killer." She laughed. "Mavis picked me up after I'd climbed most of her steps."

"She's a strong woman. I wonder if she carries Guido upstairs to bed."

David helped her into his car and drove to the old Legion Club. The morning sun warmed the air and gave the construction work a cheerful glow. A light breeze rustled through the burst of June's new green foliage, and a brilliant blue sky completed the picture. Jenny breathed deeply, her disappointments and worries temporarily dismissed.

Four men dressed in T-shirts and jeans worked at the site. David helped Jenny as they climbed over two-by-fours and skirted paint cans.

"How's it going?" David asked one of the men.

"We're on schedule. No major problems. Glenn Thompson sent some of his men over to help with the heavy work. Two are working inside now."

Jenny remembered Erin's account of her visit to the construction company and shivered. She hoped that Mendes wasn't one of them. They entered the building, and Jenny was amazed to see the transformation. Even in these early stages, the interior began to look like a theater. The second story was gone. The plywood floor was solid under foot and slanted at an acceptable angle for audience viewing. The stage filled one end and was already taking shape.

"Hey, this looks great!" Charlie Brewster surprised Jenny by giving her a big smile. "I'm glad you called me, Mr. McKnight. I brought a digital camera. I didn't bother to call Adam." He took out his BlackBerry and appeared to study its every angle and surface as though he'd never seen it, an alien object.

"You'll get some good shots, and call me 'David.' I'm glad you came. Jenny needs company after her accident."

Charlie continued to study his iPod, and Jenny knew that it was time to clear the air. "I'm glad you came too, Charlie. Isn't this exciting?" Inwardly she groaned. It wasn't exciting. Her ankle pained, her eye was still black and blue and Charlie's farewell address at the door hurt more deeply than the ankle.

Charlie's smile was forced. "I should get some good shots. David, can you give me some details about the renovation?"

"Yes. I'll show you around."

Jenny sat down on a sawhorse, and her father and Charlie moved off toward the stage. The two men from Thompson's company worked at the rear of the building, pounding and conversing in Spanish. Jenny envisioned the finished product, a theater filled with an enthusiastic audience, a stage filled with... The vision faded. Charlie's play? God forbid! Misery returned as she thought about her nightmares and accidents.

She picked up her crutches and hobbled toward the stage end of the building. As she walked away slowly, she felt a chill and cold breath on the back of her neck. She turned. No one was there. The sounds of pounding and hammering increased, high in pitch. She looked at the area where Thompson's men stood working on the walls. They paid no attention to the change and continued their pounding. Jenny stood still and covered her ears as the sound grew louder. "No, please!" she cried.

"Are you all right?" Her father and Charlie ran back to her. As she threw her arms around her father, she looked ahead toward the stage and saw the figure in her nightmare, the man with outstretched arms. The pounding stopped, and the cold breath on her neck disappeared. The terror she'd experienced in her previous nightmares suddenly vanished as she watched the specter. Although its face was blurred, she could recognize a hint of a smile, a benign facade. Its arms moved toward her, almost like a supplication, and she remembered that Louise had suggested that perhaps the spirit was a good one, not a bad one. The figure faded away into the back wall. Had it taken a second, a minute? The time was unimportant.

She stood back from her father and looked at both men. "I can't explain it, but I'm not afraid of the nightmares any more. Just now I saw the spirit again. Louise was right when she suggested that the spirit was a good one." Jenny smiled. "You can't imagine what a relief it is. All those months of worry." She shook her head and looked at Charlie. "I'm not giving up my search for Pete's killer, but it has nothing to do with your play. I don't know why, but I know that your play belongs on this stage, Charlie."

She smiled at her father. "You asked me if I was all right. You bet I'm all right." She took Charlie's hand and looked at him. "Finish your play and when the director arrives, show it to him. I was wrong, Charlie."

"I'm glad. The play's almost finished, and I'd like you to read it. Okay?" She felt a warm glow as he squeezed her hand.

* * *

David watched his daughter and Charlie and was pleased that they'd settled their differences. A nice couple, he thought. But what about Louise and Michael Jamison? He walked over to the sawhorse and sat down. He envisioned opening night, a full house. Maybe standing room only. Maybe a critic from Portland or Boston. The house lights dim, and footlights brighten the stage. A hush as the opening scene unfolds. He's sitting in front row center holding Ann's hand. He touches her knee, and she smiles.

Damn! What rubbish! He stood and faced the stage area. The renovation was far from complete, and funding was, at best, questionable. Charlie's play was probably a dud, and Louise would surely fire Jamison. David looked up at the ceiling where a scaffolding hung. The cables didn't look strong enough to hold a man with paint buckets. He hoped that an experienced builder was present. His practical mind considered insurance claims and lawsuits. He gritted his teeth and walked back to the sawhorse. As he watched Jenny and Charlie who seemed to be in another world, his mood changed. They seemed to be happy together. Life could be worse.

* * *

In the office of Hendricks Ford, George Hendricks turned off the radio's newscast. Tim Brennan's body had been found in a ditched car. He hoped that Brennan hadn't been given a bill for repair work on his car, and he prayed that there'd be no link between him and Brennan. Not now, please God! He picked up the phone and called his wife. "You know about Brennan. He's been found in his car. We have to talk."

"Are you coming home or should I come to the dealership?"

"Come to my office." Hendricks hung up the phone and studied his monthly bills. This wasn't the time to panic, to do anything that hadn't been planned with care and forethought. Stay cool, business as usual. Phrases he'd repeated silently for ten years.

When Doris arrived, George rose and kissed her cheek. "Everything's fine," he said. "Not to worry." He crossed the room and shut the door.

Doris sat down in front of his desk. "I am worried. All that business with the lobsters. Maybe someone knows about the fight."

George interrupted. "It wasn't a fight. Only a disagreement. Besides, nobody knows. We were alone at the restaurant after everyone had gone home."

"But what if someone saw you leave with Pete?"

"It was late, and everyone had left."

Doris fisted up both hands and put them against her chin. "I'm scared, George. What if that reporter finds out about you and Pete and puts that in his play?"

"Oh, my God, Doris! That's nonsense." George picked up a pencil and drummed it on his desk. "Maybe I should meet the guy and find out about his play, casually of course. He's new in town and won't know anything about my restaurant business." He laughed. "Maybe he drives a Ford, and I can offer a free tune-up."

Doris stood. "I'm going to the craft shop before I go home. I'll have a martini ready for you."

George walked with her to the office door. "It's going to be all right. Don't worry."

***

Everybody Knew Pete

Louise helped Hendricks's wife, Doris, with needlepoint patterns, trying to keep her mind on business. "I'll call you next week when our new shipment arrives," she said as Doris walked to the door. She turned away and studied the wall. No one must see the tears that dripped down onto her new green blouse. She'd call Doris next week if there was a next week and she was still here in Sowatna waiting for the axe to fall. She walked back to her office, and her mind was on auto-pilot. Make coffee, plug in computer, fill orders, pay bills. And shoot Michael Jameison. Louise put her head on her desk and moaned. She'd kept her secret for twenty-eight years, and she couldn't blow it now. The stakes were too high, and her self-esteem too low. Her right brain told her that Michael had no choice, that he'd tried and failed and that it wasn't her fault. Her left brain didn't agree. She wasn't good enough for him, not as a dancer and not as a wife. Her love for him would have been enough for both of them, and they could have worked it out if he'd given her a chance. And now he was coming to Sowatna, a small town where everyone knew everyone. Would she see him first, hope that he didn't see her and go back the way she'd come? Or would he see her first? Would he recognize her? She stood and looked in the mirror beside the door. Her wrinkles were deep ruts, her hair lifeless, her eyes red and swollen. She wasn't the girl Jamison had ditched twenty-eight years ago. Not the same girl. No, but she had survived, made it through swirling cyclonic winds of torment and misery, a survivor.

Now the woman in the mirror smiled back at her. The wrinkles had faded, her hair glistened and her eyes were bright and clear. Michael Jamison, how nice to see you, you rat, you deserter, my love.

Jenny's call shattered her reverie bringing good news. The theater was taking shape, and she and Charlie had buried the hatchet, temporarily, at least. Mavis? A strange encounter. The visit blew hot and cold, and she was glad to get home. Erin had left, and TV was a bore.

"I'll find something in the freezer for dinner. Get some rest."

Louise looked at a calendar. How many years had gone by, how many tears had been shed, and how many lies had been told? Michael's arrival would shake the walls of deceit she'd carefully erected. What if his presence in Sowatna altered her role as Aunt Louise with Jenny and slipped into reality? No, it must not happen!

Louise turned off those possibilities and poured coffee into her mug that bore the store's name and a simple logo of a cross-stitch pattern. She studied invoices, paid bills and spent the rest of the afternoon engrossed in 'Sew What?.' She remembered good advice, 'The mind is a dangerous place. Don't go in there idle and alone.'

* * *

Glenn Thompson looked at the clock across from his desk. 10:00 a.m. The highway project on route nine at Albion was on schedule, and the highway was close enough for the crew to return to their dormitory after work. Putting them up in motels was costly, and he couldn't risk too many questions. After twelve years of practice, he was now an expert on illegal immigration. Sometimes he wished that Pete Clampton was still around. His recent sources weren't as reliable, but what the hell, you took what you could get.

Mendes opened the office door without knocking. "We had a visitor yesterday, a young girl who asked too many questions."

"What was her name?"

"I don't know. She had long blonde hair."

"I think she's the one who came to our house the day before yesterday. What did she want?"

"I don't know." He gave his boss a list of supplies needed to complete the road project. Thompson studied the list, gave Mendes instructions, and returned to thoughts of Erin's visit. She'd told him about a new journalist who had written a play about Pete Clampton's murder. Was she snooping around his operation hoping to find material for the play? Did she sense any connection between Pete and himself? Was he being paranoid after all those years? He shook his head and checked his watch. It was lunch time.

* * *

Michael Jamison sat in front of a computer in the library at Skidmore College in Saratoga Springs, New York. He read Diane Martin's latest e-mail and made notes. The director's salary would be agreed upon after he'd visited Sowatna, met the people involved in the theater project and got a feel for their expectations. Hopes and dreams would not appear on his computer screen, and he'd learned from experience that each community has its own agenda. What worked in St. Paul, Minnesota, didn't necessarily fit in Albany, New York.

Jamison ran his fingers through his thick, almost shoulder-length, auburn hair that now betrayed a hint of gray. He was a trim sixty-two. Years of a regimented exercise program had maintained firm biceps and solid abs. Sitting in front of a computer was a necessary adjunct to his work as a free-lance director, but he preferred tennis, hand ball and skiing on both water and snow. The stage gave him the salary and professional fulfillment he needed and, as he studied the monitor, he looked forward to the Sowatna experience.

"Hey, Michael!" Shirley Crawford, his assistant director at Skidmore came behind him. He turned around and smiled. "We're going to miss you," she said. "You did a super job, and I hope that you'll be back next year. Everyone liked working with you."

Michael laughed. "Three productions, three different casts, and unanimous approval? Come on, Shirley, get real."

"So, okay, we had our disagreements, but standing ovations make you forget the problems. I liked your 'Bitch Box.' We filled it."

"It made a great bonfire after opening night. No one's talked to me about a contract, but I'd like to come back next year. Your theater department is excellent." He looked back at the computer. "Sowatna's theater project will be a challenge. They're creating a theater out of an old Legion Club and writing grants. I'm glad that they hired a theater architect and an acoustical engineer before they started ripping out walls."

"That's important. When will you leave here?"

"Our last performance of *Cabaret* is tomorrow night. I'd like to see Saturday night's dance program at the Saratoga Springs Art Center and be on the road by Sunday."

He turned off the computer and stood, his six-foot, five-inch body towering over Shirley. He hugged her and picked up his brief case. "I need to check the stage before tonight's performance. I'll see you at seven-thirty."

* * *

Tim Brennan's killer ate lunch at home. The place was quiet. Time to think, to plan. A vacation would be welcome, but there were too many obligations. People would notice a disappearance. The killer knew about a summer theater project that was on schedule, and there was no way to stop it. A director had been hired, and a play about Pete Clampton's murder was a possibility, God forbid!

Tim Brennan's death was necessary. Tim admitted that he'd kept their secret, but the future was uncertain. He needed more money for his drug habit, and who knew what he'd demand next month, next year? Blackmail was an ugly word, and there would be no end in sight, unless, of course, the blackmailer was no longer alive. There was no alternative. It had been so easy. Tim hadn't even seen the knife. The car was already tilted toward the ditch, and all it needed was a good shove. Fortunately the killer was strong. Lugging Pete Clampton's body down the street ten years ago hadn't been easy, but removing his boots had lightened the load. The boots were carefully hidden away, but they should have been disposed of ten years ago. Soon they'd be given a proper burial.

* * *

Colin Greene sat at his desk and doodled circles on a yellow pad. Tim Brennan's murder was a shock. He hadn't seen Tim for ten years and had often wondered if the guy had overcome his drug habit. It was doubtful. Colin would have appreciated a small thank-you for his efforts during Tim's arraignment, but when the grand jury didn't find enough evidence for a trial, Tim lit out of Sowatna in a flash. You could almost see the smoke behind him! Whoosh, and he was gone.

Colin put down his pencil and thought about his short visit with Louise at her craft shop on Tuesday. He'd wanted to ask her out for dinner but was interrupted by her niece. Bad timing, but maybe Louise wouldn't have accepted the invitation anyway. How long had they known each other? How long had Merna, his wife, languished in an Alzheimer's ward in Bangor? The years merged together like the patterns of Louise's tapestries, blending into each other. Colin looked at the calendar. Now it was June. Merna had mercifully passed away in February. Was it too soon to ask Louise out for dinner? Would his clients be too shocked to continue their client-attorney relationship?

And, hell, would anyone really care? He picked up the phone and punched in the 'Sew What?' numbers.

When Louise answered, Colin rushed in. "How about having dinner with me Saturday night?" There was a pause, and Colin's throat constricted.

"Thanks, Colin. I'd like that."

He swallowed, and his words were clear. "Good. I'll pick you up at six-thirty. Is that all right?"

"Yes. May I give you a drink?"

Colin's cup overflowed. "A Scotch would be fine. I'll make reservations at the Dolphin."

He sat back in his chair, looked up and contemplated the acoustical tiles. He remembered meeting Louise in 1988, an attractive young brunette, about five-foot eight who moved gracefully. There was an elegance about her that Colin admired. She had just arrived from St. Paul, Minnesota. Her sister, Betsy, had died suddenly of congenital heart failure, and David, her husband, was left to care for their eight-year-old daughter, Jenny. David had accepted Louise's offer to resign from her teaching position at the St. Paul Academy to help them through their tragedy. David had leaned on his friend, Colin, during those painful days, and Colin as a long-time friend who had prepared the adoption papers for David and Betsy to adopt Jenny, helped as much as he could. Colin's wife, Merna, had joined in welcoming David's sister-in-law and introduced Louise to her friends, her church, and her sewing circle. Those were good days, good years, but Merna's advancing Alzheimer's put an end to Colin's social activities. Instead, he became an advocate for the Alzheimer's center in Bangor, chairing the Board of Directors and doing as much 'pro bono' work as possible to assist the families whose lives were torn apart.

Because of his involvement in Bangor and his law practice at home, he saw little of Louise. She had opened a craft shop, and Merna had been her best customer until the disease erased her ability to follow instructions. He knew that Louise had a 'friend,' and that word was often spoken with one raised eyebrow and a half-smile. His train of thought carried him to Charlie Brewster's visit, a subliminal connection to Pete Clampton's murder. Charlie had taken a copy of the case file, mercifully incomplete. He wondered if Charlie had finished his play and whether the new director would produce it. He doodled again and wondered if there might be a part for him.

"Mr. Greene, you have a call from the county attorney, Bill Daniels." His receptionist's intercom message interrupted Colin's musings.

Colin picked up the phone. "Hi, Bill. You're calling about Tim Brennan's murder?"

"Yes. I've been at the police station most of the morning. The coroner's report was no surprise. Instant death by a knife through the heart. The report is full of medical terms, but that's the gist of it."

"And Pete Clampton was killed with a knife ten years ago."

"And Tim was the prime suspect," Daniels added. "The police are going through Brennan's car inch by inch and have found nothing. No fingerprints, not even a stray hair. Brennan must have stepped out of the car which means that he might have known his assailant. Why would he stop in the middle of rain storm and open his car door to someone he didn't know?"

"Maybe he thought the person was in trouble. It's just a thought."

"I can't help feeling guilty about this, Colin. Maybe our assumptions ten years ago were wrong, and Pete's killer is still out there."

Colin dug his pencil into his yellow pad. "And maybe the same guy killed Tim Brennan." Colin studied his doodles. "But what's the connection? Ten years is a long time to carry a grudge."

"Yes, but there can be a build-up, a rage that grows as time passes, and circumstances can change." Daniels sighed. "My desk here at the court house is piled with faxes and phone messages. I expect the governor will add his request for prompt action. I'll call you when I need someone I can trust."

* * *

David McKnight drove Jenny to the court house. She struggled up the ramp and located the county attorney's office.

"Do you have an appointment?" The receptionist looked as though she need a long coffee break and a trip to the mirror in the ladies room.

"I'm Jenny McKnight. Mr. Daniels asked me to come."

The receptionist nodded and pushed buttons. "He's expecting you. Go right in." She gestured with a thumb.

Jenny studied Bill Daniels as she lowered herself into a chair in front of his desk. She noticed that his white shirt was rumpled and that his paisley tie was askew.

He looked up, wiped his forehead and ran his fingers through his blond hair.

"It's been a crazy day," he said.

"Any leads?" Jenny asked.

"No, and the trail gets colder every minute. There was nothing in the car, and the rain washed away everything outside. No witnesses, no motive. Just a dead man in the mortuary. We hope that the experts in Portland will find something the coroner missed."

Jenny nodded. "You have a tough job right now." She leaned forward. Where to begin? Her ten-year-old vision? Her meeting with Tim? Her premonitions?

"Tim Brennan met me at my aunt's house yesterday afternoon. My friend, Erin Gregory, was there and Charlie Brewster, the new reporter, came later. Tim was anxious to leave but answered my questions."

"Do you mind a tape recorder?" Daniels asked as he switched it on.

"No problem. Tim said that he'd met Pete Clampton about a year before his murder. Tim sold drugs to Pete, and Tim had bought drugs from him. Isn't that strange?"

Daniels nodded. "Clampton must have had a source for a special kind that Brennan wanted. Did he name the drug or Pete's source?"

"He said that Pete went to Colombia often and bought the drugs there. Tim said it was 'good stuff.'"

"Did he say anything about Pete's boat that didn't come out at the hearing?"

"I don't know what was said at the hearing. Tim said that after he knew that Pete was dead, he found some drugs in Pete's cabin and snorted. He said that he and Pete were going to take a trip together, and he wondered why nobody was interested."

"The trip wasn't important because Pete was dead, and we found nothing in his log book about a scheduled trip that day or the next." Daniels excused himself and took another call.

"Yes, Harry, what do you have?" Daniels listened and made notes. "Jenny McKnight is here telling me about Tim Brennan's visit to her home." Daniels held the phone away from his ear. "Yes, we could have used the information earlier, but so far, Jenny's added nothing new. You'll get a transcript." He ended the call. "The police chief is upset because that new reporter didn't report soon enough." He turned the recorder on again. "Who was Brennan planning to meet after he left your house?"

"He said that he needed an oil change and was going to the Ford dealership. He said he had other calls to make but didn't name names." Jenny shifted in her chair. "Now I wish we'd asked for those names."

"Hindsight is twenty-twenty unfortunately." Daniels switched off the recorder and stood. "Did Brennan say anything else that might help us?"

Jenny shook her head. "He told us to be careful, nothing more." She stood and took her crutches. "I'll call my dad on my cell phone. He'll meet me here." She leaned over Daniels's desk and shook his hand. "I wish that I had more information." She looked intently at the county attorney and said, "I want to know who killed Pete Clampton and Tim Brennan, and I'm not leaving Sowatna until the killer is found."

CHAPTER NINE

Jenny's father met her in front of the county courthouse and drove her to Louise's home. "Do you need help?" he asked as Jenny reached for her crutches.

"No, I'm fine. My meeting with the county attorney was unproductive. He asked me about my visit with Tim Brennan yesterday before he was killed but was too busy to answer my questions about Tim's involvement in Pete Clampton's murder." Jenny laughed. "The police chief is upset with Charlie for not reporting Tim's visit earlier. I hope the fences will mend quickly. Thanks for the ride."

David watched Jenny as she struggled up three front steps and agonized with her. He wished that he could pick her up and carry her. When Jenny was inside, he called Ann on his cell phone. "Can you talk?" The usual question.

"Yes. Glenn's away on road work."

"I want to see you, but I'm tied up at the bank. I dropped Jenny off at Louise's. She manages well with crutches but can't drive. Of course I'm glad to help her, but I spent the morning with her and now I'm behind in my work."

"You're a good dad, sweetie. Can I help Jenny when you're too busy? I haven't seen much of her, and I'd like to know her better."

"That's a good idea, but I wish that you could pick me up and take me wherever we wanted to go, just the two of us." He rubbed his ear as he studied his e-mails that had multiplied during his absence. "I'll talk to Jenny about your offer, and I'm sure she'll accept it."

"Did you talk to Louise about the director?"

"Yes. She was in shock at first, but she'll manage somehow. She's lived this role for almost thirty years. Maybe she'd told herself that she's Jenny's aunt for so long that she now lives the part."

David's line lit up. "I have to take calls. When can we meet at the cabin?"

"I don't know Glenn's schedule. I'll call you later."

His secretary interrupted. "A call for you, Mr. McKnight."

"Yes?" As he spoke into the phone, David's voice became Mr. Bank President.

"This is Diane Martin, David. We're having an Arts Council steering committee meeting tonight at 7:00 o'clock. Can you come, and may we use your board room?"

"'Yes' to both questions. What's on the agenda?"

"The director arrives on Sunday, and we need to find housing for him. We also need a construction report. I'm sure there will be other reports and questions."

"My daughter's here for the summer and may be of some help. Also, you might want to invite someone from the Chronicle. We can always use good publicity."

"Do bring your daughter, and I've already contacted the paper. Charlie Brewster will be there."

David smiled as he hung up the phone. Nobody would sleep through tonight's meeting.

* * *

Charlie also smiled as he left the theater. Jenny's turn-about eased the tension between them, and now he could finish his play with a one-track mind. He liked his title, *'Tangled Trap Lines.'* It was vague enough to whet the audience's curiosity but strong enough to project frustration, tension, and yes, even murder. As soon as the Chronicle was put to bed Friday night, he'd spend the weekend with last-minute changes, all minor. He knew that it was good drama. He hoped that Michael Jamison would agree.

Sara greeted him as he opened the front door of the Chronicle. "Mrs. Quincy wants to see you."

The editor's door was open, so Charlie knocked and sat down in front of her desk. "I gave you my report of this morning's events at the police station. Now I'm going back for more information."

"Good." Charlotte lit a cigarillo. "I want all the latest details before we print this week's edition." She leaned back in her chair. "What do you think, Charlie? You met Brennan, and you've read the hearing file. The grand jury couldn't find enough evidence to send him to trial." She studied the florescent lighting in the ceiling. "Was he hiding something, something the killer knew?"

Charlie picked it up. "And maybe the killer threatened him or killed again with that same knife."

"Is any of this in your play?"

"No, it starts out with Pete Clampton's murder, but the play centers about the relationship between the hero and the heroine. Boy meets girl, boy loses girl, boy finds girl. The usual plot. The murder is almost incidental. During the final scene in the court room, the action focuses on their reactions. The jury, people from the audience, will be asked to render a verdict, but their decision is irrelevant."

"So what makes your play unique?"

"Intrigue, Charlotte. I've made it sound simple, but it's not. There are secrets, red herrings, unexpected twists and turns. I've sat through too many boring dramas, so I know what keeps the audience sitting on the edges of their seats, their eyes glued to the stage. When the jury returns with its verdict, the hero and heroine will be center stage, and that's the climax, the crux, the heart of the play."

"Wow! I'm intrigued, and I haven't even read it." She looked at her watch. "Now go back to the police station and get the latest developments. You'll be at the Arts Council meeting tonight?"

"Yes. Will you be there?"

"I may. I've been asked to chair the publicity committee. I'm always stuck with that job. I guess it goes with the territory. I'm also chairing the play selection committee."

Charlie drove to the police station and was relieved to see that the media people had left. Inside, the pace was hurried, the halls cluttered with people in uniform, people with clip boards, people who looked confused and harried.

The police chief's door was open, so Charlie peeked in, saw the chief chewing gum, surrounded by stacks of paper, and asked, "Anything new?"

Harry Pierce groaned. "Look at this! Reports and more reports. Did you receive the coroner's report?"

"No, it wasn't available this morning."

Pierce dug through another pile of papers, pulled one out and gave it to Charlie. "It doesn't say much. Stabbed through the heart. His blood was all over his clothes. Not much in the car. The rain must have washed away whatever was outside of the car. Time of death, probably around eight o'clock that night. The 911 call came in at eight forty-two. Rigor mortis hadn't set in completely."

Charlie chewed a nail. "Damn! I'm a journalist. I'm supposed to ask questions, get the full picture. Why didn't I ask him the names of his contacts in town?"

"Maybe your mind was on something else."

Charlie gulped. Of course. His mind had been on Jenny, her leg throbbing in a cast and her eyes burning with rage.

"So I blew it. May I use portions of the coroner's report or revise it for the readers?"

"Yes. I don't have anything else for you. The sheriff's in his office. You can talk to him"

Charlie thanked Pierce and located the sheriff who gave him the latest information. "It's almost a dead end," he said. "No weapon, no witnesses. Nothing." He leaned back in his chair. "I'm waiting for a miracle."

"So am I," Charlie said. "Please call the Chronicle when the miracle occurs."

Charlie left the police station and sat in his car contemplating his next move. Brennan had said that his car needed a check-up. Charlie started the motor and drove to Hendricks Ford.

A salesman greeted him at the door and pointed to George Hendricks's office. Charlie heard strains of a Mozart concerto as he knocked on the door.

"Come in." The voice was raspy and firm.

Charlie opened the door and hesitated. Hendricks sat at his desk behind stacks of reading material and stared at him. "Yes?" The tone was impatient, demanding.

"I'm Charlie Brewster from the Chronicle. I just started this week and..."

The tone changed as Hendricks rose and offered his hand. "Sit down, Mr. Brewster. I'm glad to know you. You'll like our little town. Not much going on, but the paper keeps us up to date. What can I do for you?"

Charlie said, "I'll probably need some work on my car in a few days after my drive up from Miami, but right now, I wanted to ask you about your visit yesterday with Tim Brennan."

Charlie noticed that Hendricks's hands shook as he shuffled papers on his desk. His tone returned to 'raspy and firm.' "I told the sheriff and the police chief everything they wanted to know. It's all in their reports that you've read. I can't remember anything else."

Charlie chewed a nail. "I hoped that you might have remembered something more this afternoon. The law enforcement people are trying to find a killer, and they need help."

"Of course, but I haven't a clue. Sorry." Hendricks shifted in his chair and smiled. "We can't solve the Brennan case, and speaking of murder, someone told me that you're writing a play about Pete Clampton's murder."

"It's about ready, and I'm hoping that the Arts Council will produce it this summer."

Hendricks leaned forward. "I'm not very busy right now. Tell me about it."

Charlie gave him a brief summary of the plot. "The murder brings the heroine and hero together, but it's not the main thrust of the play." Charlie shrugged. "I had planned to emphasize the details of the murder, but after being here for a few days, I realized that there were too many unanswered questions about the Clampton murder. Good drama needs decisive action and an ending that ties everything together. I couldn't do that, so I've revised a few scenes, and now the play focuses on relationships, not on the murder."

Charlie watched Hendricks's body language move from tension to ease. Odd, he thought. Why the change? "Did you know Pete?" he asked as he studied Hendricks.

"Everybody knew Pete. I own two restaurants, one here, the Lobster Shack in Sowatna and another in Bangor, and I bought lobsters from Pete. We did business together, but I didn't know him socially."

"Were you still buying his lobsters when he was killed?"

Hendricks shifted in his chair. "No, we had some problems so we had to find another supplier." He smiled wanly. "It was nothing, really."

Charlie picked up on 'we.' "Do you have a business partner?"

"No, just my wife, Doris, and I."

Charlie looked at his watch. "Could I speak with her this afternoon?"

Hendricks stood and glared at Charlie. "I think not. Doris has no other information for you, and I don't want to upset her." He looked down at his desk. "She has some problems." He pointed to the side of his head.

"I'm sorry. I won't bother her." Charlie stood and walked to the door. "Thanks for taking time to see me. I hope to see you on opening night."

They both laughed, but Charlie's laughter ceased as he closed the door behind him. What was it with Hendricks? The man went from cordial to aloof, from warm to ice cold. Hendricks had told him about his restaurants and buying lobsters from Pete, but he didn't tell him the reasons for changing suppliers. Problems, he said. What kind of problems? Who worked for Hendricks at the restaurants? He thought about the Lobster Shack. Maybe someone knew someone.

At the Lobster Shack, he ordered coffee and studied the employees. Most of them were too young to have known Clampton. When the waitress who looked like a freshman in high school brought his coffee, he asked, "I don't suppose you know George Hendricks who owns this restaurant."

The waitress nodded. "I know Mr. Hendricks, and I bought my last car from him." She paused. "Our assistant manager has been here for five years and knows Mr. Hendricks better than I do." She turned toward the kitchen. "I'll find him."

Charlie drank his coffee and watched a man in a soiled apron come from the kitchen. The apron was taut against his protruding belly. Gray hair held back in a black net, biceps that could lift a cauldron of boiling water with ease. His mustache sat above a smiling mouth.

"Hi, I'm Jack Barnes, Randy's dad. You know Randy in the deli?"

"Not yet, but I will." Charlie introduced himself, and Barnes sat down across from him.

"Frieda said you wanted to see me."

"Yes, George Hendricks told me that he owns this restaurant and that he used to buy lobsters from Pete Clampton. Did you know Pete?"

"Everybody knew Pete. I wasn't working here then. I worked at the Dolphin when he was killed. The restaurant's close to where Pete's boat was anchored. I worked until after midnight cleaning up the kitchen, and I heard the sirens. Naturally I went out to see what was happening, and there were the cops, an ambulance, and a fire truck. I went down the stairs to the pier and watched them take Pete's body off the boat. They'd covered him with a sheet, but I knew it was Pete."

"How did you know it was Pete?"

Barnes looked at Charlie as though the reporter had the mentality of a slug. "It was Pete's boat. Who else would it be?"

"Right. Did you see Tim Brennan, the man they arrested?"

"No, I went back upstairs to finish the kitchen. I was tired, and I wanted to get home."

Charlie took out his BlackBerry. "Did you know about George Hendricks's dealings with Pete? He told me just now that he used to buy lobsters from him."

"No. A guy from Bar Harbor was the supplier when I came here. He still is."

"Do you know anyone who was here ten years ago?"

Barnes rubbed the net on his head. "Gloria Gregory worked here at that time. She's Jacob's wife, long-suffering wife, I'd say. She doesn't even come by any more."

"Is she Erin Gregory's mother? I've met Erin."

"Yeah. Erin's a good kid. Been through big trouble at home." Barnes shook his head. "Some folks seem to survive in spite of everything."

Charlie finished his coffee and stood. "Thanks for your information, Mr. Barnes. I'll call Mrs. Gregory."

"No trouble, and no charge for the coffee this time." Barnes smiled and returned to the kitchen.

Charlie rang the bell at the Gregory residence. Gloria, Erin's mother, opened the door. "Yes?"

Charlie introduced himself and saw at once that she was in no mood to listen to a wet-behind-the-ears reporter who hadn't been in Sowatna long enough to know anything.

She offered him a chair, sat across from him and twirled a strand of long, stringy gray hair. "You work for the Chronicle. Did Charlotte send you over?"

Charlie laughed. "No, I'm on my own today." He recapped his visits with Hendricks and Barnes and took out his BlackBerry. "I'm writing a play about the Clampton murder, and I'm looking for details. Some things don't add up."

Gloria nodded. "That's for sure. Nobody asked me about Pete's dealings with Hendricks, and I didn't need to get involved because Tim Brennan wasn't indicted." She snorted. "Tim Brennan. He got what he deserved. He sold drugs to my husband, turned him into a junkie and didn't give a damn. Just wanted Jacob's money."

Gloria leaned back on the davenport and closed her eyes. Tears slid down her sunken cheeks. "Erin's gone back to Portland. Jacob's out somewhere. Life's shit."

Charlie patted her hand. "I'm sorry, and I hate to bother you, but, please, let me ask you some questions."

"You look honest and sincere, so maybe you'll understand. I worked at the Lobster Shack when Pete sold lobsters to Hendricks. Two nights before Pete was killed, I was in the cold room checking on steaks and other food that had to be kept there. It was late, maybe ten o'clock. The restaurant was closed, and I guess nobody knew that I was still there, but the door was ajar. I heard Pete come in the back door. Hendricks met him right by the cold room. I could hear everything. They got into a terrible argument. Something about the size of the lobsters and where Pete was getting them. I heard sounds of a scuffle, pushing, hitting, swearing."

Gloria wiped her eyes and sat up straight. "I was scared. What if Hendricks locked the cold room? I'd be dead before anyone found me. And what if they opened the cold room door? Finally the fighting stopped, and I heard Pete walk to the back door. I'll never forget what Hendricks said., 'I never want to see you again, Pete. You cheated and lied and I hope you rot in hell'.. Pete said something I couldn't hear. And Hendricks's last words were, 'You don't deserve to live'.

Charlie replaced his BackBerry. Gloria sighed. "I haven't told anyone about that night, Charlie. Nobody asked, and I didn't want to get involved. Erin was in high school and drinking. Jacob couldn't hold a job, and I needed the work. I tried to forget that night, but now it's all come back. Maybe George Hendricks killed Pete, but a threat doesn't mean anything in court."

Charlie took her hand. "Thanks for telling me what you heard, Mrs. Gregory. Nothing will be on the front page of the Chronicle. I'm keeping this information under wraps. I don't know if this has anything to do with Brennan's murder. For now, it's our secret."

He stood and walked to the door. "I know that your life isn't the greatest right now. Have you thought about going back to work? I'll bet the restaurants need waitresses now that the tourist season has started."

Charlie drove slowly back to the office, his mind swirling. Gloria Gregory had spilled her guts, and now the mess lay in his lap. As a journalist, his personal feelings about Hendricks must be ignored, but if Gloria's testimony was accurate, Hendricks could have killed Pete and dragged his body from his home across the street from the church, put him in his car, and positioned him at the helm of his boat. Logistically, it made sense.

He parked and walked into his office. He looked out of his window at the horizon where a cloudless blue sky met the deeper blue of the Atlantic. But what about Brennan's death? Tim had said that he needed an oil change at Hendricks Ford. Had Hendricks followed him out of town, stopped him and killed him? Why? After Pete's death, no one had questioned Brennan's testimony, that he was too stoned to remember anything. But what if Brennan had been on the boat before Hendricks dragged him in? What if Hendricks knew that Brennan was there? But why wait ten years before killing him? Again, more questions than answers. Charlie looked forward to putting the paper to bed and completing his drama. He looked up at the ceiling. Please, he thought, no more complications.

* * *

Diane Martin, the Arts Council president, met David McKnight as he unlocked the front door of the bank. "I've made copies of tonight's agenda," she said, "but I'm sure that we'll have many additions. Is Jenny coming?"

"Yes, Louise is bringing her. Jenny's worked with high school productions and knows how to build a set if it's not too complicated."

"Louise has offered to head the costume committee. Of course we have no idea what that will involve until the play is chosen. I hope that Mr. Jamison has an open mind and will listen to the committee's suggestions. Charlotte Quincy can be very persuasive."

David laughed. "Charlie Brewster has written a play based upon Pete Clampton's murder ten years ago. I hope that Jamison will read it."

Diane followed David as he switched on lights and walked back to the board room. She put her file folders and a clip board at the head table and checked her watch. As if to announce the time, one by one, twelve members of the committee entered the room and greeted each other. Louise and Jenny found chairs, and Jenny leaned her crutches against the wall behind her. Charlie followed them, smiled at Diane, and sat beside Jenny. Colin Greene came in and sat beside Louise.

Diane opened the meeting and acknowledged Charlie. "Charlotte, would you introduce our friend?"

"This is Charlie Brewster, our new reporter who got tired of Miami's rat race and decided to join the human race in Sowatna," Charlotte said. "He's also writing a play and hopes that the director will choose it." She winked at Charlie. "We may have another Tennessee Williams in our midst."

"Welcome, Charlie," Diane said, studied her notes and asked for committee reports. Joe Andrews, owner of the Sowatna Hardware and Lumber Company, stood and studied his notes. "The theater is on schedule," he said. "Glenn Thompson's men have worked well, and the equipment Glenn loaned us has been a godsend. Even the landscaping will be done in two months. Seating will be a problem, however. We can't afford theater seating."

Neil Conway, minister of the First Presbyterian Church, spoke. "The Episcopal Church is remodeling its interior and replacing their old pews. Could these be used until we can afford new seats?"

Members of the committee pondered the offer, whispered to others, and nodded. "Neil, please talk to the priest and see if we could have them. Buy them? Rent them? Whatever's possible."

"I'll check and get back to you. Does anyone else have a suggestion?"

Eleven heads shook 'no.' Joe Andrews said, "Maybe the school has chairs we can borrow if we don't get enough pews. I'll find out."

"If there's nothing else to report about the theater, let's move on to housing for the director," Diane said. "He arrives on Sunday."

The members were silent, searching for the right answer. Colin Greene said, "I'm all alone in my house, just me and Prince, my Irish setter. Jamison could stay with me."

Mavis Bianci, a new member on the committee said, "I have a better idea. The director may want solitude. The guest house behind our bed and breakfast is empty. Guido and I had planned to get it ready for couples, but there wasn't time. Right now, it's okay for one occupant."

"How much would you charge, Mavis?" Diane asked.

"We wouldn't charge anything if the Arts Council could pay for heat and lights."

David, Jenny's father, said, "I move we accept the Bianci's offer." The motion passed.

Diane said, "Jenny McKnight who teaches in Portland is here for the summer. Her father told me that she's had experience with the school's drama department. We'd like to hear your ideas." She smiled at Jenny.

"I've worked with sets and lighting for our high school's productions," Jenny said. "Building a set starts with graph paper and imagination. Lighting is crucial. We didn't always have enough pig tails or spots, but the university was generous and loaned us what we needed."

"We may have to lean on them again," Diane said. "We're glad you're here this summer, Jenny. We need you." Diane continued. "We need to talk about publicity even though a play hasn't been chosen." She looked at Charlotte Quincy. "Have you anything to report?"

"Yes," Charlotte said. "I've already gotten on the internet and checked various publications. The State Arts Council's monthly newsletter will carry a report this month, and we'll keep them informed. We need to develop a flyer that can be distributed to college campuses and local theater groups. We're compiling a list of other art associations and theater groups in the state. We'll have the flyer ready as soon as a play's been chosen and the dates established."

"What about the media?" Louise asked.

"Our local radio station has offered to work with radio and TV stations all over Maine," Charlotte said. "We'll send flyers, and the manager will make personal calls. He's been in the business for about twenty years and has connections." She shifted in her chair. "And of course all newspapers in the state will be informed of our every move. They wouldn't *dare* forget about our summer theater."

Everyone laughed. Diane looked at her watch. "Unless anyone has a burning desire to speak, the meeting's adjourned." The committee members stood and visited in small clusters.

Jenny struggled to her feet, and Charlie gave her her crutches. "It's only nine o'clock. Would you like some coffee or an ice cream?" His look took in Louise who stood beside Jenny.

"You two go ahead without me," Louise said. "I need to get home."

"We'll take my car," Charlie said. "I'll deliver your niece safely to your door."

Jenny shivered as she remembered their rush to the sidewalk, a car with blazing lights as it drove toward them, and the impact of Charlie's body upon hers. She looked at Charlie and knew that he also remembered the incident. She also noticed a preoccupation of thought as he chewed a nail and looked around the room. Was he searching for someone? His voice was stern as he gripped her shoulder.

"Let's get out of here," he said.

Jenny followed him to the door. "Are you all right? You look troubled."

"Oh, God, Jenny! I'm loaded with problems I can't solve, people I can't help. Sometimes I wish I'd never come to Sowatna."

CHAPTER TEN

Charlie put his frustrations behind him as he helped Jenny into his car and stowed her crutches in the back seat. "Would you like an ice cream?"

Jenny nodded and lay back in the seat. "Let's go to the Regal Scoop." She sat up. "What did you think of the meeting?"

"Diane keeps the train on the track. Sometimes those sessions can go on for hours because no one's in charge."

"Did you notice anything different about my dad?"

"Sorry. I have to admit that I was more interested in his daughter. Why do you ask?"

"I was sitting at the meeting, picking up a lot of energy from different people, when I saw a flash of lavender. It startled me because I usually don't see auras unless I specifically tune in on the energy that swirls around all the time. I need to block it or I'd be overcome with sensations. Then I looked at my dad, and I saw lavender light flowing from his eyes to Ann's. The flow was so intense that I wanted to get up and hug them both, tell them that it was all right." She paused. "I know that she's married, but Dad's alone, and I wish there was some way that he and Ann could find happiness together."

"Do you know her husband?"

"Not really. I've seen him at the country club with friends, that's all. He's out of town most of the time, I think. He's in the road construction business. Erin met him and wasn't impressed. Let's forget about him and enjoy our ice cream."

Charlie stopped at the Regal Scoop, took her order and rubbed her shoulder. "I knew I'd like you," he said, "in spite of our disagreements."

"They're behind us now, temporarily, but who knows what the future will bring? Except for a double dip chocolate fudge ice cream cone."

* * *

Mavis stood beside Diane waiting for the committee members to leave. She moved from side to side, impatient to discuss Jamison's housing arrangements.

When the last person had left, Diane picked up her notes and turned to Mavis. "Your offer was appreciated. I'm sure that Mr. Jamison will be very comfortable there."

"It's no trouble. I used to live in that guest house after my parents moved to the Cape twelve years ago. I worked at the school, and it was an easy walk for me. I got used to carrying heavy trays in the lunch room, so I could carry anything." She patted her thighs. "It's not all fat."

Mavis found her car and drove home, her thoughts dwelling on those two years alone in the guest house after her parents had moved to the Cape. They'd sold the cottage but rented the guest house from the Burchard estate for Mavis. "You'll be safe here, and you know the neighborhood," her mother had said. Yes, she knew the neighborhood, and she knew the pier where Pete Clampton's boat was anchored. Two idylic years. Perhaps too idyllic to last. She'd sailed with him, hauled up lobster pots with him, cooked for him, slept with him. When her parents asked her to join them in Cape Cod, Mavis was torn between love for Pete and guilt because of her parents' request. She needed to be with her parents, no longer young who needed a daughter's support, but leaving Pete would be unbearable.

She was startled and confused when Pete agreed that she should move in with her parents. "It's been great, Mavis, but it's time for both of us to move on. Find a husband and a new life. Remember the good times and think about your future."

Remember the good times? How could she forget? But, face it, he'd dumped her. He didn't want her any more-his big, fat, willing lover!

She remembered the year and the month when she made her decision. September, 1998. She'd given notice at the school, told her parents that she would join them as soon as she'd made arrangements with the Burchard estate and packed. Sadness and regret had turned into anger and a desire for revenge. She was a woman scorned, a woman with no hope for a bright future. Stuck with aging parents, she could look forward to atrophying on the Cape, becoming an old, bitter recluse, abandoned by the world. Pete should suffer for what he'd done to her. She lay awake at night planning acts of revenge. Why should he live as he always did while she languished and tore out her guts in agony? Slowly the decision was made, clear and detailed. Pete didn't deserve to live.

Mavis shook off memories of those bad years and parked her car in the driveway.

In the kitchen, she poured a cup of coffee from the carafe. In the far distances of her mind, she heard pounding. Guido was upstairs converting a walk-in closet into a bathroom. Guido, her husband who wanted babies. Mavis shivered, and her hand shook as she took the coffee cup. How could she admit that she couldn't give him what he wanted so desperately? Dear Guido who had wanted to marry her, had loved her as no one ever had, not even Pete. Guido would never abandon her. Or would he when he learned that she could have no children?

Mavis sat at the kitchen table, moved her cup away, put her arms on the table and cradled her head. Heavy sobs wracked her body as she relived her brief pregnancy that would bring shame and revulsion to her family. Pete had the solution. He knew a woman in a nearby town who, for a nominal fee, could solve her problem. Mavis agreed. There was no other choice. Whose fault was it that the abortion failed and that she could have no more children? The woman offered sympathy, refused payment. And, where was Pete who should have been there to share her agony, to hold her hand, to assure her that he loved her anyway, this fat, permanently barren woman? He was off to the shores of Colombia on a secret, unofficial, non-lobstering junket.

"Ah, you're home, my love. How was the meeting?"

Guido's voice invaded her misery. She looked up, tears falling, mouth quivering. She stood and almost collapsed on Guildo's shoulders. As they both struggled to stay upright, he stood back and smoothed her hair. "My love," he whispered. "How can I help you?"

"It's all right, Guido. I'm fine. Just tired. The meeting went well. I offered our guest cottage for the new director. I'll clean it tomorrow." She wiped her eyes, finished her coffee and took his hand. "Let's go to bed."

***

David stood with Ann as he locked the door of the bank and watched the committee members drive away.

Diane was the last to leave. "Thanks for the use of the board room," she said. "The meeting went well, don't you think?"

"Yes," Ann said. "I didn't contribute much tonight, but I want to help. Maybe I could help Jenny with the sets."

"That would be super," Diane said. "I hope to schedule another meeting next Thursday. Maybe Jamison will have selected a play by that time." She waved good night and went to her car.

"I wish I could take you home with me, Ann," David said. "My bed is so empty and cold."

"I wish so too." Ann looked at him. "I think that Jenny knows. Women sense these things."

"Maybe you're right. When we're together, even across the table from each other, I have a hard time being professional, intent on the discussions. I try not to look at you, but I'm drawn." He lifted her chin. "You're a magnet, and I'm a helpless lump of metal."

They stood together in front of the bank, held hands, then with reluctance turned away and walked to their cars. For David, there were no words to express his desire and his loneliness. A solution must be found before he lost all reason, all sanity.

***

Louise held out a cup of coffee as soon as Jenny entered the house. "An interesting meeting," she said. "Diane handled it well, and everyone seemed to agree on what's been accomplished."

"It was good of Mr. Greene to offer his home for the director, but I think that Mavis's suggestion made more sense. And now he'll be close enough for us to get acquainted."

"You're so right."

Louise's comment lacked enthusiasm, but Jenny sensed that Louise was tired. "I won't see Charlie this weekend because he'll be finishing the play. What are your plans?"

"I could close the shop on Saturday, and we could play tourist. How about a drive up to Bar Harbor? I have friends there, and the shops are enticing."

"That sounds great!" She finished her coffee and kissed Louise. "I'm so glad to be here. I haven't had any nightmares, and I think it's because the spirit knows that I'm trying to help both of us."

Louise smiled as she took their cups to the kitchen. "You're so right, honey. Sleep well."

* * *

When Charlie entered the Chronicle office on Friday morning, the air was full of the friction and frustration of press time. Charlotte moved quickly between her office and the press room barking orders, making last-minute changes, checking layouts. Charlie's report of last night's Arts Council meeting had found space on page two. He'd been given a byline, the second one in Saturday's edition. Not a small accomplishment for a new reporter.

Charlotte smiled at him. "The paper's ready to be put to bed. What are your plans for the weekend?"

"I'm going to finish the play. Jamison arrives on Sunday, and I want it ready for him to read." He paused. "I know that you're on the selection committee. Will that be a problem?"

"Of course not. We're open to all suggestions. I can't speak for the entire committee, but I'm sure that they'll be interested in your subject. What you've done with it will affect their decision, but remember, Jamison will make the final decision. That's his prerogative as director."

"So I may have a selling job," Charlie said. "Wish me luck."

He went to his office and gathered all of his files. He passed Charlotte and Sarah as he walked to the door. "I'll see you all Monday morning."

* * *

The killer was uneasy, worried yet strangely relieved now that Tim Brennan was no longer a threat. The blackmail money saved might be enough to afford a long vacation to a warm, safe place, far from Maine. The killer waited for Saturday's paper and the latest police reports. No clues had been left at the scene, but there was always a chance for a stray bit of evidence. The killer hadn't even been a suspect in Pete's death ten years ago, and that eased the tension and sleepless nights. Now, ten years later, it seemed almost as though Pete's death had never happened, that it had no connection to Tim Brennan's murder. The killer was safe. One of these nights, Pete's boots must be destroyed.

* * *

Gloria Gregory stood at the sink and washed the dishes. Jacob had left the house saying that he had business in town. Gloria didn't ask questions. She already knew the answers. Jacob had to find a new supplier now that Tim was dead, and she wanted no part of his activities. As soon as he left the house, she went through her closet to find an outfit that would be acceptable for a job interview. Charlie's suggestion had given her the courage to get out of the house and back into steady employment.

Suitably attired, she left the house and stopped at the mail box that stood at the curb. She picked up the mail, letters, overdue bills and magazines, plus ten circulars bound for the trash. As she walked past a lilac bush, she failed to notice that one of the letters had slipped out of her hand and had fallen under its branches. She didn't see the address on the envelope. 'Erin Gregory, 1954 Front St., Sowatna, ME 04401,' and she didn't see the return address, 'T. Brennan, P.O. Box 659, Portland, ME 04101.'

Gloria walked back to the house, put the mail on a table in the living room and walked briskly toward the Lobster Shack. She knew Randy, the young man who worked in the deli, and his father and prayed that she'd find work. If they weren't hiring, she would continue until someone, somewhere would give her a job. She wasn't interested in Jacob's reaction. Get a life, she had told herself, and she planned to do exactly that.

Randy welcomed her at the deli counter of the Lobster Shack. "It's good to see you, Gloria. What can I get for you?"

Gloria laughed. "A job, Randy. I want to go back to work, and I thought that maybe you'd need extra help during the tourist season."

"I'll call the boss. Just a minute."

Gloria worried when he returned too quickly. "Sorry, Gloria. He said that he didn't need anyone right now but to come back later."

"Thanks, Randy. I'll do that."

She walked away, looked up and down the street, and saw the hotel sign. Their dining room was a favorite haunt with the natives, and tourists liked their menu and gift shop. Gloria introduced herself to the manager of the restaurant who shook her head. "We have enough help right now." She studied Gloria. "But our gift shop needs a salesperson. Are you familiar with our line of merchandise?"

"Of course," Gloria said as her nose, like Pinochio's, lengthened invisibly.

"Follow me," the manager said, and Gloria trotted behind her, already seeing herself as a purveyor of Maine's finest products.

The gift shop contained a variety of merchandise, but its specialties were locally crafted or manufactured items, pottery, jewelry, art work of all sorts. The buyer had chosen well.

"We have a special collection of quilts made by local women who work with Louise Campbell at the craft shop. Louise also has some of her own work here."

"My daughter is a good friend of Louise's niece, Jenny," Gloria said. "I'd be proud to show Louise's products."

"Good. Let's go to my office and talk about your hours, salary, and all those boring but necessary details." She smiled at Gloria. "You'll like it here. We have interesting customers, and most of them are agreeable and like our line of merchandise."

Gloria wanted to skip along behind the manager. She was out of her house, gainfully employed, and, as she passed by a mirror, not too bad looking in her newly tinted and styled hairdo, acceptable make-up, and, of course, her new underwire bra.

* * *

Jenny had ridden with Louise to the craft shop Friday morning.

"You can rearrange my pattern books and straighten up the place," Louise said. "There aren't enough hours in the day to do everything." She walked to her office, plugged in the coffee pot and turned on her computer. She needed to keep busy, her mind and fingers occupied. Sunday. Michael would arrive on Sunday. She looked forward to dinner with Colin this evening, and the trip to Bar Harbor would be another welcome diversion,

At ten o'clock, Ann Thompson entered carrying a plastic bag. She smiled at Louise as she opened the bag and removed a bright green and gold quilt. She'd used pale green ties that accented the design.

"It's beautiful," Louise said. "You did excellent work."

"Thanks to you," Ann said. She looked at Jenny. "Your aunt put everything back together for me. The rest was easy." She put her hand on Jenny's shoulder. "We haven't been formally introduced, but I saw you at the meeting last night. Your dad told me that you'll be on crutches for another week, and I have time to offer transportation if everyone else is busy."

"Thank you," Jenny said. "I hate to lean on Dad and Louise too often."

"I might help in another way also," Ann said. "You mentioned working on scenery for the play, and I like to work behind the scenes. I was involved with community theater before we moved to Sowatna, and I liked making a set come alive."

Jenny smiled. "I'd like to work with you, Ann. Let's offer our fabulous talents to Mr. Jamison."

Louise moaned silently and hoped that Jenny and Ann would find a more acceptable topic for discussion. Her hopes were answered when Gloria Gregory entered the shop. Louise didn't recognize her. "May I help you?"

"Sure. I'm Gloria Gregory, and I've just got a job working at the hotel's gift shop." Louise sensed that Gloria was excited and proud, happy and anxious to talk about her new position. Ann and Jenny listened as Gloria described her work.

"The gift shop carries some of your designs, Miss Campbell, and I want to promote local crafts and art work."

Louise humphed. "Crafts are art work, Mrs. Gregory." She bit her lip. It wasn't Gloria Gregory's fault that Michael Jamison was about to ruin her life. In a softer tone, she added, "I'll be happy to send over any of our finished work. We've usually consigned our products because the gift shop wanted to control its inventory and keep down expenses."

"I'm sure they'll continue that practice," Gloria said. "I just started today and have a lot to learn."

* * *

Everybody Knew Pete

Jenny didn't know why, but Gloria Gregory's presence was disconcerting. Erin had told her about the friction at home, her father's drinking and drugging that induced her mother's anger and bitterness. Erin had moved to a motel rather than endure any more predictable tirades and accusations. And now here was Mrs. Gregory, a new gift shop employee who looked capable and self-assured. Perhaps this was a refreshing change, but Jenny was apprehensive.

As she watched Erin's mother, Jenny shivered. She felt cold and clammy. She wiped her forehead as perspiration dripped into her eyes.

Suddenly a shape formed around Mrs. Gregory. It wasn't the kind of aura Jenny had ever seen. The shape was dark, its movements fluid and wavering. Jenny moaned softly as the shape floated about Erin's mother.

"I'll be back next week to discuss your designs," Gloria said as she walked to the door.

Horrified, Jenny watched the shape form into a death's head. As the door closed behind Mrs. Gregory, Jenny screamed.

CHAPTER ELEVEN

Jenny's scream, shrill and high-pitched, filled the air of the craft shop. Louise and Ann rushed to Jenny who stood transfixed, unseeing eyes facing the front door.

"Jenny!" Louise shouted. "Wake up!"

It was as though someone had snapped his fingers, and the one under hypnosis had emerged into reality.

"Oh, God," she said, her voice quivering, "I had a vision, a horrible one. I've never seen anything like it."

"Was it an aura or a spirit?" Louise asked.

"No, not like that." She had told Louise about her occasional auras, some good, some bad. "It was a kind of a shape covering Mrs. Gregory." Jenny shivered. She couldn't describe the death's head to Louise and Ann. It was too grotesque, too foreboding.

Ann said, "I'm glad you're all right now. Louise told me that you are driving up to Bar Harbor tomorrow. That's a lovely spot. Have you been there?"

Relieved to put the vision behind her, Jenny said, "Yes, when I was in school, our family usually spent a week in Bar Harbor during the summer."

"Have a good trip," Ann said. "I'll see you at the next Arts Council meeting on Thursday." She put her quilt in its plastic bag and left the shop.

"Are you up for lunch?" Louise asked.

"I need a cup of strong coffee. Let's go to the Expresso."

* * *

When they returned, Louise busied herself in her office while Jenny assisted customers. For Louise, the hours dragged. She thought about dinner with Colin, a good friend who had stood by her when she needed help and encouragement, a friend who accepted her and didn't ask questions.

They'd seen little of each other during his wife's illness. When Merna died, Louise and everyone who knew Colin pitched in, but after the funeral, Louise backed off. She knew all about the 'casserole brigade,' the widows who brought food to the grieving husband, and who knew where an innocent tuna hot dish might lead? No, thank you. Colin's dinner invitation was unexpected and welcome. She could forget Michael Jamison for an evening.

At five o'clock, Jenny called from her place at the cash register. "We'd better close the shop if you're going to be ready for dinner at six thirty."

"You're so right," Louise said. She shut down her computer, unplugged the coffee pot and set the alarm system. There had never been a break-in, but David had insisted.

At home, Louise showered and dressed. She looked in her full-length mirror and knew that she passed inspection. Unstudied, understated elegance in a mid-calf green print skirt and matching blouse with just enough cleavage to be interesting.

"You look fabulous," Jenny said when Louise entered the kitchen to prepare a plate of crackers and brie, a Scotch for Colin, and a gin and tonic for herself.

"What can I fix for you, sweetie?" Louise asked.

She was pleased to see how adept Jenny had become with her crutches. She watched her as she looked in the refrigerator and brought out three dishes of left-overs.

"I'll have a soda and clean out the 'refrig.' Don't worry about me."

Colin rang the bell at six-thirty. Louise ran to the door. "For you," he said and thrust a bouquet of daisies into Louise's arms.

Louise smiled. "How thoughtful. Thank you."

* * *

Jenny sipped her soda and placed her food in the microwave. She could hear Louise and Colin talking in the living room. No exact words. The tone was warm but, she sensed, a bit stilted. Maybe Louise hadn't had a real date for so long that she was self-conscious, and maybe Colin was of the same mind. Middle-age dating, Jenny decided, might be awkward. Would she and Charlie find themselves in the same situation twenty years from now? Or she and whomever? Sorry, Jenny, no crystal ball.

Her cell phone rang. "Yes?" Had she willed a call from Charlie? She spoke softly. "I'm eating dinner alone. Louise is going to the Dolphin with Colin Greene."

"Let's hope they don't get run over," Charlie said. "I bought take-out, and I'm going through the play, word for word, scene by scene. If Jamison likes it, I think that Colin would make an excellent prosecuting attorney. He told me that he used to perform in college productions."

"Jamison may put out a casting call on the internet, but I hope that he'll choose as many locals as possible. I'm sure there's a lot of talent here."

"Are you going to try out?"

"No, I want to work on the sets."

Charlie laughed. "Now I won't have to worry about leading-lady rivalry." Jenny heard a slight pause as Charlie continued. "When I finish the last rewrite, I'm going to look for a house or an apartment to rent. The motel's been okay for a short time, but I want to settle in somewhere."

"I'm glad that you're sticking around. I hope you find something suitable."

"I will, and have fun in Bar Harbor."

Jenny smiled and finished her dinner. As soon as Louise and Colin left, she'd curl up on the davenport and watch TV. A quiet night.

Louise came to the kitchen door. "We're leaving now. Will you put these flowers in water? Don't wait up."

Jenny laughed. "Have a great evening. I'll see you in the morning."

She washed her dishes, found a vase for the daisies and hobbled into the living room. She sat on the davenport, switched on the TV and was startled to see only snow. She tried several channels with the same result. She stared as channel twelve's snow moved in waves, and the shape she'd seen surrounding Gloria Gregory appeared, pushing towards her.

Suddenly the dreaded death's head appeared again, and the sound became a roar. Jenny covered her ears. "No!" she screamed.

When Louise returned at nine o'clock that evening, she found Jenny curled up on the davenport holding her ears, whimpering. The

TV was on. Louise found the remote and, seeing only snow on the screen, turned off the machine. "Oh, sweetie," Louise exclaimed. "What happened?"

"The TV," Jenny whispered. "It was the shape again."

"I'm going to give you a tranquilizer and put you to bed. We can pack in the morning." She helped Jenny stand, gave her the crutches and led her to her room. Jenny fell onto the bed and cried softly. She undressed and took the pill Louise had given her. Sleep would come. Perhaps she had only imagined the TV's program. Tomorrow would be bright and filled with new surroundings. And Charlie had called. Her mind cleared and she fell into a dreamless sleep.

Jenny awoke refreshed and eager to travel. She smelled coffee and bacon. Louise was already in the kitchen.

"Good morning, sweetie," Louise said as Jenny came to the table. "We should leave at eight o'clock. Did you sleep well?"

* * *

Colin Greene sat on his back porch with a cup of strong coffee and relived his evening with Louise. She was a remarkable woman, a private person yet warm and interested in a variety of subjects. From his house above the wharf area, he could see the ocean as it met the sky. Different shades of blue meeting, blending. Far off toward the east, a storm brewed. Dark clouds whirled, a wild pattern that contrasted with the light cirrus clouds that moved gracefully above him. Their movements reminded him of Louise as she walked to the car and into the restaurant. He knew that she had danced professionally in Minnesota, but she had offered no details. As he thought about her, he realized that he knew almost nothing about her life before she came to Sowatna. Louise had thrown herself into the care of eight-year-old Jenny and, as she settled into a routine of care, she had branched out into hand work that resulted in her owning a craft shop.

Colin went back to the kitchen and returned with a refill. He sipped his coffee and thought about Louise's 'affair,' the word commonly used in Sowatna. He pushed those thoughts from his mind and recalled the dinner with her at the Dolphin. He'd call her again soon. She brightened his life, and, Lord knows, he needed a lift.

His law practice kept out the cobwebs that could form in a solitary existence, but, damn, it was lonely, especially at nights and during weekends. Sundays were the worst. He'd like to spend Sunday with Louise. Maybe next week.

* * *

Erin Gregory and a co-worker at the rehab center spent Friday night at a rock concert. The crowd was noisy and the music, loud. Erin was glad to distance herself from the Thomas J. Moore Center. She'd returned from Sowatna on Thursday to find a back-up of work that would consume her entire weekend. Tonight's concert offered a brief respite.

As the final chords of the last song faded, she and her friend moved with the crowd toward the exit. "Hey, that was great, right?" Erin said. "I'll listen to that music in my head all weekend. It'll make the work easier."

They found their car, and Erin drove back to Portland. She dropped her friend at her condo and drove home to her apartment. She didn't look forward to a long, boring weekend, but being home had been a drag. Nothing had changed.

Erin's cell phone rang at eight a.m. "Hi, mom. What's new?" She already knew the answer. "You what?" No, she didn't know the answer. "You have a job at the hotel's gift shop? That's wonderful."

She listened as her mother explained her decision to get out of the house and simply DO something. "I'm proud of you, Mom. The next time I'm home, I'll buy out the shop and give you a big bonus. Thanks for calling and brightening my day."

Erin smiled. At last her mother had broken out of the old rut. The change in her voice was refreshing, and for the first time in months, Erin looked forward to a return visit.

She started to work on the files she had brought from the center and lost all track of time. At noon, her stomach told her that nourishment was needed. A short break, and she was back at work. By three o'clock she had completed the task and thought about the rest of her weekend. A movie perhaps and visit with one of the women she knew at the center. On Monday morning, she'd be ready to assume her duties, refreshed and, thanks be to God, sober. Erin remembered those hangover mornings, the headaches, the nausea. Recovery had been painful and ugly but she had survived and now, working at the Center, she knew that if she could lead one addict down the road to a sober, meaningful life, she had would find meaning in her own life.

The climb hadn't been a straight shot to the summit. She had been in and out of love but hadn't found the man she'd dreamed of. But life was better now after her mother's phone call. Her father was a lost cause, and Erin knew enough about alcoholism to recognize the situation. His heart, kidneys, and lungs would fail, and he would die soon, coughing, wheezing, and cursing inside an oxygen tent. Her mother would need employment. Luckily she had found it now.

As Erin worked through her backlog of work, she thought about Tim Brennan. She wished that she'd asked him about his other commitments, and especially she wished that she had volunteered to drive back to Portland with him. Maybe together they could have fought off his assailant, grabbed the knife, maybe even, oh, God, killed the one who attacked them. She envisioned the scene, the pelting rain, the mud, thunder and lightning. The struggle and the victory. But who had they killed? Erin returned to her files, her vision a defeat.

* * *

David McKnight locked the front door of the bank at noon on Saturday and wondered what to do with the rest of his weekend. He wanted to call Ann but remembered the adage, 'If a man answers, hang up.' As he drove away, his cell phone rang. "Be Ann," he prayed, and it was.

"I'm free this afternoon, honey. Are you?"

"We just closed the bank, and I hoped that you'd call. Yes, I'm free. Can you meet me at the cabin?"

"I'll be there in thirty minutes."

David grinned. His weekend was now filled. Memories of today's tryst at the cabin would sustain him all through Sunday. He was glad that Jenny and Louise had left for Bar Harbor. There'd be no interruptions tomorrow, and he could dream in peace.

* * *

Ann replaced her cell phone and changed from shorts into a soft blue strapless, knee-length dress. She enjoyed dressing for David. Glenn never noticed what she wore. Glenn never noticed anything much about her. She sat and brushed her hair with vigorous strokes. Damn Glenn! Why did she stay? She looked at the calendar. June. Suddenly a decision was reached. Not a blinding flash of light, not a booming voice from above. Instead, the sure, steady knowledge that she must leave.

The summer theater project offered a challenge and a change of routine. She had agreed to work with Jenny on the sets, and she'd be with David at Arts Council meetings. The new director was to arrive tomorrow. She didn't want to lose these summer months. With luck, the play would open the weekend before Labor Day, September first. On Tuesday, September second, divorce papers would be served. 'Irreconcilable differences,' a catch-all phrase and a useful explanation.

She frowned at the mirror. What if Glenn contested the divorce? What if he knew about her extramarital affair? She slammed down her hairbrush and stood. This was not the time to wallow in 'what if's.' She knew that she'd made the right decision. She would tell David this afternoon.

David's car was parked beside the cabin when Ann arrived. She ran to the door and hugged David. Breathless, she gasped between words. "I've reached a decision. I'm leaving Glenn. I'm filing for divorce on September second."

David stood back and stared at her. "Oh, my God, Ann, I've prayed for those words for so long." He embraced her, held her body against his as though he could never release her.

Ann could feel the steady beat of his heart against her breast. She rested her head against his shoulder. "I can't explain how my decision was made. Suddenly before I left the house, I knew that the time had come, that I wanted to spend the rest of my life with you, and that I'd never have peace of mind until I took that step."

She pulled back and stared at David. "Are you sure that you want me as your wife, your companion forever in this world?" She almost feared his answer. Theirs had been a secretive, passionate affair. Perhaps there was an exotic mysticism that might dissolve in the clear light of a respectable, open life together.

"Oh, Ann, my dearest, I can't imagine life without you, and to acknowledge our love honestly," David smiled. "We know that people will talk, but that's life in a small town."

He stared at Ann. "But what about Glenn? Will he contest the divorce? And what will our lives be with him in Sowatna?" He stood back. "And what about your kids? "

"I don't have any answers," Ann said. "I only know that I want to be with you legally. No more sneaking around, worrying about discovery, fearing a scandal. Now my only worry is that I delayed this decision."

David smoothed her hair and kissed her. "Together, we can face whatever happens." He took her hand and led her to the bedroom. "Today, this afternoon. That's all we need to think about now."

* * *

Michael Jamison retired early Saturday night. He'd had a busy day packing a five month's accumulation of scripts, e-mails, and files that he'd used for his drama classes at Skidmore. His students were juniors and seniors, seriously involved in all aspects of theater. His playbills displayed a variety of genres, from *West Side Story* to *Wuthering Heights*, from *Hair* to *Hamlet*. He'd worked closely with the music and mechanical arts departments. His five months at Skidmore had been multi-cultural and multi-departmental. Shirley Crawford, his assistant, had been his strong right arm. If he were to return to the college, she'd be available because she planned to continue at Skidmore to complete a masters program in drama.

Michael cleared out his closet, packed his tennis rackets, laptop and books, and surveyed an empty, non-person two-room apartment. He had enjoyed his work at Skidmore, but now he looked forward to his new home.

He set his alarm for six-thirty and awoke Sunday morning eager for the trip to Sowatna. New surroundings and a different cast of characters. Diane Martin, the president of Sowatna's Arts Council, had called Saturday to tell him about his new lodgings. The guest house behind a bed and breakfast was available, and the owners were anxious to welcome him. A new journalist in town had written a play concerning a murder that had taken place ten years before. Diane had assured him that he had no obligation to stage the drama, but she'd appreciate his giving it careful consideration.

Michael was to call her on his cell phone when he was near his destination, and she'd meet him and guide him to the guest house. She'd asked for an approximate arrival time, but Michael hadn't a clue. "I'll call when I get there," he had said. "I don't know when that will be."

Diane's voice betrayed disappointment. "We'd planned a small reception for you."

"Thank you, but I'll be tired from the trip. Let's wait until I've settled in." The reception was a thoughtful gesture but not a welcome one. He needed time to relocate his life.

CHAPTER TWELVE

At three o'clock on Sunday afternoon, Michael stopped his car ten miles from Sowatna and punched in Diane Martin's phone number.

"I'm almost in town. Where should I meet you?"

"There's a gas station and convenience store at the corner where you'll leave the main highway and turn right toward town. I drive a gray Buick Lucerne. I'll watch for you."

Michael found the store, saw Diane's car and pulled up beside her. He lowered his right window. "I'm here."

"That's quite obvious." Diane laughed. "Follow me."

Michael trailed behind Diane. At the edge of town, she signaled right and left turns and led him to the bed and breakfast on Third Street. She turned into a driveway on the north side of the house and stopped beside the cottage that matched the main house, white clapboard with maroon shutters, a gable above the front door.

"Welcome to Sowatna," Diane said as she stepped out of her car. "I think you'll like it here."

Michael looked the cottage and the pine trees on either side of the building. "I'm sure I'll like it."

He unloaded his trunk, and Diane carried his tennis rackets and laptop. "You can carry the heavy things." She unlocked the cottage and pushed open the door with her foot.

Michael liked what he saw. Chintz and lace, an overstuffed sofa and two matching arm chairs. A stone fireplace already stocked with firewood in a heavy oak chest. The main room served as a living and dining area separated by a kitchen counter and hanging cupboards.

"The bedroom and bath are on your right," Diane said. "The bed's made up, and there are fresh towels in the bathroom." She smiled. "I checked to be sure that you would have everything you need."

Michael noticed that her smile was slightly more than cordial, and he looked out at the pine trees to conceal his amusement. Good to know that women still found him attractive, but looks can be deceiving, both hers and his. Their relationship must be on a professional level. Anything else could jeopardize the entire project.

"I'm going to be very comfortable here," he said. "I'd like to meet the owners, and of course I'd like to make an early decision about the production. I have a few ideas, but I want to meet your selection committee tomorrow if possible. I need to get a feel for what's appropriate."

"Charlotte Quincy, the editor of the Chronicle, is on the committee. If it's all right with you, I'll ask her to call a meeting for tomorrow morning at the Chronicle office."

"Good. You said that a newspaper reporter has a script. Can you call him this afternoon and ask him to bring it here? I'm always interested in local talent."

"He's not really local. He came here from Miami. Charlotte told me that he became interested in a murder that happened here ten years ago. His play's based upon that murder."

"He'll probably have an outsider's perspective of the event, and that's important. Do call him. Maybe we could have dinner together tonight."

Diane took out her cell phone and called the Blueberry Inn. When Charlie answered the switchboard's call, she told him about the director and his interest in his work.

"Ask him to meet me at the Lobster Shack at six o'clock," Charlie said. "I'll bring my manuscript."

Diane gave Michael directions to the Lobster Shack. "You'll like Charlie, but don't feel obligated to accept his work. People who were here ten years ago might not welcome a rehash of those events. It's your call, of course." She put out her hand. "I'm glad you're here, Michael. I'll see you at the Chronicle office tomorrow morning."

After he'd unpacked, Michael knocked at the back door of the bed and breakfast. Mavis greeted him. "Do sit down. Would you like a soda?"

"Thanks." Michael admired the kitchen, large and professionally furnished. He noticed that Mavis was also large and nicely furnished in a green and purple muumuu.

"How many rooms do you have?" he asked.

"Six, all with bath. We're full most of the year. Skiers and snowmobilers in the winter, tourists in the summer, and a variety of guests in the spring and fall. Guido, my husband, and I keep busy. He likes to cook too, so we both use the kitchen." She looked out of the window. "How do you like the guest house?"

"It's perfect for me, but who's paying for it? We haven't discussed my salary or any details about my work. I really must know what's expected of me."

Mavis laughed. "The Arts Council was so pleased that you'd agreed to come that they must have forgotten about a contract. David McKnight, the president of the bank, will be your source of information." She wrote his home and bank numbers on note paper. "Call him tomorrow."

"I will. Thanks for the soda." He walked back to the guest house and thought about a short nap before dinner.

* * *

That evening, Charlie drove to the Lobster Shack, his script in a box beside him. He chewed a nail. What if Jamison didn't like the play?

He pushed questions aside as he looked around the restaurant. He noticed a man dressed in a gray turtle neck and jeans jacket who sat alone. That had to be Michael.

Charlie put out his hand. "Michael Jamison?" The man nodded, and Charlie introduced himself, sat down and opened his box.

Dinner was leisurely as the men discussed the play. Charlie explained in detail his interest in Pete Clampton's murder, his frustrations regarding the investigation and his decision to revise the script that now focused on relationships, not the murder.

"I like your divided stage," Michael said. "It saves scene changes and speeds up the action."

When they finished dessert and coffee, Michael stood and took the box. "I want to read this tonight before tomorrow's meeting. I'm sure that the committee will have suggestions, and I have some also, but originality and a local theme are appealing."

They paid at the cashier's counter and shook hands. Charlie's was damp, and his food sat uncomfortably and undigested in his throat.

He was relieved that the director liked what he'd said about the play, but the actual reading of the script was of primary concern. As the author, he'd cherished every final word, but now those words were to be studied by an unbiased professional. Seeing his articles in print was now old hat. He had become inured to watching his prose used as fire-starters, wrappers for garbage, lying in fat bundles for the recycling truck. His drama was different. Those words were to be voiced, not read, to be spoken on a stage by human beings and to be heard by an audience of real people. As he drove home, Charlie wondered, would he sleep? Doubtful.

Sleep hadn't come easily, and now on Monday morning, Charlie felt like last night's warmed-over hash. His stomach churned, and his eyes were red and puffy.

He entered the newspaper office, and told Charlotte about his dinner with Jamison. "He took my manuscript, and I didn't sleep much."

Charlotte handed him a mug of steaming coffee. "You look as though you need this. I know what you're going through. I used to worry every time I sent a manuscript to a magazine or an agent. I don't have to go through that agony any more."

"Thanks." His hand shook as he took the coffee mug.

He walked into the editor's office. Charlotte had arranged chairs and given note pads and pens to five committee members. Charlie slid into a seat in the corner and chewed a nail.

Diane Martin winked at him, then stood to welcome Michael Jamison. Charlie watched the director as he entered the room carrying a briefcase. Charlotte introduced herself and offered a chair behind her desk. Jamison smiled at Charlie and shook hands with the committee members.

"It's going to be an exciting summer," Charlotte said and asked Sara to bring coffee.

Charlie studied the committee members who looked eager to present their ideas, Diane, breathless and smiling. Charlie huddled in his corner and chewed a nail. Jamison looked as though he was subtly in command. He opened his briefcase and when he brought out Charlie's manuscript, Charlie slumped even further down into his chair.

"I'm sure that you all have wonderful ideas for our production," Jamison said, "but first I'd like to tell you about a script that was given to me last evening. Its title is *Tangled Trap Lines*, and it was written by Charlie Brewster." He nodded toward Charlie, and everyone turned and looked at him. Charlie felt his cheeks grow warm.

Jamison outlined the plot and described the setting. "I read most of the night, and this is one of the finest pieces of drama I've seen in years."

Charlie sat up and smiled, then sank back on his chair. He wiped his forehead. "I hoped you'd like it."

"I'd wanted to do a musical," one committee member said, "but hiring an orchestra would be expensive."

"I'd thought about a Neil Simon but worried about royalties," another said.

"This isn't a musical, and I don't know about royalties for Charlie, but I'd like to direct this play," Jamison said. "In my mind, I've already put the set on your stage, and I've made some drawings," He gave copies to everyone. "You'll see that the stage is divided. The action moves between the court room and two living rooms. A murder has taken place, the defendant is on trial, and the heroine and hero react and interact with the action." He looked at Charlie. "We'd like to hear from the author. Charlie, have I got it right?"

Charlie stood and wiped his forehead again. "Yes." He looked at everyone as he explained, "Originally, when I read about Pete Clampton's murder, I wanted to do a play strictly about the events that led up to the murder, ending with a court room scene that tied everything together." He winked at Charlotte. "It didn't take long to realize that the answers to my questions complicated my plot instead of taking it along to a logical conclusion. There was nothing logical in what I heard."

The committee members looked puzzled, so Charlie continued. "I revised the play. The court room scene is still the play's climax, but the focus now is on relationships. The details of the murder are irrelevant."

Jamison said, "We will ask members of the audience to serve on the jury. It's been done before, and it's a twist in the plot."

Charlie said, "The jury's verdict is also irrelevant, but those who will serve as jury members will enjoy being a part of the production."

Charlotte tapped a pencil on her desk. "But what if people in the audience are too bashful to volunteer?"

Charlie laughed. "You wouldn't be too bashful, Charlotte. I hope that Michael will choose four or five people before opening night. Once those folks have climbed up the steps onto the stage, others will follow. We'll need twelve."

Charlotte said, "I'd love to serve on the jury." She looked at the director. "Now, what about the cast?"

"I've already put out a casting call on the internet, but I want to use as many local people as possible. Can you put that in your paper?"

"Of course, but I'd like to see flyers distributed at key places in town, churches, restaurants, spots where people gather. We can do the flyers, but we'll need your help with the copy."

Michael smiled at Charlie. "We can do that," he said. He took out a notebook. "I'm going to see the theater this afternoon. I met with David McKnight at the bank before this meeting, and he's taking me there."

Diane stood and looked at the committee members. "We've agreed, I think, on Michael's choice, and we can help distribute the flyers when they're ready. Our Thursday night meeting will be a busy one."

As the others left, Diane shook Charlie's hand. "I'm pleased about your play." To Michael, she said, "Did you and David at the bank discuss your contract?"

Michael nodded. "Yes, we went through every detail this morning before I came here, and I'm satisfied with the contract, salary, lodging, and my duties."

"I'm glad that you're satisfied with our arrangements." She took Michael's hand and smiled. "I'll enjoy working with you."

Charlotte stood. "Charlie, I'd like you to interview Michael for this week's edition. Call Adam Roberts when you've set a time. I want front page coverage." She smiled at the director. "We need to have the flyer ready this week. Do you have time now to work on it?"

Michael looked at Charlie. "I have time. How about you?"

"I'm ready. Let's go back to my office. I'll get more coffee."

He went to the coffee urn and thought about his play. The summer theater project was off to a good start, but lurking in the back of his mind was the horror of two unsolved murders, one just last week. But that was last week. How quickly we forget.

* * *

That afternoon, David McKnight picked Michael up at the cottage and drove to the Legion Club. Michael looked at the building and nodded. "It's a good size for your theater," Michael said, "and you have room for parking."

They walked through the open entry. "This will be double doors," David said. "We won't have a large foyer, but it will be adequate. We wanted more space for the stage area."

"You were wise to use a theater architect. It saves money down the road."

As he walked into the theater, Michael looked at the floor. "I hope you've allowed for a twenty-percent drop from the last row to the first."

"Yes, and the stage will be level with the last row. I didn't know any of this until the architect came. We'll cover the entire floor with linoleum and hope to have a carpet runner down the center aisle."

"What about seating?"

"That's a problem we haven't solved. Church pews are available, but they're not comfortable without padding, and I don't know if we can get enough folding chairs."

"I have an idea," Michael said. "Sometimes movie theaters change their seating or go out of business. I could get on the internet and check for you."

David exhaled audibly. "Theater seating would be ideal. We hadn't thought about that possibility."

They walked toward the stage, and Michael climbed up the steps. He walked back and forth and jumped several times. Then he walked to the rear of the stage and brought out a tape measure. Together they measured the depth, and Michael shook his head. "It's not deep enough. How much room is there between the edge of the stage and the first row?"

"We haven't got that far," David said. "We also don't know how much room is needed for footlights."

Michael took out his notebook and wrote. "We can work it out. I'm glad that I arrived before the last nail was pounded."

"Are we all right as far as we've gone?"

"Yes. Nothing has to be undone." He looked up at the ceiling. "I'd like to study your blueprints if you don't mind. I'd like to see exact measurements."

"I can get them from our building committee chairman. He owns the lumber company." David was troubled by Michael's request. The man was hired as the director, not as an engineer. He shrugged. But the Arts Council needed help. He thought about Diane Martin, the president who had no background in theater construction. He hoped that she would accept Michael's suggestions and that the project wouldn't hit major problems. Perhaps the council needed a Chairman of Small Details, someone who could handle the little hills before they became mountains.

* * *

That morning, Louise and Jenny had eaten breakfast together, reliving their weekend at Bar Harbor. "I'll wash the dishes. You need to open the shop," Jenny said.

"Do you want me to pick you up for lunch?"

"No, I'm going to stay here today. I want to send some e-mails and read the ones I missed while we were gone."

Charlie called at ten o'clock. "I found an apartment to rent, and I'll move in next week."

"I'm sure that you won't miss the Blueberry Inn. Where's the apartment?"

"On Maple Street, not too far from the office. I want you to see it after I'm settled. How about lunch today?"

With a smile, Jenny quickly changed her plans. "I'd like that."

Over hamburgers at Mom's Kitchen, Jenny gave a glowing account of her trip to Bar Harbor, and Charlie countered with a report on the status of *Tangled Trap Lines*.

"Jamison likes the play and wants to direct it. I gave him the script after dinner last night, and I didn't sleep much. At the meeting this morning, he announced his decision, and the committee agreed. He's put out a casting call on the internet, and we worked the rest of the morning on a flyer that announced the production and urged people to audition."

"I'm happy for you, Charlie." Jenny looked down at her plate. "I wish I were happy about me. You've completed an awesome task, revising and reworking your play, and I've completed nothing. I'm stuck on crutches, Erin's in Portland, and now I'm troubled by two murders instead of one, neither of which is solved."

"Have you seen your vision lately?"

"No, but I saw a death's head the other night." She shuddered. "I've never seen anything like that before, and I'm scared." She took Charlie's hand. "I don't know where to go or what to do. I came home to find out who killed Pete. Then Tim was killed. And remember, someone tried to run us down after dinner at the Dolphin."

"Maybe you should put your search on hold for a time. Once the Arts Council goes to work on the play, you'll be busy with the scenery." He laughed. "That's a real change of scene, right?"

Jenny nodded. "I'm looking forward to doing the sets. Ann Thompson offered to help, and I'd like to work with her. Next week I'll have a walking cast and should be able to drive. I might even visit Erin in Portland."

Charlie squeezed her hand. "Don't worry about delaying your search. When you meet Michael Jamison and start on the sets, you won't have time to be a sleuth."

As they walked to his car, Charlie said, "In the play, we know the killer. Wouldn't it be a coincidence if during the course of the play and by accident, Pete Clampton's killer were revealed?"

"I don't believe in coincidences. What will be will be."

Jenny pondered Charlie's question that afternoon as she sent an e-mail to Erin. "I hope to see you in Portland as soon as I can drive," she wrote. "Nothing's happening here,"

* * *

David and Michael completed their afternoon tour of the theater. "I'll check on theater seating and put out casting calls on the internet,"

Michael said. "The flyers will be ready tomorrow morning, and Charlotte planned to ask a Boy Scout troop to distribute them."

"We're moving right along," David said. "Call me if you need anything."

He left Michael at the guest house and drove to the craft shop. Louise had just completed a sale when he entered.

"How was the meeting?" Louise asked.

"Jamison chose Charlie's play, and the Arts Council agreed. He and I toured the theater just now, and he's satisfied with the renovation." David patted Louise's hand. "He's a good man, Louise. I wasn't prepared to like him after he practically left you standing at the altar, but he's sincere about his work. You'll have to meet him eventually, you know. Will it be difficult?"

Louise bit her lip. "Yes, it will be difficult. I was surprised and shocked when you told me about his coming here, and I'd like to spare him those reactions. I'm planning to call, tell him that I live here and make a date to meet." She smiled. "It's been almost thirty years, David. I want to look presentable."

David laughed. "Presentable? You're a knockout, Louise. The years have not only been kind, they've blessed you." Louise caught a glimpse of David's reticence. He looked at the floor. "I'm not much at flowery speeches, but you're a damned good-looking woman."

"Thanks, I'll keep that in mind when I dress for the occasion."

Louise turned the 'Open' sign to 'Closed,' and as she completed her routine, she thought about Michael. His presence in Sowatna would complicate her life. She'd promised to design and create costumes for the play, and that meant being around the director. She'd make that call this week and be prepared to accept whatever ensued.

As she drove home, she thought about her opening line. "Hi, Michael, this is Louise Campbell. Remember me?"

She couldn't envision his response.

CHAPTER THIRTEEN

On Tuesday morning, Chief Harry Pierce sat at his desk in Sowatna's police station and stared at the ceiling. He reached for a heavy wooden plaque at the edge of his desk and turned it around. 'Harry Pierce, Chief of Police.' He studied it, turned it back and thought that it ought to read 'Chief of Unsolved Murders.'

The coroner's report from Portland offered no new information on Tim Brennan's death. Brennan had used a small amount of heroin, not enough to render him incapable of self-defense. His clothing revealed no foreign matter, hair, threads, bodily fluids. The blood was his own. The car was clean. No fingerprints. And the rain had washed away anything helpful on the road or in the ditch.

Almost a week had passed, and no one had called to give an eye-witness account of the murder. George Hendricks had been interviewed because Brennan had taken his car to Hendricks Ford for an oil change. Hendricks had offered no new information. He had testified that he had been home with his wife, Doris, and she had confirmed his statement. "Tim didn't tell me where he was going, and I didn't ask."

Charlie Brewster should have come forward earlier about his meeting with Brennan that afternoon. As a crime reporter, he ought to have known the importance of each bit of information. And Gloria and Jacob Gregory, Erin's parents, should have been helpful. Why hadn't someone asked Brennan about his plans for the evening? The trail was dead, and so was Tim Brennan.

Pierce replenished his wad of gum. He dreaded his afternoon meeting with the sheriff and his deputy because they were even more frustrated than he was. The murder, outside of city limits, was under the sheriff's jurisdiction, and although they worked together, Pierce was not in charge. Usually this chain of command worked harmoniously, and Pierce understood the protocol. In the Brennan case, however, Pierce shared equally in the sheriff's concerns. Brennan had been in town before he was killed, and the people he'd seen were residents. Pierce's feelings of responsibility didn't diminish because someone waited to kill Brennan until he was out of town and in the sheriff's domain.

Pierce walked to Dispatch and studied the monitors that displayed minor disturbances. "Not much on 911 this morning," Carol said. "I may have time for a coffee break."

* * *

At ten o'clock Tuesday morning, Louise called Jenny from the craft shop. "I'll pick you up for lunch, and we'll go to the Lobster Shack."

"I hope that after x-rays next week, I'll be able to drive myself," Jenny said. "I'll meet you at the curb."

At noon, they found a table and ordered crab cakes and coffee. As they waited for their order, Louise said, "I'm going over to the deli and order lobsters and some clam chowder for dinner tonight."

She walked through the wide opening between the restaurant and the deli and gave her order to Randy behind the counter. He handed her two plastic bags, each filled with gray-green wads of seaweed, water and a squirming lobster, and a quart of clam chowder in a paper sack. She glanced to her left and noticed another customer, a tall, slender man dressed in a green turtleneck sweater and tan chinos. Michael? He had the same blue eyes, full lips and strong chin. His auburn hair showed hints of gray, but yes, it was Michael.

Louise stared at him and dropped the lobsters and the chowder. She heard Michael exclaim, "Oh, my God, Louise!" She stepped back, heard the crunch of a lobster shell, slipped on a puddle of chowder and fell to the floor.

For Louise, the next moments were in slow motion. Michael dropped his bags of lobsters. Water, wads of gray-green seaweed and lobsters mingled with Louise's purchases, and now the floor was wet and slippery. As Michael tried to help her, he fell, and they both sat on the floor staring at each other.

Louise swore silently. Where was the scene she'd scripted so carefully? Where was the park bench under a full moon, or a dinner for two at the Dolphin, she, beautifully coifed, made up and attired in a lovely, tangerine-colored, mid-calf dress that flowed and rippled gently as she moved? They'd smile at each other and recite past events. The evening would be quiet and calm as they reminisced together.

Now, God forbid, she sat facing Michael, her hair falling onto her face, her blouse and skirt covered with clam chowder, her make-up washed away in sea water.

Michael looked at her and, with care, removed a bit of clam from her nose. "Hi," he said. And suddenly they both began to laugh.

Randy leaned over the counter, surveyed the mess and said, "You two know each other?" Their laughter filled the room, then faded into quiet chuckles.

Randy came from behind the counter with a mop and a pail. "You both will have to move so I can clean up this mess."

Louise pulled down her skirt, pushed hair out of her eyes and mouth and stood. She watched Michael stand and reach for a skittering lobster. He gave the lobster to Randy and took Louise's hand.

"I can't believe you're here in Sowatna. How many years has it been, twenty?"

"Almost thirty, Michael." She turned away and picked up another lobster. She didn't want Michael to see her like this, disheveled, wet, in complete disarray. She was dressed for work in a pink shirtwaist and blue slacks. Not much makeup. She looked down at her feet. Ugh! Her sandals were soaked in clam chowder, and bits of seaweed clung to her toes.

She looked at Michael and realized that he didn't look much better. His pants were wet, and his shoulder-length auburn hair was streaked with seaweed. All of her visions of a quiet, calm, enchanting dinner or a moonlit park bench vanished in a puddle of water, seaweed and clam chowder.

So much for visions, she thought and smiled. "My niece, Jenny, is staying with me this summer. We've just ordered lunch, and I want you to meet her. Can you join us?"

"I'd like that. I'll follow you."

Louise adjusted her skirt and tried to walk without slipping in her wet sandals. She didn't know what Jenny had seen from their table in the restaurant.

"Jenny, this is Michael Jamison, our new director." Louise picked another bit of clam from her blouse. "We knew each other years ago in St. Paul." She realized that Jenny was confused by her introduction.

"I'm glad to meet you," Jenny said. "Everyone is excited about your being here."

Michael pulled up a chair and sat between Louise and Jenny. He picked up a menu and signaled a waitress. "I'm glad to be here too. I drove up from Saratoga Springs on Sunday, and I'm living in the guest house behind a bed and breakfast on Third Street."

"That's great," Jenny said. "You'll be right next door."

Louise didn't share Jenny's enthusiasm. She understood that she must be cordial, but having him next door would tax her efforts to keep her emotional sanity and to maintain her role as Jenny's aunt. She'd have three months living that role while Michael would have those months directing a cast in the theater. Who's on stage, she wondered.

* * *

Jenny had watched her aunt walk to the deli and had witnessed the entire fiasco. She thought about rushing to help Louise, but when she and the man began to laugh and talk together, she sat back in her chair and laughed also. From where she sat, the scene was hilarious. Her aunt on the floor covered with clam chowder and sea weed, the man similarly attired, and both of them laughing. She wished that she'd had a video of the event.

And who was this mysterious stranger who had turned a simple deli order into chaos? She had waited anxiously as Louise and the man came to the table. Through the introductions and Michael's lunch order, Jenny had sensed her aunt's nervousness, an ambivalence about their meeting. If Jenny's perceptions were accurate, Michael Jamison's presence in Sowatna had not been met with total delight.

* * *

During lunch, Michael's cell phone rang. It was Charlie Brewster. "I'd like to interview you this afternoon if you have time."

"I have time. Where shall we meet?"

Michael wrote directions. "I'll be at the Chronicle office at one-thirty."

For Michael, it was a relief to find a reason to leave the Lobster Shack. He'd been surprised and glad to see Louise again, but there were too many painful memories of a severed romance. He hadn't seen Louise after he'd written his letter that aborted the wedding. Maybe he'd been a coward, not accepting the consequences, but facing Louise was more than he could endure. Better to cut off the relationship completely than to agonize together. He couldn't have lived through Louise's response. He knew her well enough to know her strengths and weaknesses, and he almost knew how she would react. And the outcome would have been the same. It would simply have been cluttered with purposeless dialogue.

He realized during lunch that Louise was also uneasy. Conversation had been strained. Her niece must have sensed the tension as she directed discussions to her teaching and the Arts Council's plans. Living next door to Louise would be awkward but, dammit, he had a job to do, and the play must be a success. He'd simply have to do his job with a minimum of complications.

Now after lunch, Michael found the Chronicle office and introduced himself to the editor. He laughed when Charlotte took a black felt hat from a box behind her desk. It was decorated with a feather that almost covered her face.

"I wear this for my special guests," she said. "It was my grandmother's."

"Very nice," Michael said. Anything else would have been superfluous.

Charlie called from his office, and Michael followed the sound. A young man with a camera sat beside Charlie's desk. "This is Adam Roberts. He'll take some shots, then we'll go to work."

Michael adjusted his turtleneck sweater that had dried out and brushed off three tiny clams. As he combed his hair, wisps of gray-green seaweed fell to the floor.

"Lunch," Michael said as Charlie and Adam looked on.

Adam took twelve shots of Michael sitting and standing. He held a book, he held Charlie's script, he sat at the desk looking serious, friendly, pensive, and determined. He stood in front of the window, the ocean scene behind him. He looked at the ceiling. He held his pipe and looked artistic and wise.

"Okay," Adam said. "I think we've got it. I'll be back later."

Charlie switched on a tape recorder and began the interview. Michael knew at once that Charlie was experienced, a real professional, and the interview went smoothly.

Thirty minutes later, Charlie turned off the recorder and leaned forward. "You'll be on the front page, Michael. Now let's talk about the play. We need to put it into readable booklets for the cast. I have a cost estimate and will give it to the Council. The typesetters will have it ready by the end of the week, I hope. When do you plan to schedule auditions?"

"As soon as we have applicants. We'll need a good location. Since the theater isn't finished, can we use the high school stage?"

"I'll check with Diane. School's out except for a few summer school classes, so the stage is probably available."

Michael left the Chronicle office and drove to the pier. He sat on a wooden bench and watched the sea gulls soar, dip, and circle above the boats. There were trawlers, windjammers, tall-masted sailing boats, power boats, and indescribable boats. Further from shore, he noticed buoys that bobbed in the waves. Because he hadn't lived by the ocean, the scene was exotic. A few weekends at Myrtle Beach and Daytona were only samples of coastal living.

He walked along Front Street, admired the cobbled stones and baskets of petunias hanging from street lights. He saw a drug store, a shoe repair shop, a craft shop, and a garage. People were dressed for comfort, not for style. Tennis shoes and sandals, shorts and cut-offs. He thought about replacing his turtleneck with a lighter shirt.

He liked Charlie as a writer and as a reporter. They would work well together. He wondered about their future relationship when the director needed to alter some of the writer's deathless prose. He'd faced that situation before and knew how to soothe a writer's wounded ego.

He drove back to the guest house, made phone calls and thought about the summer in Sowatna. Although seeing Louise might cause problems, he looked forward to developing a performance in a new theater with a new cast performing a new play. The summer offered exciting challenges.

* * *

After lunch, Jenny rode home with Louise. She called the doctor's office and made an appointment for next week. She hoped that if the x-rays indicated graduation into a walking cast, she could give her crutches to the next unfortunate person and drive her own car.

She hobbled to the bottom of the staircase and looked up at the portrait of William Campbell. Was it her imagination, or did he really smile at her? She opened her laptop, located a search engine and researched Bradford, Scotland. She printed three pages of information. The Campbells were land owners, had fought with Bonnie Prince Charlie and lost everything at the Battle of Culloden in 1746. Seven mysterious deaths had occurred during the seventeenth century. Frederick Lawrence Campbell was accused of murder, and a trial was held. He was pronounced guilty and was hanged in Bradford on September 1, 1808.

When Louise returned from the craft shop, Jenny shared her information. "The Campbells were a feisty bunch. They stood by Bonnie Prince Charlie, defied the English, and died mysteriously."

Louise laughed. "I wondered about those mysterious deaths, and I also wondered about the trial of Frederick Lawrence Campbell. How old was he? Who did he kill?"

"Maybe I can search for details about the trial."

"Wait until tomorrow. I brought a DVD for tonight. We need a good laugh, and this is a great comedy."

* * *

The killer walked past Louise's craft shop and noticed a man seated on a bench by the pier and realized that it was the new director, Michael Jamison. The killer considered opening a conversation with him but dismissed the idea. Too bad that the director had chosen to produce Charlie Brewster's play about Pete Clampton's murder. It might open old wounds. Charlie had asked questions and interviewed people who were involved in the investigation. Those two women, Erin Gregory and Jenny McKnight, had also stirred up interest in

Pete's murder. Fortunately Tim Brennan had been eliminated before he had spilled his guts. The killer was uneasy. Another death might be a necessity if the right questions were asked of the right people.

* * *

Diane Martin, president of the Arts Council, phoned the director to remind him of the Council's weekly meeting on Thursday night. "I read Saturday's edition of the Chronicle and was thrilled with the publicity. The photographs were a special plus. I've already received calls from people in town who want to try out."

"That's great," Michael said. "Did you tell them that we'd have auditions as soon as we find a location?"

"Yes, and we can use the high school. I called the superintendent this morning. We can use their stage for auditions and rehearsals any evening except Wednesday."

"That's wonderful. Charlie's arranged to have the play printed in booklets. As soon as that's done, we'll notify the people."

Diane caught a hint of concern and paused. "Yes, Michael, I have a list of the callers, phone numbers and addresses."

She knew that her timing had given Michael a few seconds of worry. Fun, she thought. She liked to tease. Too much seriousness in this world. There would be plenty of time for earnest, thoughtful action later.

"If you have time, perhaps we could have lunch together," Diane suggested coyly.

Another pause, this time from Michael. "Yes, and maybe Charlie could join us. He has some great ideas about involving the Arts Council."

Diane slumped in her chair but kept a cheery tone in her voice. "Great. Call me after you've set a time with Charlie. I'll see you soon."

Diane hung up and frowned. Lunch alone with Michael would have been better. Nothing wrong with a harmless little flirtation. Of course she'd never think of going beyond a goodnight kiss, so what's the big deal? She tossed back her pony tail and sat at her computer. Time to think about next week's agenda.

* * *

Everybody Knew Pete

Colin Greene's afternoon's case work was interrupted when his intercom buzzed. "A call from Charlie Brewster," his receptionist said.

"Colin, I have a great idea." Charlie's voice was so upbeat that Colin laughed.

"What's up? Did you win an Oscar already?"

Charlie joined in the laughter. "Not yet. Listen. Auditions are set for this Friday at the high school, and I think that you should try out for the part of the prosecuting attorney."

"Are you serious? I haven't acted since college."

"So it's time for you to get back on stage. Please think about it."

"All right. Thanks for calling."

Colin sat back and thought about it. He knew that rehearsals would take place during the evening, and that's when he felt lonely and sometimes depressed. Louise, in charge of costumes, would be there. Memorization was no problem. Yes, he might audition for the part. After all, as an attorney, he really wouldn't have to act. He'd just be himself.

* * *

Michael needed an assistant to help him during auditions, someone to put faces with names and record his comments. He thought about Jenny, Louise's niece who was staying with Louise. She would be without her crutches in a few days, and he sensed that they could work well together.

He called Louise's home, and Jenny answered. "I want someone to help me during auditions, and I thought about you," Michael said. "Do you have time?"

"I'd be happy to help. Call when you need me."

Michael returned to his file and knew that he'd need more file folders as work progressed. So far, he was on schedule. But what about Diane? After he'd added Charlie to her luncheon invitation, he hoped that she had got the message. Theirs was to be a professional relationship. He'd known situations that had become untenable because of an imagined or actual romance.

He looked at the calendar and called Charlotte Quincy at the Chronicle. "Would you call the local radio station and ask them to put out a public service announcement? I'd like to schedule our first audition for Friday night at seven o'clock."

"Done. I'll also have some posters for downtown distribution. I hope that you'll have enough local people to fill all of the roles."

"That's my hope also."

* * *

The next morning, Charlie sat at his desk and finished a news story about an attempted robbery at a convenience store.

He called Jenny. "Lunch? I have two hours before my next assignment."

They found a booth at the Expresso and ordered wraps and coffee.

"Michael Jamison asked me to help him with the auditions," Jenny said. "I'm glad to have a job until we start work on the sets. Are the play booklets finished?"

"They'll be done tomorrow." He took Jenny's hand. "We're both going to be busy now. I hope there's time for us."

Charlie saw a concerned look on Jenny's face. She rubbed her eyebrow and frowned. "I don't know, Charlie. Let's not rush into something. Remember the song, *Easy Does It*? You've recently gone through a messy divorce, and me? Last month, I had to cut off a troublesome relationship with a guy I had thought was meant for me."

"And? I don't want to pry, and you don't have to tell me."

"Nothing sensational. He had other interests on the side. My roommate told me. She didn't want me to get hurt, but she knew the woman he was seeing."

"You were lucky." He sat back with a wry smile. "We'll have an interesting summer, Jenny, and I won't pressure you."

He knew that Jenny was right, and he wanted to kick himself from forgetting about his problems with his ex-wife, Dierdre. He grinned at Jenny and decided that it was all her fault. There she was, hobbling around on crutches, having nightmares, wanting to find a killer and probably in danger herself. Sympathy had become entwined with romance. Cool it, Charlie, he told himself.

He sat with Jenny at the Arts Council meeting Thursday night, and he maintained the casual relationship she'd suggested. The meeting, chaired by Diane, the president, went well. She introduced Michael who explained why he had chosen Charlie's play, *Tangled Trap Lines*.

"The play has local interest because of the murder of Pete Clampton, but it's more involved in relationships." Michael described the divided stage, the court room on stage right and living rooms on stage left. "The theater's renovation is on schedule, and I'm pleased with the work being done. I'm also pleased to be directing Charlie Brewster's play. It's excellent."

Charlie felt color rising on his cheeks. He looked at Jenny and smiled. Diane thanked Michael and called for committee reports. At the close of the meeting, Charlie visited briefly with Michael and drove to the motel. It was time to check any last-minute changes in Saturday's issue of the Chronicle.

* * *

The first audition on Friday night was a greater success than Michael had hoped for. Twenty-five people appeared, and he was pleased with their talent.

Colin Greene put his head in the door and almost tiptoed into the auditorium. "Charlie Brewster suggested that I try out for the part of the prosecuting attorney because I'm an attorney, and I know court room procedure."

"Glad you're here." Michael handed him a booklet.

Two hours went by, and Michael was able to assign parts to four people including Colin. His main concerns were about the hero and heroine, and those two roles were filled by young people who had appeared in many productions in the state. They were college students who were free for the summer. Michael also found the judge. He'd envisioned Charlotte Quincy in that role and was disappointed when she didn't appear. Instead, he chose a high school drama teacher.

Weekly Arts Council meetings became routine as the play developed. Michael was glad that all the acting parts were filled with people from Sowatna and the surrounding area. He continued to be awed by the local talent that appeared suddenly from grocery stores, the dental office, and from stay-at-home moms. Rehearsals were on schedule, and the cast would be ready for opening night on August thirtieth.

Renovation of the Legion Club continued. When the stage area was completed, Jenny and Ann Thompson followed Michael's directions for the sets. Charlie's play needed a divided stage, the court room on stage right and two interior scenes on stage left. They constructed a jury box and a judge's bench and located tables and chairs for the opposing sides in the trial. The interior scenes took more effort. The heroine's home would be Victorian and the other, simple and run-down. Jenny called it 'old attic.' Jenny asked Diane for help with furniture for both sets, and two retired teachers volunteered.

Michael used the internet to research theater seating and was rewarded with an offer from a theater in Bangor that planned to update.

"No charge," the theater manager said. "We didn't know what to do with the old seats."

The owner of Sowatna Hardware and Lumber Company agreed to transport the seats as soon as they were needed.

Renovation of the Legion Club was on schedule. Glenn Thompson's crew was efficient although communication was often difficult. Fortunately, the foreman, Mendes, appeared occasionally to translate.

Michael asked Diane about the lighting budget. "How much can we spend?"

Diane checked the proposed budget and said, "I'm afraid that it won't be adequate."

Michael heard the figure and groaned. "No, it isn't enough. Is there a college nearby?" He thought about his work at Skidmore and knew that college drama departments were usually well equipped and sometimes loaned items to reputable organizations.

Diane gave him a list of colleges and universities, and Michael spent one morning on the phone. He located people in charge, introduced himself and gave details of his production and sponsorship. He liked what he heard. Floodlights, spotlights, and pigtails were available when they were needed.

He assured the institutions that this was a first-time venture. "The Sowatna Players should be solvent and well supplied next year." Michael crossed his fingers, looked to heaven and offered a prayer.

He had seen little of Louise, and he knew that it suited both of them. They would work together when costumes were needed. Louise was sensible and would accept his directions. Right now, he enjoyed working with Jenny. She was bright and experienced in set designing.

There was something else about her that intrigued him. One evening after rehearsals were over and the cast had left, she told him about a few of her experiences as a psychic. "In high school, I saw a person dragging the body of a man toward the pier, and later that night, a lobsterman was found dead on his boat."

"Pete Clampton? Charlie told me about the murder. He had to change his play because of so much conflicting evidence and said that he'd talked to the man accused of the murder."

"Did he tell you that the accused, Tim Brennan, was also murdered this summer?"

"No, we spent most of our time working on the play." He looked down at his hands. "Sometimes I have premonitions, and once I saw an aura. I don't mention this to my friends. They'd laugh or ship me off to a place for the mentally bewildered."

Michael was relieved when Jenny didn't laugh. "I've been troubled by nightmares, visions, ever since the night of Pete Clampton's murder. Louise was right when she said that the spirit might be friendly and wanted help. I'd like to know who killed Pete Clampton, Michael. That's why I'm here."

Michael watched Jenny leave the theater, her short auburn hair shining under the house lights. Her hair was almost the color of his, he thought.

CHAPTER FOURTEEN

Breakfast was the best time of day for Jenny. She and Louise drank coffee and made plans for the day.

"I'm driving to Portland to visit Erin," Jenny said. "It's so great having a walking cast, and soon I'll be walking normally."

"The doctor was pleased with your progress," Louise said. "You healed quickly. Be careful this weekend. No more accidents, please."

Jenny laughed. "I'm sure that our great, great grandfather pushed me, but I can't prove it. Did you ever learn more about him?"

"No. Records disappeared or were burned. I spent more time at the computer last night and learned that Frederick Lawrence Campbell had killed a fisherman. They must have lived by the sea. No motive was given, and the victim's name wasn't listed. We'll never know the whole story."

"I should tell Charlie about Frederick. He might appear in Charlie's next play."

Jenny went upstairs and packed. She turned and watched the portrait of William Campbell as she started down the steps. No more sudden, catastrophic descents.

She drove to the Thomas J. Moore Center and found Erin at her computer. They hugged. "You look great," Erin said. "Let's see you walk."

Jenny limped across the room in her heavy walking cast. "So much better than crutches. I'll be shedding this boot next week."

"I'm ready to leave now. I've made dinner reservations at a new restaurant downtown. You'll like it."

For Jenny, her few days with Erin were a delight, relief to be rid of her crutches and joy to spend time with her long-time friend. Almost ten years had passed between their high school activities and their reconnecting in Sowatna. Ten years of catching up. In Sowatna, they'd been too occupied with Pete Clampton's murder to bring their lives up to date. Now over wine and lasagna, they indulged in personal histories.

Erin described her battle with alcoholism and her work at the Center. Jenny talked about teaching. Ultimately the conversation led to relationships with men, and they shared their experiences, some good, some regrettable.

"I thought that Brian was Mr. Wonderful," Jenny said. "My roommate learned that two other women also thought he was Mr. Wonderful."

"You're lucky that you found out."

"That's what Charlie said. I see him often, but I'm not ready for a romantic alliance right now." Jenny laughed. "And neither is Charlie. His divorce still haunts him."

"I've fallen for two guys who were in treatment here and thought that two alcoholics could find romance. One relapsed for the third time, and the other went back to his wife."

At midnight in Erin's apartment, Jenny made up the sleeper sofa and settled down ready for sleep.

Erin called from the bedroom. "What's happened since Tim Brennan was killed? Have they found the murderer?"

At two a.m., Jenny finished her detailed account.

"I did some sleuthing when I came back to the Center," Erin said. "Remember that we dismissed the minister who lived next door to the church? His name was Richard Evans. I wondered why he had retired, so I checked with the Presbyterian Church here. They told me that he had left Sowatna in 1999. He was forty years old, and that seemed to be awfully young for retirement."

"That's true, so why did he leave?"

"Maybe I have a suspicious mind, but we know that Pete Clampton sold drugs. What if Mr. Evans had a drug problem? What if he had bought drugs from Pete, and what if Pete, for unknown reasons, threatened to expose him?"

"Sounds like a TV thriller, Erin, so what did you do?"

Erin took a Coke from the refrigerator. "I thought about checking his records at the Center. Legally I can check billing records, but there's an ethics issue. We must preserve confidentiality. Morally we have an obligation to protect our clients. I'll talk to my supervisor, and I'll call you when I've had more time to work it out."

"It's a delicate situation. But if Evans did kill Pete, what about Tim Brennan?"

Erin sipped her Coke. "Maybe Tim knew about the drugs and threatened to expose Evans."

Jenny and Erin looked at each other. "I hate to think that a minister would kill, but I guess they're as human as anyone else. When I get home, I'm going to ask Louise about Evans. I hope you're wrong, but we have to find out."

"I'm driving home in a couple of weeks," Erin said. "We can play Nancy Drew again. Mom has a job and her phone calls are amazing. She doesn't bitch about Dad's drinking. She's making a life for herself, and I'm relieved."

"And your dad?"

"No change, and I don't expect miracles. Some folks just don't get it, Jenny. I've worked at the Center long enough to know that no matter how hard we try, there are failures."

Jenny returned to Sowatna determined to continue her investigation. That night, she sat in bed with a legal-sized yellow pad and wrote a list of suspects. 'Mavis Long Bianci, George Hendricks, Glenn Thompson, Richard Evans.' All of them lived near the church. They knew Pete Clampton, but how would they have known Tim Brennan? Jenny thought of only one reason, drugs, but Evans was the only known user. Did Tim know something that might have caused his death? A possibility. Something else pricked Jenny's brain. The investigation of Pete's murder. Where were the photographs? Why wasn't there a follow-up of Brennan's intended trip with Clampton?

She was glad to work on scenery for the play and forget the investigation until Erin's visit. She and Ann had worked as a team, and Jenny liked her. Jenny's intuition gave her a fairly accurate picture of Ann's relationship with her father, and she hoped that their future together might be assured somehow. At present, she and Ann were busy building sets. Painting, pounding and assembling flats were full-time occupations, and conversation was limited to scene two, the heroine's living room.

After all the roles had been filled, Michael asked Jenny to help him with a variety of chores.

"I needed a Chairman of Small Details," Michael had said, "and you're it."

Jenny laughed. She enjoyed working with Michael and often could anticipate his needs before he asked. She had no more nightmares but knew that the mystery remained. One evening after rehearsal, she told Michael about Pete Clampton's murder, her visions, and her determination to discover the identity of the killer.

"He or she is out there somewhere, Michael. I have to know. Charlie interviewed the photographer, the court reporter and an attorney. Colin Greene gave him the file, and Charlie was puzzled because there were no photographs. My friend, Erin Gregory, and I interviewed some people and learned nothing."

"Charlie told me that you had met with the man who was acquitted."

"Yes, and we received no answers. Tim was killed that night. Erin returned to Portland, and I've been too busy with the play to follow any leads, even if there were any."

"Louise told me of your two accidents. I hope there aren't any more."

"So do I. There's too much work to be done this summer."

* * *

Later that month on a Friday afternoon, Jenny's cell phone rang. "How would you like to take the ferry out to Isle au Bas tomorrow afternoon?" Charlie asked. "It's not far, and the island's a treasure. Great beaches, and quaint shops. Charlotte's giving me the weekend off." He laughed.

"I'd love it. Now that my boot's been removed, I can go swimming."

"We can take the two o'clock ferry, go to the beach, have a late dinner. The last ferry leaves at ten-thirty, so we won't have to hurry."

Jenny packed her swim suit and was ready when Charlie rang the door bell.

"I'm glad to have a break," Jenny said. "We've worked hard all week, and the scenery is almost finished. Michael likes most of it and made a few changes."

"How is he as a boss?"

"Very easy. He gives directions well, and the cast likes him. We're usually pounding away in back while they're rehearsing, but we can hear the dialogue and comments from the director. He sits on a stool out front, and his voice carries."

Charlie drove to the pier, parked the car and bought tickets. The dock was crowded with passengers who waited for the gangway to open. Children ran up and down the dock, and their parents whistled, called and finally shouted as the gangway ropes were released.

Jenny and Charlie found seats by a window. The sea was calm. Puffy white clouds drifted slowly across the horizon, and sailboats followed their pattern. Jenny leaned back and breathed deeply.

"It's a perfect day, Charlie."

Jenny noticed a man seated alone in a seat nearest the rear of the ferry. His face was covered as he read a newspaper. He was dressed in a brown all-weather jacket and jeans. He wore tennis shoes.

Forty-five minutes after departure, the ferry docked at Isle au Bas. Jenny and Charlie followed the passengers down the gangway and walked slowly toward the main street. The island was about two miles deep and four miles wide. Three Norwegian families had settled here in the early eighteen hundreds and had survived the bitterly cold winters, hot summers, seasons that produced an abundance of fish and seasons when there were no fish at all. When ferry service began in 1866, life on the island improved. Daily, the ferries brought people to and from the island, and because of its beaches and fishing, some people stayed on the island.

Jenny and Charlie bought sodas and walked down the street until they found a beach that offered bathrooms and changing areas. Jenny changed into her bathing suit, ran ahead of Charlie and put her toe in the water. She pulled it back.

"I think I'll just sunbathe for a while." She sat down on a rock by the shore.

Charlie laughed. "Too cold? Chicken!" He ran to the water, immersed a toe and joined Jenny on her rock. "I could skate on that stuff."

They drank sodas and watched the shore birds, razorbills, gannets, gulls, and puffins that stood in a group, all facing the east. Trawlers and windjammers sailed away from the island, and a yacht inched its way toward the pier.

"Lobstermen call those fancy yachts 'blow boats,'" Jenny said.

"Do you want to look at the shops?" Charlie asked. There was no answer as Jenny raced back to the women's changing room.

The main street of Isle au Bas was crowded with tourists. Jenny bought an agate pendant. Charlie found a ship inside a bottle, a perfect gift for Dispatch in Miami. They studied menus outside four restaurants and opted for a moderately priced, upstairs café.

Dinner was leisurely. Their table by a window offered a view of the dock area. Lobstermen readied their traps for the morning.

"I went out with a lobsterman last summer," Jenny said, "and he told me a lot about baiting and hauling in the traps. He said that he placed his buoys away from others, and he'd painted his bright pink and were easily identified."

"I want to learn more about lobstering. Maybe do a series on the lobsterers."

"You'll find lots of information in the library and on the internet, but the local scene is always more interesting than what's in the guide books."

As they finished dessert, they noticed the fog rolling in. "That's not Carl Sandberg's 'little cats' feet,'" Jenny said. "It looks more like a Maine coon cat."

They walked back to the pier and noticed tourists who looked at their watches. A man walked out of the ticket booth, looked up at the fog and shook his head. "The ferry won't leave until the fogs lifts, folks, so you might as well be off to the nearest tavern and have a beer. Here on the island, we call that 'harpoon ale.'"

Jenny and Charlie joined the group and found 'High Tide Tillie's,' a lively bistro. Its walls were decorated with pictures of ship wrecks and wave-swept rocky coasts.

"Maybe she's trying to tell us something," Charlie said.

They sat by a window and watched the fog that thickened by the minute. The bartender brought two frosted glass steins filled with beer and said, "We have a saying for that stuff out there. 'Even the birds be walkin'.'"

Charlie asked, "How long will this last?"

"God knows, and He ain't tellin', so relax. You could be in worse places."

Charlie and Jenny nodded. They'd both been in worse places.

At eleven o'clock, they noticed a change in the view. A sign across the street, people on the sidewalk. Charlie paid the bill, and they walked back to the pier. Passengers were already beginning to board as the ticket man assured them that they'd be off in a short time.

Jenny was glad to leave the tavern. She'd had too many of those frosted glass steins and needed fresh air. Charlie showed no signs of one-too-many and took her elbow as they climbed up the gangway.

The ferry moved slowly away from the dock, and Jenny felt a wave of nausea. Her head ached and her stomach did somersaults. Ten minutes later, she stood. "I need some fresh air, Charlie. I'll walk to the front of the boat and take deep breaths."

"Do you want me to go with you?"

Jenny shook her head. "I'll be fine." She pushed open the door and felt a cool breeze. She inhaled the salty sea air, and her headache was gone. She leaned over the railing and looked down at the side of the ferry. The wind had decreased, and waves lapped gently against the hull.

Suddenly she felt hands around her throat. By her neck, she was turned around and, terror-stricken, faced a tall man wearing a ski mask. A brown hat covered his head, and the brim came down almost to his nose. The mouth, muffled by the ski mask, said, "You ask too many questions."

Jenny tried to scream, but the man's grip held her throat too tightly for any sound. With one strong movement, he put his right hand around her waist, lifted her into the air and threw her into the ocean.

Jenny screamed as she fell. From the deep recesses of her brain, she remembered her senior lifesaving survival technique. She spread out her legs, one in front of her and one in back, and threw out her arms. As she hit the water, she sank only briefly but lost her breath in the icy cold water. She swallowed sea water as she surfaced, and waves washed over her while she forced herself to tread water.

"Help ! Help!" she yelled. She looked up at the ship. The man had disappeared. She saw Charlie inside the cabin, his head bent over a book. If no one found her, she knew that she would die soon. Her entire body shook, and her breathing was quick and shallow. As she treaded water, she felt her legs move more slowly.

Suddenly she heard a splash and was blinded by a beacon of light. She found a life preserver near her shoulder. Her first attempts to grab it failed. Her fingers were too numb. Next she threw both arms around it, and held on. She looked up and saw two men in black suits standing at the rail. They waved and jumped into the water. They swam to her and quickly tied a rope around her waist.

"You're okay now," one of the men said. "We're going to pull you up."

With one man on each side, Jenny felt herself being lifted up out of the water. Strong arms grabbed her, and she was pulled over the railing. The two men in black wet suits brought blankets and wrapped her tightly. They propped her up between them and hugged her.

"We're just as wet as you are, but you'll gradually feel warmer," one said.

"Weren't we going fast enough for you?" the other asked, and Jenny managed a weak smile.

"I was pushed," she said between gulps of air. She continued to shiver and felt her legs give way. The men eased her onto the deck. She began to cry. Between sobs, she said, "Please find Charlie."

A man ran to the cabin, called out, and returned with Charlie who was in shock. "My God, what happened?"

The men released her, and Charlie knelt down and put his arms around her.

Jenny sobbed. "Out on deck, someone grabbed me and threw me overboard."

"Who was it?"

"I don't know. He wore a ski mask. I didn't recognize his voice." She shivered. "He threatened me. He tried to kill me, and he almost did."

Someone brought a cup of hot chocolate, and Jenny removed her right arm from the blanket and drank slowly.

The cabin door opened, and a woman ran to Jenny. "I'm a doctor." She knelt beside Jenny, felt her pulse and looked into her eyes. "What's your name and what day is it?"

Jenny answered both questions correctly. "Good," said the doctor, "but you're pale, and your fingers are still blue." She uncovered her feet. "You're toes are blue also. You should go to the emergency room at the hospital as soon as we dock. You were in that freezing water too long."

The men who had brought her to safety returned to their positions on the ferry. When Jenny was able to stand, Charlie helped her back to her seat in the cabin. Passengers watched as Charlie dried her hair with a towel.

Jenny looked down at her feet. "I lost my sandals. I hope a fish doesn't eat them."

They smiled and held each other for the duration of the trip. When they reached the dock, two uniformed policemen pushed open one of the cabin doors. "Please stand," an officer said. "We want to talk to all of you before you leave the ship."

Children cried and men and women shouted as they milled around the aisles gathering up their belongings. The officers walked down one of the two aisles and saw Jenny, still huddled in a blanket. As they questioned her, they didn't notice a man in the back row who moved quickly up the other aisle. In all the confusion and congestion, he was out of the door before anyone saw him.

Charlie and Jenny were the last to leave the ship. One of the officers took Jenny's hand and shook his head. "We talked to the passengers, and nobody saw anything. It's a damned shame, but at least you're alive."

Jenny nodded, thanked the officers and rode with Charlie to the emergency room. The doctor on call looked familiar.

"Didn't I put your ankle in a cast last month?"

Jenny nodded. "I'm a jinx."

"You're also a lucky one," the doctor said. He checked her blood pressure, took her temperature and checked her heart and lungs. "You're okay so you can go home. Stay warm tonight, and you'll be fine tomorrow."

Charlie helped Jenny into his car and put his arm around her. "Thank God the ferry was barely moving," Charlie said. "The captain must have been worried that the fog would come back."

Jenny made little moaning sounds. "I was so scared. I thought I'd never see you again."

"Get a good night's sleep, and we'll talk tomorrow. I don't want to lose you, and I almost did. This isn't fun and games, Jenny."

He walked her to Louise's door and kissed her softly. "I'd like to take you to bed with me tonight and hold you close." He took her hand, and Jenny was surprised to feel hers still shaking.

"I'll have some hot tea before I go to bed, and I'll be fine tomorrow. Don't worry."

She closed the door behind her and went to the kitchen. Louise sat at the table drinking tea.

"You're up late," Jenny said.

"I couldn't sleep. I had a dream. Fish were all around me, and I was choking."

Jenny stared at Louise. "That's amazing." She recounted her trip home on the ferry. "The crew, Charlie, and everybody were wonderful, and the doctor says I'm okay."

Jenny saw the look of horror in her aunt's eyes as she listened to her report. Louise stood and put her arms around Jenny. "You're alive, praise God. We'll talk tomorrow."

"That's what Charlie said." She poured tea and sipped, feeling the hot liquid warming her body.

Louise gave her two extra blankets with orders to cover up and stay warm. Sleep came easily. Jenny's body had taken a beating. It was time for healing.

* * *

When the ferry had docked at Sowatna, a man dressed in a brown windbreaker jacket and jeans had mingled with the crowd. He had watched Jenny and her companion who were escorted off the ship by two crewmen, and he swore silently. She was to have been fish bait, pieces of her body sinking slowly to the black, rocky bottom of the Atlantic. That news reporter had saved her on the street that night in front of the Dolphin, and now she'd been saved again. Three times and out, he thought. And that friend of hers, Erin Gregory. She, too, was a menace. He shoved his ski mask deeper into his jacket pocket.

He'd save it for another day. He walked quickly to his car, a dark blue Ford Taurus.

* * *

Jenny awoke Sunday morning and rubbed her right ankle that was still weak from her fall downstairs. It wasn't easy treading water in the icy Atlantic, and the ankle complained. Both legs and arms were weak, and she still experienced the shock of hitting the icy water as she walked slowly downstairs. She smelled coffee. Louise was ready for church when Jenny entered the kitchen.

"There's coffee in the carafe. I'll pick you up after church, and we'll have brunch at the hotel. How are you feeling?"

"Recovering, thanks. My ankle hurts a bit, but I'm warm again. I'll call Charlie. He was worried."

Charlie's line was busy when she called. Later, she thought. She poured coffee and sat at the kitchen table. Someone had tried to kill her twice. She shivered as she remembered sinking under the water, knowing that she was about to die. She thought about Richard Evans again. Ethics be damned, she thought. If the man was a murderer, he had no right to confidentiality. She phoned Erin.

Erin's sleepy voice answered. "I just woke up. What's new?" Erin listened, speechless, as Jenny recounted her drowning experience. "Oh, my God! I'll talk to my supervisor tomorrow."

"Thanks. I know this is difficult for you."

She finished her coffee, checked the time and was ready when Louise stopped after church. They found a table set back in an alcove and ordered eggs Benedict, juice and coffee.

Jenny said, "I made a list of suspects in Pete Clampton's murder, and after last night, I think we can eliminate Mavis. The person who attacked me was definitely male. I didn't recognize his voice because he spoke through a ski mask, but it was deep and husky. He may have disguised it, of course."

Louise toyed with her coffee spoon. "Jenny, may I make a suggestion? You've had too many accidents since you've been home. I know that your fall downstairs had nothing to do with the murders, but you were almost run over and almost drowned. Isn't that enough to forget the past and live in the present? You're not having nightmares any more, so why not cool it, work on the play, and think about school this fall?"

"You may be right. I'll think about it."

As they left the hotel, Jenny didn't notice a man sitting behind a copy of the New York Times. Only his jeans and tennis shoes were visible. If she had seen him, she would have questioned his being dressed as he was last night on the ferry. Maybe he hadn't gone home. Maybe home was too far away for a drive in the middle of the night.

The phone rang as Louise opened her front door. Jenny answered. "Hi, Charlie. I called earlier."

"How are you?" he asked.

"I'm okay. Louise and I ate at the hotel."

"If you're up to it, how about a drive up the coast? We'll stay away from the water today."

Jenny laughed. "Good. I'll be ready."

* * *

Colin Greene, attorney at law, admitted to himself that taking the role of the prosecuting attorney in *Tangled Trap Lines* had been a wise move. He was able to see Louise frequently, and sometimes after rehearsals they'd have a late supper together. Louise was a good conversationalist. She listened and offered intelligent comments. He was surprised to observe no raised eyebrows, no questioning looks from his neighbors. Perhaps he'd been over-cautious. People didn't seem to care.

He liked working with Jamison. The director was experienced and able to bring out the best in his cast. The hero and heroine worked well together, and everyone followed directions. The prompter was less busy as the weeks went by.

One night during rehearsal, Colin saw his friend, David McKnight, who sat in the bleachers talking to Michael. They seemed to be in a private conversation. Probably discussing the new theater, he thought. When his scene ended, Colin joined them.

"How's the theater progressing, David?" he asked.

"We're in schedule. Charlie Brewster wants to do a page one story, and we're going to meet at the theater tomorrow morning at eight o'clock. Michael's the expert and will give Charlie the information. Would you like to join us?"

"Thanks. I'll try to be there."

* * *

The next morning, Charlie and Adam Roberts met David and Michael in front of the Legion Club. Adam pulled out his digital camera and began to take exterior shots.

"It doesn't look like much on the outside," Michael said, "but the interior is amazing."

Colin Greene joined them. "I want to see where I'm to perform."

Michael laughed. "The stage is almost completed, Colin. Let's go in."

Three men in blue coveralls were laying linoleum in front of the stage.

"Glenn Thompson's crew works here almost every day, and people from the Sowatna Hardware and Lumber Company are here too," David said. "They follow blueprints well, and we haven't had many do-overs."

Adam pointed his camera up at a platform at the rear of the room. "What's that?" he asked.

Michael answered. "That's where the control room will be, in the center. Inside will be the light board and the sound board." He looked at the young photographer.

"We'll need a technician to operate the sound and light systems. Have you had any experience?"

Adam laughed. "That's what I did in college. I'd like the job, Mr. Jamison."

"Good. You'll have a script and cue cards. We hope to have the boards installed next week. Lighting will be a borrowing effort. Two colleges in Portland and one in Bangor will loan us pig tails and spotlights. We can make the cannons to hold the spots." He pointed to the areas on either side of the control room. "The spotlights will be installed there."

Adam looked around. "Where's the stairway?"

"Well have an iron spiral stairway at the rear of the theater. There's no room for a real stairway."

"No problem," Adam said and began to photograph the stage.

They walked toward the stage, and Michael gave dimensions and discussed the wings and backstage area. "We'll buy the footlights, and the workers will build them into the front of the stage."

Colin climbed up the steps and looked at the audience. "It's going to be a fine theater, Michael. When can we use it?"

"I'm hoping that the stage will be ready for rehearsals next week."

David watched the men as they installed the flooring. These were Glenn Thompson's crew. His thoughts turned to Ann and her decision to leave her abusive husband. How would Glenn react? Was Ann in danger?

CHAPTER FIFTEEN

Erin Gregory stood at the door of her supervisor's office and considered her request. Yes, billing records were open for people with special access codes, but was it ethical? And how much information would be available? As she sat before her supervisor's desk, she worried about those questions and was relieved when she and her supervisor were able to talk person-to-person, not staff-to-supervisor. Erin gave as much information as was needed, and her supervisor agreed that a name and address search was appropriate under those circumstances.

"I don't even know if he's the same person at the same address," Erin said, "but I have to find out. Sowatna has two unsolved murders, and Jenny's almost been killed twice."

She returned to her desk and sat at her computer. Had the Reverend Richard Evans been a client at the Center? She brought up the years 2000 and 2001. On June 4, 2000, R. Evans, 1304 Regent Street, Portland, Maine, had been admitted. It was a long shot but worth pursuing.

After work, she looked at a city map and found Regent Street. It was near the downtown area and would be classified as 'depressed.' She would find empty factory buildings, low-income housing, and run-down apartment buildings. She drove slowly and located 1304, a three-story brownstone. The five steps leading to the front door were littered with beer cans and take-out plastic containers. She parked and side-stepped the litter. The interior of the building was dismal. A narrow hallway with numbered doors that needed refinishing. The hall smelled of cat pee, beer, and the sweet odor of marijuana. There was no listing information.

As she pondered her next move, a woman stuck her head out of door number four. She was young and disheveled, greasy blond hair in spikes, sallow cheeks, and her skin, a death-like pallor.

"You lookin' for somebody?" she asked.

"Yes. Richard Evans. Does he live here?"

The woman gestured with a skinny arm. "Upstairs. Number 206."

Erin thanked her and climbed the stairway, its walls covered in graffiti and grime. The door numbered 206 was ajar. She knocked, and a deep voice answered. "Come in."

Erin pushed open the door and was startled. She'd expected squalor. A quick glance revealed an overstuffed davenport and matching armchair in shades of brown and tan that matched the draperies that hung across a shiny window. A glass-topped coffee table held a bouquet of artificial red roses, a dictionary and magazines.

The man who stood before her was also a surprise. He was neatly dressed in jeans and a tan sport shirt. His brown hair was shoulder-length, tied into a ponytail. He looked at Erin with clear gray-blue eyes. A broad forehead, sharp nose, a dimple in his chin. His complexion, though healthily tanned, was clear and smooth.

Erin was so startled that she stammered when she asked, "Richard Evans?"

"Yes. What do you want?"

I'm Erin Gregory, and I work at the Thomas J. Moore Center here. We're doing a survey of clients who were with us in 2000." Erin was surprised at her own statement because it made sense.

"Come in, and we'll talk."

Erin sat on the davenport and brought out a pocket-sized notebook. "It's very confidential, Mr. Evans. We won't use your name. We only want to know if our programs are successful and what suggestions you might have to improve our service."

Evans's laugh was almost a snort. His voice was sullen, bitter. "So what do you want? A gold star? Yes, I'm clean. Did I relapse? Yes, but I quit cold turkey on my own. I don't do drugs now."

Erin decided to plunge into deep water. "I'm from Sowatna. Were you a minister there?"

Evans stood and walked to the window. With his back to her, he almost shouted, "Yes I was a goddamned minister! What's that got to do with your survey?"

He turned, and Erin saw his face crimson with anger.

"Nothing, really. I was just curious."

Evans sat down on the davenport facing her. "Sowatna was my second and last church. Have you ever had a job that you hated, one you were forced into by a family that was determined that you follow in their holy footsteps? What a load of shit they fed me, and I was too stupid to argue."

He stood and paced the floor. "So I went to a seminary, got ordained, and found a position in a little dump near the Canadian border. I hated it, so I took the call to Sowatna, and that was the last straw." He sat down and glared at her. "Stupid, suspicious people. I stuck it out for five years of hell."

"Is that when you came to the Center?"

"Yes, that was part of the agreement."

"Do you ever come back to Sowatna?"

"Sometimes." He looked down, then back to Erin, his expression almost threatening. "Why do you ask?"

"I just wondered, that's all." Erin was nervous and bit her lip. "I don't suppose you knew Pete Clampton."

Evans stood and grabbed Erin's hand. He pulled her up, and his eyes were like ice, gray-blue ice.

"What about Pete Clampton? I didn't know him. He was murdered while I was in Sowatna, and they never found out who killed him. It has nothing to do with me."

He released Erin's hand. "That's all I have to say. You can leave now."

Erin picked up her notebook and brushed back her ponytail. "Thanks for the interview. We protect our clients, so you don't have to worry about what you've told me."

She ran down the stairs and drove home, her mind whirling. Was Evans capable of murder? She knew that anger and resentment could produce violent behavior, and Evans was full of both. And he had lived next door to the church in 1998 when she and Jenny had smoked pot in the cupola, when Jenny had seen someone drag a body down the street.

She thought about the rumors that surrounded his departure from the First Presbyterian Church, rumors of missing funds and a drug problem. The latter, of course, was true according to the records at the Center.

Everybody Knew Pete

She called Jenny and told her of her visit with Evans. "He's bitter and angry. I don't know what he's doing now. When I asked him about coming back to Sowatna, he put an end to our visit. He's not telling everything he knows."

* * *

Richard Evans stood at the window of his apartment and watched Erin as she drove away. Damned woman, he thought. Was her survey legitimate? Why did she want to know about his returning to Sowatna? He thought about his time at the Center, those weeks of drying out, the agony, the night sweats. He sat down and picked up a magazine. Stay cool, he thought. But what if she returned with more questions? Like Scarlett O'Hara, he'd think about that tomorrow.

* * *

Louise's phone rang at eight-thirty as she was preparing to leave for work. She heard Michael's voice and tried to assume a respectable, formal tone. He hadn't called since their encounter at the Lobster Shack, and she couldn't, wouldn't call him. Visions of spilled chowder and seaweed still clung to her mind, and even though lunch together with Jenny had been a calming interlude, Michael hadn't asked to see her again.

Now he said "I'd like to take you to dinner Wednesday night if you're free. We don't rehearse on Wednesday."

"I'd like that. I'm chairing the costume committee and need your ideas. We haven't had time to work on costumes."

"Good. I'll pick you up at six-thirty. You choose the restaurant."

"The Dolphin's the best. I'll make a reservation." Louise hung up and mentally went through her closet. Something chic, understated, flowing perhaps. Her dreams of their first meeting had dissolved into chaos. She looked skyward. Please, not again, she prayed.

As she went to the door, Jenny came downstairs. "Do you need help at the shop? I'm not working on sets this morning."

"I can always use an assistant. Come after you've eaten."

Louise walked at a brisk pace down the street to her shop. A light breeze cooled her face, and she lifted her chin to the sky. Clumps of cotton-ball clouds drifted slowly above her. As she neared Front

Street, the air became salty, and the breeze whipped into a wind. Far out to sea, sailboats skimmed across the waves. Six lobster boats had returned to shore, and the dock was full of men and a few women securing and emptying their traps. Louise waved as she walked to her shop.

The phone rang as she unlocked the front door. It was Colin's voice.

"How about dinner Saturday night?"

Two dinner invitations in one week! Louise smiled as she said yes.

* * *

As Jenny put the breakfast dishes in the dishwasher, her cell phone rang.

"Hi," Charlie said. "How are you? I still see you on that deck, cold and wet. I covered a drowning in Miami last year, and I'll never forget it. God, Jenny, I thought you were dead."

"I was sure I'd never make it. Luckily the boat wasn't moving fast and the crew was efficient. I thought I'd never be warm again." Jenny paused. "But I'm okay now. Have you moved?"

"Yes, and that's why I called. The place is presentable finally, so I'm inviting you to dinner tonight. It'll probably be Chinese take-out."

"Sounds great. Give me your address, and I'll be there."

Jenny spent the day at Louise's craft shop and left early to dress for dinner.

"I hope you can close without me, Louise. Charlie's invited me to eat at his new apartment."

"No problem. Have a good time."

Jenny kissed Louise's cheek and ran to her car. Something in Charlie's voice told her that the evening promised to be eventful.

She rang his doorbell at six-thirty and was surprised to see a living room already settled, pictures on the walls, draperies at the windows. "It's great. Where did you get your furniture?"

Charlie laughed. "As soon as I knew that I was going to stay in Sowatna, I called the storage people in Miami. My furniture arrived three days ago. How about a drink?"

"A glass of Merlot would be nice if you have it. I don't think I'll ever drink another beer after our island trip."

Charlie put his hands on her shoulders. "It was horrible. You almost died."

Jenny noticed a tender, almost anxious tone in his voice. She looked at him, and all thought of wanting to cool their relationship vanished. She wanted him now, tonight, here in his apartment.

She spoke softly. "I thought I'd never see you again." She looked up into his eyes and felt as though her legs would give way.

Charlie moved closer and put his arms around her. He lifted her chin and kissed her passionately, kisses deep and full of desire. Jenny clung to him with her whole body and wrapped her arms around his neck and waist.

"I want you to see where I sleep," he said. "Dinner can wait." He picked her up and carried her to his bedroom.

Breathing deeply, almost panting, they undressed each other, fumbling with zippers and buttons, a bra and jockeys. Each movement was accompanied by kisses. They fell into bed together.

Jenny looked at Charlie above her and pulled him close. "It's now, isn't it?"

For Jenny, it was magic, fulfillment, pure ecstasy, and she knew that Charlie felt the magic also. They held each other, murmuring words of love, need, and desire. They moved together, and when at last they fell away, gasping for breath, Jenny knew that tonight was meant to be. She remembered a line from a favorite poem, 'Sweet is pleasure after pain.' There had been intense pain falling onto the pavement in front of a speeding car and pain as she struggled for breath in the black depths of the ocean. Now there was pleasure beyond description here with Charlie.

She raised up, leaned over and kissed him. "My love," she whispered.

Charlie looked up at her. He stroked her face and brushed back her hair. "And you're my love."

Jenny fell back on the pillow and felt for his hand. She lay close to him and shut her eyes. "I don't want this to end, ever."

Charlie gave her a lingering kiss. "I wish we could hide the clock and the calendar, but we're always invaded by reality." He sat up and reached for his shorts. "I love you, Jenny McKnight, but now I'm hungry."

Jenny joined him at the edge of the bed. "We burned up a lot of calories, and I'm hungry too."

They dressed slowly, kissing and caressing. Charlie said, "Now you can have the Merlot." He laughed. "I'll have to reheat the Chinese."

Jenny giggled. "Confusius say that sex is better than reheated chop suey." She finished dressing and walked with him into the kitchen. She sipped her wine and watched Charlie at the microwave.

He poured a glass of wine and toasted Jenny. "To my favorite, my only love, and to our future." They drank slowly.

Dinner was unhurried between kisses. "I want you to stay with me tonight," Charlie said. "Will Louise be shocked?"

"I'm sure that nothing shocks Louise, and I'm an adult. I'll call so she won't think that I've had another accident."

Charlie embraced her. "Those weren't accidents, honey. Those were 'intentionals,' and that's the problem."

After dinner, Jenny called Louise. "I'm not coming home tonight. I'll see you tomorrow."

"I understand," Louise said, and Jenny knew that she did understand. No questions from her aunt and no explanations from her niece.

* * *

The next morning, Jenny woke and felt for Charlie. His side of the bed was empty, and she smelled coffee. She dressed hurriedly and went to the kitchen.

Before she had time to admire a breakfast table set, juice poured, coffee mugs by the coffee maker, Charlie put his arms around her and whispered into her neck. "Good morning, Miss McKnight. How do you like your eggs?"

Jenny laughed. "Over easy. What can I do to help?"

"Nothing. You can do breakfast tomorrow."

Jenny laughed. "You know that I can't make a habit of this. People will talk, and you'll get bored."

"I don't care about the people, and I can't imagine boredom with you."

Everybody Knew Pete

He served eggs, bacon and toast, and Jenny realized that this man whom she now adored more than anyone she'd ever known was experienced in the kitchen. What a plus, she thought. Over a second cup of coffee, she said, "I talked to Erin in Portland. She interviewed Richard Evans, the minister who was here when Pete was murdered. Evans was angry and said nothing about his present connections with anyone here. Erin went away with questions she didn't have time to ask."

"Odd." He looked at Jenny, smiled and shook his head. "Next you'll be off to Portland for more sleuthing." He took Jenny's hand. "I don't want you to see him. You're already in danger. I can't lose you, not now, not ever."

Jenny left her chair and sat on his lap. She nuzzled his neck and whispered, "I won't go to Portland, and I'm going to be careful. I want to live too."

* * *

At six-thirty on Wednesday evening, Michael rang Louise's doorbell. He blocked the impulse to run back to his car, leave Sowatna and never return, but he knew that he had to face Louise. He also was curious. How had she reacted to his letter thirty years ago? Would he have been wiser to have told her, face to face? And what had she done with her life? Married? Had children?

His musings were cut short when Louise opened the door. Thirty years fell away as he saw that lovely, familiar smile. She looked stunning in an orange, floral print mid-calf skirt and low-cut white blouse. Her skin was unlined, her eyes clear, and her hair swept back in a chignon that was tied into an orange scarf.

Michael smiled. "You really haven't changed, Louise. Still as lovely as ever." He took her hand and led her to his car. He sensed that Louise was as nervous as he. Her conversation was stilted, formal.

When they were seated at the restaurant, Michael took her hand. "I don't know why we're both here in Sowatna, but it's good to see you. I want to know about your life." Inwardly, he wanted to know her reactions to his canceling their wedding, but he was reluctant to ask.

"I've been busy. When my sister, Betsy died, her husband asked me to move here to help raise their daughter, Jenny, who was eight years old. I had continued dance performances and taught ballet, but had no real reason to stay in St. Paul, so I moved here. It was a wise choice. Now Jenny's grown, and I have a craft shop. I'll show it to you one day."

"You never married?"

"No."

Michael noticed that she looked down, not at him, and he wondered if there had been other relationships. He hoped that there had been. Louise was too beautiful, too accomplished to have led a celibate life.

During dinner, Louise asked, "What about you, Michael? Do you still dance, and when did you become a director?"

"I've always liked directing. Remember our performances in Minnesota?" He smiled. "Dancing is for younger people, so I gradually gave it up and turned to full-time directing. I took a couple of courses in New York before I stepped out on my own."

"I heard that you were at Skidmore before coming here."

"Yes, and I hope to return this fall. I've sent in my resume and asked about a faculty position."

Michael was relieved that relationships, affairs, all those intimate subjects were avoided. He really didn't want to know about Louise's sex life, and he didn't want to discuss his. Their work together this summer must be on a professional level. He knew that their past relationship was over and long gone. They'd each moved on, and he sensed that Louise was more comfortable speaking about the present.

He relaxed as they shared a dessert and drank coffee. He took Louise's hand. "I'm glad that you're here and that we can work together. I'm excited about the play and the new theater. We have a great cast, and rehearsals are going well."

He noticed that Louise's speech and body language indicated a more relaxed mode, and he was glad to be with her. He could now bring up the subject of their first encounter.

"You look a lot different from how you looked on the floor at the Lobster Shack."

Louise laughed. "I must tell you that I'd had beautiful visions of our first meeting, and when I saw you, those visions turned into a nightmare."

"I'll always cherish the memory of you with a clam on your nose. I hope you don't mind."

They laughed together. After coffee, Michael brought out a sheet of paper. "I want to talk about costumes now." He began to write as Louise described her ideas for each character's dress. He nodded as he wrote. "Yes, you've got it, Louise. You've chosen a lot of color for the heroine, and I like the hero's simple outfit. We won't need many costume changes. Can you and your committee put everything together in time for dress rehearsal?"

"No problem." She picked up her purse, and Michael sensed that, for Louise, the evening had ended.

Michael paid the bill, and as they walked to the car, he said, "I'm glad that we could talk tonight, Louise. I felt a bit awkward at first, but now it's all right." He turned and looked at her. "Is it all right for you too?"

"Yes, Michael, it's all right. I was nervous. After all, a thirty years absence is a long time." She looked at him, and Michael noticed tears in her eyes. "I was hurt when I read your letter, deeply hurt, but I understood your dilemma."

Michael took her hand. "I've always wished that I had talked to you, but at the time, I couldn't face you, knowing how deeply you'd be hurt. Maybe I was a coward."

"We can't undo the past, and we both suffered. I admired your courage. It wasn't easy for you." She put her hand on his cheek. "What we had was special, and I think we're both stronger for our relationship."

Michael nodded. "It was special." He opened the door of the car for her and kissed her forehead. "And you're special, even with a clam on your nose."

He walked with her to her door and said goodnight. He walked back to his car and whistled a tune. A great evening, and the way had been cleared for an ideal summer's work. It was good to be in Sowatna.

He found an e-mail from Diane on his computer. "Call me tomorrow. We have to talk."

Michael groaned. The president of the Arts Council could be a thorn in his bed of roses.

CHAPTER SIXTEEN

After rehearsal on Monday, August 18, Michael spoke to the cast. "We'll have our first rehearsal in the new theater on Friday. Painting above the stage isn't finished, but the stage is ready for us."

Everyone applauded. The heroine said, "It's going to feel different."

Michael agreed. "Come early if you can and just walk around."

Jenny and Louise had watched the rehearsal. Louise said, "I'm getting better ideas for costumes now as I watch the play. I don't want their clothing to overshadow the action, but everything needs to be appropriate. One of the women needs to look more flamboyant, however. I think I'll give her a bright purple sweater."

"Maybe you could borrow Charlotte's." Charlie moved in to sit beside Jenny.

Louise laughed. "I might ask her." She looked from Charlie to Jenny and noticed that they shared a new intimacy, nothing unusual to the casual onlooker but obvious to a close associate. She missed Jenny at night as her niece moved from Louise's home to Charlie's apartment more frequently, and she wondered about Charlie's background. If he were to become a member of the family, she'd like to know more about him. Who divorced whom? It usually took two, she thought. She prayed that Jenny knew more about him than she did.

As they left the high school, Louise said, "How about coffee or a nightcap?" She looked at both of them, and Charlie looked at Jenny.

"I'd like a gin and tonic if you have it," Charlie said.

"Of course. Follow me home."

Louise made a gin and tonic for Charlie and poured Merlot for Jenny and herself. They sat in the screened porch and listened to cicadas heralding the approach of autumn. Jenny and Charlie sat together on the two-seated swing and rocked slowly. Silence was comfortable.

At last Charlie cleared his throat, and when he said, "It's time to tell you about who I am," Louise knew that she'd had a premonition.

Perhaps she'd even slipped into Charlie's mind and prompted his remark.

"I'm sure you know, Louise, that Jenny and I have more than a casual relationship."

"I've noticed that her bed hasn't been slept in recently."

Jenny laughed. "You'll have to see Charlie's apartment one day so you'll know where I am."

"Any time. I'm glad you're settled here, Charlie. Sowatna's a good town, very supportive of new ideas. Forget about all the Down East clichés. They don't exist here."

"It didn't take long to agree with you. I grew up in Chicago, but I had a refreshing impression of Maine because our family spent a few summers touring the area. Both my mom and dad were, and still are, teachers. Dad teaches in the Special Education department at Northwestern, and Mom works with the city school system in special education. They've both encouraged me to keep writing, no matter where my career takes me."

"Where did you go to school?" Louise asked.

"Northwestern. I majored in journalism, never wanted to study or do anything else."

"Have you written other plays?" Jenny asked.

"Of course. I have a trunk full of manuscripts of all kinds. If you're a writer, you write. I even write poetry that no one will ever see."

Jenny laughed. "How did you get into crime reporting?"

"There was an opening at the Miami Herald, and I took it knowing that there's enough crime in Miami to fill a reporter's day. I liked the job at first and had a great rapport with the police department. I covered a lot of murders, and that's why I was surprised not to find photographs in the Clampton file."

Louise sipped her wine. "There are many unanswered questions, Charlie. I'm glad that you switched the focus of your play." She looked intently at Charlie. "I hate to probe, but I'd like to know more about your personal life. Jenny told me that you'd recently gone through a divorce."

Charlie stood and walked to the door and back. He ran his hand through his hair and grimaced. "It was pretty awful. Dierdre and I had been married only two years. We'd dated all through high school and college, and our parents belonged to the same country club. Everyone assumed that we were the perfect couple. I don't know when she decided that life with Charlie Brewster was boring. Maybe she knew it when we were dating in college. Neither of us had dated other people, so how do you compare one guy with another? When we moved to Miami, my life at the Herald was twenty-four-seven. Dierdre worked for a software company and had a work schedule. She also had an opportunity to meet other guys who had work schedules. Order versus chaos."

He sat down and finished his drink. "I should have been more tuned into her interests. I should have known that she needed more than I was able to give. The e-mail stung, but it wasn't a total surprise."

Jenny took his hand. "I'm sorry, honey." She stood and glared at Louise. "I know that you're always concerned about me, but I wish that you hadn't gone this far. It's really not our business. Charlie has a new life here." She paused and looked down at Charlie. "And I hope that his new life includes me. I care about you deeply, Charlie, and I don't care what transpired between you and Dierdre. That's past and forgotten."

Louise stood and put her arm around Jenny. "I'm sorry. Yes, I am concerned. You deserve the best, my dear, and you've had too many problems in your life."

Charlie stood and hugged both women. "Don't worry, Louise. I love Jenny. We haven't known each other very long, but I think that we're both mature enough to know what's important in a relationship, right?" He looked at Jenny and grinned.

"You're so right," Louise said. "I'm happy for both of you. How about a refill?"

She took their glasses to the kitchen and put her head against the refrigerator. She knew that she'd overstepped in her role as aunt, and she hoped that Jenny would forgive her digging into Charlie's past. She stood back and sighed. At least she knew more about the young man now, and she was comfortable with what he'd told them. She hoped that there'd be a wedding.

* * *

The next morning Jenny received a call from Erin. "I'm free this weekend and plan to drive to Sowatna Friday after work."

"Wonderful. We're moving into the theater on Friday, so come and watch our first rehearsal on the new stage."

"I'll be there about eight-thirty, and I hope I'm not followed."

"What do you mean?"

"It's only a feeling I have. Sometimes after work, I think there's a car behind me. I'm never stopped, and there's always a long gap between my car and the other. Maybe I'm overly suspicious."

"I hope you're right. It will be great to see you this weekend. Do you want to stay with me?"

"No. Mom's a different person since she went to work at the gift shop. Dad will follow his usual routine, and I have to accept his addictions. It's his life, and I'm glad that Mom has finally accepted it also. I'll see you at the theater."

* * *

Friday night's rehearsal was chaotic as the cast adjusted to the new stage. Entrances were either too soon or too late as the actors scrambled around backstage looking for the right opening. The court room on stage right was complete with its jury box, attorneys' tables and the judge's bench. There were chairs and tables for the bailiff, the court reporter, witnesses, and the clerk of courts and two rows of seats for spectators. Colin Greene had assisted Michael with the court room area, assuring him that every item was in its proper place. The living room on stage left was late Victorian with the heavier furniture on wheels for quick set changes. The stage looked finished excerpt for a scaffolding that hung upstage above the rear of the Victorian living room. The scaffolding hung next to a second story platform that opened onto an outside fire escape. The platforms on either side of the stage were to hold spotlights regulated by Adam Roberts in the control room. No one was on the scaffolding, and only two one-gallon-sized paint cans were visible.

Jenny sat near Michael who was perched on a stool in front of the stage. He held a script and a clip board and called out directions.

"Liz, walk slowly and look back at Bruce. You're angry, remember?"

"Bruce, pull her back with more force. Good."

Jenny made notes and watched for Erin's arrival. She smiled and waved as Erin came from the rear of the theater. She sat beside Jenny and hugged her.

"How was the trip?" Jenny whispered.

"No problems. I'm sure that I wasn't being followed."

"I'm glad you're here. I'll introduce you to Michael after the show."

They sat back, and Jenny wrote Michael's directives in her notebook.

At the close of Act Three, Michael called everyone to the front of the stage. Jenny signaled to Erin who followed her up the steps to the rear of stage left.

"This is where I usually stand while Michael speaks to the cast. They'll start over on Act One, and we can watch the action from here."

As she spoke, she looked across the stage and saw Charlie enter from the wings. As she left Erin and ran to meet him, she heard a loud crash behind her. She turned and was horrified to see Erin collapsed on the floor, covered in white paint. Two heavy paint cans had fallen where she and Erin had been standing. One can had landed directly upon Erin's head, and she had dropped to the floor, an inert body covered with white paint.

Jenny and Charlie were the first to run to her, and the members of the cast followed. Charlie pulled out his cell phone and called for an ambulance.

Michael ran up the steps, looked down at Erin, then up at the scaffolding. "It's hanging only on the side closer to the audience. The cable on the other side is broken."

Charlie knelt beside Erin ignoring the paint that covered Erin and everything around her.

"Is she dead?" Jenny asked as she knelt beside Charlie. "Oh, my God, how could this happen?"

"I don't know," Charlie said. He took Erin's pulse. "It's too weak to count." Someone brought a blanket, and Charlie covered her gently.

When the ambulance arrived, three Emergency Medical Technicians took charge asking questions as they checked Erin's vital signs and lifted her onto a stretcher. One of the men shook his head. "It's bad," he said. "We'll get her to the emergency room ASAP."

Jenny sat on the floor next to Charlie and sobbed. "It should have been me. Erin wasn't the target."

Charlie stood. "Don't move. I'll be back." He ran out the side door at the rear of the theater and looked up at the fire escape. He grabbed the last step and pulled himself up, then climbed up the stairs. He pushed open the door and looked down onto the stage. The scaffolding hung on his left, swaying gently back and forth. Charlie grabbed the cable that should have held the platform and studied it. He was right. The cable had been cut.

"Jenny," he yelled, "call the police."

He ran back to the fire escape and looked around the area. At night with only a corner street light, visibility was minimal. He remembered hearing a car's motor as he climbed the fire escape. He'd looked in that direction but didn't see a car. Now he noticed Michael's BMW next to the theater. Other cars were parked on the street. He saw no one outside. He climbed down the stairs and found the cast in many stages of outrage and confusion. Erin's body had been replaced by an unpainted surface. White paint covered the rest of the area. Colin Greene appeared with a bucket of water and a floor mop. One of the actors took the mop and scrubbed the stage. More cleaning supplies appeared, and soon the stage was wet but paint-free.

"Lucky it was a waterborne paint," Michael said.

Jenny thought about Erin covered in paint and hoped that the hospital staff would be gentle and thorough. "I'm going to the hospital, Charlie."

Charlie nodded. "Call me when you learn more. I'll wait here for the police."

Michael returned to his stool and called out to the cast. "That's all for tonight. Be here on Monday, and say a prayer for Jenny's friend."

* * *

Police Chief Harry Pierce and his deputy entered the theater, and Charlie met them at the foot of the steps leading to the stage. He pointed to the scaffolding. "Someone cut the cable, Chief. Two gallons of paint fell down, and one can hit Erin Gregory's head. She's been taken to the hospital. Jenny McKnight is sure that the paint cans were aimed at her, and I think she's right."

Adam Roberts ran to Pierce's side. "You want pictures? The only way up to the platform is by the outside fire escape."

"You go first, and we'll follow," Pierce said. "Don't touch anything."

Charlie followed the police officers and brought out his BlackBerry. An ugly situation. His emotions were mixed, relief that Jenny hadn't been hit but concern for Erin. He knew that the two women were close friends. Jenny would experience guilt along with her worries.

Roberts shot the scene before Pierce moved in. He examined the cable and called to an officer. "Bring me a bolt cutter. I want to cut six inches off from the remaining end and send it to the lab." He looked at the floor and instructed his deputy to examine every inch of the scaffolding. "Whoever did this may have left us a clue, so look carefully. We'll come back in the morning when the light's better. In the meantime, we'll seal off this area."

The men climbed down the fire escape and entered the theater. Adam Roberts took photographs of the stage area and the scaffolding.

Michael met the officers and introduced himself. "We were so concerned about Jenny's friend that nobody looked up. The person who cut that cable made an easy exit."

"I heard a car drive away as I climbed the fire escape," Charlie said, "but it was too dark to identify the vehicle."

Pierce shook his head. "It won't be easy to get an identification, but we'll do the best we can. Mr. Jamison, when is your next rehearsal?"

"Monday night. The cast is free for the weekend."

"Good. My people will be able to work the area without interruptions tomorrow. You're all free to leave now, and we'll lock the doors when we leave. I want to look around tonight."

"Some of the cast mopped the floor so that we didn't track white paint all over the stage. Maybe you'll want to check whatever the mops pushed around."

"We'll do that." Pierce looked up at the scaffolding. "Damned shame, but I guess the show must go on."

Michael nodded. "Yes, and good luck."

Members of the cast and committee people left the theater quietly, each looking back at the dangling scaffold.

Michael and Charlie were the last to leave.

"I'm going to the hospital," Charlie said.

"Yes. Call me if I can help."

* * *

Charlie found Jenny in the emergency room's waiting area. She shook her head when Charlie sat beside her. "The doctors are with her now, and I called her mother. Both Mr. and Mrs. Gregory are in there, and no one's come out to give a report."

She put her head on Charlie's shoulder and sobbed. "I'm so scared. I don't like what I know about head injuries. She could die, and it's all my fault."

Charlie rubbed her back. "Don't borrow trouble. I'll get some coffee." He found a coffee pot and put a cup in her hand.

Jenny drank slowly. "I'm trying to clear my mind of gruesome thoughts. It's useless to predict anything right now."

Minutes became hours as she and Charlie drank more coffee. At midnight, a doctor came in and sat beside Jenny. "Erin has a concussion. We've taken x-rays and are concerned about internal bleeding. Her parents agreed that she should be taken to Portland where the equipment's more sophisticated. They'll do an M.R.I. and a head C.T. I've checked both eyes, and the pupils are the same size. That's a good sign. Her parents will follow the ambulance."

Jenny nodded and said, "I'd like to see her before she leaves."

"All right. Just for a minute. She's unconscious. Don't talk to her."

Jenny followed the doctor and walked to the side of Erin's bed. Her friend's face was almost as white as the paint that had been removed. Jenny stifled a sob and turned to take Mrs. Gregory's hand. "I'm so sorry," she whispered. "What can I do to help you?"

Erin's mother shook her head. "Nothing now. We're going with the ambulance."

Jenny nodded and walked back to Charlie. "There's nothing we can do. Will you take me home?"

Charlie took her arm, led her to his car and walked with her to Louise's door. "All we can do is pray. Try to sleep."

Louise met her at the door, and Jenny fell against her aunt, sobbing softly. "Erin has a concussion, and they're taking her to Portland for more tests." Jenny rubbed her eyebrows. "I can't put that death's head out of my mind, Louise. I saw it twice, once as Erin's mother left the craft shop and again on the TV."

Louise lifted Jenny's head and looked at her. "You don't know what it meant or who's the victim. A concussion isn't always fatal. She's young and healthy and will have excellent care. Let's go to bed and pray a lot."

* * *

Michael drove to the cottage and fixed a double Scotch and soda. He sat in the living room and stared at the fireplace. His hopes for a painless, eventless production were in shreds as he recalled the evening's catastrophe. He'd sat on his director's stool in front of the stage and watched, horrified, as half of the scaffolding snapped and two paint cans plummeted to the stage floor, one striking Jenny's friend. He'd noticed Jenny's quick run to meet Charlie just as the cans fell and felt pangs of guilty relief knowing that Louise's niece was safe. He knew that Monday's rehearsal would not be a good one. He'd do his best to assure his people that Erin Gregory would recover, but the cast would remember the event and forget their lines.

His cell phone rang, and he sighed as he answered. "Hi, it's me, Diane. I just heard about the accident at the theater."

"It wasn't an accident. Someone cut the scaffolding cable. The police came and sealed off the area."

"Can you rehearse on Monday?"

"We're going ahead on schedule. We have two weeks before opening night, and the cast will be ready."

"The theater seats will arrive next week, and we've arranged for installation." Diane paused. "You didn't return my call, and I want to see you. When can we talk?"

Michael glared at the phone and hoped that Diane felt a cold chill. "We could meet for breakfast tomorrow." Morning would be safe, he hoped.

"Good. I'll meet you at the Expresso at nine o'clock if that suits you."

Michael agreed, signed off and finished his Scotch. He grudgingly admitted that she hadn't bugged him too often this summer, and he hoped that her winks and coy glances were only a facade. He picked up his faxed copy of Skidmore's response to his request and smiled. In three weeks, he'd be back on their campus as an associate professor in their drama department. His future, far away from Diane, looked bright and promising.

* * *

The killer left the theater in his blue Taurus and cursed. He'd stood for two hours in an inky black corner above the stage waiting for Jenny to come backstage. He'd watched four rehearsals, sitting in the darkened back row, and he knew that she always came to that exact spot each night at the close of Act Three. It had been difficult to arrange his rehearsal-watching schedule, but this time his efforts had to succeed. He'd failed twice, and that woman continued to ask questions. He stopped the car and studied his situation. Perhaps Jenny would now be so concerned about her friend that she'd abandon her search. Fat chance, he thought. He started the car and drove away.

* * *

Gloria and Jacob Gregory followed the ambulance to Portland's General Hospital and watched as their daughter was carried into the emergency room. The clock above the reception desk read two a.m. Mechanically, Gloria answered questions, signed six documents and waited with her husband. She looked at Jacob whose face was almost as white as Erin's had been. His hands shook as he held them on each shoulder, his arms crossed. His head was bent forward, and Gloria knew that he needed a fix of some kind.

Fifteen minutes later, a young woman in a white coat came to them. "Your daughter is still unconscious. We'll know more after the tests."

"May we see her?"

"Of course, for a minute. We need to take her to x-ray immediately."

Gloria and Jacob followed the doctor into the emergency room. Behind a curtain, they found Erin whose arms were connected to tubes of liquid dripping into her veins. Her face was covered with an oxygen mask. Gloria sobbed quietly and held Jacob's hand.

"I'm going to get the guy who did this," Jacob whispered.

The doctor led them back to the waiting room. "Do you have a place to stay tonight?" she asked, and Gloria shook her head. "We have a guest room. The woman at the desk will help you."

Gloria and Jacob followed an aide and fell into bed, still fully clothed. Gloria noticed that Jacob's hands shook when he removed his shoes, but she said nothing. Sleep would come, and they would face tomorrow together.

Jenny drove to the hospital in Portland early Saturday morning and sat beside Erin's bed. A nurse had assured her that Erin's condition was stable. Her doctor would have more information. "We don't diagnose," the nurse said with a smile. She squeezed Jenny's hand. "Erin's parents were here and are having breakfast. If you stay, maybe they can go home and bring back what they need. They don't want to leave her alone."

Jenny nodded. "I can stay."

When Gloria and Jacob entered the room, Jenny repeated her offer. "We need to change and pack a few things," Gloria said. "We'll be back this afternoon."

Jenny bought a paperback at the gift shop, ate a quick lunch, and watched the intravenous liquid drip into Erin's arm. Her oxygen mask had been replaced by small tubes in her nostrils that led to a bottle beside the bed. Erin's breathing sounded normal, but her eyes were closed, and she didn't move.

Jenny dozed in her chair and waited for the Gregory's return. She'd return to Sowatna later and spend Sunday eagerly waiting for Erin's voice on her cell phone.

* * *

At nine o'clock Saturday morning, Michael sat across from Diane in a booth at the Expresso Cafe. He studied the menu and Diane who was dressed in blue. Blouse, shorts, sandals, and a blue scarf tied into her ponytail. She had dressed carefully for the occasion.

"I'm glad you came," Diane said. "You aren't able to attend our Thursday night board meetings, and I'd like to have a written report from you at our next meeting." She smiled and touched his foot under the table.

Michael drew back his foot and brought out a notebook. "Tell me what you want, and I'll have a report for you." He paused. "You heard about the accident last night."

"Yes. Will it affect the production?"

"Temporarily. We were wrecks after it happened. I called the hospital this morning and learned that Erin had been taken to Portland for tests, and Louise told me that Jenny drove there this morning. The police sealed off the area last night, but I'm sure that we'll be able to use the stage on Monday."

Diane shook her head. "Such a tragedy! I hope that it won't bother you too much." She smiled, and Michael squirmed.

How could he slip out of Diane's grasp without causing a conflict? He'd had enough after last night's fiasco. He took a deep breath and said, "Diane, I'm glad we could meet this morning because I want to clear the air between us. You're a very attractive woman, but you're married, and I'm too tied up in my work to think about any kind of romance. I like working with you. Both the Arts Council and I need your expertise, so let's keep our relationship strictly professional."

Michael was relieved when his words were interrupted by the waitress with a tray of cereal and coffee. Diane reached for her coffee and drank slowly. Michael noticed two tears. Damn, what next?

He was surprised and relieved when Diane straightened up and smiled. "You're right, Michael. I get lonely sometimes when my husband is out on his boat. Working with the Arts Council has helped, but small town life can be a bore." She drank more coffee. "Maybe what I need is a shrink, not an affair."

"You could be right. Talk to your doctor. He can recommend someone." Michael took her hand. "We have an outstanding drama with a great cast. Think about taking it on the road. You could make the contacts and bookings because you have organizational skills.

There's more to life than sitting around in Sowatna dreaming of romance."

Diane nodded and began to eat. "We might contact Booth Bay and some of the other towns along the coast." She looked up at the ceiling, and Michael knew that Diane Martin was no longer here at the Expresso Cafe. She was home at her computer with a map, a calendar, and a list of summer theaters.

After breakfast, they walked outside. Diane shook Michael's hand and said, "Give your report to Charlie, and he can bring it to next week's meeting." She looked down. "Thanks for advice and encouragement, Michael. I've been foolish, but you haven't laughed at me. The play will get a standing ovation, and maybe I'll be able to stand up and take care of my life."

Michael put his hand on her shoulder. "We all need advice and encouragement, Diane. I have my own struggles and frustrations, more than you know."

He turned and walked to his car. Diane might wonder about him and his life style, but she would only wonder, never know.

CHAPTER SEVENTEEN

Jenny sat in Erin's hospital room hoping to see some movement or hear her voice. The only movement was hospital staff checking on their patient, and the only sound came from the equipment beside Erin's bed. Jenny half-read her book as she watched and listened. She ate a quick sandwich in the hospital cafeteria and returned to her chair. Nothing had changed during her brief absence.

Gloria and Jacob Gregory arrived at three o'clock. "Has she moved?" Gloria asked.

Jenny shook her head. "I'll go home now. Call me if Erin wakes."

"We're going to stay at a motel for a few days. If Erin's still in a coma, we'll probably go home and wait for news. The doctors can't predict what will happen. They say that each case is different. I've heard so much medical jargon that my head's spinning. There's no internal bleeding, and that's a good sign."

Jenny walked to the door and looked back at her friend. She took Gloria's hand and managed a weak smile. "She's going to get well, I'm sure of that."

She arrived home and found Louise in her bedroom applying lipstick and eye shadow. "Colin is taking me to dinner," she said. "I fixed a plate for you in the refrigerator." She penciled her eyebrows and asked into the mirror, "How is Erin? Is she..."

"She's still in a coma. Her parents will stay in Portland for a few days. There's nothing we can do now."

"Charlie wants you to call him."

"Okay." Jenny's voice was toneless.

Louise hugged her. "Find something on TV or be with Charlie. You've done all you can do." Louise stood back. "Have you had any psychic moments, any premonitions?"

"No, and maybe it's better this way. I want normalcy right now."

The doorbell rang, and Louise ran to welcome Colin. "Gin and tonic?" she asked. "I'll make three. Jenny's just returned from Portland."

"How's your friend?" he asked Jenny.

She told him about her day with Erin. "You probably didn't know her, but she's had lots of ups and downs. She didn't need any more disasters in her life."

"As a small town lawyer, I probably know more than I should." He laughed. "Or want to know. Erin's father's addiction problem is common knowledge, and I'm told that her mother is now working at a gift shop. Small town folks care about each other, and it isn't merely gossip or being nosy."

Jenny felt comfortable with Louise and Colin who talked about the play and their participation.

"I have to admit that I'm enjoying my part," Colin said. "Being in a court room is natural, and I really am Josh Winters, the prosecuting attorney. I worry about the jury's verdict, even though I realize that their decision is meaningless. I'm angry when the defendant's attorney objects and relieved when the judge overrules."

Louise laughed. "Sometimes I wish that I were in the cast instead of outfitting them." She leaned back and returned mentally to *Swan Lake*. She had started as a member of the *corps de ballet* and finished her career as the prima ballerina. She smiled as she heard again the music, the applause, and, ah, the scent of a bouquet of roses as the curtain fell.

She snapped back to the present when Colin stood, gave his empty glass to Jenny and looked at Louise. "Time for dinner. Ready?"

Louise and Colin left her house and walked to his car. They both met at the passenger door. Louise laughed as she grabbed the handle. "I'm so used to doing this myself that I forget that someone might open the door for me."

Colin laughed too. "Maybe I'm the last of the breed."

After they were seated at a window table at the Dolphin, Colin said, "I'm glad we could have dinner tonight. We've been so busy with the play that there's been no time to be sociable. I'm afraid that my law practice has suffered too, but this has been a great experience."

"I've enjoyed it also. My committee people aren't professional, but they work hard, and Michael has approved our work. I'm glad we're not doing something Elizabethan. Modern makes it easier."

After dinner, Colin shifted uneasily in his chair. He looked around and saw no one close to their table. "I wanted to talk privately tonight,

Louise, but Jenny was there." He ran his finger around the rim of his water goblet. "It's so good to be here with you. I've been alone so much since Merna died. I wanted to call you sooner, but I worried about what people would think, so I just sat and didn't do anything. I've been busy with my law practice of course, but it's not the same."

He stopped to take a breath, and Louise picked up the conversation. "I've been alone most of my life except for..." She paused. "You know what I mean."

Colin nodded. "You had your life, and it was right for you at the time."

"You came to the rescue when I needed you." She smiled at Colin. "I'll always be grateful. I've thought of you so often since Merna died. It's not easy without a family to share your grief."

Colin nodded. "I wish we could have had children." He looked down at his plate. "It was my fault. I was impotent. Had mumps when I was a kid. We were both checked out, and when we discovered the problem, I offered to go along with artificial insemination, but Merna wouldn't hear of it. She said that if a baby couldn't be mine, she didn't want it."

Louise felt uneasy, wishing that she hadn't mentioned family, and she wondered if Merna could have accepted her sister's child as readily as Louise's sister, Betsy, had done.

A waitress brought the bill, ending their private conversation. They left the restaurant and walked slowly to Colin's car. This time, Louise stood back while Colin opened the door for her.

When they stopped in front of Louise's home, Colin took her hand. "The play ends on September first. I expect to see a momentous change in our relationship on September second."

Louise squeezed his hand. "I'd like that, and maybe we can do lunch occasionally before opening night."

* * *

Jenny watched Louise and Colin leave for their evening at the Dolphin. Happy people, not a care. She called Charlie and told him about her day with Erin. "Louise and Colin have gone out for dinner. I'll watch TV, I guess."

"I guess not," Charlie said. "Shall I pick you up or do you want to drive here?"

Jenny thought for only a moment. "I'll drive. I need you tonight. Louise prepared a plate for me, so I'll bring my own dinner."

Charlie met her at his door with a glass of wine and a warm embrace. They shared Louise's dinner and Charlie's pizza.

They took coffee into the living room, and Charlie said, "Tell me more about Erin."

"There isn't much to tell. She's still in a coma. Her parents will stay in Portland for a few days, and if there's no change, they'll come back here and wait."

"I've thought about the accident, and I wonder why the cable was cut at that time. If you were to be the target, how did the guy know where you'd be?"

Jenny sipped coffee and pondered the question. "I'm usually right there after the first run-through. He must have been at the high school rehearsals."

"And he took a chance that you'd be in that same place in the theater, conveniently under the scaffolding."

"That took careful planning. And how did he know that we were at the restaurant the night the car tried to hit us, what time we left, how long we sat on the pier and when we crossed the street to your car?"

"How did he know when we took the ferry to Isle au Bas? He's been watching you, Jenny. Maybe he has people who keep him informed."

"Maybe. I'm scared and confused. I haven't seen my spirit lately. I almost wish that he'd come back and help me."

"If you scream tonight, I'll know why." He took their cups and went to the kitchen. "I just bought a new DVD, a comedy. We can watch it before you invite your spirit to join us in bed."

* * *

"Jury!" Jenny sat up and looked at the clock. Three a.m. Why had she screamed out that word?

Charlie stirred beside her and mumbled, "You saw the spirit?"

"No. I saw the word 'jury' in bright lights, and it woke me up. Why?"

Charlie sat up beside her. "If you were dreaming about the play, you know that the jury will be chosen from the audience. My editor, Charlotte, has agreed to serve. Michael wants about four or five people already prepared to come on stage. He says that others will follow once they see a few brave souls climb the steps."

Jenny nodded and spoke slowly, her mind in low gear. "I think that we should ask Charlotte to invite both George Hendricks and Glenn Thompson. Richard Evans in Portland probably won't show, but if he does, he should be with the panel. It's important. These three people are suspects. They live or lived near the church, and I want them on the jury."

"Do you think that the murderer will suddenly admit his guilt in front of the opening night audience?"

Jenny laughed. "I don't know, but I wouldn't want to wreck opening night." She leaned back and studied the ceiling. "Supposing those people were to practice during dress rehearsal the night before?"

"That makes sense. Will you talk to Michael? What does he know about your premonitions and spirits?"

"I've told him about what I saw the night of Pete Clampton's murder and the visions. He wasn't shocked and said he understood. I think he'll agree to my jury selection plan."

Charlie reached over and put his arms around her. He kissed her and stroked her hair. "And now that we've settled that problem, I'm having a problem also." He took her hand and brought it down. "Only you can help me," he whispered.

Jenny nodded. "We can help each other. It's 'mutual aid.'" She fondled him, moved closer and put her left leg around his body. "I want you too," she whispered.

* * *

Michael Jamison called Charlie Monday morning. "I'm never available for the Arts Council's board meetings on Thursday night, and Diane wants a report. I'll prepare one this week, and I'd like you to present it."

"I can do that," Charlie said. "I attend so that I'll have a fresh news story for the Saturday edition. It's always a late night for me, but Charlotte Quincy, the editor, wants the latest news. Stop by any time and leave it with Sara at the front desk."

"I'll do that on Wednesday."

Michael hung up and started work on his report. He remembered Jenny's morning call about selecting the jury and wanted to discuss it with Charlotte at the Chronicle office. He stopped at the front desk, and Sara mouthed a kiss. "Charlotte's in her office. Knock first."

Michael heard Charlotte's cough as he knocked and pushed open the door. She stubbed out her cigarillo and brought out her feathered hat. "Theater business brings out the glitz." She laughed. "What can I do for you this morning?"

"Diane wants a report for the Arts Council meeting. I'll bring it here on Wednesday. Charlie said that he'd present it for me." He sat down. "I have a rather unusual request. Jenny McKnight called me this morning and asked if you would line up a few more jurors who would agree to practice during dress rehearsal. You've already agreed to serve, and she gave me a list of others she wants on the panel. She specifically asked for George Hendricks and Glenn Thompson, men I don't know. She said it was important."

Charlotte chewed a pencil, put it down, and looked at Michael.

"I could ask them, but what if they decline?"

Michael laughed. "Jenny said that your powers of persuasion would convince them of their importance in the drama. This isn't my idea, but Jenny's been such a great help to me this summer that I can't turn down her request."

Charlotte smiled. "All right, I'll do it. Perhaps I'll ask the librarian also. How many does she want?"

"She didn't specify. I think that if four of you walk up on stage, the other eight will follow. If not, the judge who is already at the bench could ask for more from the audience. I'm quite sure that the jury box will be filled with wannabe thespians." Michael stood. "Thanks, Charlotte. I'll be waiting for the results of your calls."

* * *

George Hendricks's phone rang. He listened to Charlotte Quincy's request and said, "I was on a jury once a few years ago." He paused and considered the situation. Why not, he thought. "Yes, I could be there on August twenty-eighth. What time?"

He listened and made notes on his calendar. He hung up and pondered the call. Why should he be present at dress rehearsal? He knew that the play was based upon Pete Clampton's murder. He didn't want to be involved, but he knew Charlotte well enough to know that she would have persisted. Weird and puzzling. He was sorry that he'd accepted the job. He punched in his home phone number and told his wife, Doris, about the call.

"Oh, my God!" Doris exclaimed. "You can't be on the jury. Why did she ask you? What does she know?"

"Cool it, Doris. I'm sure that it doesn't mean anything. I can't go back on my word. If I call back, she will wonder why. I'm sorry I bothered you."

He heard a loud sigh from his wife. "I'll take the boat out today. Maybe I can think more clearly out with the lobster traps."

Hendricks returned to the invoices on his desk and shook his head. His life this summer had been crammed with misfortunes and accidents. He'd planned carefully, but nothing had worked out. And now he was to be on stage in Charlie Brewster's play. He put his head in his hands and wished that he were anywhere but in Sowatna, Maine, U.S.A

* * *

Glenn Thompson answered Charlotte's call at his desk. He listened patiently as she explained the need for rehearsed jurors. "If you're not walking up on stage, nobody's going to follow, and they need twelve jurors."

"Why me?" he asked. "Can't you find someone else?"

"Glenn, you've done so much for the theater, offering your crew to help with the renovation. You'll probably get a standing ovation when you walk up those steps."

Thompson smiled. He'd like a little recognition for his efforts, and even though he knew that Brewster's play was based upon Pete Clampton's murder, no one knew of his involvement in Pete's activities. His presence on stage would surely proclaim his innocence of any wrongdoing.

"I can help you," he said, "but why must I be there for dress rehearsal?"

"The director wants to go through that part of the first act. He doesn't want any last-minute glitches on opening night."

"Okay, I'll be there. What time?"

Thompson wrote on a sticky note pad and posted it on the wall behind his desk. He called Ann. "I'm to be part of the jury for Charlie Brewster's play and have to be there for dress rehearsal. Have you finished work on the scenery?"

"Almost. We'll have to wait for the police to finish their investigation before we can complete the sets."

"What investigation?"

"You weren't home Friday night, and I forgot to tell you about Erin Gregory's accident. Part of the scaffolding fell, and a can of paint hit her on the head. She's in Portland General with a concussion."

"That's terrible. I remember when she came to our house to talk about the play. I hope that she recovers." And Glenn really did hope for her recovery.

* * *

Charlotte completed her calls and was pleased that everyone had accepted. The librarian was especially glad to be part of the jury. "Life in a library can be a bit dull," she said.

Thompson and Hendricks hadn't been enthusiastic but had agreed. She sensed something in their voices that made her uneasy. She attributed her feelings to her life as a newspaper woman, one who could smell a story before it occurred.

Charlie knocked on her office door at eight-thirty. "What do you have for me this morning?"

"You're looking especially chipper. You must have had a good weekend in spite of the accident at the theater."

Charlie smiled. "I feel great, and it wasn't an accident. I'm going to the police department this morning and talk to the people. Maybe Dispatch knows something."

"Yes. We need a news report from them. I'd like a report on Erin Gregory also. Hospitals are reluctant to give out information, but maybe you can learn something."

"I'll try." He sat down. "I'm worried about Jenny. She blames herself for Erin's accident. Jenny's had two attempts on her life and believes that the paint calls were meant for her. She's probably right."

"Does all this have anything to do with jury selection during dress rehearsal?"

"I think so." He told Charlotte about what Jenny saw the night of Pete Clampton's murder. "She's had nightmares and suspects the people who live or lived near the church." He didn't acknowledge when and where Jenny had screamed 'Jury.'

He left the newspaper office and drove to the police station. Carol Hughes sat at her computer and watched two monitors. She turned and greeted Charlie. "Nothing new to report. Ask Chief Pierce. Maybe he knows something."

Charlie saw Pierce at his desk. "I talked to Dispatch, and she suggested that I talk to you."

Pierce grumbled. "Our people worked at the theater most of the weekend and found nothing, not even in the sweepings after the paint cans fell. I gave the piece of cable to one of our men who drove to the lab in Portland early this morning. Every bolt cutter has its own pattern. Almost like a fingerprint. When they send back a blow-up, we'll try to get a match in town, but it will take time."

Charlie took out his BlackBerry. "What can you give me for this week's paper?"

"I'm sure that you've already written about the event. All I can tell you is that our people have worked hard all weekend and that the cast can rehearse again tonight. Don't mention the bolt cutters, please."

"I understand. I'd like to write that you're close to an identification, but that's wishful thinking, not news."

"Right. I'll call you when it's no longer wishful thinking."

Charlie left the station and found the number for Erin's hospital nurses station. "I'd like to speak to Mr. or Mrs. Gregory, please." He waited several minutes until Erin's mother answered.

"There's no change in my daughter's condition. I'll stay a few days and go home if there's no improvement." She spoke more softly. "Can you ask Jenny to check on my husband? He didn't come back here with me, and I'm worried."

Everybody Knew Pete

Charlie knew about her husband's addiction problem and understood her concern. "I'll talk to Jenny. She'll call you."

He knew that the hospital staff would give no patient information, so he could only report what Gloria had said. No story there.

He called Jenny's cell phone. "Lunch at the Lobster Shack?"

"Yes. I'm at the craft shop helping Louise unpack supplies. Did you call Michael about the jury?"

"Yes. I'll give you a full report at lunch." He looked around. No one was near him, but still he whispered, "Last night was so great. I can't wait to see you."

"Mmm," Jenny said. "It was marvelous. I'll see you at noon. Stop at the craft shop, and we'll walk over to the Lobster Shack."

Charlie returned the Chronicle office and wrote the requested articles. He returned to Charlotte's office. "I wish I have something spectacular to report," he said. "The police have no leads, and Erin's still in a coma."

"Maybe we'll have to invent a catastrophe,"

"We've had enough real ones. How about a headline, 'Nothing Happened This Week'?"

Charlotte's phone rang. She answered and listened for a moment, then reached into a box behind her desk. She pulled out a blue velvet hat adorned with three blue roses and put it on. "Okay, what else do you know, Harry?" She made notes and gave them to Charlie. "Yes, he'll be right over."

She hung up. "I always put on one of my grandmother's hats when there's bad news. Someone knocked a police officer unconscious and stole the piece of cable."

"I'll be there in minutes." He drove to police headquarters and found Dispatch at her computer. "What happened?"

"Go over to the garage where we keep our police cars. Chief Pierce is there with a doctor. The garage is two blocks north."

Charlie found the garage. It was a brown, wood-sided building set back from the street, large enough for six cars. The building was surrounded on three sides by tall pine trees. The double doors were open. Charlie found the Chief and a doctor bent over the body of a man who lay on the floor next to a police car. Charlie took out his BlackBerry and waited for Pierce to notice him.

"It's crazy, Charlie," Pierce said. "I gave Williams the piece of cable at six o'clock this morning. At nine o'clock, I tried to reach him on the police radio, and when he didn't answer, I came here to take my car and look for him. I didn't expect to see his car because I assumed that he was already en route to Portland."

The doctor stood. "I've checked his vital signs and have called for an ambulance. He's had a nasty crack on his head, but it's not serious. He'll be all right, but I want him checked at the hospital."

"We'll check the car for fingerprints before we open any doors, but I'm sure that we won't find that piece of cable." Pierce unwrapped a stick of gum. "It's inexcusable! I should have walked to the car with him. I should have known that someone might want that evidence. Dumb!"

An ambulance braked to a stop in front of the garage, and two emergency medical technicians moved Williams into the back of the vehicle. The doctor followed the ambulance to the hospital, and Charlie and Pierce were left to look at the place where Williams had lain. Pierce chewed, and Charlie worked his fingers on his BlackBerry. The garage was eerily quiet.

"What other evidence do we have?" Pierce asked, already knowing the answer. "This has been a summer of riddles and impossible situations. A man is murdered, a woman is pushed overboard on a ferry, another gets hit on the head with a paint can and we have no clues. I'll be glad when the summer's over, and we can go back to the usual misdemeanors of a small town. I'd almost welcome 'disorderly conduct'."

Charlie nodded and thought about Jenny's spirits and her scream last night. "Maybe your prayers will be answered before Labor Day."

CHAPTER EIGHTEEN

Mavis Bianci sat at her kitchen table and studied a new cook book that specialized in breakfasts and brunches. By mid-August, she'd exhausted all of her old favorites and wanted to find new dishes that would please their guests.

Guido came into the kitchen and kissed his wife's hand.

Mavis laughed. "You're impossible, Guido. Sit down, and let me bring you a cup of coffee. There were only six people here this morning, so the pot's quite full."

"I'm glad to have this time to talk to you, Mavis. Yesterday I received a call from my nephew, Ernesto, in Rome. Remember that he called us this summer to say that his wife was to have a baby?"

"Yes. That was good news."

"Now he is desperate. He cried. Of course he always was emotional, but I hadn't heard him cry before."

"What was his problem?"

"It is his wife. She died two days ago. I didn't know her well, but I remember their wedding in Napoli. It was so beautiful." Guido sat at the table and drank his coffee.

"I'm so sorry. How did she die?"

"She was having the baby, and something went wrong. She hemorrhaged and died."

"Oh, no!" She put her hand to her mouth. "That's terrible, Guido. Such a tragedy. How is the baby?"

"The baby is fine, but Ernesto doesn't want to keep him. That is why he called me. He said that the baby would always remind him of Rosa, and he doesn't even want to look at him. I think my nephew should see a psychologist, but our family in Italy is too old-fashioned to consider it."

He took Mavis's hand in his and stroked it. "I wish that we could be there with him."

Mavis nodded. "So do I. What can we do?"

"He wants us to take the baby, adopt him, give him a home here."

Mavis studied the open cook book on the table. She couldn't look at Guido. She thought about her own problem, knowing that she must tell Guido that she couldn't have his babies. She knew that she'd been wrong not telling him about her situation before they were married, but she wanted to be Mrs. Guido Bianci, not fat and unattractive Mavis Long. She'd feared that Guido would have looked somewhere else for a wife, someone who could give him the *bambinos* he dreamed about, so she'd kept her secret. Ever since they'd opened the bed and breakfast, she'd known that she must confess, but the day never came. How could she break such tragic news to the man she now loved?

She looked up at Guido. "Would you like to have the baby?"

Guido's smile was radiant. "Oh, yes. Ernesto said that my sister agreed to fly here with him if we would take him."

Mavis put her head on the table and began to cry, deep, gut-wrenching sobs. Now had to be the time to reveal the terrible truth that she had kept hidden. She clutched Guido's hand and, between sobs and moans, told why she couldn't have children. "I knew that you wanted a family, and I was afraid that you'd never marry me if you knew."

Guido stroked her hair, and lifted her chin. "Look at me, my love. Do I look any different now that I know? No, I am no different. I love you, and we will have a good life together." He took her hand and stroked it. "And now we will have a baby. He may not be completely ours, but he is part of my family, and now he will be part of ours, yours and mine."

He gave her a tissue, and she wiped her eyes. "Yes, he will be ours," she said, "but I feel bad about your nephew. Do they have other children?"

"A boy and a girl. He will always be sad about losing Rosa, but he will be happy to know that her baby will have a good home."

Mavis stood and refilled their cups. "I've been so happy here with you, Guido. I'll have to buy some baby books and forget about cook books for a while. When will your sister arrive?"

"I will call today and tell the family that we are so happy to adopt the baby. I am sure that my sister will bring the baby as soon as possible." Guido finished his coffee and stood behind Mavis. He put his hands on her shoulders and whispered in her ear. "I have a secret too, my sweet. You must not tell anyone."

Mavis turned to look at him, fear and questioning in her eyes.

"Yes. My secret is that I like to crochet. My grandmother taught me. I have been to our neighbor Louise's craft shop and have looked at patterns for baby things, bonnets, Afghans, booties, all the things a baby might use."

Mavis stood, laughed and kissed him. "I love your secret, and I'll never tell anyone. You must find out how much the baby weighs, then go to the craft shop and buy patterns and lots of blue yarn."

* * *

Charlie left the police department's garage knowing that Chief Harry Pierce would spend a nail-biting day worrying about his officer and blaming himself for the theft of the piece of cable. Maybe the police could locate the other end of the bolt cutter's slice, and maybe his officer would recover quickly and be able to identify his assailant.

He returned to the newspaper office and transcribed his information. Just before noon, he walked to the craft shop and found Jenny sitting on the floor of the back room unpacking boxes of supplies.

"Louise always wants a full supply ready for people who will spend a cold, dreary winter working on a tapestry, a baby blanket, or a quilt."

Charlie sat beside her. "If you're in Portland with your third graders, I may have to take up needlepoint to keep my sanity."

Jenny kissed his nose. "Don't worry. I'll come back often for more 'mutual aid.' Shall we ask Louise to join us for lunch?"

"Yes. She'll be interested in your jury selection plan too." He stood and saluted. "Charlie Brewster reporting, ma'am. Charlotte called Glenn Thompson, George Hendricks and the librarian, and all three agreed to show up the night of dress rehearsal."

"I'm relieved. I don't know why it's important, but I have to trust my instincts."

"Nothing would surprise me in this town," Charlie said. "I just spent the morning reporting an assault and a theft in the garage of the police department. It was a difficult assignment because the chief asked me not to divulge the object of the theft. Officer Williams is in the hospital after being hit on the head and knocked unconscious. Read all about it in Saturday's paper."

They found Louise busy with a customer. Jenny recognized Ann Thompson and smiled. "I hope that the paint that came down from the scaffolding Friday night didn't damage our flats. I left the theater too quickly to check."

"So did I," Ann said. "Apparently bad news doesn't always travel fast because my husband, Glenn, said that he didn't know about the incident." She took a package from Louise. "I'm finishing a quilt and needed extra yarn. Quilting keeps my mind occupied." She looked at Jenny. "It's lonely sometimes."

Jenny nodded. She sensed that Ann wanted to say, *It's lonely when I can't be with your father.*

"It's not good to be lonely," Jenny said. "I understand."

As soon as Ann left the shop, Charlie said. "How about lunch, Louise? Jenny and I are going to the Lobster Shack."

"I'd like that. Give me a minute to comb my hair and close the shop."

They found Michael sitting alone in a booth. "Sit down and join me," he said. He looked at Louise and grinned. "No clam chowder on the menu today."

"Don't remind me. Will we be able to rehearse tonight?"

"Yes. I've been at the theater all morning. The police removed all the yellow tape, and people at the lumber yard are unloading theater seats. The spiral stairway leading to the control room is being installed, and tomorrow the control room will be ready to handle the sound and lighting systems."

"I'll ask Adam Roberts to photograph the theater for Saturday's edition," Charlie said. "He'll want to climb those steps as soon as the control room is ready for use, so he might as well take pictures at the same time."

Jenny asked, "Michael, how will you communicate with Adam when he's in the control booth?"

"We'll have walkie-talkies, but the booth won't be enclosed, and I have a loud voice. He'll have a script, and we'll work together on the lighting. I'm not worried about the sound system because the theater is small, and we won't have any special effects."

Charlie asked, "Will there be a problem bringing the jury members up on stage?"

Michael finished his sandwich and fingered his gold chain. "I hope not. I've decided to introduce the play. I'll come on stage after the lights are dimmed, welcome the audience and explain that, without a curtain, scene changes will be made in full view. I'll tell them about jury selection and ask them to consider being part of the panel. Finally, I'll introduce you, Charlie. You can either be backstage or in the front row, whichever you prefer."

"I'll probably want to be backstage. I'll be too nervous to sit quietly."

Jenny laughed. "I'll hold your hand so you won't bite your nails."

"I'll want to rehearse those jury members who Charlotte called because I want that first act to move along quickly. If there's too much hesitation at that point in the play, momentum could be lost."

"Charlotte would be a good lead-off person," Charlie said.

"You're so right," Louise said. "She'll get the rest of the jury up on the stage in seconds."

"We'll practice the order of their appearance during dress rehearsal the night before the play opens. It won't take long."

After lunch, Charlie walked back to the craft shop with Jenny. "I'm going to the hospital to get a report on Williams," Charlie said. "I'll talk to you later."

He drove to the emergency entrance, asked for Officer Williams and was told to check at the front desk. He was directed to room 106 and found Williams in bed visiting with Chief Pierce.

"Excuse me. I don't want to intrude."

"Come in. I'm okay and can go home this afternoon. I suppose that you want to know what happened. Sit down, and I'll tell you what I know, but it isn't much."

Charlie took out his BlackBerry. "Did you see the person who hit you?"

"No. I had opened the trunk and was bent over putting the cable inside. That's all I can remember until I found myself on a gurney in the emergency room. I had this god-awful headache, and I couldn't see very well. Everything was hazy and spinning around."

Pierce spoke. "We checked the garage thoroughly and couldn't find anything. We couldn't find the instrument that the assailant might have used to hit Williams, and of course we couldn't find the cable."

"Was the trunk still open?" Charlie asked.

"Yes. We checked for fingerprints and found old smudges. Nothing new and well defined."

"There wasn't anyone around when I unlocked the garage this morning. It was still pretty dark, so there could have been someone I didn't see."

"Cars?"

"A few. I didn't pay any attention to them. Why would I?"

"Can you think of anything else that our readers might want to know?"

Williams closed his eyes. "Yeah, something else. I thought I heard music when I walked to the car, real faint. Kind of funny, isn't it?"

"As my mom would say, 'funny peculiar.'" Charlie pocketed the BlackBerry. "I don't want to tire you out, so I'll go now. If you think of something, call me. Here's my card."

Chief Pierce followed Charlie as he left the room. "I've asked my men to locate the other end of the cable, but they haven't found it. This is serious, Charlie. Of course I blame myself for not going with Williams to the garage this morning."

"Wouldn't that have been highly irregular and almost insulting to Williams? Your men are trained to take care of themselves, and who would have expected a problem? Don't beat up on yourself, Chief."

"You're right, and Williams is okay." He turned back to the room, and Charlie heard a faint, "But I wish we had that damned cable."

* * *

Louise and Jenny closed the shop, ate an early dinner and entered the theater at six-thirty.

Michael stood at the back trying to move the circular stairway. "It's solid. I've climbed it, and the control booth is also well built." He patted one of four wooden pillars that supported the structure above them. "Adam won't fall into the audience."

"Has all the sound equipment arrived?" Jenny asked.

"Most of it. I expect another shipment tomorrow. As soon as we have all the pieces, I'll call Adam. Together, we'll get it up and running."

Louise looked at the stage. The scaffolding was gone, and the set looked complete. "Is the painting done?" she asked.

"Yes. Two men who work at the lumber yard came yesterday. They put up their own scaffolding and finished the job in about three hours. How does it look?"

"Perfect," Jenny said. "No one would ever believe the condition it was in Friday night." She turned to welcome her father who had just entered. "Hi, Dad, what do you think of the theater now?"

"It looks like it's ready for opening night," David said.

"Diane asked me for a written report," Michael said. "Charlie will read it because I can't be there."

David walked down the aisle and said to Jenny, "Have you seen Ann lately?"

"Not since Friday. I drove to Portland on Saturday to see Erin."

David nodded and walked back up the aisle, greeting members of the cast on their way down to the stage. Jenny watched him leave and sensed that he was concerned about Ann. Did he worry about her? Was she in trouble?

* * *

Police Chief Harry Pierce returned to headquarters and called to his deputy.

"Williams is doing well," Officer Marling said.

"Yes, I'm glad that he can go home today." Pierce unwrapped a stick of gum and popped it in his mouth. "We have to find the other end of that cable. Take another man with you, and go back to the theater. We left the scaffolding hanging just as it was, and if it's still there, bring back the other end of the cable. I called Thompson Construction Company this morning and told Glenn what had happened. He was surprised, said he was sorry and hoped no one was hurt. I told him about Erin Gregory."

"If the cable's there, we'll bring it back."

"Good, and this time we'll guard it with our lives."

After Marling and Tom Lopez, another officer, left, Pierce returned to his desk that was now covered with memos and legal forms. He thought about Williams and wondered again how he could have been ambushed.

Ten minutes later, Marling called. "The scaffolding's been removed, Chief. Paint cans, everything. The painting looks finished. Someone else must have done the job on Sunday. What should we do?"

"Drive out to Thompson's and ask them to give you the cable. There shouldn't be a problem."

"Okay, we're on our way."

The two officers followed orders and pulled into the parking area at the construction company. "You might as well stay in the car," Marling said. "This shouldn't take long."

He opened the office door and found Thompson at his desk. "Good morning," Marling said. "Chief Pierce needs the other end of the cable that was cut Friday night. The scaffolding wasn't in the theater this morning, so I assumed that your men had removed it."

"Yes, the guys brought it back here, and I told them to take the whole damned mess to the closest landfill. I didn't even want to look at it."

Marling was puzzled. "But couldn't you have used the scaffolding and the rest of the cable? Seems like a waste of good materials."

"The stuff wasn't worth saving."

"Could you tell me where your people took the scaffolding and the cable? It's important to Chief Pierce, and if you don't want it, I might as well get it and bring it to headquarters."

"The truck left this morning and hasn't come back. I have no idea where they went."

He sat down and worked his computer. Marling knew that the interview had ended. Now what? He returned to the car, called headquarters and told Chief Pierce about the material. "He didn't know where his men took the stuff. I don't know what to do."

"Stay where you are and wait while I check out landfill locations in the area."

Everybody Knew Pete

Marling and his companion sat and waited. Five minutes later, Pierce called and gave him directions to two of the closest landfills. "I'm sure the men wouldn't have driven much farther. Check them out."

Marling found the nearest landfill and stopped by a dump truck with its tailgate open and noticed two men shoveling dirt into the landfill. "Wait!" Marling called. "I need to talk to you."

The men stopped their work, and one of them asked, "Do you have a problem? We have orders to fill the area."

"I understand, but I want to find out if a truck has been here recently and dropped off some material."

One of the men said, "We saw a truck stop and throw out some stuff. They weren't here long and left in a hurry."

"Do you know where they threw the material?" Marling asked.

"Yeah, over there. We've just finished filling that part of the landfill."

Marling swore under his breath. "Do you have an extra shovel?"

The first man grinned. "Sure. Look behind the front seat."

Marling found the shovel, and he and Lopez drove to the area that Jake had indicated. Marling took off his jacket, rolled up the sleeves of his clean blue shirt and began to dig. He worked until his eyes filled with sweat that poured down from his forehead. He'd found two mangled bicycles, seven treadless tires, fourteen bags from McDonalds, six broken skate boards and fourteen battered lobster traps, but no scaffolding. He sat down under a pine tree and handed Lopez the shovel. "Your turn. Maybe you should move more to the left."

Lopez removed his jacket and began to throw dirt into the area that Marling had cleared. Fifteen minutes later, his shovel hit something metal. He dug quickly and brought out the end of a quarter-inch, vinyl coated cable. "I think I've found it," he called. Marling ran, and the two men pulled on the cable. It took two of them to bring the scaffolding up to the surface.

Lopez looked at Marling and raised his right thumb. "This wasn't in my job description, but now I could moonlight as a ditch-digger."

Marling laughed. "Yeah, and now we have to load it into the trunk. Ready?"

They pulled the scaffolding to firmer ground and released the cable that had been cut. They threw the scaffolding back into the landfill and carried the cable to the trunk of the police car. Marling waved to the men in the dump truck and drove back to the station.

Pierce thanked them as both men slumped into chairs in his office. "As soon as you've showered, I want both of you to take the cable to headquarters in Portland. We'll keep an eye on that patrol car until you leave town."

* * *

Thompson opened his office door and watched the police car leave. He didn't care where they went or if they found the scaffold. When Pierce had told him about Erin Gregory's condition, he lost interest in completing the interior of the theater. His men had worked hard to finish the job in time for Labor Day weekend, and the paint can hitting Erin soured the entire project. He was sorry that he'd agreed to serve on that stupid jury. Charlotte had finagled his acceptance, appealing to his vanity. A smart woman.

The phone rang. "Yes? It's what? Okay, I'll be there." He pounded his fist on the desk. His contract for ten miles of new highway resurfacing one hundred miles from home had meant the difference between breaking even and making a profit this quarter, and now a piece of heavy machinery had broken down. He called his best mechanic and told him about the problem. "I'll pick you up in half and hour. I don't know how long this will take, at least two days, so pack a toothbrush."

He called Ann. "I have to leave for a couple of days. We're having a problem with the new road work." He leaned back in his chair and stared at the ceiling. One problem after another. Would he ever find peace?

CHAPTER NINETEEN

Monday night's play practice was, as Michael predicted, dismal. The cast was listless. If lines were remembered, they dragged, and entrances were late. He almost called "Cut," and sent them home, but he knew that they had to work through this night, experience the remembrance of Friday night's horror and put it behind them.

At the end of Act Three, Jenny walked to the back of stage left and stood in her usual spot. She looked up, and Michael sensed that she almost expected another disaster. He nodded and smiled wanly. Everyone walked his own path of anxiety. He walked one also. The last two weeks of rehearsal, whether they occurred on Broadway or Main Street, were always stressful, exciting, emotional strings taut with anticipation and worry. He knew it all, but each time it was new in different ways. He'd never experienced Friday night's chaos, but there had been other instances of almost equal catastrophes, and he knew that all would be forgotten as soon as the first line was spoken on opening night.

Michael jumped down from his stool and stood close to the footlight area. "Okay, let's take a break and relax. I know what all of you are going through because I feel it too. So look around. Notice the seating. Inspect the new stairway leading up to the control booth."

He told them about the sound and light equipment. "Adam Roberts will be our technician, and he and I will work together as soon as all the equipment arrives. The footlights will be installed tomorrow." He looked up at the platforms on either side of the stage. "When the spotlights arrive, we'll need to make canisters for them. Does anyone know a welder?"

"I do," one of the cast members said. "I'll call him tomorrow."

Michael gave him his cell phone number. "Thanks. Ask him to call me." He walked to the back of the theater, and the cast moved off to try the new seats, drink a soda, and visit.

The next run-through was an improvement, and as he and Jenny sat together making notes, Michael said, "I'm relieved that we finished tonight's practice without major problems. Our heroine was so nervous when we started that I thought she might lose it completely."

"She's had enough experience not to panic. I'm feeling better too. I didn't call Erin's room today. I didn't want to bother anyone."

"Good thinking. They'll call when there's news."

Michael locked the theater as they left. "I'm working on a report for the Arts Council meeting. Charlie's going to read it."

Michael noticed a change in Jenny's voice when she said, "He'll present it well. Have a good night."

Michael smiled. "I will. I'm glad tonight's over." He drove back to the cottage, switched on the TV and fixed a Scotch and soda. He leaned back in his chair and thought about Jenny, so young, so full of life. He wished that he could have had a daughter just like her.

*　*　*

Jenny awoke in her own bed Tuesday morning and wished that she'd spent the night with Charlie. Monday night's rehearsal had been a bummer, and she hadn't been in the mood for sweet talk, wine or sex. Now she looked at the clock and thought about another dull day. But what about Erin?

She called the hospital and asked for Erin's room. Gloria Gregory answered. "There's nothing to report," she said. "The doctors come in and go out, and nobody says anything. I may come home at the end of the week. I'm concerned about Jacob. When I call home, his words are slurred, and I know he's been drinking."

"Can I help?"

"No one can help, Jenny. I finally learned that after too many years of screaming and crying. The gift shop owner told me to take two weeks off to stay with Erin. I may stay one week here, then come home and decide what to do with my life. If Erin dies...,"

Jenny heard sobs and knew that Gloria was breaking down. "Would you like me to come to the hospital today?"

"Yes, if you're not busy."

"I'll come, and you can take some time off, maybe see a movie, have a manicure, something away from the hospital."

Jenny heard sighs and more sobs. She knew that Gloria needed a change of scene.

Everybody Knew Pete

The drive to Portland was uneventful. Jenny found Erin's mother sitting in a chair by Erin's bed. She held a magazine with one hand and Erin's hand with the other. Gloria stood and hugged Jenny. "Thank you for coming." She looked at her watch. "Give me four hours. That's all I need."

Jenny nodded. "Don't worry. Erin and I will be fine. I brought a book, and maybe I'll read to her."

Gloria nodded and left the room. Jenny sat down and took out a paperback. "I'm going to read to you, Erin, and if you can hear me, squeeze my hand."

Jenny read until her voice became hoarse. There was no squeeze, so she continued silently. An hour later, she went to the ladies room, and bought a soda at the pop machine. When she returned, she noticed a man who walked away from her in the hall, his brown hair swinging in a pony tail. Odd, she thought as she faintly recalled that same figure during her last visit. She'd caught a glimpse of his face, a broad forehead and a dimple in his chin. She'd dismissed him then. Now, she was puzzled. She entered Erin's room and picked up her book. Two more hours and no movement in Erin's bed. Jenny put her head down on the bed and cried.

Gloria returned sporting a new hair-do. "I even had it colored," she said.

"You look fabulous. I'm glad that I could be here."

They walked to the corner of the room and talked quietly as though Erin might hear them. "Do you want me to stop at your house to see Jacob?"

Gloria shook her head. "He'll think that I asked you to check on him. I'm going to drive home on Friday if there's no change. I'll call you this weekend."

Jenny drove home and called Charlie. "Have you had dinner? If not, I'd like to see you."

Jenny could almost see Charlie's smile. "I'll pick you up. I heard about a new restaurant up the coast with tables for two."

Jenny showered, wrote a note for Louise, and put a toothbrush and her birth control pills in her purse.

* * *

Diane had prepared an agenda for Thursday night's Arts Council meeting. She knew that it would be a long one.

"The meeting will please come to order." Diane stood at the end of a long table and studied the Arts Council members. She smiled at Jenny and Charlie who sat next to each other. Charlie held a file folder.

David presented his finance report, and everyone sat up and listened. "The news isn't good right now," he said, "and we have two weeks before opening night, but the Biancis agreed to pay for the utilities on the guest house as a contribution to the Arts Council." Smiles all around.

"We have no accounts receivable, but we can expect rather hefty bills next week. Fortunately they won't come due until the first of the month, and by that time we'll have ticket receipts." More smiles.

He gave a detailed report of expenditures, and there were no questions.

"Now let's hear about publicity," Diane said and looked at Charlotte.

"I'm not presenting a bill now," Charlotte said, "but here's what we've done and what we plan to do."

She told them about the flyers that were distributed and the radio and TV stations that had been given full reports. "Radio stations allot time for public service announcements, and we hope to saturate the media with news items. We're using the internet and e-mail. If there's anyone in Maine who doesn't know about our summer production, he must live in a cave on an island with no means of communication."

"How about programs for the performance?" a member asked.

"We're working on them with Charlie, Michael and an artist who's giving us her time. We have asked several businesses in town for advertising to defray printing costs. That's standard operating procedure, good publicity for the donors and a big help to our finance committee."

There were no more questions, so Diane asked Charlie to read Michael's report. The director had outlined every aspect of the production. He praised the cast for their talent and their long rehearsal hours. He included a short reference to Friday night's incident but gave no details. All of the members knew about Erin's tragic accident and interrupted Charlie's reading, each with his own theory about

Everybody Knew Pete

who had done it, and how could this happen, and would there be a lawsuit. Finally Diane pounded the gavel, and Charlie continued Michael's report with references to the new seating, the control booth, and the lighting and sound systems.

Diane asked. "Are there any questions?" There were none. She noticed a smile on Jenny's face when Charlie finished his report.

Diane was about to close the meeting when there was a loud pounding at the door.

Charlie who had stood by the door to give his report, opened it, and Jacob Gregory staggered in, his eyes wide and bloodshot. "Don't anybody move," he shouted. His words were slurred and venomous. "You're all sittin' around here nice and comfortable, and my little girl is maybe dyin' in Portland. My God, can't you find the guy who did that to her? You started this whole damned mess with your damned play, and now my kid's unconscious."

Jacob fell against a chair and sat on the floor. "I went to the cops, and they wouldn't do nothing, so I come here." He covered his face and sobbed. "Can't anybody do something?" He stood and leaned against the wall. "Ain't nobody can help. Ain't nobody."

He lurched toward the door and shuffled out. The members heard him bump against walls and furniture as he left the building. No one spoke.

"I guess the meeting's over," Diane said. "Thank you for coming."

Jenny stood and took Charlie aside. "I'm going to stay with Louise tonight. You'll be busy transcribing your notes for the paper."

Charlie nodded. "I'll miss you, but it's going to be a short night. I'll call you in the morning."

Jenny left with the other committee members, and Charlie looked back at Diane who had put her head on the table. He walked over and put his hand on her shoulder. "It was a good meeting. I'm sorry it ended this way. We can't do anything for Erin's father or for Erin. Can I give you a ride home?"

Diane looked up. "Thanks, Charlie, but I have my car. Would you like to follow me and have a nightcap? My husband's home and we can tell him about what happened."

"Okay. We could all use a drink."

Diane nodded, picked up her papers and walked with Charlie to her car. She thought about breakfast with Michael. Perhaps if they hadn't had their little talk, she might have looked for fun with Charlie. Instead, she thought about Erin Gregory, the play and, if it was a success, a traveling troupe presenting *Tangled Trap Lines* everywhere in Maine.

* * *

"We put the paper to bed," Charlotte said when Charlie came into her office Friday morning. "How long did you work last night to finish your article about the Arts Council meeting?"

Charlie's smile indicated fatigue as he slumped into a chair. "I finished about two o'clock. It was a good meeting. I had a drink with Diane and her husband afterward, but I left in a hurry to write my article. Diane's husband is a sailor. He'd be an interesting subject for a profile."

"After the play is over, you might consider a series about people in town. Louise Campbell and her craft shop come to mind."

Charlie nodded. "And maybe one on her niece."

Charlotte laughed. "You couldn't be objective. Pick someone you're not in love with."

"Is it that obvious?"

"People have organized a wedding date pool. I'm in it."

Charlie's groan was followed by a grin. "Life in a small town. I'm going to the police department to find out about the cable. Maybe they've had a lab report."

"Do check it out." She leaned back in her chair. "Take the rest of the day and the weekend off. Come back Monday for next week's assignments. You've earned a vacation."

"Thanks, I'll do that." He whistled as he left the Chronicle office.

At the police station, Charlie greeted Dispatch who nodded briefly and returned to her monitors. "The Chief's in his office going through phone books."

Pierce looked up when Charlie put his head in the door. "Come in. We received the lab report yesterday, and I'm checking to see who probably has bolt cutters. I called the Hardware and Lumber Company, and Lopez is on his way to compare the cutters their people use with the print-out we received. We'll check the auto dealerships, private contractors, anyone in town who might use one."

"How about the telephone company and other communications people?"

"I've made a list, and it's a long one. This process could take weeks, but we have to know."

"How's Williams?"

"He's back at work and says he feels all right. He was lucky."

"Luckier than Erin Gregory. Jenny McKnight visited her on Tuesday, and there was no change."

"Erin's father came in late yesterday afternoon. He'd had too much to drink, and he cussed out everyone he could find. Officer Marling finally talked him into leaving."

"I know. He broke up the Arts Council meeting last night. A sad case. Call me on my cell phone if you find a match. Charlotte gave me the weekend off." He whistled as he left the station. A whole weekend ahead of him. He hoped that Jenny was available.

CHAPTER TWENTY

Jenny and Louise ate a hurried dinner. It was dress rehearsal night, Friday, August twenty-ninth. "I don't know why I'm so nervous," Jenny said. "I have no lines to speak."

"I'm nervous too. I worry that a seam might break. What if the heroine's skirt falls to the floor?"

Jenny laughed. "That's why we have dress rehearsal. Better now than on opening night."

"You're so right. More coffee?"

"No, I think we should leave for the theater."

When they arrived, Michael met them at the door. "Jenny, I can't find page two of Act Three. Do you have it?"

"No, but I'll look." She thumbed through the pages on her clip board. "Here it is. Adam wanted to check the script when he was down here last night."

She knew that Michael had dress-rehearsal jitters. She'd seen it in the eyes of drama department high school teachers. She smiled as Ann Thompson sat down beside her.

"My husband, Glenn, is still in the car and won't come in until Michael needs him. I think that he's nervous about being a jurist."

Jenny laughed. "Everybody's nervous. Ask him to come in and sit in the back row with George Hendricks and the librarian."

"All right." She left, and Charlie took her seat. He squeezed Jenny's hand and grinned. "Big night. I don't know where to sit."

"Wait until Michael gives directions." She leaned over and kissed his cheek. "I want to be with you after the show."

"Mmm. I want to be with you too. These last two weeks have been crazy. Most nights I'm not very good company. The police are still checking bolt cutters, and Charlotte's kept me running all over the county picking up news reports. I learned more about the lobster haul than I wanted to know, and everybody's doing Lobster Days, Crab Days and Old Maine Days. It's the end of the tourist season, and everyone wants to cash in before Labor Day."

Diane sat down beside Louise. "Michael asked me to come. I'm to introduce all of you." She smiled at Jenny and Louise. "This is so exciting. I wonder if he wants me to say anything before the play begins."

"I don't know," Jenny said. "I'm sure that he'll tell you what to do and what to say."

Michael walked to the footlight area, and everyone listened. "Tonight we're going to go through Act One with no interruptions. When we've finished, I'll make comments. Charlie, I want you backstage so I can introduce you before the play begins." He looked at Diane. "You can come up with Charlie because I'm going to introduce you also." He looked toward the back row. "Jurors, please come down and sit in the second row." He waited until all four were seated. "Charlotte, when I ask for jurors from the audience, I want you to jump up right away." He looked at the other three. "I'd like you to follow Charlotte in this order, Glenn Thompson, then Genevieve Upton and George Hendricks. I expect that others will follow."

He turned to the bailiff. "Usually the entire jury speaks the oath in unison, but I want you to administer the oath individually so that the audience will hear each person's name. Most people will know you, and you may even receive applause. You may acknowledge it if you wish."

The four jurors looked at each other and laughed.

"I will enter stage right and welcome everyone. "I'll introduce Charlie." He smiled at the author. "But no speeches, please. You can say something at the end of the play while you and the cast receive a standing ovation." Michael beamed at the cast. "Of course you all will have the audience on its feet, right?"

The cast nodded and laughed.

Michael looked up at the control booth. "I'll acknowledge you too, Adam." He looked at the actors, the jurors, and the others in the audience. "Adam and I have worked together, and he's followed the script perfectly. You, the cast, have worked with him this week and know how complicated his job is as he focuses on each set at the proper time and works the floodlights and spotlights." He looked up. "Take a bow, Adam."

Adam waved to everyone and called down, "It's been a blast. I hope that all goes well tomorrow night."

"Okay," Michael said. "Let's start. Cast, I want you backstage now. As soon as I've introduced Adam, I want you to take your places on stage. I will have explained what will happen without a curtain, how the cast will appear and how the sets on stage left will be changed. Charlie, you and Diane can go to the wings next to stage right."

Charlie, Diane and the actors and actresses climbed the steps. The courtroom people walked behind the flats on stage right, and the living room cast walked to stage left. No one spoke, and Jenny who sat in the audience knew that each one was thinking his own thoughts and trying to remember his first lines. She thought about Charlie backstage biting his nails and thinking about what he would say at the end of the performance.

Michael climbed the steps, walked to the center of the stage and stood close to the footlights. Adam put a spotlight on him, and he began to speak.

"Good evening, ladies and gentlemen. Welcome to the opening performance of *Tangled Trap Lines* presented by the Sowatna Arts Council. I am Michael Jamison, the director." Michael looked both right and left to the people in the wings. "Okay, everybody, that's about all I'm going to say now as an introduction, so Charlie, be ready."

He looked to stage right. "I'm proud to introduce Charlie Brewster, author of our play tonight." Charlie came out and stood beside Michael. "I won't give my opening night remarks now, but I want you to get the feel of being onstage with me."

Charlie grinned. "Okay, and I can't say anything now, right?" Michael nodded. "That's good because I'll be too nervous to talk anyway."

Jenny heard laughs from backstage.

"Now this is when I'll introduce Diane who will be backstage. Charlie, stay on the stage until Diane introduces members of the Arts Council who are in the audience." Michael looked at both sides of the stage. "Are we all right so far? Any questions?" There were none. "That's good. I'll ask the audience to turn and acknowledge Adam. As soon as the applause ends, the cast will enter from both sides and take their places. Judge, I want you to stay off the stage until the bailiff says his lines."

The judge nodded, and Michael continued. "Okay, people. I've just acknowledged Adam, the applause has ended, so take your places on stage. As soon as you have taken your places, I'll say something like 'And now the Sowatna players present *Tangled Trap Lines*.' I'll exit stage right, and as soon as I'm off, bailiff, you can open the play. Let's take it from there, and we'll go through the first act with no interruptions."

Michael walked to the wings, and the bailiff began to speak. "Hear ye, hear ye, the circuit court of New Bradford, Maine, with Judge Ruth Carlson presiding is now in session. All rise"

The judge entered the stage from the door close to the bailiff's chair and took her place at the bench. She looked at the attorneys and their aides and said, "This is the case of the state of Maine versus the accused, Brian Potter. I am Judge Ruth Carlson. Bailiff, bring in the accused."

The bailiff opened the door and led the accused murderer to his place at a table upstage next to his attorney.

After Potter had taken his place, the judge said, "We will now ask the jurors to take their places." The actress who portrayed the judge looked anxiously into the audience.

Charlotte in the second row took her cue and walked toward the steps, a spotlight followed. Louise and Jenny in the front row gasped. Charlotte walked on stage in an orange and black plaid suit. She wore her grandmother's wide-brimmed silk hat with a massive black feather that bobbed with each step.

Louise and Jenny looked at each other, and Jenny whispered, "I'll bet that Michael will make some reference to jurors' attire."

The bailiff made an effort to keep his voice steady as he said, "Do you solemnly swear to fairly try the issues in the case of the State of Maine versus Brian Potter and to render a just verdict?"

"I do," Charlotte said and walked to a seat in the jury box.

Michael walked to the edge of the stage. "More light, Adam. Give the jurors more light."

Glenn Thompson who had entered the theater with Ann, got up slowly and climbed the steps, a bright spotlight accenting his movements.

When he turned and faced the audience, Jenny in the front row stared at him for a moment, then jumped to her feet. She ran up the steps to the stage and grabbed Thompson's arm. "Stop! You killed Pete Clampton!"

"What the hell!" Thompson shoved Jenny's arm away. He glared at Jenny who stood in front of him. Michael ran to the center of the stage, and the entire cast looked on, transfixed and puzzled.

Louise ran up the steps and put her arm around Jenny. "Is this true? Is this what's been haunting you all these years?"

"Yes, it's true." Jenny continued to stare at Thompson.

Charlie ran onto the stage from the wings and took her arm. "What are you saying, Jenny? What's happened to you?"

Jenny shook him off. "It was the lights when he was on the stage. It was the lights that blinded me that night ten years ago when I left the church."

Thompson leered at Jenny. "You have a foul mouth and a big imagination. What are you talking about?"

Jenny spoke quickly, her words loud and clear. "I ran across the street when the lights of your car hit me in the face. I saw you drive up the street and turn in at your driveway." She turned to Charlie. "I'd forgotten about those lights until just now. The spotlights brought it all back."

"And that's why you didn't move out of the way that night after dinner at the Dolphin when the car came at us." Charlie looked at Thompson. "Did you drive that car?"

"I don't know what you're talking about, either one of you." He glared at Michael. "You're the director. Get these people off the stage." He lifted his arm, ready to strike Jenny.

Louise put her arms around Jenny and stared at Thompson. "Don't touch her, Glenn. She's telling the truth."

Ann ran up the steps and put her hand on her husband's arm. "I don't know what's going on, Glenn, but you don't have to answer." She looked at Jenny. "How can you accuse my husband of murder?"

"Because it's true." She broke away from Louise and faced Ann. "I saw him. I saw him drag the body of Pete Clampton down the street to his car, and I saw him drive back."

Thompson laughed. "Oh, sure, I could drag a man all the way from my house past the church? You think I'm some kind of an Atlas, a guy who could carry the world on his back?"

"But you did. I saw you." Jenny was desperate.

Ann stood by her husband's side and took his hand. "You must be crazy, Jenny. Everybody knows that you have these wild visions and nightmares. And this was ten years ago. My God, you were a high school kid, probably high on pot. What were you doing out that night?"

"I admit that my friend Erin and I smoked pot in the cupola of the church, but I only took one puff. I looked out the window and saw someone drag a body down the street. I didn't know who either of them were. I heard about Pete Clampton's murder the next day."

"And you think I was the one who carried Pete's body? My God, I couldn't have carried him two steps. Even without boots, he'd weigh a ton."

Colin Greene, who had stayed behind his prosecutor's table, ran up and grabbed Thompson's arm. "How did you know that Pete didn't wear boots that night? That evidence was never revealed, not even in the grand jury hearing."

Thompson stammered. "Somebody must have told me."

Colin said, "The boots are important. We have to find them."

"Over my dead body!" Thompson yelled.

"We can get a search warrant, Glenn," Colin said.

Thompson walked to edge of the stage and turned and looked at everyone. "You're crazy if you think I'm going to stay here on this stage and be a part of your shitty play and listen to a crazy woman."

He walked down the steps and strode up the center aisle. Jenny yelled after him, "You killed Pete Clampton, and you probably killed Tim Brennan, and you tried to kill me. You're a murderer, Glenn Thompson."

Ann looked at Jenny. "I don't understand any of this. Glenn's right. You're crazy!"

Jenny's response was silenced by a loud noise that came from the back of the theater. It sounded as though someone had fired a gun. Because of the footlights and the spots, no one could see beyond the first two rows. Charlie was the first to run up the aisle, and everyone on the stage followed.

As they ran, they heard a man's voice that shouted, "You almost killed my little girl, you dirty bastard!"

Thompson lay in the middle of the aisle, his body facing the back row. Blood spurted from his forehead. Charlie looked in the direction Thompson faced and saw a man slumped down on a seat next to the aisle, his outstretched hand dangling near a gun on the floor.

Charlie passed by Thompson and knelt by the man in the seat. He recognized him. "Jacob Gregory!"

Jenny stood in the aisle and stared at Erin's father. Suddenly she screamed as she saw the death's head again that now covered his body. "Oh, God! Is he dead?"

Charlie nodded. "Maybe he had a heart attack or a stroke." He pulled out his cell and called police headquarters. "Carol, Charlie at the theater. We have a dead body here, maybe two."

"We'll be right there. Ten four."

Ann sat on the floor next to her husband. Tears fell as she held his hand. "Why did this happen? Glenn didn't kill anybody." She stared at Jenny. "You did this. You drove him off the stage. You killed him." She put her head on Glenn's chest and sobbed.

Charlie knelt and felt Thompson's pulse. He shook his head, stood and put his arm around Jenny. "Wait until the police arrive. There's nothing anyone can do now."

Michael looked at the dead bodies and turned to the cast, the three jurors, Louise and Diane. "Let's all go back to the stage and sit down. Charlie's right. We can't do anything."

The people walked slowly down the aisle and looked back at Jacob Gregory and Glenn Thompson. Ann still sat by her husband. She rocked back and forth and moaned. Jenny stood in the aisle between Louise and Charlie. They held each other, and Jenny wept silently.

Three police officers and four emergency medical technicians ran into the theater. Chief Pierce looked at the bodies. "Where's Adam Roberts? Is he here?"

Everybody Knew Pete

Adam had run down the steps as soon as he heard the shot. "I'm here with my camera, Chief," he said.

"Good. Go to work." Adam took pictures, choking back the bile in his throat. When he finished, Pierce said, "Okay, take the bodies to the mortuary now."

Michael helped Ann to her feet. She looked down at the body of her husband. "No, no, I want to go with him"

"I'm sorry, Mrs. Thompson," Pierce said. "We have to take them now. We have to find out how they died."

"I know how Glenn died!" Ann pointed her finger at Jenny. "You killed him. That's how he died."

Michael took Ann's arm and led her slowly down the aisle to the front row. "I'll get you a glass of water. Just sit here for a while. The police will probably want to talk to you."

Ann slumped down into a seat. She covered her face with both hands, and her shoulders shook as she cried.

The ambulance people lifted the bodies onto stretchers. An officer put on clear latex gloves and placed the gun in a plastic bag. Two of the men looked around the area and shook their heads. Marling spoke. "Nothing here, Chief. The floor's clean." Pierce nodded.

Colin Greene walked back up the aisle. "Is there anything I can do?"

"Yes. Tell me what happened." Pierce sat down in an aisle seat and brought out an iPod and a notebook. "I need both."

Colin gave him a detailed report beginning with Glenn Thompson's entrance on the stage. "I don't know what Jenny saw, but when she accused him of killing Pete Clampton, he got angry and stormed off the stage. I don't think that anyone saw Jacob Gregory in the back row."

Pierce looked at Jenny. "What did you see?"

"It was the lights on Glenn Thompson when he walked up the steps." She described her being in the church the night of Pete Clampton's murder. "Tonight when the spotlights hit him, it all came back. When I left the church, his headlights blinded me for a minute, but I caught a glimpse of his face and saw the car turn into his driveway. I must have blocked it out, but twice bright lights have scared me, made me stop, not move."

Charlie said, "I had to push her out of the way that night after dinner when a car came at us as we crossed the street."

"What kind of a car was it?"

"I don't know. It was a dark color. The light wasn't good, and we were both too shocked lying in the street."

Pierce looked at Jenny. "I had just joined the force when Pete was killed, but I remember the case. The grand jury acquitted Tim Brennan."

Jenny nodded. "I would have testified if Tim had been charged. As long as there was no trial, I didn't feel the need to tell anyone."

Colin said, "Thompson made a strange remark. He said that he couldn't have carried Pete Clampton's body from his house to the car because the man would have been too heavy, even without boots."

Pierce looked puzzled.

"The police report mentioned Pete's not wearing boots, but that information was never given out, not at the grand jury hearing, not to anyone. The police wanted to keep it quiet, probably hoping that it might be part of the evidence if later, someone else had been arrested and charged with the crime."

"I suppose we could get a search warrant and look for those boots, but I'm sure that if Thompson had them, he would have disposed of them long ago. Why keep them for ten years?"

"You won't need a search warrant." Ann had walked slowly back up the aisle and had heard their conversation. "You can search the house, but you won't find anything. Glenn's innocent."

"Thanks, Mrs. Thompson," Pierce said. "I think that we'll have to look even though we probably won't find anything. Can we come tomorrow?" Ann nodded.

Diane took Ann's hand. "You shouldn't be alone tonight. Please come and stay with us."

Ann stared at Diane, not seeing her. "It's too much. Glenn's dead. I don't know where to go or what to do."

"Don't worry. We can help."

Michael stood in front of the stage, and his hand shook as he took a handkerchief from his pocket. "There's an old saying, 'The show must go on,' and it must. I'd like to try another dress rehearsal tomorrow morning beginning at ten o'clock for those of you who can attend. You three jurors will have to lead the way. You might want to enlist the help of your friends to fill the jury box quickly. Charlotte, we need to talk before you leave."

Jenny, Louise and Charlie stood together with their arms around each other. Jenny put her head on Charlie's shoulder and cried softly. Her legs felt weak, and she shivered. Colin joined them and took Louise's hand. He looked at his watch. "It's early yet. Please come to my house for a drink. We could all use one." He turned to Michael. "You might need a drink also."

Michael nodded. "I'll follow your car." He spoke quietly to Charlotte, then returned to the others who followed him. Michael was about to switch off the lights when he turned and looked back at the stage. "*Tangled Trap Lines*, indeed. Tonight we had tangled lives and tangled emotions. Let's hope that they untangle tomorrow night."

Jenny and Louise had ridden together. Charlie helped Jenny into Louise's car. Jenny sat down, gripped Louise's hand and leaned on her shoulder. The others followed Louise. Five stunned, shocked and saddened people, each with his own fears and concerns.

At Colin's house, Jenny waited for Charlie. "You go ahead, Louise. I'll come in a minute."

Colin took Louise's hand and opened the door. "I can't believe any of it," he said. "Everything about the play has gone smoothly. People learned their lines, the sets went up, the lighting was perfect. Except for Erin's accident, there were no major problems, not even minor ones, and now this."

Louise stared at Colin. "I must believe Jenny, but what if she's wrong? Two men are dead, and the play might fold after the first line is spoken. You're not professionals. Michael can say that the show must go on, but what if it can't?"

"It will go on, Louise." Michael came and stood beside her. He took her hand. "You know that life isn't always the way we want it. We both know what it's like when our lives suddenly change. We move ahead because we have to, because there's no other sensible way." He sat down and wiped his forehead. He looked up at Colin. "I'd like a double Scotch and soda if you have it."

"You're entitled." He welcomed Jenny and Charlie. "I'm taking drink orders. Charlie can help."

They walked to the kitchen, and Jenny sat down between Louise and Michael.

Louise squeezed Jenny's arm, then turned to Michael. "Can you pull the cast together tomorrow?"

"I hope so. In my short time here, I've learned that people in Maine are strong and can accept whatever comes."

"It must be the winters," Louise said. "We're a hardy bunch, and we know that spring will always come."

Colin and Charlie returned with drinks for everyone.

Michael raised his glass. "To life!"

"To life!" they repeated.

Michael finished his drink and stood. "I can find my way back to the cottage." He looked at all of them. "There's good news at the bed and breakfast. Mavis and Guido have a new baby. Guido's nephew's wife in Rome died in childbirth which is tragic, but Guido's sister brought the baby to them. The Biancis are going to adopt him."

"That's good news. A new life," Louise said.

Michael closed the front door behind him, and Colin took empty glasses to the kitchen.

Jenny finished her drink and said to Louise, "I'm going home with Charlie tonight."

"I understand." She smiled at both of them. "I'll see you tomorrow at ten o'clock."

Colin came from the kitchen and said goodnight to Charlie and Jenny. Louise stood. "I must go too."

"How about another drink, Louise. I'd like one." Colin took her glass and went to the kitchen.

Louise followed him. "It's nice to be in your home again."

He made two drinks and led her back into the living room. "Will you be all right tonight?"

"I don't know how I'll get through the night. I'm so worried about Jenny, but I'm glad that she's with Charlie." She sipped her drink. "And I'm used to being alone."

"So am I. It's not fun." He looked at her and smiled. "One night we won't be alone. One night we'll be together, I hope."

Louise stared at him. "Am I supposed to clutch my bosom and say, 'Oh, this is so sudden,' or should I be honest and tell you that one night I'd like to be with you also?"

She stood, and Colin put his arms around her. He lifted her chin and kissed her, a long, passionate kiss. "If you stayed tonight, we'd both think that our emotions had gone wild because of what happened at the theater. When you stay, it will be under different circumstances." They kissed again. "Perhaps after an opening night."

CHAPTER TWENTY-ONE

Jenny's cell phone rang at seven-thirty, Saturday morning. She rolled over in bed and felt for her cell phone on the night stand beside Charlie's bed. "Yes? Who is it?" she mumbled.

"This is Chief Pierce. We need you. Mrs. Gregory is here."

"Who was that?" He rolled over and kissed her.

"Chief Pierce. Gloria Gregory's at headquarters, and he wants me to come."

"I'll go with you." He jumped out of bed and dressed quickly. Jenny dressed, and they ran to the car. She combed her hair and brushed her teeth with a finger and a sample tube of toothpaste she'd picked up at a motel.

When they entered Pierce's office, Gloria stood and put her arms around Jenny. "I went to the mortuary last night after they called me. I'd returned from Portland yesterday afternoon. I couldn't believe it. Jacob was laid out on a table covered with a sheet. I identified him, and they asked questions. A doctor was there, and he said that Jacob had died of a massive heart attack." She wiped her eyes with a tissue. "I knew that his health was bad, but I never expected this. He must have been roaring drunk. He'd never kill someone if he had been sober."

She sat down and sobbed. "I worried about him while I was with Erin. I knew that he'd drink when he was alone. He loved Erin so much." She covered her face with both hands and cried.

Jenny knelt in front of her and took her hands. "This is a terrible shock, Mrs. Gregory. Last night was a nightmare for all of us."

Charlie leaned against the wall and worked his BlackBerry. He had no comforting words. He could only take notes and hate being a reporter.

Pierce said, "We searched Jacob's clothing, and we found this letter. Mrs. Gregory has read it and knows now why her husband brought his gun to the theater."

He held out a water-stained envelope, and Jenny saw that it was addressed to Erin Gregory. She opened the envelope and read the letter. It was dated June 4, 2008, and signed by Tim Brennan.

"That's the day he was killed," Jenny said. "Where has it been all this time?"

"I think I know," Gloria said. "I asked Jacob to rake the yard, now that fall's coming on. When I got home yesterday, he was in the front yard with a rake. He said that he'd found a letter under a bush, didn't know how long it had been there. He had put it in his pocket, and I forgot about it until a letter was found in Jacob's pocket. By the looks of it, this is the one he found."

Jenny scanned the letter and gave it to Charlie. "Now we know why Tim told us to be careful, and now we know who killed him."

Charlie took the letter and read it aloud. "'Dear Erin, I'm leaving for Portland now. Remember our visit this afternoon when I told you to be careful? I have to be careful too because I know who killed Pete Clampton. I haven't told anyone because I made a deal with Glenn Thompson. He'd give me the stuff I wanted for nothing, the best Colombian, he said. All I had to do was make up a story about Pete's death. So I did. When I got busted by the cops, they sent me to treatment and that's when I met you. After I left the Center, I really planned to stay off the drugs, and when I saw Thompson, I told him I didn't need any more stuff, but I sure could use some money. He knew what I meant, and he didn't like it. Finally he agreed.'"

Charlie stopped reading. "But we all know that Tim was back on the stuff and was pushing drugs."

Gloria nodded. "Yes, he was at our house, and Jacob bought heroin from him."

Charlie nodded and continued reading. "'I couldn't stay off the stuff. Sorry, Erin. You tried. So I found a supplier, and that took more money than Thompson had given me. I went to see Thompson this afternoon. He gave me money for a month's supply but said that our deal was over. He said that after ten years, no one would believe anyone on drugs, and there was a thing called a 'statute of limitations.' I don't know what that means, but I guess the case against Pete is closed for good, so you might as well know what really happened the night Pete was killed.'"

Charlie wiped his forehead. "This is tough. I can still see him as he walked out of Louise's house that day. Of course he wouldn't tell us that he was going to see Thompson. He must have had a plan when he walked out."

"Maybe that's why he told us to be careful," Jenny said. "He knew what Glenn Thompson was capable of."

Charlie read on. "'The night of the murder, I boarded Pete's boat about eleven o'clock. Pete hadn't planned to leave port until about two a.m., but I wanted to see him and learn more about our trip. He hadn't given me any details. Nobody was on the boat. I went down to the cabin and found some stuff. I must have taken a lot because I fell asleep. I heard a noise and pushed open the door enough so I could see what was happening. I saw Glenn Thompson carry Pete's body onto the boat. I recognized Thompson because I'd met him before on the boat. Thompson lifted Pete's body and propped him up on his captain's chair. I thought it was funny that Pete had no shoes. Maybe they were too heavy. I sneezed, and Glenn saw me. He pulled out a knife, and I think he would have killed me, but I told him that I wouldn't tell if he could just get me the good stuff that I'd found in Pete's cabin. I know it was crazy, but I didn't know what else to say. Thompson thought I was a nut case, I guess. Anyway he agreed. I took some more stuff out of Pete's cabin, and Thompson followed me out. I was still stoned, so I sat down on the pier and took some more stuff. I guess I passed out because the next thing I knew, the cops grabbed me and took me to jail. I'm writing all this because I don't know what Thompson will do. He's mad, and he's killed once, but I'm going to see him again after I mail this letter. The money he gave me today was nothing, and I think I'm entitled to a lot more. After all, I've saved his hide for ten years. I'll call you next week when I'm in Portland. See you later.'"

Charlie sighed and put the letter on Pierce's desk. "He signed his name, mailed the letter, but he never made it to Portland."

Jenny patted Gloria's shoulder. "I'm so sorry about your husband, but he did a brave thing. He killed a murderer." She looked at Charlie. "Last night when I accused Glenn, he must have known that the police would follow up and learn the truth eventually."

Pierce said, "I think that Thompson would have cracked. We would have looked for Pete's boots, and even if he'd disposed of them, he'd have panicked as we searched the house." He stood and put his hand on Gloria's shoulder. "I'm sorry about all of this, sorry about Jacob, sorry about Erin. Has there been any change?"

Gloria shook her head. "I want to see her. Will you go with me, Jenny?"

"Of course." She looked at Charlie. "Are you going to the theater this morning for dress rehearsal?"

"Yes, and I'll tell them about Tim's letter. I hope that Ann won't be there because she should be told about this by the police or someone close to her."

Pierce said, "I'll go to her house this morning and show her the letter. She'll be in shock. Her husband's death, and now this." He shook his head. "I hope that her children will be there. She's going to need support."

Jenny nodded. "I hope that she can accept the truth." She wondered how her father would react. Jenny felt that in time she could forgive Ann. Glenn was her husband, and wife should stand up and defend him. Or should she? Did she know the truth about Glenn and play the role of the grieving widow? Jenny shook her head. No, Ann's was no performance last night. She meant every word.

Jenny walked with Gloria to her car. "I need to stop at Louise's for a minute. Come in and have some coffee."

"I could use a cup," Gloria said. She wiped her eyes as she drove. "I'm glad that you're coming with me."

Gloria stopped at Louise's home, and Jenny ran upstairs to shower and change. Gloria walked with Louise into the kitchen. She drank coffee and told Louise about Tim's letter.

"I don't believe that about Pete and the drugs," Louise said. "I knew Pete." She paused and looked out of her kitchen window toward the ocean. "He was..." She turned, and Jenny, who had entered the kitchen, saw tears in her eyes.

"I'm sorry, Louise," Jenny said, "but I think that Tim was writing the truth."

Louise nodded. "Pete was a good person. At least I thought so." She looked back at the window. "If what Tim wrote is true, then

Glenn must have killed him." She stared at Jenny. "And he must have tried to kill you too."

"But I didn't know him that well. I recognized him that night in his car because I'd seen him at the country club and at church, but I never really knew him. And that was ten years ago. Why would he want to kill me now?"

"He must have known that you and Erin were asking questions."

Jenny poured a cup of coffee. "That night on the ferry, the man who threw me overboard said, 'You ask too many questions.'"

"It's also possible that he saw you that night after he killed Pete. You said last night that the lights of his car blinded you."

"But would he remember a high school kid ten years later?"

"He would if he'd just killed someone and didn't want anyone to know."

Jenny sat down at the table and sipped her coffee. "I still don't know how he knew where I was after dinner at the Dolphin and on the Isle au Bas ferry."

"And now he's dead," Gloria said. "You may never know." She stood. "Thank you for the coffee. I need Jenny today." She took Louise's hand. "Jacob was a gentle man, a quiet man. He only went crazy after he'd been drinking. He'd been hitting the bottle a lot since Erin was hurt, and I couldn't be in two places at once." She shook her head. "But it wouldn't have mattered. I never could keep him from drinking."

"I know. Now Jacob's at peace," Louise said, "and he died a hero. He killed a murderer. Remember that."

Gloria nodded. "It makes today a bit easier."

For Jenny, the ride to Portland was a respite from her own concerns and worries. She thought about her aunt's reaction to Pete's drug dealings. Unbelief, regret, tears. She thought about the two dead men at the mortuary and the people left behind to grieve and question. She knew that Gloria would come through unbroken, unbeaten. She wasn't sure about Ann.

When they entered the hospital and walked toward Erin's room, a nurse came to them with outstretched arms. She put her arms around Gloria and smiled. "Erin's waking, Mrs. Gregory. She's going to be all right."

"Praise God! When did this happen?"

"An hour ago. I went to her room and noticed a smile on her face. She didn't open her eyes, but her skin had changed from its usual pallor to a normal color. Her breathing was normal, and she looked so peaceful. Just now, she moved and put her hand to her head."

Gloria and Jenny ran to Erin's room and pushed open the door. The head of Erin's bed had been raised. Her eyes were open, and she moved her fingers.

Gloria ran to the bed and put her arms around her daughter. She cried, looked at Erin, and cried again. A nurse, with gentle hands, pulled Gloria away. "We mustn't jostle her."

Gloria looked up at the nurse and smiled. "I know. I'm her mother."

"Let's give your daughter time to adjust."

That morning, the excitement in room 329 was silently high-pitched. A doctor came and left. Two nurses came and left. Three more doctors came and left. Erin was bathed, fussed over, and two hours later was told that she might dangle her feet if she wished.

Slowly Erin was helped to sit up and put her feet over the side of the bed. She looked at her mother and at Jenny. "I'm okay," she said. Her speech was slurred, and she breathed deeply between each word.

Gloria beamed at Jenny. "It's a miracle."

A nurse brought a tray with milk, a glass of juice, and a soda cracker, and said, "This is her first solid food in almost two weeks."

"Mmm?" Erin looked puzzled.

"That's all right, sweetie," Gloria said. "You had an accident."

Erin drank the juice slowly. She nibbled the cracker and lay back on the bed. "Head aches."

One of the doctors opened the door and beckoned Gloria. Outside in the hall, the doctor said, "Erin's going to have headaches for a while, and she may be unsteady on her feet. I want an ophthalmologist to check her vision, and we'll do some other tests."

"Is she going to be all right?"

"I'm sure that she'll be fine. She's young and healthy. It may take a few days for her to bounce back, perhaps a week, but everything looks good."

Gloria shook the doctor's hand. "Thank you. I have to go home this afternoon, but I'll be back early tomorrow."

"Don't hurry. She's in good hands, and she needs time now to rest and adjust to where she is and what's happened to her."

* * *

Ann Thomson's morning was a continuation of last night's horror. She had been taken to the mortuary to identify her husband officially. Diane was with her, waited in the car and brought her back to the Martin home. Diane gave her a nightgown and an over-the-counter sleep aid that did nothing. She dozed occasionally but was awake most of the night.

At eight o'clock, Diane knocked on her bedroom door. "Chief Pierce is on the phone. He'd like to meet you at your house in half an hour."

Ann got up and dressed. Diane gave her a cup of coffee and drove her to her home. Ann felt like a robot, following orders mechanically. She walked to the door next to the driveway that led to her kitchen and sat at the table.

Diane stood in the doorway. "Do you want me to stay?"

Ann shook her head. "I'll be all right. Thanks for last night."

Diane left, and Ann went upstairs to shower and change before Pierce's visit. He'd talked about searching the house for Pete Clampton's boots. Ann smiled. Let them come, she thought. She shivered as she looked around the bedroom. So many memories of nights in this room, nights when Glenn's anger had spilled over into a rage that had to be quelled with a few well-aimed blows at his wife's buttocks or her stomach. The blows were followed by apologies, promises and, frequently, sex. Of course the children didn't know. How could they?

The door bell rang, and she hurried to answer. Pierce wore a grim look as he walked into the living room.

"I'll make coffee," Ann said.

Pierce shook his head. "No thanks. We have to talk."

Ann stood before him, hands on hips. "I suppose that you want to search the house for those boots. Be my guest."

She was surprised when Pierce took her hand. "Sit down, Ann. I have a letter for you to read, but first I have to talk to you about Glenn."

Ann sat and stared at Pierce, and her stares became blurred with tears as Pierce told her the truth about her husband. Numb, chilled, her mind filled with visions of death, unwanted death and the growing knowledge that Glenn Thompson had killed. She put her head down and sobbed.

Pierce said nothing until Ann's sobbing ebbed. "We have a letter that Tim Brennan wrote just before he was killed." He gave her the letter and waited until she had read all of it.

She gave the letter to Pierce. "It doesn't matter any more about the boots, but if they're here, I think I know where to look." She stood, unsteady on her feet, and led him downstairs to Glenn's room. "This was his special place, and I had orders to keep out."

The walls of the room were covered in dark wood paneling. A thick brown carpet, mounted heads of deer and antelope, a massive desk with neat piles of memo pads and business cards, a table that held a TV. A six-foot chest stood in one corner. It was locked.

"I'll get some tools," Ann said. She left the room and returned with a hammer and a screwdriver. Pierce broke the lock and opened the lid. Inside were two wool blankets. Under the blankets was a pair of well-worn boots, the kind that lobstermen wear when they're out in the ocean with their traps.

Tears fell from Ann's eyes as Pierce lifted them out of the chest. "I didn't wear gloves," he said. "We don't need to worry about fingerprints."

Upstairs, Ann found a plastic bag for the boots. "I need coffee." She plugged in the coffee maker. "I had this ready for breakfast this morning. I made it before we drove to the theater last night, Glenn and I."

"I'll have a cup too. God, I hate this, Ann."

"I know, Harry. That's your job."

They sat in the kitchen and waited for the coffee. "What will you do now?" he asked.

"I don't know. I called the kids last night before I went to the mortuary. They'll be here this morning. It's going to be such a shock for them. They loved their father."

Pierce finished his coffee, picked up the boots and walked to the door with Ann. As he opened the door of his squad car, he saw a green SUV pull into the driveway. "Your kids are here," he called. "You'll be okay."

Ann nodded and went to the side door. Kevin and Janet ran to their mother and hugged her. "Oh, Mom," Janet cried, "What happened? How did he die?"

Kevin stood back. "Is he really dead?'

Ann nodded and told them about the shooting. "It was horrible. He died instantly, blood all over."

They sat at the kitchen table as Ann described the scene at the theater. She said nothing about Pierce's visit. Tim's letter and the boots would come later.

"Why did the guy shoot my dad?" Kevin asked.

"It was a private matter. The man was drunk."

Janet put her head on the table and sobbed. Kevin stared at the ceiling. "You're okay?" he asked.

Ann nodded. "I'll get through it now that you're here."

Kevin stood and put his arms around his mother's shoulders. "I'm so glad you're okay. I thought that maybe Dad had hit you again and that you decided that you'd had enough."

Ann looked up and stared at her son. "What do you mean?"

"Come off it, Mom," he said. "Janet and I knew that Dad knocked you around. You never said anything, and we didn't know what to do."

"I talked to my high school counselor once," Janet said, "but she didn't want to get involved. She thought that I was probably exaggerating, acting emotional over nothing."

Ann looked at her children. "I didn't want you to know. It had nothing to do with you, and I was able to cope." She sat back in her chair and thought about her hours at the cabin with David. Yes, she'd been able to cope, thanks to a pair of arms that held her, hands that stroked her back and would never, never hit with brutal force.

She put her head on the table and thought about the words she'd spoken to David's daughter last night, how she'd lashed out at her as the girl had spoken the truth about her husband. Would Jenny forgive her? Would David?

She looked up at her son and daughter. "We'll get through this together. You're going to hear terrible news about your father, and I want you to brave the storm and hold your heads up high. We can't change the past." She took their hands. "I'm glad you're here. I couldn't go through this without you."

* * *

Pierce left the Thompson home, returned to headquarters and drafted Marling and Williams. "We're going out to Thompson's construction company, and I don't know what we'll find. Did Bill send over the search warrant?"

"Yes," Marling answered. "I have the county attorney's document in my pocket."

When they stopped at the construction company, it looked deserted, but Pierce noted the neat appearance of the yard. He knocked on the office door, and a dark-skinned, heavy-set man in jeans and a brown sweat shirt opened it.

He glared at Pierce and looked beyond him at the police car. "What do you want?"

Pierce flashed his badge, introduced his men and asked, "Are you in charge when Thompson's not here?"

The man nodded. "I am Oscar Mendes, Mr. Thompson's foreman." He didn't move away from the door, and his eyes were narrow slits. "Mr. Thompson isn't here."

"I know, and that's why we're here." He gave Mendes a brief account of last night's shooting. "Thompson's dead, and we need to look around. I have a search warrant." Pierce spoke quickly as he looked at Mendes, not certain what the man's reaction would be.

Mendes moved back. He looked more confused than angry. "You can look around. I don't know what to do about the men." He sat down in Thompson's chair. "Do you want to talk to the men? They don't speak English, but I can interpret for you."

At that moment, Pierce had a sixth sense. He sat down. "Where do your men come from? I noticed a building near the office that looked like a dormitory. Do the men live there?"

Mendes nodded. "Mr. Thompson brings them here and they stay for a while, then they leave in a van."

"How many leave at one time?"

"Six maybe."

"You know where they came from and where they're going, so you might as well tell us now. It will save time later, and if you cooperate, we may be able to help you."

Mendes looked at the floor. "I have worked for Mr. Thompson for over twelve years. I came here with the first group of people that Mr. Clampton brought."

Pierce stood and looked down at Mendes. "Are you telling me that Pete Clampton brought illegal immigrants to Sowatna?"

Mendes nodded. "We met Clampton's boat out at sea, and he brought us here. Some of us were sick. It was a long trip from Central America to the place where we met Clampton's boat."

Pierce sat down again and looked up at Marling and Williams. "Can you believe this? My God! Pete had a thriving business. Drugs and illegals. I wonder what else he did in his spare time."

"Caught lobsters," Marling said. "When I had my car fixed at Hendricks Ford last year, Mr. Hendricks said that he used to buy lobsters from Pete for his restaurants."

Pierce shook his head. "We'll have to call in the Drug Enforcement Agency and the immigration people. This is too much for headquarters." He sighed and looked at Mendes. "You might as well show us the dormitory, Oscar. We'll need the names and addresses of your crew. Williams, call the department and ask them to send another squad car. You and Marling can start with the names and go through the files here. I need to get back to the real world."

Pierce walked to the office door. "You help my men, *comprende*? I'm leaving now."

He drove back to headquarters still pondering the secret life of Pete Clampton.

CHAPTER TWENTY-TWO

David McKnight, president of the Old Maine Bank & Trust Company, father of Jenny McKnight and lover of Ann Thompson, sat in his black leather arm chair in front of his TV. He checked his watch. Six a.m. It was Saturday now. He leaned forward and put both hands on his forehead. Slowly he stood and moved to the kitchen. In robot movements, he made coffee and sat at the kitchen table. He rubbed the stubble on his chin and looked at his wrinkled sport coat and moaned. What had happened to his life?

The events of the last twelve hours had shattered his dreams and his hopes. He relived again last night's dress rehearsal.

Jenny had stood, run to Glenn Thompson and accused him of murder while he had sat with Louise, stunned, speechless. Louise had run up the steps to join Jenny, and still he sat. When Ann grabbed Jenny's arm and shouted accusations, he had stood, ready to rush forward and comfort his daughter, but what could he do? If he comforted Jenny, he'd lose Ann. If he comforted Ann, he'd lose Jenny. So he had stood in the front row, his emotions torn and twisted. When Jacob fired his gun and Ann ran to her husband, he could do nothing. He had tried to reach Jenny but stopped when Charlie became his daughter's comforter. Helpless, unable to take action, he had walked to the side door of the theater and driven home, numb, unbelieving, his world a meaningless, formless mass of swirling molecules. Nothing stable, nothing recognizable.

He had come home and sat in front of the TV, and he had sat there all night. He may have dozed. Now it was Saturday morning, and, still in shock, he wondered what to do. Should he call Jenny? Should he call Ann? Should he drink two bottles of Scotch and slip into the abyss? He couldn't call anyone at six o'clock, and he feared that he wouldn't die with two fifths of Scotch in his stomach. He'd merely be violently ill. So he sat in his kitchen and did nothing.

He felt better after three cups of coffee. He showered and dressed. Ann would need him this morning, he thought. He drove to her house and was startled to see a police car in front. As he passed slowly, he saw a green SUV pull into her driveway. He drove on to the cabin. He wouldn't find Ann there, but he'd find comforting memories.

* * *

Charlie drove to the theater at ten o'clock, Saturday morning. As he started down the aisle, he paused at the last row. The body of Jacob Gregory was gone, but Charlie could still see the man sprawled across the arm of the seat, his eyes and mouth open. Charlie sidestepped around the place on the aisle where the body of Glenn Thompson had lain. The floor was clean now, but Charlie could still see the blood.

He found Michael perched on his stool with his clipboard. The actors milled around on stage, unsure of their places. Louise moved about, straightening a collar, adjusting a skirt. She waved to Charlie.

Michael smiled at Charlie and called to the cast. "Okay, let's take it from the top." The actors moved quickly to their places on or off the stage. "Bailiff, you may begin."

Charlie noticed that the first lines were unsteady, barely audible, but as the play progressed, the actor within came forth, and by the middle of Act One, the play moved smoothly. Michael made notes on his clipboard and gave suggestions at the close of each act. His words were upbeat and encouraging. The director knew how to bring out the best in his cast.

After he'd made comments and suggestions at the end of Act Three, Michael turned to Charlie. "What do you think of your play, Mr. Author?"

Charlie laughed. "It's great. While I was listening this morning, I asked myself, did I actually write those lines?"

"It went well considering last night's fiasco." He called to the players. "Be here at seven o'clock tonight. We want to start promptly at eight."

"Do you have time for lunch?" Charlie asked.

"Yes. I'll meet you at the Expresso."

Lunch was hurried, but coffee was leisurely. "I'm sure you noticed Charlotte's attire last night," Michael said.

Charlie laughed. "I thought she was upstaging the actors."

Michael smiled. "We had a short visit before I left. 'Understated' will be tonight's dress."

"When I first arrived in Sowatna, Colin Greene told me that Charlotte had a keen mind and atrocious taste in clothes. He was right."

They finished lunch, and Charlie drove to police headquarters. He stopped at the front desk, and Sharon said, "You can stick your head in the door, but you might not get any farther. Chief Pierce has been on the phone straight time."

Charlie did put his head in the door, and Pierce beckoned him to a chair. He put down the phone and unwrapped a stick of gum. "I went to the Thompson house this morning. I had to tell Ann the terrible truth about her husband. After she read the letter, we went downstairs and found Pete's boots. She's going to need real guts to survive, but her kids came as I left. She won't be alone."

He told Charlie about his trip to the Thompson Construction Company.

"Marling and Williams are there now going through the files. Thompson was a neatnik, so I'm sure that everything's been recorded even though the entire operation was totally illegal. The immigration people told me to hold the workers there, and my officers will patrol the place until the authorities arrive tomorrow."

Charlie had worked his BlackBerry. "I have enough information for about ten pages in the Chronicle. Charlotte should be pleased."

Pierce was serious. "It's dicey, Charlie. Pete didn't have a family, but Thompson has a wife and kids here."

"I know, and I'll discuss everything with Charlotte before anything goes to press. She's a wise woman, and she'll make the right decisions."

Pierce nodded. "What's crazy is that we don't even know the motive behind Pete's murder. Why did Thompson kill him? I think it had something to do with the illegals Pete brought in, but I don't know, and I think that Oscar Mendes knows more than what he said this morning. We'll bring him in for questioning."

"I guess it really doesn't matter any more. That was then, but if Thompson was still importing illegal immigrants, that's now."

"Right. We need to know who Thompson was dealing with after he killed Pete."

Charlie left the station and called Jenny on his cell phone. He listened as Jenny told him about Erin's recovery. "It's a miracle. She's going to be all right."

"When are you coming home?"

"I'm leaving now. I'll just have time for a quick snack and a change of clothes before the performance."

"And what are your plans after the play?"

"I'm thinking of a quiet supper with the author. Soft music, a glass of wine. I might wear something delicate and slinky."

"Your plan sounds perfect, but I think that the play's author will probably want you to remove that something delicate and slinky. It might wrinkle."

Charlie heard a soft giggle. Opening night promised to be a greater success than he imagined.

Jenny told Louise the good news about Erin as soon as she came home. "I can't wait to see her tomorrow. She'll have a lot of catching up to do."

She and Louise had a bowl of soup and changed for the performance. "I want to be there early enough to check the sets."

"And I want to be sure that everyone's dressed properly. Last-minute alterations can be a problem."

They sat down in the front row and looked at the stage. At seven o'clock, it was ready for Act One. Cast members walked around, not going anywhere. "Opening night jitters," Jenny said. "I feel it too."

Michael walked onto the stage, nodded to Louise and Jenny and visited with the cast. As soon as they were all present, he looked at his watch. "Thirty minutes until show time. This is it, our magic moment, the night we've dreamed and worried about. You've given six weeks of your summer for tonight, and when the last line is spoken, you'll know that it was worth every minute. Break a leg."

Voices and nods of approval. Jenny saw admiration in the eyes of each cast member. Michael would always be a special person in their lives. For the younger ones, he might have led them into a career in the theater. For Jenny too, he was special. They had formed a bond this summer, and she hoped that they'd meet again. She wanted, needed to stay close to him. She couldn't explain her feelings for Michael. Why try? She thought about the first time they'd met and remembered that ridiculous scene in the deli when her aunt and Michael had slipped to the floor and laughed. When they came to the table, Louise had been tense, nervous. She'd known Michael in St. Paul, she had said. Nothing more. Tonight, Jenny turned to Louise and saw admiration in her eyes also. Was there something more? Jenny couldn't ask. If Louise had wanted to elaborate on her brief explanation at the Lobster Shack, she would have done so. She had never mentioned it again, and Jenny, knowing that her aunt was a private person, hadn't asked.

Now they sat together as the audience filled every seat. At eight o'clock, Michael came on stage and welcomed everyone.

"You are in for a special treat tonight, the premier showing of Charlie Brewster's new drama, *Tangled Trap Lines*. You'll notice that we have no curtain and that the stage is divided into two scenes, the court room and a living room. Lights turned off and on will indicate which side of the stage to watch, and because the trial involves past and present actions on stage left, the transition will move smoothly."

He turned and smiled off stage. "Now I want you to meet the author. Charlie will speak later and perhaps take questions from the audience." Michael gave him a questioning look as Charlie walked out from the wings.

"And please welcome Diane Martin, President of the Sowatna Arts Council." He motioned for Diane to join them on the stage.

"Thank you," Diane said. "This is our first annual summer theater presentation. Next year we may have a curtain and carpeting." The audience laughed. She praised Michael and the cast for six weeks of hard work and introduced the members of the Arts Council who were in the audience.

Michael took the microphone from Diane, and she and Charlie walked off to the wings. Michael looked up at the control booth. "Adam Roberts is our sound and light technician. We're grateful for his expertise and the hours he's spent connecting all of the equipment." Adam waved, and the audience applauded.

Michael continued. "You have noticed the court room. Every murder trial must have a jury. Tonight we need twelve of you to serve on the panel." He paused as the audience considered this new twist in audience participation. "The cast will take their places, the house lights will dim only slightly, and when the judge asks the bailiff to bring in the jury, that's your cue to come from the audience and walk up these steps. Ready?"

He smiled at the audience. "And now, the Sowatna Arts Council proudly presents *Tangled Trap Lines*."

Michael walked to the wings as the audience applauded.

The bailiff's lines, "Hear ye, hear ye," were clear, and the judge appeared when announced. Jenny in the front row crossed her fingers when the judge asked the jury to come forward. She saw Charlotte Quincy neatly and sedately attired in a black suit and matching, featherless hat ascend the steps and walk to the jury box. Because of Jenny's accusation and the ensuing drama, neither Genevieve Upton nor George Hendricks had had a chance to practice, but they followed Charlotte as they'd been instructed. Jenny uncrossed her fingers as nine more from the audience came forward and took the oath.

The first act went well, and Jenny was totally engulfed in the action and dialogue. She knew that Charlie was no ordinary newspaper reporter. The man she loved was a literary genius! At the close of Act One and after the applause, the cast walked to the wings, and jury returned to their seats.

Michael returned to the center of the stage with his microphone. "Wasn't our jury wonderful?" Following the applause, he said. "You can return to the jury box at the beginning of the next act and remain there until the judge asks you to retire and return with your verdict. Is Brian Potter guilty or innocent? His life is in your hands." Jenny heard nervous laughter from the jurors.

Michael continued. "You will notice that there is no intermission between the acts. Intermission will occur during the jury's deliberations. Jury, you may return to the jury box."

Acts Two and Three were almost perfect, and Jenny was again awed by the talent and dedication of the cast. When the jury filed out through the door next to the jury box, Adam turned on the house lights. People stood and stretched. Many walked outside to have a cigarette or to get some fresh air.

Ten minutes later, Adam blinked the house lights, and people returned to their seats. The footlights came on and floodlights illumined the court room. The judge, bailiff, court reporter, clerk of courts, the accused and his attorneys, the prosecuting attorney and his staff, the heroine and the spectators waited as the jury returned and sat in the jury box.

"Has the jury returned with a verdict?" the judge asked.

"Yes, your honor," Charlotte said. She handed the bailiff a note, and the bailiff gave it to the judge who returned it to him.

"Will you please read the verdict?"

"We find the defendant not guilty."

The hero shook hands with his attorney, and the heroine left her seat in the spectators' section and ran to embrace the hero.

"Now will you marry me?" he asked. "Our lives are beginning all over again."

The actors in the court room paused and looked at the audience. They were joined by those who came from the wings, and the entire cast walked to the front of the stage and bowed.

The audience rose to its feet, applauded and whistled. Michael came on stage, and the cast joined the applause. Michael waited and motioned for silence. The audience sat, and Michael spoke.

"Weren't they fantastic?" He acknowledged the cast and beckoned Charlie from the wings. "Charlie, we have a hit on our hands if tonight's audience is any indication." More applause. Michael waved to the control booth. "Thanks, Adam." He paused. "I also want to thank two people who have worked behind the scenes, Louise Campbell who was in charge of costumes and Jenny McKnight who was my assistant and in charge of the sets."

"Now, Charlie," Michael said, "I'm sure that you want to say something and perhaps take questions from the audience."

Jenny had never seen Charlie so embarrassed and tongue tied. She watched him lift his shoulders and push back his hair. He took the microphone and smiled at the audience. He thanked everyone in the audience, everyone on stage, everyone behind the stage and his parents who couldn't be here tonight but he surely wish that they had been in the audience. Jenny put her hands over her face and tried not to laugh.

Charlie must have seen her because he straightened up and asked for questions.

"How long did it take to write the play?" someone asked.

"It's been in my head for about four years, ever since I read about the murder of Pete Clampton while I was a reporter for the Miami Herald."

Another asked, "What was so special about that case?"

"I'd covered murders for the paper, but this one intrigued me because of the setting and the people involved. The grand jury's verdict seemed inconclusive, and I thought that there were several loose ends." He looked at Jenny. "I didn't realize how many loose ends there were until I started asking questions here, and that's why I shifted the play's focus to the relationships between the characters."

Another stood. "I've taught creative writing courses at a university and have read and seen dozens of dramas. Mr. Brewster, yours is one of the finest pieces of dramatic writing I've heard in years."

Charlie was speechless during the applause.

Diane Martin walked to the center of the stage. "If you enjoyed tonight's performance, tell your friends. There will be a two o'clock matinee and an eight o'clock evening performance tomorrow and a final performance Monday evening at eight. Thank you all for coming."

The audience rose and walked slowly to the exits. Cast members hugged, laughed, and yawned. Charlotte and the other eleven still stood in the jury box. Diane shook Charlotte's hand. "You were wonderful, but I'm curious. When you retired to study the case and render a verdict, what did Michael and Charlie say to you?"

Charlotte and the others laughed. "Charlie told us that our verdict should be 'not guilty,' but if it weren't, the cast had other lines memorized for a 'guilty' verdict. He said that the verdict itself wasn't important because the inner strengths of the hero and heroine had developed throughout the drama, and the audience would know that guilty or not, they would each find inner peace and the real meaning of a true relationship."

Diane nodded. "That's what makes Charlie's play such a masterpiece. I became so involved with the main characters that

I forgot where I was. Charlie's dialogue was clear and natural. I actually knew those people."

The librarian said, "I felt it too. I read a lot, and I know what holds a reader's or an audience's attention. Charlie has that gift. At first I wasn't keen on sitting in the jury box during the entire performance, but I became so interested in the play that I, like Diane, forgot where I was."

Jenny climbed the steps and hugged Charlie. "It's all so wonderful, and everyone was wonderful, and you're wonderful." She giggled. "Isn't that wonderful?"

"I'll remember that line for my next play," Charlie said and laughed.

Michael broke away from a crowd of drama enthusiasts and put his arm around Jenny. "I hope that Adam got it all on his video. It'll be a great addition to my library, and if it's good enough, it could be shown at special gatherings." He looked at Charlie. "I'm going to find out about a copyright. The play should be submitted to high-level contests, but you don't want anyone to take it from you. It can happen. I have a friend in the publishing business who can walk you through the procedures. He's good, and he's honest."

"Thanks, Michael. I'll still up there in the stratosphere. When I come down tomorrow, we'll talk." He turned to Jenny. "Right now, Jenny and I have a date."

They left the theater and found Charlie's car. He climbed behind the wheel and leaned back against the seat. "I can't believe tonight. It was a beautiful, fantastic dream."

Jenny took his hand. "Yes." She had so much to say but couldn't find the words. A once-in-a-lifetime euphoria filled every corner of her mind.

Charlie started the car. "I have a bottle of wine breathing and a pizza ready to heat. Okay?"

Jenny nodded. "It sounds ideal, a perfect ending for opening night."

"As the play's hero said, 'Now will you marry me? Our lives are beginning all over again.'"

* * *

Louise joined everyone on the stage as the audience left the theater. She told the cast, "You're in charge of your costumes until the play ends on Monday night. We don't want any lost items."

Colin laughed. "I wear my costume every day in my law office. I wouldn't dare lose any of it." He took Louise's hand and led her away from the others. "What are your plans for the evening?" He looked at his watch. "I know it's too late for a five-course dinner, but we could have something light. I didn't eat much before the play."

"I didn't either. I can make an omelet at my house."

"That would be perfect. I'll follow you home."

Louise's mind raced as she left the theater. She remembered Colin's words after he'd kissed her, something about opening night. Would the omelet end the evening, and if it didn't? She thought she knew the answer.

* * *

George and Doris Hendricks left the theater after congratulating Michael and Charlie. Doris took George's hand as they walked to the car. "The play was excellent. I don't know how they pulled it together after last night."

George shook his head. "It was really amazing. I can still hear Jenny screaming at Glenn, and that shot! It sounded like a cannon."

"Was she correct? Did Glenn really kill Pete?"

"I think so. Glenn and I used to have a few beers together. He knew that I bought lobsters from Pete, so one night last year, after we'd had more than a few beers, I told him about my dealings with Pete. I thought he was ripping me off but I couldn't prove it. Glenn told me that Pete had transported immigrants to work for him, and he thought, too, that Pete was charging too much. There was something in his eyes, and it wasn't the beer. I can't explain it."

When they were home, Doris asked, "How about a drink? I could use one." She went to the kitchen and poured two shot glasses of Chivas Regal. "To hell with soda tonight," she said, "I need something strong."

George looked puzzled. "Why? Is something wrong?"

Everybody Knew Pete

Doris downed her drink and stared at George. "No, something's right." She sat down and looked at the floor. "All these years, I was afraid that you had killed Pete Clampton."

"What?" George stood over her. "What are you saying? You think that I could kill someone? What kind of a guy do you think I am?"

Doris looked up at him. "I knew that you had an argument with Pete about the lobsters. You came home that night with daggers in your eyes. You swore and said that Pete was a thief and a cheat and didn't deserve to live. That's what you said, George. And two days later, Pete was found dead on his boat."

George went to the kitchen and returned with the bottle of Scotch. He poured each of them another shot. "I was mad. I admit it, but dammit, Doris, I'd never kill anyone. You should know that."

Doris nodded. "But then you were upset when you heard about Charlie Brewster's play, and that made me even more suspicious. Why do you think I spend so much time on my boat? I have to get away from here, even from you, George."

"And you've kept this evil thing in your mind all these years and never asked me for the truth?"

Doris sipped her drink. "I guess I was afraid to ask."

George stood. "I'm going to bed, and I'll sleep in the guest room. I have a lot to think about. I won't sleep much."

"I understand." She looked up at her husband. "I'm sorry, George. I know that I overreact sometimes. I've handled it badly. I went sailing instead of telling you about my fears. I was wrong."

"I was wrong too. I shouldn't have unloaded my anger on you." He walked upstairs, got his pajamas and lay down in the guest room. He stared up at the ceiling. What had happened since the 'I do's'? They'd both lost something, and he wondered if they'd ever find it again.

CHAPTER TWENTY-THREE

Jenny lay close to Charlie and, as she awoke, she reached for his hand. "Mmm," she whispered. "It's nice to find a hand beside me."

"How do you like what the hand's attached to?" He moved her hand down his body.

"That's nice too." She raised up. "Tell me again what you like."

He told her and showed her. For Jenny, it was always the first time with Charlie, the first time she'd given and taken freely and completely. They lay together taking deep breaths.

Charlie stroked her hair. "I love you, Jenny. I meant what I said last night. I want to marry you. I never thought I could say those words again to anyone. I came here hurt and bleeding, and a young woman, a psychic, licked my wounds and made me whole again. Is that what's known as a psychic phenomenon?"

Jenny smiled. "I wasn't looking for romance either. I came home to rid myself of nightmares and visions. Now my only vision is you in bed with me. It's too good to be true, so it must be a vision."

Charlie rubbed her back. "When the play's over, we need to do some serious planning. Will you like this apartment after you're Mrs. Charlie Brewster?"

Jenny sat up, leaned over and kissed his eyebrows. "I will love this apartment after we're married, but I won't be Mrs. Charlie Brewster. I want to keep my own name, darling. Our adorable children can be Brewsters, but I'll still be Jenny McKnight."

Charlie laughed. "That's fine with me. You can have any name you want. Just be my wife."

They rose, showered together, dressed and ate a hurried breakfast. "I won't take time for church this morning because I want to drive to Portland. Erin should be fully awake by now. Will you need me during the matinee?"

"No. I'll tell Michael where you are, and he'll understand. Erin's accident was hard on him too, and he'll be relieved that she's mending."

The drive to Portland was uneventful. She ran into the hospital and found Erin sitting up in bed, her eyes bright and focused.

Jenny hugged her carefully. "They told us not to jostle you."

Erin smiled. "I've been jostled, poked and examined thoroughly. The people here have been efficient and kind, and God, Jenny, I'm glad I'm alive to appreciate them. I can't believe that today is the last day of August. It's frightening to have lost so many days out of my life."

"But you're alive, thank God. If you had died..." Jenny caught herself before the tears came. "You weren't the target that night. I was. Glenn Thompson had it all planned perfectly."

"Tell me what happened Friday night at dress rehearsal. Mom didn't know the whole story, and she was so upset about Dad that she really didn't want details."

Jenny told her what she needed to hear. "I'm so sorry about your dad, Erin, but he died a hero. Did your mother show you the letter that Tim wrote to you the day he was killed?"

"No, the police have it. Mom thinks that she must have dropped it when she picked up the mail in our box in front of the house. It was under that bush, and nobody saw it until Dad raked the yard."

Erin moved in bed and put her hand on her forehead. "I need to take something for my headache. She reached across her table and found a bottle of aspirin. "I take these when I need them. It's not often." She lay back in bed. "Now tell me all about opening night."

Jenny gave her a complete report. "Charlie's play was a smashing success. Michael's a fine director, and the cast outdid themselves. They rehearsed yesterday morning and somehow managed to pull it all together. They're real troupers."

"And Charlie?"

Jenny felt her cheeks grow warm. "I won't say it was love at first sight, and I was so angry when he told us to forget about our investigation."

Erin laughed. "I remember. He was a real schmuck." She sighed. "The path of true love is never straight. It is true love, isn't it?"

"I'm sure it is. He recited the last line of his play when he asked me to marry him, and I said yes. I'll look for a teaching job next year in Sowatna."

"I'm happy for you. Have you had any more visions?"

"No. The last one occurred when your father died." Jenny didn't want to describe her vision. The death's head was gruesome, and she knew that she'd never see it again.

They heard a knock on the door, and a man slowly pushed it open. Both Jenny and Erin stared at him, Jenny because she'd never seen him before, and Erin because she recognized him.

"Richard Evans!" Erin exclaimed. "How did you know I was here?"

Evans walked to her bed and stroked her hand. "I knew because I've been in and out of this room since August nineteenth, the day after you were brought here."

"I don't understand," Erin said. She waved at Jenny. "This is my friend, Jenny McKnight. She was with me on the stage."

"I know all about the accident. I'd been following you for weeks, afraid that something like this might happen. That was my assignment."

"Your what?" Jenny asked. "What do you mean?"

Evans sat down and gave Jenny a card. She read it aloud. "Richard E. Evans, Special Investigator, Drug Enforcement Agency." She looked at Evans. "You're a narcotics agent?"

Evans nodded. "I've been with the department ever since I left the Center, sober and in need of employment. I wanted to get away from the church and do something meaningful. I felt that I'd wasted too much time in a career I hated. I'd used drugs and knew what they did to people, so I joined the department."

"But you live in such a poor part of town," Erin said. "Don't they pay you enough?"

Evans laughed. "I live there because these are the folks that need help. You almost blew my cover when you came to see me, Erin."

"No wonder you were so angry. But why did you follow me?"

"The department has been watching Glenn Thompson ever since Pete Clampton was killed ten years ago. Sometimes it takes that long. He always covered his tracks, picking up shipments at places you'd never expect. We didn't learn about his illegal immigrants until we grabbed one of his men and charged him with possession of a controlled substance."

Jenny shook her head. "I don't get it. A big agency with so many employees, and you couldn't nab Glenn Thompson?"

"We don't always win the first race. You'll be interested in this, Jenny. When we picked up this little guy in Sowatna for possession, he was scared out of his pants. He cried, said he didn't want to go home and was only doing what his boss told him to do."

"And what was that?"

"Spy on you, Jenny. He was a little fellow, dark skin and hair, and he wore dark coveralls. He had a pocket-sized walkie-talkie, and he watched you and reported to Thompson."

Jenny was stunned. "That's how Glenn knew when we left the Dolphin that night and when we took the Isle au Bas ferry."

"Yes. You wouldn't have noticed him. He was careful and almost invisible."

"I can't wait to tell Charlie. He may want to put this in his next play."

"I attended the play last night," Evans said. "It was a winner." He looked at his watch. "You'll miss the matinee today."

"I know, but I wanted to see Erin." Jenny sensed that Evans wanted to speak to Erin alone. She stood and kissed Erin. "I'll come back tomorrow. Is there anything you need at home?"

Erin shook her head. "Mom will be here later this afternoon. Thanks. I'll see you tomorrow."

Jenny walked to her car and punched in Charlie's number on her cell phone. "You'd better sit down, honey. Richard Evans, the former Reverend Evans, is a narc who has been following Erin to protect her, and now he's with her at the hospital."

Jenny thought that her phone had died when Charlie said at last, "A narc, and he's been following Erin to protect her? He didn't do a very good job the night of dress rehearsal."

"He wasn't there. When she came to the theater that night, she said that no one was following her. Maybe Evans was on another case."

"That's possible. I have a lot of questions, but they can wait because I have to be at the theater."

"I'll see you after the play. You won't have much time between the matinee and the evening performance."

"No, but I'll be with you, and you can help me put my clothes back on."

"You're a sex fiend, Mr. Brewster. I'd report you to the authorities, but I was thinking along those same lines."

* * *

Louise rolled over in her bed and looked at the clock. Six a.m. She rolled back and touched Colin's shoulder.

"It's time to wake up. You should leave before the church crowd arrives and sees your car parked in front of my house."

Colin kissed her cheek. "Yes. If we were in New York City, no one would notice."

"You're so right, but the police might have towed your car, and you'd have a ticket for all-night parking."

Colin sat up and began to dress. "I should have driven home about four o'clock, but I didn't want to leave you." He looked down at her. "I've wanted this for us for so long."

Louise got up and put her arms around Colin. "You've always been a special person to me but not in a sexual way. We've been friends for a long time, and you've helped me when I needed you. I'll always treasure your caring about me."

She kissed him with deep emotion. "When you kissed me after dress rehearsal, something inside hit me on the forehead and said, 'You dummy! Where have you been? You know that you've always cared for him. You're finally waking up.'"

Colin put his hands on her shoulders. "It's never too late to wake up."

She helped him button his shirt. "May I make coffee for you before you leave?"

"No, I must get home. I have a better idea. I'll see you in church, and we'll have brunch together. I won't have to be at the theater until one-thirty. Will you come to the matinee?"

"I won't miss any of the performances. I might be needed."

Colin ran down the stairs, and Louise heard the front door slam and his car's motor start. She lay back in bed and hugged his pillow. She had put sexual instincts behind her and busied herself with her craft shop and Jenny. She thought about Michael, her first real love after high school and college romances. Having sex with him was something you did secretly, and that was part of the thrill. She didn't know if Michael found sex to be as exciting as she did, and after she read his letter, she wondered if he'd only performed because that's what he was supposed to do. Dear Michael. She was glad now that he'd come to Sowatna. She admired his skill as a director, his empathy with the cast. She knew that the people respected and liked him. A special person in her life. She wondered about his association with Jenny, his daughter. Could he ever imagine that Jenny might be his? He'd lived almost thirty years never knowing that he had fathered a child.

As Louise dressed, she looked in the mirror and silently asked her image if she should divulge Jenny's true identity. The image shook her head. No. Only David knew that Louise was Jenny's mother. Don't rock the boat, she thought. The waves of a shocking revelation might sink the craft that had sailed smoothly for thirty years. Michael might see himself in Jenny and wonder, but he would never know.

She went next door to the Presbyterian Church and half-listened to Neil Conway's sermon. Her thoughts were of Colin who sat in a pew two rows ahead of her. He didn't turn his head or acknowledge her presence, and Louise smiled. They would meet after church, and brunch would give them an opportunity to talk about last night. And after last night? In her mind, she pushed the future ahead where it belonged.

* * *

When Jenny left her hospital room, Erin studied Richard Evans. She remembered the interview, and confusion reigned supreme.

"I still can't understand your being with the drug agency, following me, coming here while I was in a coma."

Evans laughed. "I enjoyed the assignment. The more I learned about you, the more I enjoyed it. You're an excellent employee at the Center, and you've helped many people. When you came in here unconscious, I beat up on myself. Maybe if I could have followed you, I might have prevented the accident."

"It wasn't an accident. Jenny told me that Glenn Thompson planned it well, but Jenny left to meet Charlie, and I moved over to her spot on the stage. I don't know why. It was an automatic move. Did you know Tim Brennan?"

"No. Someone else had his case. I'm sorry that he was killed, but I don't think he'd have ever kicked the habit."

"I wish I knew who sold Dad his drugs after Tim was killed."

"So do I. Too many unanswered questions."

"This whole affair has been filled with unanswered questions, Mr. Evans. Why did Glenn kill Pete?"

"We'll find out, and call me Richard."

Erin smiled. "I hope that I can be released soon. I'm anxious to get back to work and lead a normal life."

"My life is never normal, but I'd like to be a part of yours. How about dinner after work sometime when you're feeling better?"

"I'd like that."

Evans stood. "I must leave, but I'll be back. I can take you home when they dismiss you."

"Thanks. I'll call if I need you."

Evans left, and Erin lay back in bed. She was tired and shocked to learn Evans's identity. She dozed until her mother knocked.

"I brought lunch," Gloria said. "Tomorrow I'll be signing papers and making funeral arrangements. I called Jacob's closest relatives yesterday and talked to a reporter and the police department. Everyone's helpful, trying to make it easier for me."

Erin's smile was weak. "I wish that I could help now, but I don't know how long I'll be here. I had a visitor this morning."

Gloria nodded as she listened to Erin's report of Evans's visit. "Nothing surprises me any more. I'm sorry that he didn't follow you Friday night."

"He couldn't have prevented the accident. No one could. I have to catch up on my life, adjust to what happened Friday night. Guilt too, wishing that I could have helped Dad."

"We both know that we couldn't help him, but we'll still feel guilty. The next few days will be tough, but I'll manage. All I have to do is think about your recovery, and nothing will be too difficult."

* * *

Sunday's matinee was smooth and uneventful. Michael's introduction and Diane and Charlie's remarks were appropriate. Every seat was filled, and jury members came up from the audience when asked.

Louise had spent time with Colin before the show, helped with his tie, gave him her comb. Charlie smiled. Maybe there'd be a double wedding.

After the matinee, he rushed home to meet Jenny. She had found two turkey dinners in his freezer and made iced tea. He kissed her. "Now tell me more about Richard Evans."

"I was amazed when he told me how Glenn Thompson knew about our dinner date and our ferry trip. I don't remember seeing anyone lurking, but Evans said that the man who followed me was small and almost inconspicuous."

"What about Evans?"

"He's good looking, has a ponytail, dresses well, and I think he has more than a professional interest in Erin. Of course he's much too old for her."

"Hey, what's fifteen or so years among friends?"

"Of course, and it takes men longer to mature."

Charlie reached over and patted her cheek. "Sexist comments are off limits, unless you're talking about going to bed." He looked at his watch. "And just enough time before dinner."

* * *

Jenny sat with Charlie in the wings during Sunday night's performance. They drank sodas and acknowledged the cast as they made entrances and exits. Charlie's closing remarks were relaxed and informative, and the questions from the audience gave him an opportunity to explain his change of focus from the murder of Pete Clampton to relationships.

He cleared his throat. "By now, most of you have learned who killed Pete Clampton ten years ago. Everyone is shocked and saddened. Many of you have known the Thompson family for a long time, and Glenn's crew worked hard this summer to complete the renovation. We don't know why Pete was killed. We may never know. Please give your support to the family."

Diane stood by Charlie and took the microphone. "Thank you for coming. Tomorrow night will be our final performance. Come back and bring your friends."

As the audience left, Jenny joined Charlie and Diane. "It went well tonight, but I'm sure that you're all exhausted after two performances in one day."

"Yes," Diane said, "but the adrenaline flows. Tuesday morning will be a downer."

"Not if you start thinking about next year."

Michael came from backstage. "I have some ideas for next year, but it's important to have an Arts Council meeting next week while everything's fresh. This weekend has been a shocker, an upper and a downer. Too much adrenaline for everyone. We'll all need a few days to digest it."

Louise and Colin walked to the footlights. "I almost forgot my first lines at the beginning of the play," Colin said.

"That's normal," Michael said, "and you didn't hesitate. I'm pleased with all three performances. It was hard to make it work after the first dress rehearsal."

Jenny stood back and rubbed her eyebrows. "It was awful," she said, almost in a whisper. "I can't imagine what Ann's going through." She stopped. How would Ann feel now knowing that her husband had killed a man? Would she remember her accusations as Glenn stormed off the stage? And what about David, her dad? She hoped that one day she might be able to talk with him about what happened that night. Now she wanted to be with Louise. She couldn't explain her need for family. She only knew that they needed to support each other. Tragedy had not had a mere ripple effect, it was a tsunami!

Jenny took Charlie's hand and led him aside. "I'm going to stay with Louise tonight if she's alone. I haven't had time to talk to her or my dad, and I need to reconnect. Can you understand?"

"No, but I'll try. I thought you might want to stay with her the night of dress rehearsal, but if you need each other tonight, that's where you belong." He kissed her forehead. "I'll see you tomorrow. It's a holiday. We could have a picnic, maybe with Louise and Colin and your dad."

"That's a great idea." Jenny walked back to the center of the stage. "Hey everybody, tomorrow's Labor Day. I know that we've all had a rough time, but how about a picnic in the park? We can call our friends. Everyone's welcome."

"I'll drag my husband off his sailboat and make a salad," Diane said.

"I have steaks in my freezer," Colin said, "and there's a grill at the park."

"I'll do hors d'oeuvres," Charlie offered.

"I have some cheese and crackers," Michael said.

Jenny took Louise's hand and whispered, "I'd like to stay at home with you tonight if you're alone."

"Is it that obvious?" Louise whispered back.

Jenny giggled. "To me, it is."

Louise and Jenny joined their friends, and Louise said, "Jenny and I are going home and think about tomorrow, the picnic and the last performance. We'll meet everyone at the park at two o'clock, okay?"

Jenny led Charlie to the wings and kissed him. "I'll miss you tonight. Keep the bed warm for me."

Charlie hugged her. "Your pillow will be a poor substitute, but I'll survive."

They walked back to the others.

"I'll ride back with you, Louise," Jenny said.

When Colin looked at Louise and said, "I'll see you tomorrow," Jenny knew that she had ruined his plans for a night alone with Louise. She wanted to assure him that he could be with her aunt after tomorrow night's performance, but there was no opportunity to see him alone. Instead, she looked at him, winked and hoped that he understood her need to be with Louise.

CHAPTER TWENTY-FOUR

Police Chief Harry Pierce ate a hurried breakfast Sunday morning and thought about Glenn Thompson. Why had he killed Pete Clampton and why were illegal immigrants working for him? Dead men don't talk.

He brushed aside attending church and a day off and called his deputy. Marling agreed to visit Oscar Mendes again.

Pierce and Marling drove to the construction company office. As they stopped, Mendes came out and stood at the door.

"We need to talk, Mendes," Pierce said. "Do you want to talk here or at the police station?"

"Am I under arrest?"

"No, but we need information. If you cooperate, it will be easier for all of us. Where are your men?"

"They are in the dormitory. People from the immigration office are guarding them, bringing food, asking questions. The men are worried and afraid." He motioned Pierce to come inside. "We can talk here."

Pierce brought out a recording device and sat down at Thompson's desk. "Tell me again the year you came to Maine."

"I came from Colombia in 1996. Pete Clampton met our boat, and he brought me and five other men here."

"How did you board Pete's boat?"

"It was easy. We came alongside his boat and jumped on. Pete and the other captain made the arrangements, and they knew what to do."

"Do you think that Thompson had been working with Clampton before you came?"

"Yes. I don't know how long."

"What about the drugs?"

"We carried them. Clampton kept them on his boat, and Thompson drove us here."

"How long do the men stay?"

"Six months. Mr. Thompson feeds them and pays them well. They are sent home with money. They do not complain and are happy to go home to their families. They do not want to stay here."

Pierce nodded. "Now I want to know about Pete's murder."

Mendes stood and looked out of the window. "I do not want to talk about it."

"Oscar, do you want to go to jail for the rest of your life? You are involved in the crime of illegal entry into this country and have remained silent for twelve years. If you work with us now, we may be able to help you. If not, you are at the court's mercy."

Mendes sat and covered his face. "I have lived with this for ten years. Mr. Thompson was good to me, but I always did what he asked me to do."

"Did he ask you to help him kill Pete Clampton?"

"No, but I was there. I rode with him that night to Pete's boat, and Pete rode with us toward Mr. Thompson's house. He parked his car east of the church because he did not want his wife to hear the car. We walked to his house and went downstairs to his den. He said that no one could hear us. I sat in a corner while he and Pete talked."

"Did you expect trouble?" Marling asked.

"Not at first. They talked about the drugs and the men. I did not understand all of the words, but they argued. Clampton said he needed more money, and Mr. Thompson said no and he would tell the police about the drugs."

"The fight was only about the drugs?" Pierce asked.

"No. Clampton said that he would have a passenger that night and could only bring back five men. Mr. Thompson told him that they had an agreement. It was six or none. It was warm in the room. Clampton took off his jacket and said that he would call the police. He grabbed the phone, and Mr. Thompson took a knife from his desk and stabbed Clampton. I was scared."

"What did you do?"

"I had to help Mr. Thompson. I wasn't a citizen then, and he said that he would report me to the authorities if I didn't help. We put Pete's jacket on him, wiped up the blood and washed the floor. Mr. Thompson was very neat. After I helped Mr. Thompson carry Pete outside, he told me to go home. He said that he would take care of the body." He shuddered.

Pierce wiped his forehead and turned off the recorder.

"I think that we have enough now, Oscar. This is serious, but we will help you if we can. Don't leave town. I'm going to post two of my men at the dormitory. One of my officers will take you to the station tomorrow morning at eight o'clock. It's Labor Day, but I'll be there."

The officers stood, and Pierce asked, "Why did Thompson put a tail on Jenny McKnight and try to kill her?"

"Mr. Thompson was worried. He told me that he had to kill Tim Brennan because Brennan was going to tell the police everything, and when he heard about the girl asking questions, he knew that she would find out. He said that Brennan had told him about the girl, that she would not give up until she found out who killed Pete." Mendes sat down and stared at Pierce. "She asked to be killed, that's what Mr. Thompson said."

Pierce shook his head. He and Marling walked to the car. "When Mendes comes tomorrow, we'll ask about who's bringing in the drugs and the illegals now. I didn't want to talk about it this morning. We have enough evidence against him to send him to jail as an accomplice, but I want all the facts about Thompson's operation before we arrest him."

Marling went home, and Pierce drove to headquarters. He listened to the tape recorder and made notes. Tomorrow he would have the whole story.

* * *

David awoke Sunday morning and decided that yesterday's inaction and depression must end. He had wanted to see Ann, but when he drove to her home on Saturday, he'd seen a police car and an SUV and knew that he couldn't stop.

Sunday morning might find her alone. He was relieved to note the absence of the police and the SUV, so he stopped and rang the bell. Ann opened the door and stared at him. David stepped back, startled by her appearance. She wore a gray bathrobe, and her feet were bare. Gone was her loving smile. In its place a questioning, almost frightened expression. She held the collar of her bathrobe to her throat.

"May I come in? I wanted to come yesterday, but you had company." He took her hand and led her to the davenport. She sat and looked at the floor. David asked, "Are you all right? What can I do?"

Ann's voice was almost a whisper. "I don't know. Everything's mixed up. Glenn's dead. He killed Pete. We found the boots." She shivered.

"Your kids are with you?"

"I think they came yesterday. They went somewhere." She stood, rubbed her arms and paced up and down. "It's my fault. I'm alone now."

David rose and tried to comfort her. He brushed back her hair. "It's okay," he said. "I love you, and when this is over, we'll have our time together,"

Ann broke away and ran to the kitchen. She turned back and looked at David. "No. Not now. Glenn's dead. It's my fault, our fault. I can't think. Go away now."

David nodded and walked to the door. Ann needed the kind of help that he couldn't give. Would her children recognize her need for reassurance and perhaps therapy? He'd call and talk to them as a banker concerned about her business transactions.

He drove home, sat down and wept. What was his future with Ann? She would find a psychiatrist who might bring her back. Who could help him? He made coffee and considered his situation. Jenny didn't need him. Louise was interested in Colin. He looked at the clock. One-thirty. The matinee would begin at two. He'd missed opening night, and the play might be a diversion.

He found a seat in the front row and sat down beside Louise. She smiled, and he leaned back.

"Are you all right?" she asked.

"Is it obvious that my world has fallen apart?"

"Worlds fall apart. You know that mine did."

David nodded and took her hand. "Yes. I'll have to find a way to put the pieces back together."

Michael came on stage to welcome the audience, and David relaxed. He looked around the theater that he had helped to finance. Sometimes you win one, he thought.

Louise nudged him before the play began. "We're having a picnic in the park about two o'clock tomorrow afternoon. Please come and bring something to pass."

David smiled. "I'm not a cook, so I'll bring the wine."

* * *

Labor Day wasn't a holiday for Chief Pierce as he sat at his desk at eight a.m. and waited for Williams and Mendes to arrive.

"Wait in your office. I may need you," Pierce said to Williams as the two men entered his office. "Thanks for bringing him here."

Pierce turned on his recorder, and Mendes sat. He removed his cap and twisted it. "I told you everything yesterday," he said.

"Not all. Let's go back. We know that Pete brought illegals and drugs into the U.S. What happened after Glenn killed him?"

Mendes looked at the floor. "Mr. Thompson trusted me and told me to take care of his work."

Pierce was astounded. "You mean you continued to bring in drugs and illegals?"

"Not drugs. Mr. Thompson said he didn't want anything more to do with drugs. That is why Tim Brennan and he fought. Brennan wanted more drugs, now that he was using them again. Mr. Thompson told him that he didn't have any and swore at him. He said something like, 'Get your own drugs, and get out of here.' Brennan said he would need more money for drugs and that if he didn't get the money, he would tell the police about Clampton's murder. Then he left Mr. Thompson's office."

"Did Thomson kill Brennan?"

Mendes nodded. "I helped him clean his car when he came back. I worked late that night. Mr. Thompson shook so bad that he could hardly wipe off the mud, and he hated a dirty car."

"And you are now in charge of bringing the men here?"

"Yes. I know the people in Colombia."

"One more thing." Pierce put his face close to Mendes. My officer, Williams, was ambushed in the garage. I want to how anyone knew the contents of William's trunk, who hit him, and what was the weapon."

Mendes pulled back and snorted. "You guys think you're so smart. Mr. Thompson came back to the theater that night and listened at the back door while your men cut the cable. He heard your instructions, and the next morning, I waited outside the garage. When your officer came in, all I had to do was find the right time and hit him with my blackjack and take the cable. Mr. Thompson knew that the cable could be traced."

"Williams said he heard music before he was hit."

"I like music. Is it against the law?"

Pierce turned off the recorder and leaned back in his chair. "There's no law against music, but there's a law against attack with a deadly weapon. I will have to arrest you for the attack, as an accomplice to murder and for bringing in illegal immigrants. These are serious charges, but you have cooperated, and that will help your case."

Pierce followed all legal procedures and asked Mendes if he wished to make a call or hire a lawyer. Mendes shook his head. Pierce called Williams for handcuffs, and he and the officer led him to a cell. Mendes walked between the two men, his head bent and his shoulders stooped.

Pierce returned to his office with Williams. "We have a full confession. Call one of our people to watch him. I'll contact the immigration authorities, and we should wrap up this case in a few days." He looked at the calendar. Labor Day. He'd labored enough. It was time to go home.

* * *

Seven-thirty p.m., the evening of Labor Day, September first. The final performance of *Tangled Trap Lines* would begin in thirty minutes. The cast inspected each other's attire, and Louise made a final check before leaving the stage. Jenny inspected the backdrops and props, then joined Louise in the front row.

Charlie waved to Jenny from the wings as Diane looked in a mirror and applied lipstick. Michael joined Charlie, and all three looked out at the audience as people filled the theater.

At eight o'clock, Michael came out and welcomed everyone. "This is our last performance. It's been a pleasure for me to work with such a fine cast and all of the people here who have made this production a success." Following applause, Michael continued. "After tonight's performance we must strike the set. You can help us as we clear the stage. Two trucks will be outside, ready to load everything."

Charlie's and Diane's remarks were brief, and the play began. Following the last words of Act Three, the cast took a final bow. The heroine gave Michael a bouquet of roses, and the cast and the audience applauded.

Many came up from the audience, and the stage was bare in thirty minutes. Michael and Charlie stood together. "It's been a success, and the picnic was a blast," Charlie said. "It's been an amazing summer. When do you leave?"

"I hope to leave tomorrow and e-mail my report for the Arts Council. I'll call you about publication. You and your play have a great future."

"I may write another if all the facts about Pete Clampton's murder are ever revealed. Now we only know who killed him."

"I'll be interested in knowing the whole story. Keep me informed."

Jenny came from the back of the stage. "We'll miss you. I hope that you'll return and direct another play." She hugged him. "I've enjoyed working with you. I'd like the job again."

Michael laughed. "You're hired." He shook hands with Louise. "Please thank David and the Arts Council members for all they did this summer." He said to Diane, "You did a masterful job. You pulled everyone together as a team. The Sowatna Players have a great future."

Diane hugged him. "It was worth the effort. I hope you'll return."

Michael waved and ran out the side exit. He hated goodbyes, and saying goodbye to Jenny had been difficult. He felt a bond between them. He knew that she was David's daughter, but was she? He would always wonder.

* * *

Jenny watched Michael's departure and looked at the empty stage. "It's sad to say goodbye, but what a success it's been!"

Charlie held her hand. "And what a summer!"

Louise and Colin joined them, and Louise said, "Let's go back to the house and have a drink. I'll call David. At the picnic, he said that he wanted to know about our last performance."

Jenny and Charlie parked in front of Louise's home. "Will you stay with me tonight?" Charlie asked. Her answer was a lingering kiss.

Colin and Louise came from the kitchen with drinks.

David had arrived. He accepted a drink and smiled at Louise. "Thanks, I needed this." He looked around at all of them. "I need to talk," he said, "and I hope you'll understand. Ann Thompson and I were…"

"Dad," Jenny filled her father's silence. "I know that you and Ann love each other. It's been obvious all summer, and I understand."

David looked at them and saw approving nods. "Ann was going to file for a divorce, and we were going to be married, but now I think that she's traumatized. I saw her yesterday."

"She's had a terrible shock," Louise said. "Her husband was shot, and she learned that he'd killed at least one person, maybe two. That's no ordinary revelation."

"It's going to take time," Colin said. "I'm sure that her children will hire the best doctors. Trauma can be treated, but it doesn't happen overnight. How about you, David? Can you wait?"

"Of course." He looked at Jenny. "I'm glad that you and Charlie have worked out your problems. You will have a wonderful future together."

"I'm going to apply for a teaching position in Sowatna as long as Charlie's here."

"I may have to write another play about Pete Clampton's murder as soon as I have all the facts. I called Pierce this morning, and he told me about Mendes. He brought him in this morning, and Mendes gave him the full story, not only about Pete's murder, but also about Brennan. He wanted to kill you too, Jenny, because he knew that you'd never give up until you found out who killed Pete."

Jenny stood and walked to the east window. Street lights illumined the waterfront. "Pete had a busy life bringing in drugs and illegal immigrants. He must have been clever to avoid arrest."

Louise walked to the window and put her arm around Jenny. "He knew this area better than anyone. I..." She choked back a sob.

Colin rose and took her hand. "It's all right. He wasn't all bad." He paused. "Charlie's been bugging me about the pictures Adam Roberts, Senior, took the night of the murder. I think we should show them."

Louise nodded. "Yes, it's time." She went upstairs and returned with a packet. She gave them to Charlie.

"Good God!" Charlie said as he flipped through a dozen pictures, pictures of Pete slumped over the wheel, pictures of a coffee mug bearing the 'Sew What?' logo, pictures of a woman's sweater slung over a chair.

He stared at Louise. "Yours?"

Louise nodded. "Colin knew that Pete and I had a relationship. When Brennan was brought in, the county attorney appointed Colin to represent him."

Colin broke in. "I had immediate access to the police report and the photographs, and I didn't want to involve Louise. I knew that she hadn't killed him, for God's sake, but her things on the boat would have incriminated her."

He took her hand. "It's been our secret for a long time."

"Who else knew?" Charlie asked.

"The police chief who retired five years ago and the county attorney. When you called on Bill Daniels, Jenny, he hustled you out because he was afraid that you'd ask about the pictures."

Jenny sat back on the davenport and looked at Louise. "I'm not shocked, but I'm amazed that you kept your secret so well."

David sat quietly in his chair, still engrossed in his own problems. He looked up and spoke slowly. "Louise has kept her own council for ten years, and now I can add more to the story. Didn't anyone ever wonder what Pete did with all that money? He'd sold drugs, he'd supplied workers for Glenn Thompson who paid him well, and he sold lobsters, a lot of them to George Hendricks for his restaurants."

"I wondered," Charlie said, "but there were so many unanswered questions that none of us thought about the profits."

"Wonder no more," David said. "I brought something tonight to show all of you." He pulled three photographs from his sport coat pocket. "Pete's grandfather came from County Cork, Ireland, and raised his family here. Pete never returned to his roots, but he kept in touch with people in his grandfather's home town, Oysterhaven. One day he came to me and asked to set up a trust fund with his money. He wanted the interest to be used for a special project in Oysterhaven, and after ten years, the entire amount was to be sent there. Next week will mark the end of the ten-year period, so now I can tell you what Pete did."

He showed the photographs to everyone, and a stunned silence followed. Louise looked at David. "I can't believe this. The sign in front of the building reads 'Peter Clampton Home for Boys.'"

David nodded. "His grandfather told him about the poverty he'd left behind in Ireland and asked his grandson to remember the people. Pete not only remembered, he set up the trust fund, and everything he earned was poured into it."

Louise nodded. "Pete didn't spend money on himself. He kept his boat in working order, but there were no frills." She looked at Colin. "Our relationship lasted only about six weeks, but I have no regrets. We both knew that it couldn't last, that our paths were meant to cross briefly, and we had our farewell dinner together the night he was killed."

Louise sat on the davenport, leaned back and shut her eyes. "I remember every detail. We had oyster stew and white wine. Pete had lit candles and covered the table with a white cloth. We lingered over coffee and talked about our separate futures. He said that he wanted the best for me, and life on a lobster boat wasn't best. We kissed, and I left about nine o'clock. I looked back at his boat, and he waved. I never saw him again."

Colin sat beside her. "Remembering isn't easy."

Louise smiled. "No, but it doesn't hurt so much any more. And you were so helpful, Colin. You covered for me, and I'll always be grateful."

Jenny and Charlie stood and walked to the door. Charlie turned and said, "When I started asking questions about Pete Clampton, the answer always was 'Everybody knew Pete.' But they didn't really know him, did they? A complex man, a dealer in drugs and illegals and a benefactor of homeless boys." He took Jenny's hand. "Thanks for the drinks. We'll see you tomorrow."

David stood and followed them. "I'll be busy this week arranging for the transfer of funds to a bank in Oysterhaven. I've been the trust officer." He left with Jenny and Charlie and walked to his car.

"Wonders will never cease," Charlie said. "Let's set a date for our wedding before another earth-shaking revelation occurs."

"I'm still wondering about the connection between New Bradford, the location of your play, and Bradford, Scotland, the home of my ancestors."

"Maybe we should plan a Bradford honeymoon and find the answer." He kissed her and started the car.

Louise and Colin sat together and held hands. "What a night," Colin said. "The play was a success, Michael's on his way to a teaching position at Skidmore, Charlie's going to be a successful playwright, and *your daughter, Jenny*, will be a lovely bride."

Louise sat up and stared at him. "What do you mean, Colin?"

He smiled. "I handled all of the adoption papers for David and Betsy, Louise. I had just started to work at the law firm, and I was given the assignment. Betsy and David were so excited to have your baby, and of course the mother's name was on the adoption papers."

Louise began to cry. "When I moved here after my sister's death, I was determined that no one would ever know."

"No one knows, my dear, and no one will ever know. I won't ask you about Jenny's father. We both know who he is, and I'm sure you didn't tell Michael."

Louise shook her head and smiled. "That's our secret now. I thought it was only mine, but I'm glad to share it with you."

They walked to the porch and sat on the swing. They rocked slowly. Colin put his arm around Louise and kissed her. "We'll have so much to share together. Remember the last line of the play, 'Now will you marry me? Our lives are beginning all over again.'"

ABOUT THE AUTHOR

Marian Mathews Hersrud, a Minneapolis native. has lived in South Dakota most of her life. Her first two novels, "Sweet Thunder" and "Spirits and Black Leather" take place during motorcycle rallies in Sturgis, SD. She is also a freelance writer whose articles have appeared in The South Dakota Magazine, The Educational Record and Pan Gaia. She served on the South Dakota Board of Regents and on several educational boards. Because of such a wide variety of interests, Hersrud is able to present many different characters and unusual events. She and her husband Morry are now Florida residents.